THE MIDAS MEN

Also by Jonathan Evans

MISFIRE

Jonathan Evans

The Midas Men

Futura
Macdonald & Co
London & Sydney

A Futura Book

First published in Great Britain in 1981
by Michael Joseph Ltd

First Futura Edition 1983

ISBN 0 7088 2297 0

Printed and bound in Great Britain by
Collins, Glasgow

A BPCC plc Company

Futura Publications
A Division of Macdonald & Co (Publishers) Ltd
Maxwell House
74 Worship Street
London EC2A 2EN

For Chris and Carole, with love

Author's Note

Although events described in this book are based upon fact, it is a work of fiction. All the characters are fictitious and any resemblance to actual persons, living or dead, is purely coincidental.

Winchester, 1981

'Here's the rule for bargains: Do other men, for they would do you. That's the true business precept.'

Charles Dickens: *Martin Chuzzlewit*

Prologue

Psychiatrists who have studied the phenomenon conclude that although the truly rich differ mentally in substantial ways from other people, nearly all have the linking bond of greed. Poor people can be greedy too, of course. But they don't have the means to indulge themselves, any more than they can pay a psychiatrist to hear secrets they would probably prefer to remain hidden anyway. R.L. Bains, whose personal fortune was estimated at two billion dollars, had never consulted a psychiatrist because he associated such people with madness and sure as hell knew he wasn't mad. Had an examination occurred, however, he would have concealed his overwhelming ambition to accumulate even more wealth, because Bains was a very private man. This trait was unusual for Texas, but then Bains enjoyed the unusual.

His father had been a cantankerous man who had established the family fortune from oil and disdained his son's ability to maintain the business. But from his teens, Bains had determined to better the old man: one of his greatest regrets was that his father had died before he had been able to prove his expertise in the world commodity markets which, by the time he was thirty, had more than doubled the amount his father had bequeathed in his will.

The idea of cornering the world's silver supplies was flamboyant, even for a man who favoured the unusual.

Despite his father's doubts, Bains never forgot that oil was the basis for his other business dealings. He ran the company personally, travelled extensively and had naturally formed links with the oil producers of the Middle East.

A particular friendship had developed with Prince Tewfik Hassan, predominantly because they had known and liked each other at Harvard. Of equal importance, however, was Hassan's membership of the Saudi ruling family and the confident expectation that he would eventually become its head. Bains considered kings the best friends to have. He had always imagined that the advantage of his association with Hassan would come from oil. Then, when he calculated the sums that would be necessary to cover the world silver markets, in hedges and maintenance margins, he realised that he didn't have sufficient liquid capital and foresaw another benefit.

The Texan and the Arab were similar in many ways, both men whose domination by strong-willed families in their youth had created a determination to prove themselves. Hassan's response to the other man's approach was immediate. Within a month, the prince had pledged his personal fortune of £100,000,000 to the enterprise.

Bains planned everything with the utmost care. Through nominees and intermediary companies, he placed automatic purchase orders with brokers operating in New York, London, Zurich and Tokyo, initially cautious that the spread should be wide enough to hide from any jobber or trader the fact that there was a concerted purchase being made. In four months, they were showing a profit of £250,000,000. An OPEC price rise had its usual whiplash effect, fuelling Western inflation and creating an uncertainty with paper money; and a bullish market forced up metal prices even further, so that in the succeeding two months, the profit increased by a further £150,000,000.

Paradoxically, the disaster came from Bains' meticulous attention to detail, and it might have gone unnoticed but for a market analyst in London's Leadenhall Street whose hobby was crosswords and whose mind was therefore often occupied with conundrums.

Throughout any day's trading on any of the world's stock markets, prices rise and fall like a kite in an uncertain wind; the expertise in speculation is guessing the highs and the lows and making a quick profit. Bains didn't want a quick profit. He wanted manipulative ownership. So his automatic purchase orders were made within thirty minutes of the markets opening; experience had proved to Bains that over a period of time, this established a price average covering any margin commitment for which he might be liable. The mistake was his failure to protect his anonymity by allowing some of his purchases to be sold, which was what would have happened during normal trading. The analyst identified the trend and then followed it, curiously, first on the London market and then, with increasing interest, on the rest of the main metal exchanges. A man who completes crosswords doesn't immediately write down the most obvious answer to a clue and so the analyst waited for over a month, until he was quite sure, before reporting the information to the jobbers who employed him for precisely this purpose.

Discreet inquiries among brokers enabled the analyst to isolate Bains' nominee companies and then, as the pressure increased, a broker's clerk whispered the name and within twenty-four hours the Texas billionaire was linked.

A single brick breaking loose from a dam is usually the initial cause of a flood. The association of R.L. Bains and his Croesus-type wealth with massive silver purchases had the same cumulative effect.

There was the rush to buy, matched by an eagerness to sell for a quick profit when the prices rocketed, and the surging value persuaded people to buy again, increasing the upward spiral.

Bains had never lost — ever — and he allowed arrogance to override his business acumen. He could have deflated the over-blown value within days had he taken a short-term loss and sold heavily. But he was already locked into purchases against the future value of silver, stretching forward over a six-month period. To have brought about a market crash, however temporarily, would have meant his being contracted to pay high for low value.

Greed was now added to the arrogance. The surging prices had already transformed his original £400,000,000 profit into £820,000,000. And Bains couldn't bring himself to suffer a loss, however short. So he took the first positive, unthinking gamble of his career and decided to stay bullish. That meant continuing his purchases at the rising market price, hoping that the frenzy would explode itself, just like dynamite is the last resort to extinguish an uncontrollable well fire. The only explosion was in the continuing upward price.

By now Bains had exhausted not only his own liquidity but the £100,000,000 provided by Prince Hassan and was deeply into the arranged loans with the banks. Brokers became nervous and began calling their maintenance margins. Bains had already surrendered the second mortgages on his real estate and assigned his companies. And for the first time in his life, he was refused an extension of credit. The only thing Bains had left was silver. To cover his debts, he was at last forced to act as he should have done months before and sell, to raise liquidity.

Coincidence defeated him. The Bank of Venezuela possessed forty million ounces of silver, which at its peak of £30 an ounce represented £120,000,000. They decided to capitalise to raise foreign currency at the very moment when Bains began to sell, and silver brokers with whom he had extended contracts decided to unload as well, to cut their losses. The sudden selling of such volume burst the bubble. In two weeks of frantic, world-wide dealing, the silver price plummeted from its peak of £30 an ounce to £9. Bains was trapped again, this time with the nightmare of all stock market speculators. He had bought astronomically high and was selling disastrously low.

The plunge levelled out, of course. And, slowly, the price rose again. When the market began to lift, Bains was able to arrange credit to carry him forward and by the end of a year his losses were reduced to £100,000,000. Which meant he remained a very rich man.

Prince Hassan's losses were the same, because he and Bains had established themselves as equal partners. But the Saudi prince's £100,000,000 represented his personal fortune and he suffered loss of face. In the Middle East, as in Asia, the loss of money through speculation is a disgrace for an ordinary man; for a man destined one day to be king, it was unthinkable. To recover face, Prince Hassan had to recover his fortune. And he didn't have a year, like R.L. Bains.

Chapter One

During the flight from Moscow, the Ilyushin 11-76T had encountered unexpected head winds and so it was thirty minutes behind schedule when it landed at Amsterdam's Schipol airport. It was directed at once by airport control to the freight section, where diplomats from the Soviet embassy were already waiting.

Dutch intelligence had been advised earlier of the intended arrival from the filed flight plan, and so identification of the aircraft was the second message they received that day. A computer check upon that identification disclosed the NATO interest. A normal information request had been registered with all allied intelligence services from the moment of the Ilyushin's first appearance at the Paris Air Show in 1971. A priority designation and the codename Candid had come later, when it was learned that as well as being in commercial service with Aeroflot, the aircraft had become the standard transport vehicle for the Soviet armed forces, with more than a hundred attached to front-line squadrons.

From the Paris exhibition, the external configurations and equipment were well established, both from visual examination and from extensive photographing. The NATO interest was concentrated entirely upon cockpit modifications and particularly on the range and type of radar fitments.

An intelligence team reached the airport within an hour of touchdown and almost immediately resigned themselves to failure. The aircraft and its cargo were protected by absolute diplomatic clearance. In fact, the degree to which the embassy personnel were invoking their diplomatic status was intriguing to those who watched. The only Dutch being permitted anywhere near the aircraft were the crew of the fuel bowser. Otherwise, everything was being handled by Russians, even the aircraft cleaning and cargo loading.

Aware that they were duplicating information already available but unable to think of anything more constructive, the intelligence men photographed the plane extensively, using long-range lenses. They photographed the cargo pallets as well, accepting as they did so that the effort was probably just as pointless; the wooden crates were quite anonymous and could have contained anything. From the effort involved in lifting them, whatever it was appeared heavy.

The loading took two hours. When it was completed, the Russians who had done the labouring work left in the two lorries and an escort car, leaving only a small group of senior diplomats. They stood by their cars, watching the Ilyushin taxi towards the departure runway. By 5 pm there was a build-up of traffic. The Ilyushin was allocated position ten in the take-off queue, which was stationary to permit the landing of a backlog of passenger aircraft. Through binoculars, the intelligence team watched the growing impatience of the embassy staff. At 5-30 pm there appeared to be a huddled conference. They entered their cars, waited a further ten minutes and then, in a regimented line, looped the perimeter road to join the main highway back to the embassy in Andries Bickerweg Street.

It was 6-15 pm before the Ilyushin was directed for take-off and by that time the four Soloviev D-30 turbofan engines, individually mounted in underwing pods, had been running for over an hour. Matching the earlier impatience of his embassy colleagues, the pilot over-revved them, causing the engines to overheat. The aircraft lifted with a take-off speed of just over 114 knots and was 100 feet in the air when two of the fan blades in the bypass section of the outer port engine sheared through metal fatigue. The blocked engine shuddered violently, vibrating the entire aircraft and then the pod snapped right away from the wing. For what appeared a long time but was, in fact, barely seconds, the huge transporter hung in the air. Then it dipped to starboard and ploughed sideways into a marsh field a mile from the airport.

The intelligence teams got to the crash scene at the same time as the ambulance and fire services. The navigator, who was housed in the glazed nose section directly below the flight deck, was killed instantly. The pilot lost an arm and was deeply unconscious and it was not until the post-mortem examination that the co-pilot's fatal internal intestinal rupture was discovered.

Despite the extensive damage to the cockpit, the intelligence men were able to expose four rolls of film, recording all the fitments and establishing a radar installation far more sophisticated than that imagined by NATO electronics experts. They had already been warned by radio of the hastily approaching embassy personnel when they turned to the cargo. They opened eight cases at random, using crowbars clamped to the side of the hold, and knowing the damage could be explained by the crash.

'Christ!' exclaimed the section head, going from box to box and staring down at the dull reflection of the gold that lay there. From the standardised ingot weights assessed against the number of crates carried, it took them three days to calculate the total value at £150,000,000. And to identify, from the assay marks which remained, the predominant source as the Witwatersrand mines of South African Grain, Ore and Mineral Incorporated.

Another brick breaking loose from another dam.

Chapter Two

The knock was hesitant, but not as timid as he had expected. As if in confirmation of his thoughts, she rapped again, louder this time. Marius Metzinger did not respond at once, wanting every advantage, no matter how miniscule. He allowed a third summons before he moved, not just opening the door but pulling it wide apart and confronting her suddenly. The only reaction from Ann Talbot was a slight widening of the eyes; she didn't start back, as he thought she might.

'I was worried I might have mistaken the time, when you didn't reply,' she said. Her voice was properly respectful, but only just. Metzinger decided she was very sure of herself. The awareness pleased him, even though he had already been fairly confident of the sort of woman she was from the dossier that had taken enquiry agents almost a year to assemble. He was glad the opportunity to utilise the information had occurred.

'No,' he said. 'You didn't mistake the time.' He stood back for her to enter the suite, the best at Claridge's. Metzinger was a large, barrel-bellied man aware of his size and of his ability to overpower people. But as she passed, Ann Talbot didn't seem overawed either by him or by their venue.

'Sit there,' he said, indicating a chair positioned near the desk which had been specially installed for Metzinger's stay in London. He was a man who enjoyed his wealth and privilege and it was obvious. As well as the desk, there was a stock market tape machine near the window and the cords of additional telephones ribboned messily across the carpet.

Ann Talbot did as she was instructed, pulling a large briefcase close to her, as if in expectation of some work. She was a ripe bodied, full-featured woman. Her suit was severe but cleverly cut to show the heaviness of her breasts, and Metzinger decided the way she had of nipping her bottom lip between whitely even teeth was not nervousness but a discreetly cultivated mannerism, to make her appear provocative. Perhaps it was going to be easier than even he imagined. As he watched, she took heavily rimmed spectacles from her briefcase and put them on, reinforcing the impression that she was expecting the meeting to be on a business level. At the same time she patted into place the thick black hair strained back into a bun at the nape of her neck.

Metzinger gestured towards the bar. 'Would you like a drink?'

'No thank you.'

'Were you surprised at my asking you to come here, instead of our meeting at the office?'

'Yes,' she said after a pause, catching her bottom lip between her teeth.

'What did you tell Richard Jenkins?' The curtness of the question concealed Metzinger's apprehension at what he was setting out to achieve. It wouldn't have mattered, had Jenkins simply been the managing director of their United Kingdom division. But he was one of the founder directors of South African Grain, Ore and Mineral Incorporated, with a seat on the SAGOMI parent board in Pretoria. And he'd been one of the most vigorous opponents, the last time Metzinger had attempted to upset the English control of the combine.

'Just that you'd asked me to call by,' said Ann.

'Was he curious?'

'I don't know.'

According to the enquiry agents, Jenkins' affair with his personal assistant had ended a year earlier, before her present involvement with James Collington, but Metzinger supposed there could still be some lingering jealousy. Fleetingly he was amused at the thought of Jenkins imagining that he might become sexually involved with her.

'What about your curiosity?' he said.

'There's obviously a good enough reason,' she said. 'It's not really for me to question, is it?'

Instead of replying, Metzinger moved past towards a window overlooking the streets far below. It was one of those muddily grey November afternoons that he hated in England, not yet four but already necessary for cars to use their lights, an opaque mist clouding out the shapes of the stores in Oxford Street. He looked forward to getting back to the warmth of South Africa. Metzinger turned, the movement as abrupt as his opening of the door.

'For the past seven months,' he announced, 'you have been involved in an affair with my son-in-law: you've practically set up home together, at Princes Gate.' Metzinger had rehearsed the attack for maximum effect, wanting to steamroller her into a collapse. He strode back into the room, indicating the manilla folders on a low table close to where she was sitting. 'I have documentary evidence,' he said. 'Photographs, statements, everything.'

Metzinger gazed at the woman intently, waiting for the reaction. She used the spectacles for her escape, slowly removing them, replacing them in their case and then just as painstakingly putting that into her briefcase, all the while keeping her face away from him. When she did look up, she was quite controlled. 'Yes,' she said, in simple admission.

The reaction momentarily off-balanced Metzinger. He had expected a denial, maybe even tears. He decided to maintain the pressure: 'And before that, you were sleeping with Richard Jenkins.'

Ann looked at the assembled evidence. 'You've gone to a lot of trouble.'

'You'd be surprised how much,' said Metzinger honestly.

She continued to look at the folders. 'It makes me seem like a tart,' she said.

'Yes,' agreed Metzinger. 'It does.'

She moved to snap back at him, her face defiantly hard, then apparently changed her mind. Instead she gestured around the suite. 'Now I know why it had to be here.'

Not yet you don't, thought Metzinger. 'At the moment my daughter and Collington are only separated,' he said. 'What I've assembled here guarantees her divorce. And considerable embarrassment for you.'

'Divorces aren't publicised, not any more,' she said.

Metzinger laughed at her. 'Collington is a well-known man. With the influence I've got, I could get the publicity, even without the divorce action. And when it happened, you'd have to leave the company: he might be chairman, but he could never retain you on the staff if there were a scandal. South Africans are very moral people: the shareholders wouldn't have it. So you'd lose £15,000 a year as well as your reputation.'

'There's one thing you've overlooked,' said the woman.

'What?'

'What if James *wanted* the divorce? What if he wanted to marry me?'

Metzinger moved away from her, going back to the window. It was completely dark now; the mist had thickened into a fog. He had expected it to take longer, but her question obviated the need to protract it. 'I suppose you think you know Collington well?' he said, not looking at her.

He heard her snigger, imagining a naïvety in the question. 'I should, shouldn't I?'

Metzinger turned to face her. 'Then how do you think he'd react to knowing that while he's in South Africa, which he is most of the time, you average three nights a week with a rather unsuccessful stockbroker named Peter Brading, whose child you had aborted seven months ago in a Harley Street clinic?'

The barrier fell away, for a few moments. She blinked against the tears and her shoulders sagged. The recovery was equally quick, her attitude moving from bewilderment to outrage. 'Who the hell do you think you are!' she erupted. 'You're the deputy chairman of the company I work for, nothing more. I don't have to sit and take crap from you.'

Metzinger regarded her expressionlessly. 'Yes you do,' he said. He spoke quietly, conversationally almost, and at first the threat did not register with her.

'What do you want?' she said warily.

'Co-operation,' said Metzinger.

'Co-operation?'

'About Collington. And Jenkins, if it's appropriate.'

'You want me to spy for you!'

'I suppose that's what it amounts to.'

'That's prepostrous!'

'No, it's not.'

'Then it's blackmail.'

'All I'm asking for is information from an employee of my company,' qualified Metzinger. 'In return for which I'm prepared to do nothing to jeopardise your well-paid job or whatever you get up to here in London with Collington.'

She hesitated and Metzinger pushed the folders across the table towards her. 'These are copies,' he said. 'I'd like you to take them and read them tonight. To get some idea of how messy everything could become.'

The hesitation continued for a little longer and then she reached out, picking up the enquiry agents' reports and fitting them into her briefcase. As she re-fastened it she gave an abrupt, sneering laugh and said, 'When this began I actually thought you had some genuine concern for your daughter and Collington.'

The suggestion seemed to surprise Metzinger. 'I *am* concerned for Hannah,' he said. 'About Collington, I feel entirely different.'

Metzinger did not drink, so he shook his head against the steward's invitation for a departure aperitif. He unfastened his safety belt, gazing down at the receding amber lights of London airport and reflecting on the visit. Ann Talbot had surprised him. He had only previously come across her as an efficient assistant in a multi-national business environment and he was curious at the attraction she had for Collington. And not just Collington, he remembered; Jenkins, too. Metzinger was not a man who categorised women in whom he had little interest, but she had appeared to him an obvious type, despite the attempted protection of formal suits, heavy glasses and pulled-back hair. The complete opposite, in fact, to the natural sophistication of Hannah. Perhaps it was the difference between them that Collington found appealing. Metzinger sighed, dismissing the thought. Whatever the reason, it hardly mattered; Hannah's marriage to Collington was over, thank God. Just as his supremacy in SAGOMI was to be over. Within a year, judged Metzinger; with luck, maybe even less. And then the company would be under Afrikaner control.

Metzinger leaned back against the headrest, closing his eyes. There was a fitting irony that he was returning to South Africa for the funeral of the man who'd beaten him the last time he'd attempted to gain control, but whose death had provided him with a second chance. He'd taken more precautions on this occasion than he had on the last, even resorting to sexual pressure, which he found distasteful. But it was necessary to win.

Obediently Metzinger responded to the seatbelt announcement, securing himself for the Amsterdam landing. On its final approach, the aircraft passed over the skeletal wreckage of the Soviet transporter.

It was to be several days before Metzinger learned that most of its gold cargo had come from his company's mines. And even longer before he reached the decision to use this information as a way of removing Collington completely from the board, to achieve an absolute victory.

Chapter Three

It was considered an emergency, so the meeting was convened early in the morning. The streets of Moscow were even clearer of traffic than usual and so the two outsiders arrived early at the grey stone, seven-storey building dominating Dzerzhinsky Square, the headquarters of the Komitet Gosudarstvennoy Bezopasnosti, the Soviet intelligence service.

Insurance was the purpose of the meeting, much to the annoyance of the man acting as host. Dimitri Krotkov was the head of the Directorate responsible for all clandestine activities outside the country and in the beginning of the gold-buying operation had been treated as such, closely involved in its inception and planning. He'd provided one of his best deep-penetration operatives by activating Brigitte re Jong in Amsterdam to act as broker, and she had succeeded brilliantly. So brilliantly, in fact, that other ministries had become aware of what was happening and intruded themselves, gauging the benefits of association. And if the plane hadn't crashed, it would have continued that way. But now they had a problem. So they came running back to him, expecting his experts to give the reassurances they wanted and guarantee there weren't going to be any difficulties arising out of the accident. Which was typical. Soviet government was fettered by prestige-seeking ministers and responsibility-avoiding bureaucrats, anxious for their dachas in the hills and the Zils in which they could drive unobstructed along the traffic-free lane in the centre of Moscow roads and their concessions at the foreign currency stores, and shit scared of anything going wrong.

Krotkov looked sympathetically across to the man on his left. Because everyone knew how highly the scheme was considered and the benefits that might accrue from it, Nikolai Leonov had initially been fought over by the various ministries, like a bone among hungry dogs. How long, wondered Krotkov, would it be before the dogs tried to bury him?

Leonov was chief planner at the Foreign Ministry, but it was under the Finance administration that he had been operating the scheme. And the Finance Minister was Igor Struve, who was so adept at side-stepping trouble that he had survived from the era of Stalin. Leonov was in a worse position than he was, decided Krotkov. Poor sod.

The third man in the room was Viktor Simenov, controller of the scientific and technical division. It was Simenov who had to determine whether or not the Ilyushin had been brought down by sabotage, and the degree of unauthorised entry before the return of the embassy personnel. It was he who had produced the files and assessments which were mounded, several inches high, before each of them, the various stages of the investigation differentiated by the colour of the folders.

'Shall we begin?' suggested Krotkov. He was a fat, disordered man, his shirt and suit bulging around him. Leonov made a sharp comparison. He was fastidiously neat, his collar stiffly white, his well-cut, almost Western-style suit freshly pressed. Krotkov appeared to become aware of the difference between them, pulling upright in his chair and securing all four buttons of his jacket. This in fact accentuated his obesity, making his appearance worse.

'Of course,' agreed Leonov.

'Have you studied everything?' enquired Krotkov, speaking directly to Leonov.

'To the point of exhaustion,' said Leonov. When the scheme had begun so spectacularly, he had been confident of getting an ambassadorship as a reward. It was frightening how quickly the attitudes had been changing since the crash. Turning to the technical expert he said, 'I am aware of the efforts to which you have gone over this. But it comes down to one, simple question. Was the gold discovered?'

Simenov shifted uncomfortably. 'I know the point of concern,' he said.

'So what's the answer?' intruded Krotkov.

Simenov was a scientist, not an operational member of the KGB: from across the table, Leonov imagined the man more comfortable in a white laboratory coat than the wedding-and-funeral suit he was wearing. Simenov separated the files before him, refusing to be flustered.

'Quite obviously there was entry into the cockpit section,' he said. 'The crew had been extracted by the time the embassy people returned and forensically we were able to establish the presence of others all over the area.'

'What about the hold?' persisted Leonov gently.

Simenov extracted a paper, offering it for consideration. 'The fuselage was cracked in more than one place. At the worst spot it was possible for a man to enter and leave without obstruction.'

Leonov saw Krotkov about to speak and thrust up his hand, stopping the man, to allow Simenov to continue at his own pace. Krotkov frowned but said nothing.

'Eight cases containing gold ingots appeared to be smashed . . . .' said Simenov.

'. . . *appeared*,' qualified Leonov, deciding the interruption sufficiently important.

'Embedded in the wood were minute fragments of metal,' said the scientist. 'But there was also a great deal of jagged metal all around, in the hold. The opening of the boxes could be consistent with their coming into contact with that metal.'

Leonov shook his head, refusing the man's caution. 'Forensically it should have been possible to discover if the shards embedded in the wood were Russian or Western metal,' he insisted.

'Yes,' agreed Simenov. 'It was definitely steel manufactured within the Soviet Union.'

'There are crowbars and other escape equipment carried in the luggage holds of such aircraft,' said Krotkov, showing the attention with which he had studied the reports.

'I was particularly careful to check the emplacement of each,' said Simenov. 'Two were still in their clamps. Three more were displaced, but they could have been dislodged by the force of the crash: certainly they were nowhere near the opened boxes.'

'What about the crash?' demanded Krotkov. 'Could it have been sabotage, an attempt to discover the contents of the boxes?'

Simenov shook his head. 'Of that I am quite sure,' he said. 'The engine broke away from the wing after the fan blades sheared, through metal fatigue. It was definitely an accident.'

'So the likelihood of there being any foreign intelligence people immediately available to enter the hold is unlikely?' Krotkov demanded.

Leonov nodded, approving the point the other man had raised, but then said: 'It needn't have been an intelligence man.'

'I have tried to make the report as extensive as possible,' said Simenov. 'And to do that I considered the accounts of our embassy personnel, who were at the scene. I even cabled for additional details from Holland. Our officials all say that as far as they could ascertain, everyone at the crash site was attached to the rescue services.'

'Who would be concerned only with injured crewmen,' pointed out Krotkov hopefully.

A faint hope, assessed Leonov, looking towards the intelligence chief: too faint. Leonov had read all the reports and assessments and was irritated at their inconclusiveness. He had come to Dzerzhinsky Square determined to get a positive answer, either way. And was getting no further than he had from the files. He hesitated, uncertainly. He was going to have to disclose the details of the operation to make Simenov understand the importance. He coughed, gazing down at the unhelpful dossiers, weighing the words before uttering them.

'You are both members of State Security and as such need little reminder of the secrecy oaths you have taken. But I'm going to make that reminder, nevertheless. Because what I am about to say is a State secret of the highest importance . . .'

Krotkov frowned, but decided to forgive the impudence because of the pressure upon the man. Simenov shifted with the apprehension that he had shown at the beginning of the meeting.

'The Soviet Union is facing a crisis,' resumed Leonov. 'It is a crisis which, if discovered and manipulated by the West, could lead to our very destruction . . . .'

For the first time he looked up, alert for their reaction. Both men were staring at him. Simenov looked disbelieving.

'At the moment,' took up Leonov, 'we are concealing satisfactorily the extent of our difficulties. There is only one weakness in the proposals we have adopted to resolve them.' He paused again for them to appreciate what he was about to say.

'And that is the fact that we are buying vast quantities of gold on the Western market. If that knowledge were to become known by a Western intelligence agency and correctly analysed by our enemies, then as I said, we could be destroyed.'

'An attack . . . but I don't understand . . .' blurted Simenov.

'I do not mean any sort of nuclear offensive,' Leonov cut off, the impatience spurred by his concern. 'Forget all the May Day nonsense of tanks and rockets and soldiery. Despite every effort, the closest control, the harvests of the Soviet Union have consistently failed for the past five years . . .'

Simenov was quite still now, but Krotkov was nodding at the confirmation of something he already knew.

'There are levels of diplomacy,' lectured Leonov. 'There are public, aggressive stances. And then there are realities. America overproduces grain to such a degree that without government intervention, their crop agriculture would collapse.'

Leonov stopped yet again, reluctant to make a concession even among men whom he knew to be no risk. Haltingly, he said: 'We need grain. They have it. The balance, in our favour, was that we were the world's second biggest gold producer . . .'

'Were?' said Krotkov. He was responsible for things outside the country, not internal affairs, and he didn't know of the difficulties at which Leonov was hinting.

Leonov sighed. 'Gold production of the Soviet Union is another State secret,' he said, in unnecessary warning to both of them. 'Because of the volatile nature of the world's metal and money markets, we have allowed it to be interpreted that our gold production figures range between 280 and 350 tonnes a year.'

'What are the true figures?' Krotkov demanded.

'The decision was taken several years ago,' continued Leonov, committed now and seeing no point in holding back. 'In the middle '70s, with the unlimited work force at our disposal and no serious mine difficulties against us, we were able to produce an average of 320 tonnes. This enabled us to stockpile, in the event of difficulties . . .'

'Which have arisen?' anticipated Krotkov.

Leonov made a reluctant gesture of agreement. 'Our most productive mine was Muruntau, in the south-west Soviet. And then there was Zod, close to the Turkish border. Both are open-pit workings, which have divided advantages: they're easy to operate when the weather is good, but impossible when it is bad. And the same floods which have destroyed our crops have flooded our open mines. At Zod there have also been labour difficulties.'

'What's our commitment to America?' said Krotkov.

'Vast,' conceded Leonov. 'Even before the grain problems, our financial experts had calculated the over-extension of the United States dollar, linked as it is to the Eurodollar and oil payments. After the election of the new American President, our embassy in Washington reported the desire to strengthen the dollar. It gave us an advantage when we made the wheat request. We pledged payment for the wheat in gold so that they could mount a currency support operation. We averted famine and they averted a further weakening of their dollar.'

'Muruntau and Zod are practically unworkable,' reminded Krotkov.

'We weren't worried at first,' conceded Leonov. 'We've sufficient drainage equipment. No manpower shortage. Our engineers miscalculated the erosion problems and the resultant cave-ins. After pumping the floods out, the mines practically had to be re-dug. We actually had Muruntau in production and there was still some stockpile left.'

'The crops failed again this year,' said Krotkov.

'And the mines flooded again,' admitted Leonov. 'To avert a famine so widespread that it would unquestionably have resulted in uprisings throughout every republic in the Soviet, we had to exhaust our disposable stockpile to buy wheat, and when that went, we had to establish a nominee company in the West to buy and then ship to us secretly gold with which to purchase the grain. This in turn enabled the United States to stage their gold sales and support their dollar openly.'

'Holy Mother of God,' said Simenov, who was religious but usually managed to conceal it in surroundings where such a revelation might be damaging. Neither of the other two men appeared to be aware of the lapse.

'It's still an equal balance,' said Krotkov, over-extending himself in his confidence.

'No!' rejected Leonov at once. 'It's impossible to assess with absolute accuracy, but we calculate that the Federal Reserve Bank in New York holds something like 800 tonnes. That's stockpile sufficient to bluff through any demand we might artificially create. They could sustain a run against reserves. We couldn't. It wouldn't take them longer than a month, two at the most, to guess what had happened to us.'

Leonov turned to look directly at Simenov. 'To deprive us of grain to feed two hundred and sixty-three million people would be far more devastating than any atomic or neutron bomb,' he said. 'The foreign currency reserves to buy gold on the open market are limited. If anyone realised what we were doing, we could be brought to our knees.'

'Oh God,' said Simenov, uncaring this time.

'So that's why I must know, with absolute certainty, whether you think anyone saw the gold in Amsterdam,' said Leonov patiently. 'That information, in the hands of the proper analyst, could be the end of us.'

He stared, waiting, at the other man.

Simenov seemed to be debating his reply. He actually started to fumble through the folders, as if in search of a fact which had eluded them all, and then he snatched away, conscious of it being a nervous reaction.

'You have to know, with absolute accuracy?' he enquired, establishing a term of reference.

'With absolute accuracy,' echoed Leonov for emphasis.

Simenov shook his head, helplessly. 'I can't give that assurance,' he admitted. 'I think the breaking of the boxes was accidental and I don't think anyone apart from those from the embassy knew what the contents were . . .' He stopped, swallowing again. 'But I can't be sure.'

Although the man tried to conceal it, Krotkov saw the moment of despair that registered on Leonov's face, confirming the pressure that was already being imposed. And he recognised that he could become a scapegoat, as easily as the other man. But Dimitri Krotkov was a clever man. His record of service wasn't quite as long as that of the Finance Minister, but he'd survived from the days of Khrushchev, which was still impressive. And he intended to go on surviving. Krotkov wondered if Leonov would ever realise how fortunate he was in having him as an ally.

Chapter Four

Collington got back to the SAGOMI building first, but he knew his car was only minutes ahead of the rest. He considered waiting for them in the vestibule, and then decided against it: they might identify it as concern and that would be bad tactics. Collington knew tactics were going to be important for what lay ahead.

He smiled at the Afrikaner liftboy, greeting him by name, and the man smiled back and called him boss. As the elevator snatched upwards, Collington wondered idly how many of those following would even notice the presence of the man. He frowned at the criticism: it was stupid hostility, anticipating the arguments that were to come. He should be considering how Metzinger and his section of the board would seek advantages from Walter Simpson's death, not worrying about their racism. He hoped to be able to do something about one, but not about the other.

He didn't go directly into the boardroom but instead to his penthouse office alongside. Two walls were almost entirely of glass and Collington stood, staring out over the South African capital. It was the time of day when the sun bleached everything, making the white buildings all around even whiter. Simpson had joked about it the first time they had met, reciting the Noel Coward warning about the midday sun and mad dogs and Englishmen and then changing the banter, abruptly, forecasting that one day people being treated like dogs would finally bite back. Perhaps that was what had made him think of apartheid in the lift. Certainly his mind had been upon Walter Simpson — and not just the problem his death had created.

The circumstances of Collington's life meant there had been few men whom he could admire. But he'd admired Simpson; respected him, too. A father figure, thought Collington. He frowned at the idea. Never, until now, had he conceded the presence of such a person in his life.

There hadn't been one in the Barnado's home, at Kingston. The orphanage officials had discouraged attachments like that. Or afterwards. British Rail had insisted upon suitability reports and Collington knew that the stationmaster at Richmond had actually praised the independent self-confidence in listing him the best junior porter on the station. And this quality had been isolated again in the Army character assessments by the officers who promoted him, unaware that it extended to nighttime excursions in blacked-out National Service lorries during the Berlin airlift, running from one divided section to another the contraband which was the carefully concealed beginning of his entrepreneurial career.

Father figure, thought Collington again. That was undoubtedly what Simpson had become: a father figure who had adopted him and over fifteen years curbed the excessive enthusiasm and developed the maturity for him to head a multi-national the size of SAGOMI. It seemed a long time since that first meeting on a clingingly damp October day in London. He had been suspicious at first, remembered Collington, wanting to know why the takeover of his Rhodesian company by SAGOMI was already so far advanced without any involvement by the controlling English directors, but realising almost at once, from the blankness of Simpson's expression, that the man knew nothing whatsoever about it. And Simpson unsure if the approach were genuine or that of a provocateur. Simpson's questioning had meant that he had learned everything about him at that first meeting. About the orphanage and the porter's job at Richmond: even about Berlin, although he had avoided specifics. To have done otherwise would have made him seem a crook and he'd never considered himself that. An opportunist, accurately gauging the potential of an unusual situation, perhaps. But never a criminal. He'd refused to run drugs or medical supplies or human cargo. He had transported status symbol washing-machines from the American to the Soviet sector in exchange for vodka. From the French, he had shipped wine. And from the British, cigarettes. In twelve months he had amassed £7500 and lost interest in returning to the early shift at Richmond. He supposed it was the Berlin experience that made him think immediately of washing-machines when he was demobilised into a Britain emerging from the austerity of post-war restrictions and shortages. He had bought washing-machines from the factory and sold direct, undercutting by twenty per cent the retail prices in the high streets of Richmond and Twickenham and Hounslow. After washing-machines there had been refrigerators. And then television sets. Gauging the public response to television had probably been his most astute move. At the end of three years he had had a personal fortune of £60,000 and experienced the first unease of boredom; which was why the buy-out approach from one of the major manufacturers had been so welcome. The take-over proposal had intrigued him, too. Not just because it came at exactly the right time, but because of the nature of the initial proposal. It was a low cash offer, backed by a share portfolio and an invitation to sit on the board. He had refused, insisting on an outright cash settlement, but learned for the first time that one company could take over another without any money changing hands; it was a lesson he committed to his ever receptive memory.

Collington considered that coincidence had been partly responsible for his success. It was coincidence which had made the Army utilise his ability with timetables and freight problems. Coincidence again that he had been sent to Berlin and its money-making environment. Coincidence that his demobilisation had come at the beginning of the consumer boom. And coincidence that he should have decided with his buy-out money to holiday in the then-named Rhodesia. In two days he'd become bored by swimming pools, decided to tour and by the end of the week recognised the under-developed potential of the country. Within three months he had settled there permanently. He had founded a commodity brokerage and negotiated future contracts on the tobacco and produce from dozens of farms, and within a year he had had to establish a transport division to handle it. He had bought a farm of his own, with a manager to run it, and it had been at a farmers' annual dinner at Salisbury's Meikles Hotel that he'd met Hannah Metzinger. That, too, had involved coincidence, although he hadn't known at the time that her father was connected with one of the biggest mining corporations in South Africa. The coincidence of that had emerged much later, after the opposed marriage and the near estrangement, when he had agreed with the neighbouring farmer upon whose land the gold lode was discovered to set up a development company and work it, with experts imported from South Africa's Witwatersrand.

Metzinger's approach had been surprising because of the hostility which existed between them, particularly after the marriage to Hannah. In every other respect, the suggestion of a SAGOMI take-over made sound, practical sense. Already the political uncertainty of the country, just prior to illegal independence, was sufficient to make Collington think of moving on. SAGOMI had superior trading experience in metals, and appeared prepared to take the risk in Rhodesia where Collington was not.

Despite the feeling between him and his father-in-law, it was not suspicion which initially prompted Collington to examine the share register. He did it in order to study the construction of the various companies and learn their government by interlocking boards of directors, rising like a pyramid with the controlling SAGOMI directors at the top. The realisation that he was dealing only with Afrikaners who didn't control the company was accidental — coincidence again — but it needed Simpson, over a civilised, unhurried lunch in the subdued elegance of London's Connaught Hotel, to explain it, once he'd satisfied himself of Collington's integrity.

The SAGOMI board was determined by the holding of 'A' shares in the original Witwatersrand mining company. The English directors maintained supremacy with three hundred shares, against the two hundred and fifty held by Metzinger's Afrikaner caucus. It was the simplest arithmetic, but it illustrated the deep Afrikaner resentment, not just in SAGOMI but throughout South African commerce, that the majority of their major businesses were British dominated.

Simpson had long feared an attempted coup and identified it as being the take-over of Collington's company. The only way the balance of power could be altered was by a vote of no confidence from the shareholders, on a motion showing British neglect. He guessed Metzinger intended to get that no-confidence motion by bringing the take-over to the point of actually obtaining Collington's legally binding agreement. And then making the announcement immediately before the annual meeting, to show that the acquisition of such a valuable holding had been solely the work of Afrikaners maintaining the success of the company, without the support of the English.

Collington had never forgotten how they had confronted deviousness with deviousness.

Already he had been aware of the wealth of SAGOMI from his share register investigation. The meeting with Simpson convinced him that to achieve their apparent stability, the company had sacrificed opportunities to expand further: and that if he became a part of it he would become even more successful. At Simpson's urging, he agreed to appear to accept the terms of the take-over. And to continue as a pawn in the negotiations, accepting without any contractural backing Simpson's assurance of protection if they were successful in resisting Metzinger.

Under Simpson's instruction, Collington returned to South Africa to negotiate with Metzinger not simply for a cash settlement, but for the secondary 'A' share apportionment in SAGOMI that had been floated to raise development money in the first year of the Witwatersrand operation. And to insist that Bruce Jamieson, the neighbouring farmer on whose land the gold was actually located, should be treated equally. There were two hundred secondary shares, carrying none of the voting power — and therefore the importance — of the normal 'A' holdings. They had all been owned by the Afrikaners who had used their purchase to gain access to the company in the first place. Confident that there was no danger, Metzinger and his two fellow Afrikaner directors surrendered them to Collington, dismissing it as a minor sacrifice that would contribute to their absolute coup.

Metzinger delayed until the last possible moment his revelation of the take-over, wrongly expecting the week before the annual meeting to be occupied by the panicked arrival from London of the rest of the board.

But Collington had kept Simpson informed of every stage of the deal. On the day when Metzinger planned to make the surprise, embarrassing announcement, all the English directors were assembled in Pretoria. They summoned a full meeting of the SAGOMI board to coincide with it, giving the impression of complete awareness of what had been happening, and approved the merger. Once that had been made irrevocable, Simpson proposed an alteration of the share structure, elevating the secondary 'A' shares to voting power. It had been a vicious, angry meeting, with Metzinger and the Afrikaners attempting every opposition and being met at every effort by Simpson and Richard Jenkins. With insufficient votes to prevent the adoption of Simpson's suggestion, the Afrikaners were outmanœuvred.

When Simpson had spoken of rewards, Collington hadn't expected the deputy chairmanship. Nor the chairmanship that followed two years later, when he'd adjusted to the power of a corporation spanning two continents and was setting out to work towards the expansion which had brought SAGOMI to its present position. Collington knew there were many men who would have resented the speed with which he established his own control; objected, through jealousy and hurt pride, at the suggestion of the chairmanship which Simpson held. But it had never happened, not once. And it was not until today that Collington fully recognised that Simpson had groomed him to succeed, conscious of his age and of the need to pass on the corporation of which he had been justly proud to someone who had filled the place of the son he never had.

Groomed him but for one omission, thought Collington angrily. The annoyance burned through him at the thought of his incredible mistake. It had been Simpson's, too, he supposed, but he exonerated the man. Simpson had been ill, dying. It was unfair to apportion any responsibility to him. There was only one person to blame for the oversight and Collington accepted the responsibility.

Collington turned at the sound from behind, and saw his father-in-law framed in the doorway. Collington was a big man, well over six feet, but although he didn't have the height, Metzinger appeared bigger. The large-bodied impression was not of fat, but of muscle, broad shoulders and huge hands, and hair cropped militarily short around his unlined, tanned face.

A Boer and proud of it, remembered Collington. That had been Metzinger's own description of himself, the day Collington had travelled from Salisbury to Pretoria to tell the man of his intention to marry Hannah. Metzinger had offered it as the reason for opposing the marriage, not wanting his daughter to marry outside the Afrikaner caste system.

Hannah had prepared Collington, just as she was prepared to ignore the anticipated objections, listing the Voortrekker commemorations in which her father had taken part and recounting the efforts to which he had gone, locating the spot in the

English-built concentration camp where he believed his grandmother had died so that he could erect a headstone in her memory. The year-long search had reflected the fetish Metzinger had about his ancestry and his country's history. At his ranch, on the outskirts of the capital, he had preserved and restored three covered wagons in which the Boers had fled into the Transvaal from the Cape, and the walls of the house were filled with original pictures and prints of the Voortrekkers.

'A sad day,' greeted Metzinger.

'Yes,' agreed Collington. It was not surprising that Janet Simpson had refused his offer to travel back from the funeral, going instead with Metzinger, decided Collington. There had never been any friendship between them, despite Simpson's attempts to create one. How the hell could he have forgotten Janet's Afrikaner ancestry!

'He'll be sadly missed.' Metzinger succeeded in making the platitude sound sincere.

'Yes,' said Collington again. The brevity was intentional, in the hope of drawing Metzinger in advance of the board meeting.

'Surprised he wanted to be buried here and not back in England, with his first wife?'

'Not really,' said Collington. 'I think he'd come to regard South Africa as his home.'

Where did he regard as home? wondered Collington. The Rhodesian farm, maybe, when he and Hannah lived there in the first years of their marriage. And the house in Pretoria, before the separation. Now he had no feeling of permanence anywhere. Perhaps it was the sub-conscious affect of an orphanage upbringing. It had been months since he'd thought back that far. If he were Metzinger, he supposed he would have paid investigators to probe through the records and discover who his parents were; sought them out, to discover if he were an orphan through death or illegitimacy. The idea had actually occurred to him, fleetingly, years before. And he had discarded it just as quickly. If they were dead, he would have found strangers to mourn. If he were illegitimate, he would have been an embarrassing reminder of his mother's mistake. It was best left as it was. Unlike Metzinger, Collington was more concerned with the future than the past. And Simpson's death made the future uncertain.

'I dropped Janet off on the way back,' said Metzinger. 'She's taking it very well.'

'Walter had been ill for some time,' reminded Collington. He would have liked to have known more of the discussion between Metzinger and Janet Simpson on their return from the funeral.

'Still a shock, though.'

'Yes.' Metzinger was playing with him, decided Collington. He'd been right in anticipating a difficult meeting.

'The others are in the boardroom,' said the deputy chairman.

'We'd better go in then,' said Collington. He strode across the room towards Metzinger. For a moment he paused beside his father-in-law, creating the comparison. The nickname 'Tiny' had first been given to Collington in the Barnado's home when, at the age of seventeen, he had been six feet tall. It had stuck when he joined British Rail with a uniform two sizes too small because they only came in stock sizes, and it was permanent by the time he entered the army for his National Service. His growth had stopped there. Army records had listed him at 6′ 6″: they'd had trouble with the uniforms there too. The tailoring was better now, but Collington never tried to minimise his height. Rather, he saw it as an advantage, conscious of the impression it created. Metzinger used his size the same way.

There was a momentary hesitation and Collington gestured the older man to precede him. The other directors were arranged at the conference table like opposing armies in some biblical encounter, drawn up on either side of a valley, English to the right, Afrikaners to the left. He nodded, generally, and there were answering gestures in return.

Collington took his place at the head, looking down at the others present. He purposely looked to the left first. Immediately beside him was Metzinger, as deputy chairman. Next to Metzinger was Louis de Villiers, a thin, bespectacled man who had begun his career as an accountant and spent too much time at meetings scrutinising accounts. The third Afrikaner was Jan Wassenaar, a company lawyer. He was a sparse, reserved man, rarely allowing any emotion or feeling to reach his face. He reminded Collington of the dried-out trees he and Paul had photographed when he had taken his son on safari near the Kalahari. They'd been together as a family then, remembered Collington; his predominant recollection was how much he and Hannah had laughed. It seemed so long since they had found anything to laugh about. Collington put aside the reflection, continuing down the table. Rupert Brooking occupied the seat to his right. He was a languid, indulged man whose accountant had recommended he buy his way into a directorship of the Witwatersrand mining company years before, rightly feeling that the man might otherwise squander his inheritance. His elevation to the parent board had occurred almost automatically. Simpson had recognised Brooking as pliable and kept him under tight control. But now Simpson was gone. Which meant Brooking was a weakness, someone who would always sway with the majority, anxious for the easiest way out.

The Englishman next to him was Henry Platt. He was an accountant, like de Villiers. And like de Villiers, he looked it. But they were quite different men. De Villiers constantly imagined trickery. Platt's only interest was profit and he was impatient with any extenuating circumstances which might temporarily prevent it. Several times he and Collington had clashed over Platt's automatic reaction to cut off or close down any of their enterprises which was suffering a decline.

The chair in which Walter Simpson had always sat on such occasions had been left empty, as a mark of respect. Bruce Jamieson sat beyond. Collington smiled briefly at the man with whom he had developed the Zimbabwe gold mine and Jamieson smiled back. It was a paradox, thought Collington, that he regarded Simpson as having been far closer to him than Jamieson, whom he had known much longer. There had been house visiting and parties, more in Salisbury than here, but Collington had always found it difficult to think of the man as anything more than a business partner. There was an element of puritanism in Jamieson, which would account for his reserve towards Collington since the marriage break-up. Reminded of Hannah again, Collington thought back to the funeral and the surprise approach from his wife. It had been two months since their last contact and this time there had been none of the former hostility; she'd actually appeared pleased to see him.

Her invitation, just as he was leaving, had momentarily confused him, so that he had fallen back on the half excuse about pressure of work and said he didn't know if he could manage the visit she suggested. The confrontation had added to a day of uncertainties. He'd been lying about the work, he realised. There wasn't any reason why he shouldn't go out to Parkstown later, apart from the apprehension at what she might say.

The fifth chair which Richard Jenkins, the other English director, should have occupied, was empty. Jenkins' inability to get there from London was a complication he didn't need. Jenkins was a blunt, plainspeaking man whose support would have been useful against the pressure Collington was anticipating.

'Apology for absence,' began Collington formally. 'Richard Jenkins is kept in London. He sends his regrets.'

'I would have thought the circumstances demanded the effort,' said Wassenaar, needing to score at the smallest opportunity.

'He had apologised,' repeated Collington.

'What voting indication?' demanded Metzinger.

'Proxy, vested with the chairman,' said Collington. He passed sideways the authority that Jenkins had sent so that the Afrikaner could see it. Metzinger read it carefully and then returned it. First Wassenaar, now Metzinger; they were declaring themselves immediately.

Collington indicated the empty chair to his right. 'The death of Walter Simpson has created a vacancy upon this board,' he said, still formal. 'I have convened this meeting to consider replacements.'

'Any nominations?' asked Brooking at once. He was given to neutral questions so that he could appear to be contributing, but rarely said anything that could be construed as controversial.

'Several,' said Collington, moving to circulate the names around the table.

'Is there a necessity for a replacement?' asked Wassenaar.

'Necessity?' echoed Collington. He would have expected this challenge to come from Metzinger. Perhaps they had rehearsed the attack.

As if in confirmation, Metzinger said: 'There is no stipulation in the minutes governing the composition of the parent board that there should be nine directors.'

There wasn't, Collington knew. He had checked, the day of Simpson's death, and realised the oversight that was too late to correct. He'd been right in his anticipation of the Afrikaner pressure.

'Surely the composition is established by fact,' he said, aware of the weakness of the argument.

De Villiers, with his clerk-like mind, had been studying the replacement nominations. He looked up, coming to the support of the other South Africans. 'No one on this list has sufficient qualifying shareholding in any of the subsidiary companies,' he said. 'There would have to be a share adjustment.'

'Little more than a formality,' said Collington. He was not a man who liked unsound arguments and was irritated by the hollowness of what he was saying.

'A great deal more than a formality,' corrected Metzinger. He paused, challenging Collington to resume the argument. When Collington remained silent, Metzinger took several sheets of paper from his briefcase and laid them out before him. When he looked up, there was a faint smile of satisfaction. The bastard had undertaken a lot of preparation, thought Collington.

'Witwatersrand 'A' shares are an essential for a place upon this board,' insisted Metzinger. He took a gold pen from an inside pocket, making tiny ticks against the names listed in front of him. 'Of the voting shares in Witwatersrand the chairman and Jamieson hold one fifty each, Platt one hundred, with Jenkins apportioned thirty and Brooking twenty . . . .' Metzinger looked up, again inviting Collington to argue. Collington stared back, expressionlessly. He knew what Metzinger intended to do. And like the forgotten share inheritance he had realised after Simpson's death, he was powerless to dispute it. Why hadn't he recognised earlier the possible danger? Simpson had been ill for almost six months. And for the last two of those it had been obvious that it was terminal.

His preoccupation with Hannah and Ann? He frowned at the thought. If that were the case, then he was guilty of stupidity, as well. Before he had always been able to keep his private life absolutely separate from any business consideration.

'As founder shareholder, the late Walter Simpson held two hundred shares. I have one hundred and fifty and Wassenaar and de Villiers hold fifty each,' continued Metzinger.

The challenge came down to simple arithmetic, just like the lunch all those years ago at the Connaught, Collington recognised. With Simpson alive and as a result of the secondary share adjustment at the time of the gold lode take-over, the English side of the board had held overwhelming superiority with four hundred and fifty shares against the South African two hundred and fifty. But if Simpson's two hundred shares were switched, the division would be reversed, the Afrikaners controlling four hundred and fifty against the English three fifty.

'Simpson's shares become available,' said Platt, taking the lure that Metzinger intended. 'We merely apportion to Mrs Simpson sufficient non-voting shares to compensate for the capital represented in those necessary for transfer to the next nomination.'

Metzinger didn't speak at once, prolonging his enjoyment. At last he announced. 'Mrs Simpson does not wish to dispose of her voting shares. Although not seeking board nomination, she intends to retain possession.'

From the English side there was the silence of complete awareness.

'A temporary reluctance, surely,' came in Brooking, forgetting his usual caution. 'Confusion of grief, that sort of thing. Once the situation is explained, she'll understand she's not being deprived of any income . . . .'

'It has been explained,' cut off Metzinger impatiently. 'Mrs Simpson is withstanding the grief remarkably well. It was she who raised the subject with me. She asked me to make it quite clear at this meeting that she will not surrender the voting shares she has been left in Simpson's will.'

Brooking, like Jamieson before him, looked to Collington for guidance. Collington was gazing beyond the man to Platt. The accountant made a brief calculation on the pad before him, hesitated uncertainly and then said, 'There could be a disposal between directors Metzinger, de Villiers and Wassenaar, to enable a new director to be brought on to the board.'

'Why from the South African representation?' challenged de Villiers logically and at once. 'Why can't there be an adjustment from the English side of the board?'

No reason at all, thought Collington. Except that it would further diminish their share control. So what was more important, share strength or directorship superiority? He looked down at the list of nominations he had prepared. Not one upon whom he would be able to rely for unquestioned support. So all he was considering was numbers. And numerically he was still in control.

'This is not a discussion I consider should be continued in the absence of a director,' said Jamieson, speaking for the first time and moving the talk away from a direct confrontation.

Collington looked towards the man gratefully. 'It is not a decision that *has* to be made now,' he said. 'It could be left for the annual meeting.'

He knew Metzinger would also have anticipated this possibility. By the time they faced the shareholders, Metzinger would have ensured sufficient votes against the parent board being increased, unless the nominee was an Afrikaner.

As if aware of Collington's thoughts, Metzinger said, 'We would be quite happy for the matter to be considered then.'

The meeting was ending far more quickly than Collington had expected. He wouldn't propose it at the shareholders' meeting, he decided. He'd have to content himself with the reduced strength.

'Director nomination was the only purpose of this meeting,' said Collington. 'Is there any other business?'

'I think a formal letter should be written to Mrs Simpson, inviting her to dispose of her voting shares,' said Jamieson.

Metzinger turned quickly to the man. 'Are you doubting me?' he said. It was the first time since the start of the meeting that the Afrikaner had given way to anger. It was a thoughtless lapse.

'Of course not!' said Jamieson, emphasising his astonishment to heighten the other man's mistake. 'It would be a proper thing for this board to do.'

'I agree,' said Collington quickly. 'Is that a formal proposal?'

'Yes,' said the man.

'I second,' said Platt.

'In favour?' persisted Collington. Just like a biblical encounter, he thought again. The Afrikaners sat still. Every hand went up on the English side.

'Carried, with the proxy vote of Jenkins,' said Collington. It was a pointless victory but he still felt some satisfaction. 'Any other business?' he invited again.

From around the table there were varying gestures, but Collington rose to end the meeting. The South Africans came up in a group, de Villiers and Wassenaar looking to Metzinger for direction. Metzinger hesitated and for a moment Collington thought he was going to speak. Instead the man jerked his head in a swift gesture of farewell and led the other two from the room.

The four English directors stood about, unsure what to do. Collington remained silent, considering what had happened. He had been outmanœuvred and that hadn't happened for many years. He was both irritated and worried by the realisation.

'It'll be important for none of us to miss any meetings in future,' said Jamieson.

'Yes,' agreed Collington.

'I'm surprised Walter Simpson didn't foresee the attack,' said Platt.

'We should all have anticipated it,' said Collington, coming to the immediate defence of the man. 'And me more than most. I made a mistake and I'm sorry for it.'

'Worried?' asked Platt.

Collington hesitated for a moment. 'Maybe I'd grown complacent,' he said.

'We're all equally to blame,' said Platt. 'We let things become slack; it's been too easy for too long.'

'Little point in jumping at shadows,' said Jamieson objectively. 'They've won a battle, not the war.'

Platt began gathering his papers into his briefcase. 'Don't forget how they fought the Boer War,' he said. 'Guerrilla tactics, all the time.'

And that would be a strategy Metzinger would know about better than any of them, reflected Collington.

Ann had been in conference with Richard Jenkins when the call came from Pretoria, so she had known at once who it was. It would have been easy to get on to the line, to go to her own office and instruct the switchboard to transfer the connection when the first conversation was over and then tell Collington of Metzinger's pressure and about Peter whom she needed for companionship but didn't love and admit she was in a mess and ask for help and forgiveness. She'd even half rehearsed the phrases, for the letters she hadn't written and the telephone calls she hadn't made. And then, as she left Jenkins' room for her own in the SAGOMI building just off Threadneedle Street, she thought again of the photographs and the reports in the manila envelopes that Metzinger had left and sat staring at the telephone until she knew Collington had gone.

The summons from Jenkins had been immediate and the concern was obvious; there was no embarrassment between them about their ended affair. It had resolved into a friendship and Ann knew he trusted her completely, which heightened her feeling of helplessness. He briefed her on what had happened in South Africa and itemised Collington's concern, actually asking her to prepare position papers on any activities within their British division of the corporation which might be vulnerable in the Afrikaners' attack. Initially Jenkins was too preoccupied with his own reaction to what had happened in Pretoria to notice her dispirited response, but finally he looked up, frowning, and said, 'Is anything wrong?'

'No,' she said. 'Why?'

Jenkins shrugged. 'You seem a little odd, that's all.'

'Could control of the company actually switch, because of this?' she asked, to move the conversation on.

'Too early to say,' said Jenkins. 'We're going to have to watch ourselves.'

'Richard . . .' she blurted impulsively, wanting to tell him.

Jenkins had gone back to the notes he had made during his conversation with Collington. He looked up, frowning again. 'What?'

For several moments they stared at each other. Then Ann said, 'Nothing.'

'Sure you're all right?'

'Positive.'

'James can handle it,' said the man, misunderstanding the reason for her attitude and coming as close as he ever had to acknowledging the relationship he knew existed between her and Collington. 'He's worried, but he's sure he can handle it.'

'Of course,' she said.

Ann had been back in her own office for thirty minutes when the telephone sounded and momentarily she thought it was Jenkins, with something he had forgotten. And then she became aware of the nasal intonation and recognised Metzinger's voice.

'I'm monitoring the switchboard here,' said the Afrikaner. 'There was a call this afternoon to London.'

'Yes,' she said dully.

'What about?'

Ann didn't reply for several moments, and Metzinger said, 'Did you read that stuff I left you?'

'Yes,' she said.

'So what was it about?'

Haltingly, actually moving her pen through the notes she had made, Ann recounted her meeting with Jenkins. At the end Metzinger said, 'Is that all?'

'That's all.'

'Sure?'

'Of course I'm sure.'

'I want a copy of the position papers.'

Ann felt a physical disgust at talking with the man. 'I've got to go,' she said.

'You've started well,' said Metzinger.

And by disclosing what she had done in this conversation, she had committed herself even more deeply, Ann realised.

'Keep it up,' said Metzinger, concluding the conversation.

Slowly Ann replaced the receiver, bringing her hand back against her forehead. 'Oh Christ!' she moaned into the empty room.

Chapter Five

Generals who win wars accept the honours on behalf of their armies and there is a parallel with the selection for the Presidency of the United States of America. Behind every successful candidate there are legions of men committed to the campaign. John William Pemberton's win was achieved, however, with a military precision unusual even for American politics. It fulfilled not only his own overweening ambition but that of a dynastic Boston family whose founder had amassed millions from the country's thrust to maturity at the turn of the century and whose descendants, over the succeeding eighty years, had gained all but the ultimate office in government service.

Under the patronage system of American politics, it is easier for presidents to reward their lieutenants than it is for modern generals. And for Pemberton it was easier than most, because he was sure of those around him. The leaders of his campaign were men who had been vetted and tested and then selected with particular care, each supremely qualified to run what was planned — just as the campaign had been planned — to be a brilliant administration.

Henry Moreton was one of the men chosen to help Pemberton earn a place in history. And he knew it. Moreton had come from the Harvard Business School, with an honours degree and a rare sense of dedication, to serve as Finance Director of Pemberton's election machine. And distinguished himself as the ideal worker. Without sycophancy or insincerity, he had subjugated personal ambition and a great deal of his personal life to one exclusive, all important goal — to get Pemberton into the White House. Not once, throughout the four years, was the election machinery threatened by a shortage of money.

It was a remarkable achievement and one for which Pemberton, not Moreton, earned the credit. Moreton wanted reward, not congratulation. And he got it. His selection as Secretary to the Treasury was one of the first appointments announced by Pemberton when he moved into Pennsylvannia Avenue.

Because there had been no evidence of ambition during the time he served upon the President's staff, there were those who imagined that Moreton was a rarity in Washington, a man actually *without* ambition. Which was quite untrue. Moreton had plotted his career with the personal neatness with which he kept his ledger and account books. He had worked with such obsessiveness precisely to gain the Treasury appointment. Having got it, he intended to benefit from it. The decision in no way impinged upon his loyalty to the President. Everything he did would continue to be in support of the man, but at last he had a public, recognisable appointment. And Moreton wanted to be recognised. During the run up, he had established himself as a meticulous financial planner. Now he wanted appreciation as a financial innovator. The chance to prove himself arrived sooner than he had expected.

Pemberton had come to office on a pledge of strength, calculating the appeal of a commitment to restore America's honour and prestige throughout the world. It didn't take long for political commentators to mock that undertaking by comparison with a falteringly weak dollar.

Moreton had always been fascinated by the frequent references at Harvard to the inherent, almost mystical appeal of precious metals over any other form of currency, even to hardened financiers. The memory of those early lessons came within the first minutes of the cabinet meeting, when he heard for the first time of the Soviet request for wheat and grain sales, following the successive Russian harvest failures which the CIA had already reported from their aerial reconnaissance.

Moreton's presence at the meeting had been little more than a courtesy gesture from the President, but he dominated the discussion after the Soviet gold offer was disclosed. It provided, argued Moreton, a unique opportunity to underpin the dollar. World gold supplies were controlled by two producers, South Africa and the Soviet Union. And South Africa, conscious of the power it gave them, curtailed its output. The Soviet approach provided America with the opportunity to establish gold reserves greater than those already held in the Federal Reserve Bank in New York. Moreton's argument was that if they established sufficient reserves, they could resume their monthly open-market gold sales and it would only be a matter of weeks before the metal markets recognised what they would believe to be a miscalculation of the size of the U.S. reserves. They could allow leaks from the Treasury to encourage the speculation. And then confirm their holdings at the much higher figure.

The effect, insisted Moreton, would be automatic and involve them in no further effort at all. Supported by the unshakeable belief in the strength of gold, the dollar would harden. The chance to disperse the grain stored in hoppers throughout the mid-West would be an additional advantage and increase Pemberton's backing in states like Iowa and Oklahoma where he had not shown particularly well during the election.

The simplicity of the argument carried the meeting. The gold for grain treaty was secretly concluded and in the course of nine months, America's reserves had increased sufficiently for Moreton to announce the monthly gold sales.

When he first proposed the idea he had intended waiting longer, but so smoothly was the agreement running that Moreton saw no point in delaying any further: he'd been in the shadows for almost five years and he was anxious for the sunlight.

It had been necessary to disclose what was happening to the senior permanent advisers at the Treasury and some argued against a premature resumption of sales. If, for any reason, they had to suspend them after a few months, speculators would imagine a bluff to conceal a shortage, rather than a surplus of gold. And then the whole scheme would backfire, draining the dollar even further. But it was a minority opinion and Moreton had no difficulty in convincing them eventually that nothing could go wrong.

On the day that Nikolai Leonov left the KGB headquarters in Moscow having found nothing to allay his worries, Henry Moreton arrived early at the *Sans Souci* for his meeting. The sales had started and with them the rumours. And Moreton was lunching with a feature writer for *Fortune* magazine. It was the beginning of his campaign for recognition.

Chapter Six

Long after his call to Richard Jenkins in London, Collington sat hunched at his desk. Jenkins had been right in his blunt assessment. A bloody nuisance, the man had said. But they still had numerical superiority. Collington found it a weak assurance. He'd been beaten. Outflanked and outmanœuvred and beaten, like someone playing Monopoly for the first time and not knowing the rules. There was no excuse, not even distraction of Hannah and Ann. From the time of his very first association with SAGOMI he had been warned of Metzinger's determination to gain control, and because of the share deal that had been evolved then, he should have remembered the inherent danger of the size of Simpson's holding. It was a crass oversight.

Pointlessly Collington jabbed through his diary, knowing before he turned the pages that he had no further appointments that day.

So what about Hannah? There was no reason why he shouldn't go. And he was definitely curious. Perhaps she had made her mind up, ahead of him. And wanted a divorce. He supposed he would give it to her, if she asked; that was the agreement they had made when they had decided to separate. Which would mean he was free to marry Ann. In London, Ann was increasingly being recognised as someone more than just a mistress. It would be formalising an existing situation. But did he want to? He wasn't sure, Collington realised.

He left the room impatiently, announcing to his personal staff as he passed through the outer office that he would not be returning that day. It was just four, he saw, as the lift descended. In the early days he hadn't been able to quit in the middle of the afternoon. Then he'd worked as if clocks hadn't been invented, his life regulated by the work to be done, not by the sweep of a second or a minute hand.

The heat had gone from the day, so Collington lowered the hood of the Corniche, moving out on to one of the feed roads into Church Street and then turning westwards, travelling through the heart of the city. Far away on the hills, the clouds were gathering in preparation for a familiar thunderstorm, and Collington decided he would have to cover the car before going in to see Hannah. He was moving through the oldest part of the city, by the Raadzaal and the Reserve Bank and the Kruger monument in Church Square, and as he did frequently, Collington stared around, trying to find some attraction in the capital. And as always, he failed. For Collington there was an impression of flatness about Pretoria, cupped between the hills, that created for him a feeling of impermanence. He preferred the snag-toothed skyscrapers of Cape Town, with its proper mountains. Or Johannesburg. But at least Pretoria had the jacaranda trees as compensation, Collington reflected, turning off Church Street on to the highway leading to Parkstown. Purple and sapphire flowers blossomed on either side of him, almost artificial in their profusion. Beyond the trees, the clipped lawn and barbered hedges and the methodical sprinklers began their established pattern as he entered the residential suburb.

He turned familiarly into the driveway, gazing from side to side for any changes in the gardens that bordered the approach to the house. There were more jacaranda trees and roses, with their identity labelled at the base, and more sprinklers, in case the thunderstorms which always came didn't erupt, just once. The same as last time, thought Collington — even the bloom of the roses.

He parked carefully to the side of the colonnaded entrance and as he got from the car saw Hannah, standing at the door.

'I wasn't sure you'd come,' she said as he mounted the steps.

'Neither was I,' lied Collington.

He stopped, uncertainly, on the porch. Hannah hesitated too, caught by the same difficulty. She was the one to resolve it, offering her cheek. Collington stooped, coming into the briefest contact. Like strangers, he thought. But better than last time. Then there had been the lawyers and the formal talks about access to Paul, which was unnecessary anyway because the boy was at boarding school in England.

Hannah maintained the lead, turning and going ahead of him

into the house. He followed slowly behind her, looking around him. Had this seemed like home, he wondered, thinking back to his reflections earlier in the day. He supposed it had, while he lived there. But he hadn't thought about it, from the day he'd left.

She went into the smaller sitting-room, the one that led out to the pool. Without knowing why, he had expected people to be there, but it was deserted.

'Outside or in?' she asked.

'I think it's going to rain,' said Collington. And he'd forgotten to put the hood up on the car.

'Inside then,' she accepted. 'Booze or tea?'

'Tea.'

He watched as Hannah rang the small bell and gave the order. The boy was new and looked at Collington without recognition.

'If such a thing can be, it was a nice funeral,' she said.

She'd chosen a neutral comment, thought Collington; just like Brooking.

'Yes,' he said. He tried to think of something more to add. 'Janet seemed to take it well.'

'She's as tough as hell,' judged Hannah.

'She's retaining the voting shares in Witwatersrand,' said Collington. Hannah would learn that soon enough, so he wasn't volunteering anything.

'Is that a problem for you?'

'Inconvenient,' said Collington dismissively.

He stared at the woman sitting opposite him, admitting the excitement. She was tall, which matched his own height, and big-bodied, the firmness of her breasts and hips accentuated by the dress into which she had changed after the funeral. In the battling weeks before they had parted there had been a haggardness, but that had gone now. She had obviously been sunbathing and the tan pointed up the greyness of her eyes and contrasted with the blond hair reaching almost to her shoulders, longer than he remembered. Conscious of his attention, she made an embarrassed gesture.

'I had a letter from Paul today,' she said. 'He wrote that you had a marvellous time in London.'

'I owe him a letter,' admitted Collington. He was surprised, if that had been his son's judgment. He had extended the last of his regular visits to London to take the boy out on one of his exeats.

He had told Paul that he and Hannah were separating and had taken all the guilt, without mentioning Ann, and Paul had said he understood. Collington had known the boy was lying. The entire weekend had been artificial, each trying to help the other and failing. The relief when they parted had been mutual.

'He said you explained. About us,' said Hannah.

'I thought it was right he should know.'

'I think you should have discussed it with me first.'

'Why?'

'Because it would have been the proper thing to do, for a start. The decisions about him are supposed to be joint now, remember?'

'It was the honest thing to do.'

'And upsetting, for him.'

'We *are* separated, for Christ's sake!'

'I thought it was supposed to be a trial.'

'It is.'

'Then what if we decide it's a mistake and get back together? There would have been no need for him to have known at all.'

'I'm sorry,' said Collington. 'I thought it was for the best.'

The houseboy returned with the tea, setting it out on the table before them. Hannah poured, remembering how he liked it.

'How are you?' she said, offering him the cup.

'Fine. You?'

'Fine.'

They smiled, both aware of the awkwardness.

'How was London?' she said, breaking the silence.

'Cold. And wet,' shrugged Collington. Had that been a casual remark? Or had she discovered about Ann? It would have been logical for her lawyers to suggest enquiries to provide grounds for a divorce.

'I don't suppose this should be happening,' said Hannah. 'After the last time we were supposed to meet only through lawyers.'

'I won't tell if you don't!' said Collington.

She smiled again, but almost immediately became serious. 'I'm sorry for all those things that were said.'

'Most of them were true.'

'I'm still sorry.'

Was she offering a reconciliation, ahead of the time they had decided upon for a decision, wondered Collington suddenly. Inexplicably, he was surprised.

'I'm not enjoying it,' she said in sudden admission.

Collington found her truthfulness disconcerting. He moved to speak, but she held up her hands, stopping him. 'Don't think I'm pleading for you to come back,' she qualified quickly. 'That's the trouble. I'm unhappy when you're here and I'm unhappy when you're not . . . .' She made an uncertain movement. 'Why can't we sort ourselves out?'

'I don't know.'

'What do you want to do?'

'That was the point of the separation, for us to decide.'

'Why six months? It doesn't take that long for two people to make up their minds about whether they want to stay married or not.'

'I don't know what I want to do.'

She put her cup down on a side table, too hard, so that the china clattered against the saucer. 'What sort of an answer is that?'

'An honest one. Do you want a divorce?'

'No,' she said immediately.

'I thought that's why you asked me here.'

She shrugged her shoulders. 'I'm not sure why I did. I was cross, I suppose, about your telling Paul.'

'So you haven't . . .'

'. . . met anyone else,' she completed for him. 'Sounds like something from a movie, doesn't it?'

'Have you?' he persisted.

'No. Have you?'

Now was the time for the honesty he had been portraying a few minutes earlier. At once came the contradiction. The time for that had been months before, when his behaviour had made their living together impossible. And when Hannah had asked him then, he had denied it. So an admission now would be a confession of a lie, as well as adultery.

'No,' he said, despising his cowardice.

'Paul asked in his letter what we were going to do.'

'What did you say?'

'I haven't written back yet.'

'From what he said, there seem to be quite a few kids with

divorced parents at his school.'

'I'm not interested in other children, just Paul.'

Outside the late afternoon had grown dark with storm clouds. It would start to rain soon, Collington realised, remembering the car.

'When is he due home, on holiday?'

'Not for some time.'

'Why don't we get together then?'

'Mightn't that confuse him, after being told we're apart?'

'I thought he might like the idea of us remaining friends . . . knowing we don't hate each other.'

'I could never hate you,' she said, her voice softening.

She could if she discovered the truth, thought Collington. 'I could never hate you, either,' he said.

'Nor is there reason not to see each other.'

'No,' he said.

'I'm glad you came.'

'So am I.'

'I wasn't really angry, about Paul. It's best he knows. If we're ever going to sort ourselves out at all, it will be by being honest.'

'Yes,' he said. He experienced a sudden sensation of claustrophobia and wondered if she were aware of his discomfort. 'There are some things I've got to do,' he said.

She frowned, recognising the attempt to get away. 'Of course.'

She went with him to the door and once more offered her cheek. He kissed her, as lightly as before. At the car he turned and said, 'Perhaps I could call you sometime?'

Hannah hesitated and then said, 'Yes, why don't you?'

Collington turned the car back on to the looped drive, pressing the control for the hood to come up. Christ, what a bloody hypocrite! James Collington, the man of integrity and fair dealing. Yet with a woman he loved he cheated and lied through cowardice. And he still loved her, he decided. He forced himself to concede that one of the underlying reasons for going there that afternoon, perhaps *the* reason, had been to discover if the feeling were still there. It had taken him only a few minutes to realise it was. Which solved nothing, he thought miserably. Because he knew that if he had been in London, with Ann, he would have felt the same for her. So why couldn't he have done what any other man would have attempted in his favoured circumstances? He had homes in both capitals, thousands of miles apart. So why couldn't he have remained with Hannah in South Africa and Ann in London? Because he couldn't sustain the deceit, he realised. He could lie and run, but he couldn't maintain the artifice all the time. Perhaps that was some sort of integrity, he attempted to reassure himself. But it was convoluted.

He began to enter the city, able to pick out the SAGOMI skyscraper block at the top of which was the penthouse into which he had moved from Parkstown. The building brought him back to that afternoon's meeting and the clash with Metzinger.

Was it as dramatic as he was attempting to make it? The English control had been weakened, unquestionably. And he doubted if he could find a way to restore it. But just weakened: not lost. And neither would it be, providing he was careful and avoided a repetition of the mistake that he had made over Simpson's holdings.

The storm broke in a sudden flurry of rain and hail, with the lightning twitching over the hills. Collington coasted the car carefully into the underground car park, grateful for the shelter. He took the basement lift to the first floor, then transferred to the separate elevator linking him directly to the penthouse.

Daniel was waiting in the hallway. Collington gave the houseboy his briefcase and ordered a gin, then walked into the main room. The curtains were still undrawn. The storm was worse than usual, huge black clouds squatting on the hills and parts of the city itself, concealing them completely. As high as he was, Collington could see the water funnelling along the streets below, temporarily flooding the drains. He stayed there, watching the fury of the weather exhaust itself and then lessen, until the rain stopped completely, the curtain of clouds gradually lifting. He heard the clock chime seven behind him. Seven o'clock: an evening before him, with no plans to fill it. Should he have invited Hannah to dinner? He didn't think she had expected it. He wasn't sure it would have been a good idea, anyway.

Collington cupped both hands around his glass, staring unseeingly into it. He was held by a feeling he had rarely known before and its strangeness worried him. He frowned, trying to identify it, automatically thinking of his encounter with Hannah.

And then he recognised that it had nothing to do with her. It was the company — and his place in it. There was a division now, responsible for investigating and recommending and then completing take-overs. And country and area managing directors, who dealt with the officials and politicians in whatever part of the world they were established. Even the final decisions came to him with suggestions and then several alternatives, everything minuted and stereotyped, so that all he had to do was to read his lines, like an actor.

There wasn't enough for him to do any more. And he was bored.

The solution had come suddenly to Ann, and the more she thought of it the more obvious it seemed. Irritatingly so, because she could have done it before Metzinger's call and so refused to give the details of Collington's conversation from Pretoria. But it wasn't too late. She didn't love Peter, any more than she believed he loved her. They had drifted into the relationship, through loneliness she supposed, and maintained it because it was convenient and because they were used to each other. That was why there had never been any thought of having the baby. If she had believed for a moment that there had been a possibility of their marrying, she wouldn't have gone to the clinic where the doctor had presented his bill before the operation and the nurses' unspoken criticism hardened when she'd listed her religion as Catholic.

All she had to do was end it. End it and then tell James all about it during his next trip to London: explain it was something that had begun before they got together and which she had stupidly allowed to continue. Despite his upbringing, Collington was one of the most complete and sophisticated men she had ever known. He'd understand readily enough, once she explained.

Ann stirred, checking the time; she wanted everything to be ready when Peter arrived. She prepared the table and opened the wine and stopped at the entrance to the kitchen, knowing there was nothing that needed to be made ready there. It was to be a simple meal, everything cold except for the steaks. Now that she'd finally made the decision she wanted to announce it properly, sensibly, not jumping up and down from the table every few minutes, like some embarrassed schoolgirl.

He was late, Ann realised. Which was unusual, because he had a thing about time. He would have telephoned if there had been a delay at the office. So it was probably the traffic. It was bad, sometimes, coming out of the City. Ann lighted a cigarette and decided she didn't want it, so she stubbed it out again. She began worrying her lip between her teeth, which she always did when she was uncertain, gazing around for some activity. The ice was melting. She hurried some into a glass, before the gin — a mistake, because she couldn't properly judge how much she put into the glass. She added a little more, filled it with tonic and then sat waiting, forward on the edge of her chair. It was right to end it with Peter: they both knew it was an aimless, drifting affair, something that would have to finish one day. He'd be more affected than her, Ann knew. And not just because she had another involvement and he didn't, at least not as far as she suspected. She had always dominated and Peter had always been happy to follow. Another reason for breaking off; it was wrong for anyone to be as dependent upon a woman as Peter was. One day he'd probably realise she'd been kinder, by being cruel. Ann put her glass down, annoyed at the attempted reassurance. She wasn't thinking of being kinder to Peter. She was thinking of herself. Of being in a hopeless situation and trying something, anything, to get out of it. And she would get out of it. She'd get out of it and she'd warn James and then help him screw Metzinger.

She was not a tart. It might seem so, from those flat, unemotional reports and those blurred pictures, which made it appear she was always hurrying in and out of houses and apartments, but the truth was far different. The affair with Jenkins had been like hundreds of others, something that had developed between an attractive, charismatic employer and a personal assistant who spent more time with him than his wife. It had been fun and neither of them had taken it seriously, and when it had ended they had remained friends. She'd never been a danger to Jenkins' marriage and she knew she wasn't to James's. He and Hannah had been apart before their involvement, and arguing about a separation for even longer. Not a tart, she decided again.

She was at the drinks table, refilling her glass, when she heard someone at the door. She turned and at once felt a sweep of compassion for the man standing there. Peter Brading was a thin, haphazard man upon whom clothes always appeared to sit awkwardly, so that his shirt collar seemed too large and his jacket to be retreating from his shoulders. He dropped his briefcase heavily, and sighed, with matching effect.

'Drink?' she said.

He nodded. 'A big one.'

'Bad day?'

'Bloody awful.'

He came further into the room, accepting the tumbler and going to the chair in which she had recently been sitting. He sat slump-shouldered, staring down into the glass. 'Lost three clients today,' he announced, like a small boy confessing a wrongdoing.

'Three!'

He looked up at her surprise. 'It's a record,' he confirmed bitterly. 'The firm's never had three withdrawals in a single day.'

'All yours?' Ann asked gently.

Brading nodded again. 'They complained of consistent losses over the last two years. And they were right: I hadn't recommended one good portfolio.'

'What's going to happen?'

Brading shrugged. 'There's a directors' meeting next week.'

'Serious?'

'They could ask for my resignation, I suppose.'

'Will they?'

'I don't know.'

Ann looked beyond him to the carefully arranged table and the open wine and then into the kitchen, where the steaks lay in readiness before the grill. It couldn't be tonight, she realised. When then? With the resignation meeting a week away, the timing wasn't going to improve. Christ, she thought, what a stupid, hopeless, bloody awful mess.

Chapter Seven

It was during the British war against the Zulus, when they fought as allies, that the Afrikaners developed the protective device of assembling their wagons in a circle or laager. Ironically, during the first Boer war against the British which followed within four years, and then again during the second at the turn of the century, it became an established defensive position and it remains the mental attitude of a country confronting ostracism and embargoes from its policy of separate development, between black and white. In practical terms, they have improved on covered wagons. The laager is now formed by the Department of National Security from Pretoria's Skinner Street and so important is its function considered that its Director is frequently accorded a seat in Cabinet discussion.

It was a responsibility of which Louis Knoetze was very aware. Which was why his response was immediate when the Dutch intelligence service contacted him after the Ilyushin crash; their request for consultation extended beyond a mysterious gold cargo.

Until the overthrow of the Shah, South Africa obtained ninety per cent of its oil from Iran. One of the first acts of the Ayatollah Khomeini was to join the other Middle East oil producers and forbid open sales to Pretoria. Surprisingly for a country to which many Afrikaners can trace family links, Holland supported the blockade more strongly than any other in the west, only just stopping short of formal legislation. The fervency of the Dutch feeling created a paradox, because it was in Holland that Knoetze established his nominee companies to make secret purchases of spot oil contracts from the huge Europort depot at Rotterdam, to make up the shortfall created by the Iranian stoppage.

Knoetze flew to Zurich for his meeting with the Dutch intelligence man. Hans van der Welk was a bespectacled, balding Dutchman who walked with a limp inflicted by Gestapo torture in 1943 when they had unsuccessfully tried to make him disclose the

Jewish escape route through the Netherlands. The gold provided him with the opportunity for which he had been looking for months, ever since his service had ascertained that the South African companies were buying oil, although not the extent of the operation. He knew from the strength of opposition to South Africa within his country that if the surreptitious purchasing were to become public, the embarrassment would be sufficient to bring down the government.

They met over lunch at the Baur au Lac, with Van der Welk insisting upon the role of host because he considered himself in the stronger position and therefore wanted to appear generous, in everything. Knoetze was a pragmatic man, so he accepted his inferior role without irritation or offence, letting the other intelligence chief take the lead. Van der Welk dealt out his information with the care of an expert card player, producing the photographs of what was proveably South African gold but refusing any information about its discovery until Knoetze disclosed his oil purchasing arrangements. Knoetze had flown to Switzerland prepared. He appeared to attempt a token argument, in an effort to gain some bargaining position, and then finally produced despatch and shipment dockets. Van der Welk took his time, comparing them against material of his own. Finally, deciding they were genuine, which was a mistake because they were not, he volunteered the details of the Ilyushin crash and the size of the gold shipment. It was an indication of Knoetze's professionalism that he controlled his bewilderment at the revelation, intent for the moment on safeguarding his uninterrupted oil supplies.

'We want it to stop,' said Van der Welk.

'We don't,' said Knoetze.

The opposition surprised the Dutchman, who imagined he retained control. Seizing the other man's hesitation, Knoetze said, 'I will guarantee that any commercial activity within your country will remain discreet.'

Van der Welk shook his head. 'I couldn't accept that.'

'That's unfortunate,' said Knoetze.

'But unavoidable,' countered Van der Welk.

'I wasn't thinking of South Africa,' said Knoetze.

'I don't understand.'

'After your country's support of the manic regime in Iran, it would be embarrassing if what we are discussing today were to become public knowledge.'

'It's precisely for that reason that I've arranged this meeting,' said Van der Welk patiently. 'And why it has to stop.'

'If our activities had to be curtailed, I would try, of course, to prevent any disclosure of what's been happening,' said Knoetze gently. 'But I couldn't give any guarantee. Not the sort of guarantee I could offer if everything were to continue undisturbed.'

Van der Welk's face tightened as he realised how he had been outplayed. 'Full disclosure would cause a political upheaval in my country,' he accepted.

'Unfortunate, as I said,' remained Knoetze. He waited, anticipating Van der Welk's move.

'I imagine the discovery of South African gold on a Soviet airliner would cause some surprise,' said the Dutchman, trying to fight back.

'But only surprise,' qualified Knoetze. 'My government wouldn't be affected. The fact that it occurred on Dutch soil would be an unfortunate coincidence, coupled with the publicity about the oil purchase.'

'This meeting began with the offer of co-operation,' said Van der Welk.

'Which I appreciate,' said Knoetze.

'That's difficult to accept.'

'We each have to do everything we can, for our respective countries,' said Knoetze, content with the victory.

Van der Welk rose stiffly from the table, gesturing with the documents that Knoetze had supplied about the South African nominee companies. 'These will be watched,' he said, recognising the weakness of his counter attack. 'At the slightest legal infringement, no matter how small, I shall move against them.'

'I understand,' said Knoetze, letting the man have the point. He rose, offering his hand. Van der Welk considered it and then turned, walking abruptly away from the table. Knoetze watched him go, unoffended, even amused that in the end he had been left to pay the bill.

Knoetze was a complete professional. Even before he left the hotel he had relegated the resolved oil difficulty and was concentrating upon the gold cargo. The oil had been straightforward and easy, but the gold was not. And because of the necessary handling of the Dutch security chief, he'd closed the door on any help from Holland. Which meant it had to come from South Africa. In any other country, the investigation might have taken weeks or even months. But Knoetze decided there might be a short cut through the Broederbond.

The Broederbond is the most secure laager of all, a tightly controlled, absolutely secret society of 12,000 leading Afrikaners who have moulded it to become the framework of white South African society. Formed originally to oppose the English attempts to anglicise the Afrikaner population after their defeat in the second Boer war, it is composed of self-contained, separate cells answerable to a controlling council and for over half a century has resisted every official attempt at disbandment. Now it is inviolate. So powerful is the Broederbond that it is synonymous with the ruling Nationalist Party. Nearly every government minister and almost every MP belongs to it. So, too, do the leaders of its armed forces, its university professors and its leading industrialists. Louis Knoetze was a Broeder and proud of it. Not as proud as Marius Metzinger, of course, but then very few people were as fervent an Afrikaner as he was.

Before his departure from Switzerland, Knoetze made contact with Metzinger through his office in Pretoria, not wanting there to be any delay in a meeting when he returned.

Although they were Broeders and should have come together as friends, Louis Knoetze found it difficult to regard Metzinger as such, although Metzinger seemed sincere in the friendship he offered. But it hadn't always been the case, Knoetze remembered. Metzinger was from an established family, with a tradition of pride and wealth. And he had showed it, as a social reminder, during their encounters years before in the Pretoria cell of the Broederbond. At that time Knoetze had been a farm labourer's son, a lowly constable, and Metzinger had maintained the gulf until Knoetze had started to progress through the security service and his ability had become recognised. Knoetze had little doubt that Metzinger had forgotten that early reserve. But he hadn't. And never would. In some ways, it was fortunate; it removed any embarrassment at using the man, as he intended.

Knoetze had never before visited Metzinger's farm, even though he was acceptable now as the country's security chief, and he undertook the tour with interest, staring with contempt at the pictures of Lord Kitchener, haltered in a Sam Browne and stiff in official uniform and polished boots, disembarking at Cape Town to take his part in the Boer war. And then with even greater hostility at the picture of Lord Milner, the worst enemy, a governor who had refused to consider the Dutch immigrants as anything other than upstart insurgents who should be crushed without mercy.

Metzinger had arranged the photographic gallery of his house to the maximum effect. There were pictures of Milner in cockaded hat and official sash with his gleaming landau at glittering champagne receptions. And alongside were prints of Afrikaner women and children, after their incarceration in Kitchener's concentration camps. Plump, shimmering English wives were compared to peasant-capped Boer women, attempting to nourish stick-limbed babies from empty, spaniel-eared breasts. English teenagers, crimped pantaloons crisp beneath lace dresses, cavorted with croquet mallets alongside images of swollen-bellied youngsters who had known death before puberty. And then there was the surrender at Vereeniging, in May 1902, leaders like Botha and De Wet and De la Rey and Kemp and Beyers, heroes dressed in canvas and rags after three years of bitter guerilla war, contrasted again with the costumed and bemedalled British negotiators.

Knoetze, who was not a man given to emotion, turned away blinking rapidly and said, 'That's a wonderful exhibition. Our children should pass by that record of events every day, as they enter school.'

'And the children of other nations,' said Metzinger bitterly. 'The nations that criticise us.'

Silent in agreement, the two men walked towards the huge barn in which Metzinger housed the covered wagons.

'These actually went on the trek?' demanded Knoetze in awe.

'All three,' assured Metzinger. 'A few wheel-spokes have been restored, and the hoods, of course. But otherwise they're original.'

There was silence again, as two men might stand before a shrine.

'It has made me proud to come here today,' said Knoetze, finally.

'I am glad you did,' said Metzinger politely.

Knoetze turned to the other man, reminded of the purpose of his visit and appearing embarrassed at the recollection. 'This isn't a social occasion,' he said.

Metzinger stared back, without surprise. 'Shall we go back to the house?'

'It would be more convenient. I've things I want to show you,' said the intelligence chief, gesturing with the briefcase he had carried throughout the tour and which he had refused to surrender, even to the security of his own driver.

Metzinger led the way from the barn, across the square and into the farmhouse. The boy arrived in automatic attendance, but Metzinger dismissed him immediately, wanting to know the reason for Knoetze's visit and irritated by any interruption.

'You must understand this is not an official visit,' said Knoetze, in further warning.

Metzinger nodded.

'Broeder to Broeder,' emphasised the security chief.

'Broeder to Broeder,' accepted Metzinger.

Unspeaking, Knoetze took from his briefcase the pictures of the gold ingots bearing the South African government stamp and then the minor company imprint from which it had been so easy to establish their source as SAGOMI.

Metzinger studied the pictures and looked up, open-eyed in curiosity. 'Our gold,' he said, as if he were surprised at the need for identification.

'Disposed of where?' demanded Knoetze.

Metzinger's expression of curiosity widened. 'Where else can it be disposed of?' he questioned back, in return. 'The government can be the only purchaser, by law.'

'You've no idea how these ingots came to be in the possession of the Soviet Union, then?'

'The Soviet Union!'

Knoetze, who was an accomplished interrogator, noted the other man's astonishment. It was quite genuine, he decided. Succinctly, he gave the details of the discovery, recognising again the incredulity that registered upon Metzinger's face when he disclosed the value of the shipment that had been discovered in the Soviet plane.

'Stolen?' queried Metzinger at once.

'There are no reports,' said Knoetze. 'And we would have known about the loss of bullion of this value.'

'Genuine purchase, then?'

'Unquestionably.'

'But the Soviet Union is a producer of gold. Why should it want to buy?'

'That's what I want to find out,' said Knoetze. 'And that's why I came here today.'

Metzinger frowned. 'I'm not sure I understand,' he said.

'There are several different ways to get through a maze,' said Knoetze. 'The easiest is to start from the inside and work outwards: in that direction you never get blocked by a cul-de-sac.'

Chapter Eight

Metzinger's call for an unscheduled meeting, so soon after the boardroom confrontation, was an unnecessary reminder to Collington of the recurring problem of his weakened control. Jenkins responded as he had promised, arriving in South Africa within forty-eight hours of Collington's call and Brooking reluctantly broke a vacation in France, flying in a day before. They assembled in advance in Collington's office suite, Platt and Jenkins arriving together, followed by Jamieson and Brooking.

'What's this all about?' demanded Brooking at once. His irritation made him more forceful than usual.

'I don't know,' admitted Collington. 'There's no requirement under the company rules for a reason to be given.'

'Haven't you asked Metzinger directly?' said Platt.

'If he'd wanted to tell us, he'd have listed it in his request,' said Collington. 'I didn't think it was good tactics to ask openly.'

'Nothing we haven't overlooked, like last time?' suggested Jenkins.

Collington shook his head positively. 'One mistake was enough,' he said. 'I've had reports prepared on everything: individual shareholdings, voting strengths, proportional directorships . . . the lot.'

'Was there a reply from Mrs Simpson to the formal request for sale?' asked Jamieson, referring to his suggestion at the previous meeting.

'Exactly what we thought it would be,' said Collington. 'She hasn't the slightest intention of selling.'

'Metzinger's really stitched her up, hasn't he?' said Platt.

'It's something we're going to have to learn to live with,' predicted Jenkins. 'It's going to be damned difficult and sometimes impossibly inconvenient, but we're stuck with it.'

Collington led the way through the linking door into the boardroom. Metzinger, de Villiers and Wassenaar were already assembled and were looking expectantly towards the approaching Englishmen. Collington remembered that at the previous meeting, where he'd loosened their control, Metzinger had been unable to keep from his face the expectation of success. There was no expression of satisfaction this time.

Collington waited until everyone was seated, then read out the formal notice convening the meeting and the article of formation which gave Metzinger the right to demand it. As he had expected, Metzinger recorded possession of Mrs Simpson's proxy.

Metzinger's demeanour was quite different from before, recognised Collington. He turned to the man and when he did so became conscious that alongside Metzinger's chair there were at least three briefcases.

'Shall we begin?' offered Collington.

Metzinger nodded, looking around the table at each of them before speaking. Then he said: 'I want it understood that the discussion which is to take place this morning must remain absolutely secret. The need for that will become obvious, but I want now to propose the formal exclusion of all secretarial staff.'

'Seconded,' said de Villiers at once.

Collington stared again at the man to his right, apprehensively. Seeing the look, Metzinger said: 'I do so on the understanding that a further motion can be put forward, if anyone disagrees with my request, and that the Minute clerk can be recalled.'

'I'd like to move an amendment,' said Jenkins from the other side of the table. 'I propose that this board goes into private session to consider the reasons for secrecy but that at the end of any explanation, the decision to remain in unrecorded session be put to the vote.'

'Seconded,' said Platt, matching the other accountant's reaction.

'I will not argue with that,' said Metzinger.

This time Collington managed to keep from his face any reaction to the man's behaviour. He had been expecting opposition and instead was receiving co-operation. He moved the formal vote, which was unanimous, and then sat back while the secretaries and the Minute clerk filed out.

While the room was being cleared, Metzinger leaned sideways, bringing his briefcases on to the table and taking from them what appeared to be identical folders. He slid them across the polished table, one for each director.

He looked to the doors to satisfy himself that only the eight of them remained in the room, and then he opened his folder. Everyone else did the same. The first photograph was an external shot of the crashed Soviet aircraft in the Amsterdam field. It was taken in such a way that the word Aeroflot was clearly identifiable.

'A Soviet transporter which crashed in Holland six weeks ago,' began Metzinger, his opening as dramatic as the picture. 'And upon which, according to the best estimates available, was found something approximating to the entire supply of gold which this company has made available to the South African government over the last three months.'

They were clearly handling classified intelligence material, Collington realised worriedly. It would have come from a Broederbond link. Collington knew from Hannah that Metzinger belonged and guessed that de Villiers and Wassenaar did too. It was logical that membership within the South African security services would be high.

Like any businessman in South Africa, Collington was aware of the Broederbond and its controlling power within the country. He was instinctively uneasy about secret societies, particularly a society which had evolved the theory of apartheid to maintain Afrikaner supremacy. But now wasn't the moment to think of moral integrity: now was the time to thank Christ it gave them access to secret information.

Metzinger had paused, looking again to each man in the room, conscious of the astonishment they all showed. Louis Knoetze's file was very complete and Metzinger started to take the board through it, document by document and photograph by photograph.

The picture immediately beneath that of the crashed Ilyushin was of a woman. It had obviously been taken with a concealed camera, but the quality was still sufficient to show a petite, dark-haired girl of about thirty-five, studiously bespectacled, a briefcase in her hand. There appeared to be a canal or waterway in the background.

'Brigitte re Jong,' identified Metzinger, obviously enjoying his command of the meeting. 'She heads the brokerage company which legitimately purchased the metal. It's a firm that's existed for a number of years and appears to be a properly conducted, bona fide business.'

'Is she Russian?' demanded Jamieson.

'There's a birth record of a Brigitte re Jong being born in Utrecht in June 1946,' said Metzinger, going back to his files. 'She was illegitimate, the result of some wartime liaison. A lot of records appear to have been misplaced or simply not kept during that time. But she certainly entered Utrecht University in 1964 and graduated three years later with an honours degree in economics.'

'She must *know* for whom she's buying,' insisted Platt.

'It's a possibility, but there isn't any proof,' said Metzinger. 'She's been thoroughly investigated since our government discovered the gold shipment. She seems to be nothing more than a successful businesswoman.'

'That doesn't make sense,' protested Platt.

From a third briefcase Metzinger took further files. 'It does,' he said. 'The business is a pyramid construction. Her company, König Nepthaven, was purchased a year ago by a Zurich firm, Zilgiesser and Bosche. They're headquartered in the Jupiterstrasse: all the directors are lawyers . . .'

'Fronting as nominees,' interrupted Platt.

Metzinger nodded. 'From Zilgiesser and Bosche, everything goes into bank holdings. Protected by Swiss anonymity.'

'What else?' said de Villiers.

Metzinger moved on through pictures of the aircraft interior and the exterior of the brokerage house, this time with a slightly clearer image of the woman, and then circulated the reports which Knoetze had assembled after the Zurich meeting with the Dutch intelligence official. It was an hour before they looked up from the files in front of them. Metzinger had maintained the commentary throughout. He reached forward for a glass of water when he finished and said hoarsely, 'Now is the time to vote on the re-entry of any secretarial staff.'

'I don't think that will be necessary,' said Collington at once.

'Are we sure this is genuine?' asked Platt, showing his accountant's caution.

'Unquestionably so,' said Metzinger. 'I can guarantee the source as impeccable.'

'Is this an official approach?' Collington asked. If it were, it should have come to him, as chairman. But in the circumstances, he wasn't concerned with the propriety: he just wanted as much information as possible.

Metzinger hesitated, selecting the words. 'The government is aware of today's meeting,' he said.

It wasn't quite an answer to his question, decided Collington.

'Why have they involved us?' asked Jenkins.

'Because they don't understand it,' said Metzinger simply. 'We're gold producers . . . supposed experts. They want our assistance.'

Metzinger had every justification for summoning the meeting as he had done, decided Collington. And he had been quite wrong in anticipating another confrontation. Today there was no animosity between the two sides; they were working together smoothly against what could erupt into a major difficulty for the company.

'After South Africa, the Soviet Union is the world's biggest gold producer,' said Collington, in an unnecessary reminder. 'It exports, not buys. Why the purchases, on this scale?'

'A cornering operation, to unbalance free world currencies?' suggested de Villiers.

'No one is on a gold standard any more,' argued Platt.

'There's always an effect, gold standard or not,' said the other accountant.

'We control our sales,' pointed out Wassenaar. 'South Africa has the corner. No one could ever hope to get market control with the reserves we hold'.

'There must have been earlier purchases,' said Jenkins.

'It's believed there were,' said Metzinger, 'Although not on the single scale of that in the Amsterdam plane. So far the government has traced contracts through Amsterdam and Zurich amounting to about £300,000,000.'

'What about Russian production?' asked Jamieson. He looked to Collington for a reply.

'Precise figures aren't known,' he said. 'The last survey Consolidated Gold Fields made of production throughout the Communist world estimated Soviet output at between 280 and 350 tonnes a year.'

'That's less than previous estimates,' said de Villiers, a man always concerned with figures. 'The assessment in 1977 was 444 tonnes. And in 1970 it was put at 346.'

Platt was groping through his own briefcase. He emerged as the South African accountant finished talking, gesturing with a statistics book. 'That doesn't balance,' he said. 'In the three years, from 1976 to '78, the Russians sold more than 400 tonnes on the open market, each year. And open sales are continuing.'

'It's possible they've had mining difficulties,' speculated Jenkins. 'It's a known fact that because of weather conditions they can only operate their Siberian mines for five months of the year.'

'But where's the logic in their buying bullion at a market price, to re-offer it as Soviet gold?' said de Villiers. 'They would just be spending their foreign currency one month and replacing it the next. It's a pointless exercise.'

'And dangerous,' supported Platt. 'If there were a sudden fluctuation, they could find themselves buying high and selling low and actually *losing* money.'

'I'm not surprised at the government bewilderment,' said Collington.

'No one expects instant answers,' said Metzinger, enjoying the fact his information was from Cabinet level. 'I was asked to initiate a discussion and keep people informed.'

'What official action is the government taking?' said Jenkins.

Metzinger was glad he had spent so much time with Knoetze, rehearsing everything he was likely to be asked. He shook his head. 'At the moment, nothing. Why should they? There's nothing illegal in what's happening: it's a legitimate market operation.'

'But it couldn't be allowed to continue,' insisted Jenkins. 'Not with Pretoria's expressed attitude to the Soviet Union. If the government's claims are true and the increasing unrest among the blacks is Communist supported, it could be turned to appear that South Africa was financing guerillas pledged to its overthrow.'

'That's a somewhat convoluted scenario,' said Metzinger. 'But that's the sort of concern uppermost in their minds. What if the transaction isn't financial? What if, for some reason we can guess, Moscow has evolved something that will create a political embarrassment for us?'

'I can't imagine what it might be,' said Jamieson.

'I can't imagine why the world's second biggest gold producer is buying back,' snapped Wassenaar, showing the first division between the two groups.

'I don't want us to be used as any sort of shuttlecock,' said Collington, irritated at the lapse between the two men.

Metzinger seemed equally annoyed, glancing at both of them before turning back to Collington and saying, 'Neither does the government. That was in their minds as much as anything else when they informed us.'

The concern would be at the possibility of any embarrassment to the government rather than the company, Collington knew, but there didn't seem any purpose in making the qualification. Where was his own concern?'

Inexplicably, Metzinger's disclosures had produced excitement rather than apprehension. Unlike the irritation caused by board-room structures, it created a positive challenge, and it had been a long time since he had confronted anything like that. And he didn't want to lose it.

'What resolution do you want from this meeting?' he asked Metzinger.

The South African appeared surprised at the question. 'I don't think we can make one,' he said. 'None of us has come up with anything so far.'

'We haven't made any enquiries yet,' defended Jenkins, gesturing with the file before him.

'I gave an undertaking that the files would not leave my safe-keeping,' said Metzinger.

'You want them back!' said Jenkins.

'Everything,' insisted Metzinger. 'The material is far too sensitive for any risk to be taken.'

'How can we initiate anything, without documents?' persisted Jenkins.

'Anything we do has got to be as circumspect as possible,' warned Metzinger. 'I don't want any leaks traced to this board.'

'I think that is a valid point,' said Collington, in rare support of the other man.

'I don't like this at all,' said Platt, a man used to the conformity of accounts and numbers. 'We could become involved in God knows what sort of difficulty and there's nothing we can do to prevent it.'

'I think that until there has been some resolve we should agree to fortnightly meetings,' suggested Wassenaar.

There were nods of agreement around the table.

'And the chairman should be empowered, in the interim, to take what action he considers fit,' added Jamieson.

Collington looked to the Afrikaners, watching for the division to become obvious.

'After consultation with the deputy chairman,' qualified de Villiers.

It was the best he could hope for, Collington accepted. 'Of course there would be consultation,' he said. Feeling he could make the concession, he went on: 'Realistically, it is through the deputy chairman that we are likely to get most assistance over this.'

That wasn't necessarily true, thought Collington, as the idea came to him. But it wouldn't hurt for the Afrikaners to believe their superiority until he had explored it further.

The business club was just off Church Square, with a view of the Union Buildings. Metzinger, de Villiers and Wassenaar were founder members, with a table permanently held for them near the window. They went straight to it, ignoring the bar, beckoning immediately to the waiter so they could give their order and talk uninterrupted. Among themselves they spoke Afrikaans.

'You didn't hold anything back?' asked Wassenaar.

'No,' said Metzinger. 'They know as much as we do.'

'And Knoetze can't provide any more?' said de Villiers.

'Not at the moment.'

'It would be good to get some advantage out of this, after the way we cornered Simpson's shareholding,' said Wassenaar, reflectively.

'I've considered that, too,' assured Metzinger. 'But we've got to know more about this Russian business before we attempt any sort of side benefit.'

'What do you think Collington will do?' asked de Villiers.

Their meal began to arrive and the three men waited. When the waiters had finished, Metzinger said, confidently: 'Attempt something clever, as always.'

'Do you think he'll keep the undertaking to consult?' pressed Wassenaar.

Metzinger paused, fork half-way to his mouth. 'Yes,' he said. 'He feels like I do at the moment: the company is more important than individual personalities. And he knows that through the 'Bond I'm far more likely to get information than he is. He needs the consultation more than we do.' He smiled, in private satisfaction. 'I know I'll be able to anticipate anything Collington does. Or thinks of doing,' he said heavily.

'A boardroom advantage would be good,' repeated Wassenaar, unable to get the idea from his mind.

'I'll be alert for it, if the opportunity arises,' promised Metzinger.

It occurred, three days later, when African National Congress guerrillas infiltrated into the Transvaal from Mozambique and almost completely destroyed at Sasolberg and Secuna the £3,000,000,000 oil-from-coal plants which South Africa had developed to meet its energy needs, confronted by the increasing embargo from world producers.

Metzinger didn't recognise it at first, however. It was not until after Collington's initial success that the idea came to him.

Nine thousand miles away from the refinery explosions, in office surroundings more appropriate to Wall Street than to Moscow, Nikolai Leonov flustered nervously between tape machines linked to metal markets throughout the world, noting closing prices and end-of-day trading volumes and then breaking down the information to give to the computer programmers. He wanted an average and so had been working constantly for three days to prepare an unequivocal case for the Finance Minister, snatching uneasy sleep on an army cot set up in the corner of his secretary's office and existing on sandwiches and coffee brought in from the canteen. What was happening to him was monstrous, decided Leonov. The Ilyushin crash had created sufficient difficulty, without the behaviour of Igor Struve.

After the three days Leonov was almost convinced, but because a mistake would have been so disastrous and because somewhere in the world, throughout the twenty-four hours, there is a metal market in operation, he committed a further day, to be absolutely sure.

He had allowed for every explicable spasm and fluctuation, anxious only for a global interpretation. Even so, he was constantly over-cautious, calling in three analysts from Struve's ministry so that the Finance Minister would have independent confirmation if he wanted it.

The answer from the experts concurred with Leonov's own conclusion. The diplomat allowed himself another twenty-four hours to recover from the fatigue, before seeking a meeting with Krotkov. He had appreciated the indications of help from the KGB chief and wanted to talk through the problem with a friend.

'The market has remained utterly stable,' reported Leonov. 'If the gold had been discovered in Amsterdam I would have expected some evidence, through the amount offered for trading. Over two months, there has been no change whatsoever: there's not a market trend I can't account for quite logically.'

The unkempt intelligence men smiled, his face puddling into fat. 'So there's no problem?'

'Not externally,' qualified Leonov.

'What's happening?'

'The Finance Ministry is trying to minimise the operation,' disclosed Leonov.

'Minimise it?'

'I've been told I can't have any addition to the budget allowed to buy on the open market.'

'It's a decision that will have to be altered,' said Krotkov, simply. 'We've just got confirmation of crop disease in the Ukraine. Our agronomists there estimate a grain and wheat yield down a third, even on the reduced levels forecast.'

Leonov pressed his eyes shut. 'Perhaps now they'll allow me more money,' he said.

And then again, perhaps they won't, thought Krotkov.

Henry Moreton decided things were going perfectly. The gold sales and the rumours had been consummately balanced. The dollar had hardened, perceptibly. Against some currencies it had been by as much as ten to fifteen points, but those currencies were weak in their own right and Moreton attached considerably more importance to the showing against the German mark and the Japanese yen. In both cases, it had been exactly what he had forecast to the President. Pemberton was impressed, Moreton knew. The administration praise was beginning to circulate. There had been an approach for co-operation on a *Time* magazine front-cover profile but Moreton had refused, calculating that people might suspect a personality push following so closely after the *Fortune* article. It had been a well-phrased refusal, of course, leaving the door open for another approach later on. Moreton had even hinted when and was sure the editor had taken the point. A month, he calculated. By then he would have got it just right.

Chapter Nine

Collington's interest in diamonds extended back to his days as a Barnado boy when, at the annual fair on Hampton Court Green, he had always aimed above all to win the rings on the hoopla stall, imagining that the glittering paste was diamonds.

SAGOMI's diamond division was one of the early expansions Collington had initiated after joining the board; now they controlled six mines, sub-licensed to De Beers. Collington had remembered his Hampton Court fantasies when he made his first on-site visit, surprised how much more attractive the fairground imitations were than the real thing in its raw state.

It was a fleeting reflection. A far greater surprise was to learn that only a proportion of the dull, uninteresting pebbles remained for cutting and polishing in South Africa. The rest went to Israel, to be turned into gems that represented the country's chief export.

Collington had involved himself personally with the Israeli firms, just as he had involved himself in every aspect of the company's growth in those early years, and he had retained his friendship with the leading diamond merchants in Tel Aviv, Jerusalem and Haifa. It was of them he thought in the closing stages of the board meeting at which Metzinger had disclosed the Soviet gold purchases.

There had been an analysts' report about Israel, two weeks earlier. Admittedly it was about the increased availability of diamond cutters, but it was the source of that additional labour that had registered with Collington as Metzinger spoke, giving him the idea.

The analysts' department was one of Collington's most successful innovations: the basis, in fact, for his public reputation as a flamboyant entrepeneur, with a genius gift for take-over and development. The reality was that Collington rarely moved without first dissecting the company or business with the care with which he had studied SAGOMI's construction. The analysts had been created to make such examinations. Over the years, their function had been extended to include political information and any other knowledge from which any of the divisions might benefit. The passing reference to Mordechai Levy's staff increase, enabling him to make additional diamond purchases, provided exactly the sort of detail Collington needed.

It had been four years since their last meeting, but Mordechai Levy showed no surprise at Collington's call. Levy had no plans that would take him out of Israel in the coming weeks, he said. So he would be delighted to renew their friendship, if Collington were passing through. It was Levy who chose the Sunday; he always felt like good food and wine after the Saturday shabaht fast.

Collington was buoyant at the prospect of personal activity after so long — of initiating something rather than sanctioning it with a tick or an initial. He prepared for it with his customary care, withholding the need for the information but otherwise briefing Geoffrey Wall completely. Wall had been sent to South Africa on temporary secondment from SAGOMI's New York division and had made one of the biggest impacts Collington could recall. There was a brashness about the man's ambition, but it was backed by solid ability and efficiency. It had been recognised early by the section heads under whom he worked and commented on in the official reports that were submitted to Collington, who had years before determined, with the international spread of their group, that middle- and upper-echelon managers were vital to its continued success. In order to assess the man before his ultimate return to New York and possible chairmanship of their division there, Collington made him his personal assistant. He knew he was going to miss him when the time came to transfer him back to America.

Collington carried to the penthouse the intelligence file that Wall had produced, to brief himself on the night before his flight to Tel Aviv. He assimilated it with his usual speed and then moved restlessly about the apartment, needing activity but unsure what it should be. He could go to the business club, but didn't want that sort of environment. He consciously tried to put the other idea from his mind and then became irritated at his own stupidity. Hannah had agreed he could call, the last time. And she may have heard back from Paul.

She answered the telephone herself, and he thought he detected a lift in her voice when she recognised him. She hesitated at the dinner invitation and when he said he'd understand if she had other engagements, she blurted hurriedly that she hadn't and then stopped talking, appearing annoyed at the immediate denial.

As he drove towards Parkstown to collect her, Collington tried to subdue the confidence that had grown from his reading of Wall's assessment. The Israeli trip could easily be pointless, an idea which seemed good but wasn't, on investigation. If that happened, they would be dependent again on Metzinger's sources. It was official intelligence, so obviously the enquiries would be continued and the board might learn something further. But the security people couldn't be having too much success: there was a degree of logic in their approach to Metzinger and through him to the board, but not as much as the Afrikaner had attempted to convey. Certainly they wouldn't have bothered if they hadn't encountered difficulties.

Hannah appeared on the porch, like before. This time there was no hesitation. Collington leaned forward and they kissed quite naturally.

'Time for a drink?' she invited.

'Sure.'

They went to the small drawing-room and she prepared the drinks herself, handing him the martini and standing back for his approval.

'Perfect,' he said. The first time they had ever slept together, at Meikles Hotel, they had had room service deliver the gin and the vermouth and she had made the drink exactly the way he liked it. It had remained one of their intimacies.

She drank the same, touching glasses with him and then moving to the couch. She was wearing a simple black sheath dress, fastened just at one shoulder by a diamond pin. Collington didn't think she was wearing a bra.

'You've had your hair cut,' he said.

She smiled, appearing pleased that he had noticed, automatically moving her hand up towards it. 'Like it?'

'Very much,' he said honestly.

'You sounded very bright on the telephone.'

'No particular reason,' he said. 'I'm going away on a trip.'

She frowned. 'You're always going away on trips. What's so different about this one?'

'Nothing, like I said. Maybe the chance of more business.'

She shook her head. 'Always business.'

Had he neglected her before the break-up? He didn't think so. There had been the trips, certainly; five, sometimes six months of the year, he supposed. But he'd occasionally taken her with him, and tried to spend more time than usual with her at the end of each one.

'That's how it's always been.'

'Not always,' she said. 'There seemed to be more time, in Salisbury.'

The suggestion surprised him. He had been starting out then, doing something new, anxious to build and expand. He would have thought he had been busier in Rhodesia than he was now.

'I don't like inactivity,' he said.

'You don't have to remind me,' she said, freshening his glass from the pitcher. 'How long will you be away?'

Collington shrugged. 'Not long. A week maybe.'

'So you'll be back for Paul's vacation?'

Collington sipped his drink to conceal his embarrassment. He'd forgotten about their son's homecoming and the thought of their getting together. 'Of course,' he said.

'I had another letter,' said Hannah. 'He asked if we were friends and repeated what he told you about there being quite a few boys at the school whose parents are divorced. Most of them seem to hate each other.'

'How did you reply?'

'That of course we were friends. And that we always would be.' Hannah spoke looking directly at him and Collington shifted uncomfortably under the gaze. 'Shall we go?' he said.

She hesitated, then rose. 'Certainly.'

Because he knew she liked it, he had chosen the restaurant near Summit Hill, where the voortrekker pilgrims had erected their monument after the commemorative march in 1938. She identified the route and turned to him, smiling. 'I wondered if we'd come here,' she said. 'You brought me here on our first date in Pretoria.'

'*You* brought me,' he qualified. 'I didn't know of the place.'

'I was trying to impress you,' she confessed.

At the restaurant they were recognised and greeted by name and led to the table Collington had stipulated.

'What sort of outing were you thinking of, for Paul?' Hannah asked, once they had ordered.

'I thought we'd decide between us,' he said. 'Down to the coast, maybe. Or perhaps inland. He seemed to enjoy the safari last time.'

'I wonder if he wouldn't just prefer to be at home,' she said, almost a private thought.

'I thought the idea was for us to be together with him,' said Collington.

'It is.'

'So Parkstown isn't possible, is it?' he said.

'No,' she said slowly, 'I suppose not.' She seemed to expect him to respond but when he didn't, she said, 'Why tonight?'

'I don't understand.'

'The invitation here, to dinner, and this special restaurant?'

He'd chosen Monument Hill because he knew she liked it, not for nostalgic reasons. Collington realised he had been somewhat thoughtless. 'I said I might call, last time.'

'I thought it might be something more than that,' she pressed.

He looked away from her. 'I hoped we wouldn't get involved in this sort of conversation.'

'That was hardly likely, was it?'

'I suppose not,' he admitted.

There was a silence, each seeking a change of subject.

'Where's the trip?' she said.

'Israel.'

She looked surprised. 'Don't go there often, do you?'

'Not recently,' he said.

'Coming straight back?'

To reduce the curiosity that a special visit might have aroused, he had told Levy he was calling into Israel on his way to England. 'I might go on to London,' he said. If he did, then Ann would expect a commitment. She hadn't given him an ultimatum the last time because she was too sensible a woman, but it hadn't been difficult to gauge from her attitude that she expected a decision. And she deserved one: just like Hannah. Rome would be nearer, he thought, suddenly. But perhaps she would expect a decision in Rome as well.

'Will you try to see Paul?'

'Of course.'

'He didn't mention the holiday in his letter.'

Their food arrived and they began eating. 'Bet I know something that you don't,' she said, between mouthfuls.

'What?'

'Daddy's walking out.'

'Walking out?' frowned Collington, baffled by the expression.

'Seeing a woman.'

Collington stared at her, allowing his surprise to show. Metzinger's wife had died two years after Hannah had been born, so she had no memory at all of her mother. What Collington knew of Metzinger's background had come from Walter Simpson, and because Metzinger was a private man, that wasn't very much. According to Simpson, the marriage had been the nearest thing to an arranged affair between two established Afrikaner families, but as sometimes happens, a sincere and devoted love had developed between them. Metzinger had been devastated by her death, initially coming near to the point of a nervous breakdown and then immersing himself in the businesses, needing constant activity. And never once, since that time, had he shown the slightest interest in another woman.

'Who?' he asked.

'Janet Simpson,' announced Hannah.

Collington shook his head. 'I don't believe it!' he said.

'Neither did I, at first. I've always known they were friends. It was Daddy who introduced her to Walter. Apparently, since the funeral they've been together quite a lot. I was actually asked about it at the luncheon club last week.'

They leant back as a waiter removed the remains of their meal, and Collington said: 'How do you feel about it?'

Hannah hesitated before replying. 'I don't think I feel anything in particular,' she said.

'Do you think they'll get married?'

'God knows,' said Hannah. 'Daddy hasn't even talked about it to me. But I think he would, if it became as serious as that. He's a very moral man, you know. That's why he disapproves of what's happened to us.'

'Does he ever talk to you about that?'

The waiter returned and Collington ordered brandy, leading

Hannah away from the table to a verandah overlooking the hill.

'Not much,' she replied, when they had sat down. 'When I told him, he said he wasn't surprised and that he'd known it wouldn't work from the start.'

'Does he know we've met since the separation?'

'I haven't said anything. Don't you want him to know?'

'It hardly matters, either way,' said Collington.

He offered her more brandy but she refused and so he led the way out of the restaurant. There was no conversation between them on the way back to Parkstown. He halted the car in the driveway, without turning the engine off.

'I didn't mean to be difficult, back in the restaurant,' she said.

'You weren't.'

'Thanks for being gallant, but I know I tried to force the pace.'

Both were staring straight ahead as they talked.

'We agreed six months,' reminded Collington.

'But it didn't *have* to last that long.'

'You've made your mind up then?'

'I think so.' She turned for the first time, waiting.

'I've got to be away early tomorrow,' he said.

'Sure,' she said, disappointed. 'The trip.'

'I'll call you when I get back.'

'All right.'

'Perhaps you will have heard from Paul by then.'

'I'll write him tomorrow.'

Silence began to settle between them and Collington abruptly got out of the car, going round to the passenger door and opening it for her. She seemed uncertain about getting out and then swung her legs sideways.

'Thanks for the evening,' she said, offering her cheek. Collington kissed her, then walked into the porchway and opened the door for her. She closed the door softly behind her.

Collington waited for several moments and then went back to the car. It was a warm night and he lowered the hood going down the driveway, wanting the breeze.

He could go back if he wanted to, he knew.

The meetings at Metzinger's farmhouse had begun casually,

without regularity at first, and then it had gradually become an established practice for them to gather on the last Wednesday of every month. They had left the dining-room and were now grouped around the huge, unlighted fire of the living area, the brandy bottle and balloons on the table between them. Metzinger gestured to de Villiers and Wassenaar, inviting them to help themselves.

'Damage is damned bad at the Sasol plants,' said de Villiers. He had relations in Johannesburg and had just returned from a visit there.

'How serious?' said Metzinger.

'Suggestions are that it will take a year to repair, with hardly any production at all during that time.'

Wassenaar made a whistling noise of surprise. 'Bastards!' he said vehemently. 'Did they find out who did it?'

De Villiers shook his head. 'Too many blacks there to guarantee the necessary security. It was obviously done with inside help.'

'I think we should step up the raids into Mozambique and Rhodesia,' said Wassenaar, pointedly refusing to use the word Zimbabwe. 'That's what the whites did, during the Rhodesian war. Hit the bastards in their camps.'

'Rhodesia lost the war,' reminded Metzinger.

'They wouldn't have done if we hadn't bowed to world pressure and withdrawn our support.'

'I had lunch with Knoetze today,' disclosed Metzinger. 'He said the government is worried: certainly they expect the guerrilla activity to get worse.'

'Did you tell him about our meeting. And what Collington is going to do?'

Metzinger nodded. 'He thought it was a clever idea. It's not the sort of enquiry he could make as easily, so he was quite happy for Collington to become committed.'

'Is that the word he used?' enquired Wassenaar, curiously.

'What?'

'Committed?'

Metzinger frowned, in recollection. 'Yes,' he said. 'It was.'

Wassenaar took his time, pouring some more brandy and swirling it around, enjoying the aroma. 'How big a step is it from commitment to over-commitment?' he said, smiling at the other two men.

Ann determined that it would have to be tonight. On the telephone she had easily evaded Collington's curiosity, saying that the distance over which they were speaking was the cause of any apparent strangeness in her voice, but she knew she would not be able to maintain the pretence when they met. And the circumstances were right. Peter had survived the directors' meeting. There'd been a warning and he was properly worried, but at least they hadn't demanded the resignation that he had expected. And sufficient time had passed for her not to be crowding him with one crisis on top of another. Ann decided that the delay had actually been to her advantage. She had thought more deeply about ending the affair and concluded that to do so in the flat they had occupied more or less permanently for six months would have been a mistake. A restaurant was the proper place: a neutral, crowded restaurant where the surroundings would inhibit any dramatics. She hoped Peter wouldn't take it badly; she really didn't want to hurt him any more than was unavoidable.

She arrived first and sat quite confidently at the table to which she was shown. She was conscious of the looks from the men in the room and answered them openly, not provocative but challenging, staring each one down. Just as she was going to stare Metzinger down. She was going to get enormous pleasure, exposing Metzinger for the bastard that he was. How would Collington react when she told him? Ann considered the question curiously, recognising for the first time that she had never seen James show any indication of anger. There had been many occasions when it should have arisen, when some negotiation of which she had been part had gone wrong through someone's incompetence or through a mistake, but never once had there been any outburst. She decided it must be a strain for him always to remain as cool as that. Perhaps Metzinger would occasion the first outburst: it would certainly be appropriate.

Peter flustered into the restaurant, giving his usual impression of having someone in pursuit. He approached smiling, sitting down with an exaggerated sigh. 'I'm not late,' he said, at once defensive.

'I know,' said Ann. 'I was early.'

When the waiter came to take his drinks order, Ann suggested they choose the food as well, anxious now that she had made her decision not to prolong the meal.

'Cheers,' he said, raising his glass to her as soon as it was delivered.

Ann sipped her drink in response. He looked so vulnerable, she thought.

'Good day?' he asked.

She made a rocking motion with her hands. 'Not bad. I'm going away.'

He looked up at her intently. 'Where?'

'Rome. It's business.'

He smiled, relieved. 'Won't be for long, then?'

'I think it might be.'

He grimaced, half smiling. 'What's that mean?'

The temptation to avoid the answer swept over her, but Ann forced herself to respond. 'I don't think it's a very good idea for us to go on.' It wasn't what she had intended to say: she had produced a cliché and she had prepared herself much better than that. She had wanted them to come to it gradually, almost naturally, so that there would have been some warning to him. This was all too rushed and clumsy.

'Go on?'

'You know what I mean.' She'd sounded irritated and she hadn't meant that, either.

'Why not?' he said.

'Because there isn't any point!' Too sharp again: Jesus, she was handling this badly.

Peter was about to reply, but the waiters arrived with their meal. They both pulled back, neither looking directly at the other. When the waiters left, Peter said, 'As far as I'm concerned, there's every point.'

'We've become a convenience to each other,' said Ann, trying to remember the phrases she'd rehearsed. 'But that's all it is, a convenience. We spend our evenings together because we're lonely and we sleep together because we need that, too. But it's only because it's convenient: because it's less trouble to go on than to be honest with each other. You don't . . .'

'. . . I love you,' burst out Peter.

Ann sat staring across the tiny table, the untouched food in front of her. Hesitantly she shook her head. 'No,' she said doubtfully.

'I love you,' he said again. 'I thought you loved me.'

'Why now?' she said. 'Why now and not when I was having the baby?'

'I agreed with you then.'

'Agreed with me!'

'I didn't think you wanted it.'

'Oh Christ!'

'Don't you love me, Ann?'

She made a vague gesture. 'I don't know.'

'That can't be so,' he said, showing unusual positiveness. 'You either do or you don't.'

'No,' she said brutally. It wasn't as definite as that, she knew. Truthfully she wasn't sure how she felt, but she was tired of the aimlessness of their relationship. She wanted some definite decision, and weighed against the association with Collington and the pressure being imposed by Metzinger, she was right to do what she was doing now. Peter would understand. Not now, perhaps, any more than she did, completely. But when he thought about it, rationally, he'd understand. She stared across at him, trying to convince herself. He seemed to shrink before her, to become even more awkward in his formalised, waistcoated suit.

'I see,' he said. His words came out unevenly.

'You will,' she said hopefully.

'Of course.'

'I didn't mean to hurt you.'

'You haven't.'

'We haven't got to act for each other, Peter. I know I've hurt you and I know I've hurt myself.'

'Why then?' he demanded, desperately.

'Because it's right.'

'For whom?'

Me, thought Ann. Because it's selfishly right for me. And selfish or not, she had to do it. There had been enough wrong starts: she might not have the chance again. Was Collington a chance? He was apart from his wife, certainly. And said he loved her. But she wasn't sure. She wasn't sure about anything.

'I want to finish,' she said, sounding more positive than she felt.

'I don't know what to say.'

And she had thought she would know, but hadn't got it right.

'We could stay friends,' she said, thinking of her relationship with Richard Jenkins.

'No.'

'I'm sorry.'

'So am I,' he said bitterly.

'It's best,' she said. 'You'll come to see it's best.'

'I won't. Never.'

Chapter Ten

Collington travelled alone, without the usual entourage of aides and secretaries. And found himself enjoying it. The customs queues at Tel Aviv airport were more unruly than most, but he stood quite contentedly in the sort of line he usually bypassed, standing back unprotesting when people twice pushed in ahead of him. Levy had offered a car and Collington had refused that, too: he would have even hired a smaller vehicle if his size hadn't made the driving uncomfortable.

Like Berlin again, he thought. And certainly like the early days in England, having to think for himself and rely on nobody else. It gave him a strange feeling — an impression of freedom.

He took the car through the clotted, anger-fuelled traffic of the city, calm among the hooting and the hand-shaking, and picked up the Jerusalem road without any difficulty. He could be away the following day, he calculated; certainly the day after that, even if anything unexpected came up. Ann had sounded excited on the telephone at the suggestion they should meet in Rome, and he was looking forward to it, too. But the accusation pricked at him irritatingly. He was trying to avoid a decision by not going to London. Worse, it meant that he wouldn't be going to see Paul, as he had promised Hannah. But in London he would have had to make the commitment. And he wasn't ready yet. Would he ever be? he wondered.

The road ribboned away through the orange and ochre hills, their outlines blurred by the heat shimmer. It was difficult to imagine the history in every twist and turn of the highway. Far ahead the road lifted towards the rise upon which Jerusalem was built, and as he got closer Collington could make out the enclosing walls. Perhaps he would have time for sightseeing, he thought, as he entered: he'd never been to the old city of the Dome of the Rock or seen the Dead Sea scrolls.

He made one wrong turning, became aware of it almost

immediately and was quickly re-directed towards the King David Hotel. Levy's call came as he was unpacking and they agreed upon an hour.

Collington was already in the ground-floor bar when the Israeli flustered through the door, halting momentarily and staring around. Collington rose, hand extended, and Levy started forward again, bellowing the greeting when he was still yards away. He was a small, fleshy man who advertised his profession with the diamond rings on each of his little fingers. He was an immigrant from New York and favoured American silk suits and plump cigars, which he smoked through a stunted holder.

Collington stood, letting his hand be pumped and his shoulder slapped, aware of the attention throughout the bar and conscious that because of their differing physiques they must look an odd couple.

Levy ordered whisky, touched glasses and said: 'It's good to see you again.'

'And you,' said Collington.

The Israeli looked around, apparently aware for the first time that Collington was alone.

'No staff?' he asked curiously.

'No.'

At once Levy's exuberance diminished. 'No problems, I hope.'

Collington smiled at the immediate concern that business might be bad. 'No,' he said. 'No problems.'

Levy gestured for more drinks, looking unconvinced. 'You don't normally stop by,' he said. 'You haven't for a few years now, anyhow.'

'And you don't normally increase your diamond purchases by as much as twenty per cent,' parried Collington.

Levy's face opened into a strangely boyish grin. 'For me, business is good,' he said contentedly.

'Twenty per cent is more than good,' encouraged Collington. He didn't think it would be difficult, getting Levy to boast.

Collington had made a table reservation and they stopped talking when the head waiter approached. Remembering Levy's remark about enjoying food after the sabbath fast, Collington spent some time over the order.

'Twenty per cent is fantastic,' agreed Levy. 'Bad times for

some mean good times for others.'

Collington frowned, pretending not to understand.

'People don't trust money,' said Levy. 'But they trust things . . . .' He grinned again, preparing Collington for the rehearsed joke. 'Diamonds are more than a girl's best friend,' he said.

Collington laughed politely: there had rarely been a meeting when Levy hadn't said that. It was his favourite song.

Collington stood, leading the way into the dining-room. Once they were seated, he said: 'It must be difficult for you to meet such demand.'

Levy nodded seriously. 'It would have been,' he conceded, 'but everyone needs a little luck and I got it. There's no difficulty getting cutters and polishers.'

'There used to be,' said Collington. He had absorbed every fact in the analysts' report, even down to the annoyance that Israel had expressed a few years before that the South Africans were enticing craftsmen to work for firms in Johannesburg and Cape Town.

'It was a problem,' said Levy. 'But the immigration from Russia has increased. Last month alone I took on five extra cutters who came here from Kiev.'

Levy had meant what he said about his Sunday enjoyment of food, thought Collington, watching the man eat. He allowed a pause and then said: 'I didn't think the Russians gave exit visas to craftsmen.'

Levy shrugged. 'It's a mystery,' he said. 'It hasn't happened before.'

'Perhaps they've trouble with their own mines,' said Collington. As he spoke, he looked down at his plate, wanting the remark to appear a casual aside rather than a lure to get Levy to repeat anything that the newly arrived immigrants might have said about conditions in the Soviet Union.

'I asked,' said Levy, taking the bait. 'There was no indication of it.'

Collington waited, hopefully, but Levy appeared to be concentrating upon the meal. 'Always difficult, assessing the production in Russia,' he said.

'Things aren't good there,' agreed Levy.

It was coming, thought Collington. Slowly, but it was coming. 'Not good?' he said.

'Thought *you* might have told *me*,' said Levy.

Collington pushed away his plate, shaking his head at the other man's remark. 'Told you what?'

Levy stopped eating too, with apparent reluctance. 'The gold,' he said simply.

Collington forced himself to look directly at the other man, attempting to keep his face devoid of expression.

'Don't you have an intelligence section in your corporation?' demanded Levy.

'Yes. They've reported nothing about Soviet gold.'

'No drop in their sales?'

'No,' answered Collington honestly. That had been one of the first statistics he had checked, after Metzinger's disclosure.

'It's only rumours, I suppose,' conceded Levy. 'But I should have thought they would have been picked up . . .' He paused, spooning cheesecake into his mouth. 'But the stories among those who have just left talk of a lot of disruption, throughout their industry . . . .'

'It happens from time to time,' said Collington, knowing the scepticism would prod the other man's memory.

'It doesn't seem to be temporary. Or even seasonal, as it would be in those parts of the country subjected to a heavy winter. It's reckoned to be serious and prolonged.'

'What causes?' asked Collington. He changed his attitude, knowing that Levy would expect the interest and be suspicious if he didn't show it.

'A combination, as far as I can gather,' said the Israeli. 'The Russians always operate with antiquated equipment: apparently there's been a lot of plant failure. Zod is near the Turkish border and has a lot of Muslim workers. The authorities tried to suppress the incursion into Afghanistan, of course, but they don't appear to have been very successful. There's been a very high rate of absenteeism and even talk of sabotage, in protest.'

Richard Jenkins had guessed at mining difficulties at their emergency meeting, remembered Collington. And been argued down by both accountants because of the illogicality and danger of open-market purchasing. But that was unquestionably what was happening. And it *was* illogical and dangerous. He'd exchanged one mystery for another.

'The facts don't fit,' said Collington, wanting to talk it through with an astute, sharp-minded man. 'If there had been a reduction in Soviet gold output, then there would have been a reduction in what they offered on the Western market to obtain their foreign currency. And I've already said there's been no drop in their sales, not for months.'

Levy shrugged dismissively at the contradiction. 'I'm only repeating rumours,' he said.

Which an air crash in Amsterdam had confirmed, thought Collington. He had pressed Levy far enough, he decided. He didn't want their friendship endangered by Levy realising how the encounter had been manipulated, even though he was quite sure Levy would have done exactly the same in similar circumstances.

'Perhaps it's a good job you're not in the gold business,' he said.

'If I were, I'd buy from South Africa,' said Levy. 'It's less uncertain.'

'Production is very high,' said Collington, wanting to give the impression of volunteering information as well as seeking it. 'There's an extensive government stockpile.'

Levy was intent upon what Collington was saying. 'No danger of a price drop through over-production?'

'The South African government controls that well enough,' said Collington.

'And diamonds?'

'No problem at all.'

'I'm thinking of expanding, buying quite a lot of new plant.'

Collington hesitated, unhappy at the commitment the other man was demanding from him. If the Soviet gold difficulty became public knowledge there might be a vibration on the metal markets. But it wouldn't be severe over an extended period. South Africa could easily move to cover any shortfall. And Levy was thinking of diamonds anyway, more than gold.

'I can't see any danger in the investment,' he said.

'There are some more Russian immigrants wanting jobs,' said Levy. 'They'll be pleased that we met.'

Levy accepted cognac with the coffee, holding the goblet sideways over the steaming cup to warm it. 'It's pitiful to see them when they first arrive,' he continued reflectively. 'I came here from New York through ideology and a belief that this was the

Promised Land which should be restored to the Jews . . .' He looked up, fearing that he was expressing himself badly. 'That's their motivation too, of course,' he said hurriedly. 'But I'd never know the oppression of Europe, neither during the Holocaust or in the East. I'd never had to wear a Star of David on my jacket. Or worry about my children starving . . .'

This sort of conversation, like the joke about diamonds being more than a girl's best friend, was not unusual at some time during a meeting with Levy, and Collington's concentration began to falter as part of his mind became occupied with what he had learned from the Israeli.

'. . . and they are starving, apparently,' continued Levy, sipping the liquor. 'People I've got coming to me now say that this is the sixth year in succession that there have been crop failures . . . in some of the eastern provinces, people are actually begging in the streets . . .'

Collington renewed concentration, alert to the additional information. 'Russia can always buy from Western surpluses,' he said.

'I suppose they are,' said Levy, snapping out of his reverie. 'But it never seems to be enough.'

They had more brandy in the lounge and Collington promised to stay longer on his next visit. He allowed the conversation to return to diamond production so he could reassure Levy once more that there wasn't any danger with his planned expansion.

It was past midnight when Collington walked the other man solicitously to his car. They shook hands and Collington said, 'Longer next time, I promise.'

'I'll keep you to it,' said Levy.

Collington started to turn away but the Israeli retained his hand, preventing him. 'I hope you got it, James,' he said.

'Got it?'

'Whatever it was you came here to learn.'

Collington actually considered cancelling the visit to Rome in his eagerness to follow the leads that Levy had provided. And then he confronted the other reason and realised he would be running away from the encounter with Ann. He arrived in Italy the day before her and used the time to assemble the information he had gathered in a written assessment before calling Geoffrey Wall in Pretoria. He kept him on the telephone for over an hour, stipulating the information he wanted prepared for his return.

As he drove to the airport to meet her, Collington recognised that he was avoiding nothing by meeting her in Rome rather than London. It was still decision time. So what was he going to do? The weekend would provide the answer.

Collington stood slightly back from the crush around the arrival barrier so that he saw her before she located him. She was one of the first passengers to emerge, striding confidently forward as she gazed around for him. She was wearing a beige chamois travelling suit with a matching wide-brimmed hat and large sunglasses: she looked sensational and was receiving a lot of attention. Collington felt a pop of satisfaction, knowing she was his.

The first surge of anxiety went through Ann when she couldn't see him. She shrugged irritably away from the man beside her, not hearing what he said. She had imagined the scene of her arrival, Collington waiting for her with the smile that would make her uncertainty disappear, and now he wasn't there and all the rehearsals in the new suit and the last minute preparations in the cramped aircraft toilet had been pointless. Then she saw him. She was glad of the protection afforded by her sunglasses and hat, because the tiny whimper of relief was lost, but she recovered quickly and took them off with one movement as she hurried towards him. Her hair had been caught up without any clasp under her hat and billowed around her face as she released it. He had to push it aside to kiss her. Ann clung tightly to him, wanting the reassurance of his arms around her: he'd smiled as she had known he would, yet the uncertainty was still there.

Collington felt the envy of the men who had watched her, minutes earlier. 'Hello,' he said.

'You were spying on me!' she said, in mock accusation.

'Admiring,' he said. 'Like a lot of others.'

'Jealous?' she said, hopefully.

'Very,' he replied. Was that true? he asked himself. If he properly loved her, wouldn't he have felt jealousy rather than pride of possession at the way the men had ogled?

Collington had got hold of a porter. He identified her luggage quickly and within half an hour they were in the car and on their way back to the city. She sat facing Collington and ignoring the countryside. He was aware of her grave expression. 'What's the matter?' he asked.

'Nothing,' she said, trying to prevent the abrupt smile appearing too obvious.

'You seem very serious.'

'Nothing,' she said again.

'Any problems in London?'

Momentarily she hesitated. Then she said, 'No. Did you expect there to be?'

He glanced at her again. 'No,' he said. 'Did you tell Richard you were coming here to see me?'

What was the point of that question? she wondered. He hadn't seemed concerned with discretion before. 'No,' she said. 'There wasn't any reason.'

She was alert for his response. The shrug seemed one of disinterest.

'Did he tell you about the Afrikaner move on the board?' said Collington.

Ann turned away, sharply, staring out at the passing view at last. 'Yes,' she said, her voice indistinct.

'There are some funny things happening,' he said. Should he tell her about Israel? It would mean disclosing the details of the gold cargo and they had taken a boardroom decision about secrecy. But there were few things involving the company with which she wasn't familiar and he knew he could trust her discretion absolutely.

'I thought this was a holiday,' she said, quickly.

'It is.'

'No shop then,' she insisted.

'No shop,' he smiled, reaching out for her hand. She seemed to misunderstand the gesture, holding her tightly-knitted fingers in her lap for several moments before responding. 'What's the matter?' he said again.

'I told you. Nothing.'

'You sure?'

'Positive.' If she weren't careful, it was going to be a disaster. She didn't think she could tell him about Metzinger: not today, anyway.

'You don't seem very relaxed,' he said.

'I'm excited at our being together.'

They were both relieved by the arrival at the Grand Hôtel. Collington had insisted upon a corner suite, so there was an elevated view of the Spanish Steps and the Rome streets beyond. There were roses on the side tables and champagne ready in the cooler. Ann twirled in the middle of the room, hands clasped tightly to her chest. 'This is fabulous!' she said and Collington smiled at the reappearance of her usual attitude. He always thought of her like this: constantly enthusiastic, every sentence an exclamation. She took her jacket off. Underneath she was wearing a tight oatmeal-coloured sweater and her nipples were showing. Hannah hadn't been wearing a bra under the black dress, the night before he'd left Pretoria. Collington made much of opening the wine, angry at the comparison. But why should he be? Wasn't that what he was supposed to be doing, comparing and deciding? Yes, he thought. But not like this: this made both of them whores.

'What are we going to do?' she demanded.

'What do you want to do?'

'Be a tourist!'

He handed her the glass, holding her eyes. They clinked rims and said 'cheers' together, and then she smiled and said, 'Sorry about the car. I really was nervous.'

This was the only way they had ever known each other, outside their business lives. With the aphrodisiac of the illicit about them, both trying to impress the other. She had wanted to make an impact at the airport, and he had attempted to impress her with the champagne and flowers. Could he sustain this perpetual zestfulness?

'You haven't been nervous before,' he said.

'I am now.' The sharpness surprised both of them. Her lip came between her teeth and she said, 'I'm sorry.'

Collington took the glass from her and placed it, with his own, on a side table. Then he reached out and pulled her to him, not trying to kiss her but just holding her against him. He felt her trembling. 'What is it?' he said, quietly. 'What is it darling?'

She shook her head against his chest. 'I'm frightened of losing you,' she said.

Collington winced, glad she was unable to see his reaction. She was waiting for him to say something. He strained for the right words, but they wouldn't come. 'What are you talking about?' he asked.

She pulled away from him. 'I'm doing a pretty good job of spoiling everything, aren't I?'

'You're usually more fun,' he said gently. 'I thought we were going to be tourists?'

'Not yet,' she said. 'I've missed you.'

'I've missed you, too.'

'Let's go to bed.'

He was frightened. The realisation gouged his stomach. The impotence extended beyond the physical to become mental as well. It was as if it were their first meeting, as if she were a stranger. He blinked rapidly, trying to concentrate upon her.

'Don't you want to?' she said.

'Of course I do.'

'Shouldn't you be suggesting it, rather than me?'

He reached out for her hand. It was a sumptuous apartment, the bedroom especially so. The walls were covered in wild silk and there was an elaborate bed, with satin sheets as well as coverlets, and the closets were set with mirrors on the outside; looking slowly from one to another, to see the different images of anyone undressing, produced the same effect as the ancient erotica of the amusement arcade peep show. Ann became aware of his attention and preened herself, because she knew she had a good body and was proud of it. Collington stared at the puppy-nosed breasts and the hard, push-back belly and the tangled pubic puff and willed himself to be aroused. He felt nothing.

She got into bed first, throwing back the satin so that he could see her lying there. She had one hand behind her head, pulling up her breasts. 'I love you,' she said.

Their time in bed together was the only time when the words didn't end with an exclamation.

He moved towards her hurriedly, wanting to shield his difficulty. He kissed her, hurriedly again, trying to create an arousal, and she misunderstood it as passion, snatching at him and pulling his head down into her. She covered his hand with hers, forcing it between her legs and then up, into her mouth, and then she reached out for him and he felt her tense.

'I'm sorry,' he said.

'Oh God!'

'It's not you . . . I want you . . .'

'It doesn't seem like it.'

'I'm sorry,' he said again. 'Please forgive me.' He lay with his head against her breast so that he wouldn't have to meet her eyes, his frantic hand resting now on her thigh.

'Have I done anything wrong?' she asked tensely. She wouldn't tell him anything now, not after this.

'Of course not.'

'Then why?'

'I don't know.'

'I didn't expect this.'

'Do you think I did?'

'It's supposed to be flattering, for it to happen to a woman.'

'I don't see how.'

'Neither do I,' she said. 'I've just heard it said.'

An unidentifiable emotion engulfed him and then he realised he was close to tears. He was frightened by his weakness. He lay with his eyes tightly shut, his muscles tensed against a breakdown, and shook his head, unable to speak. She was holding him with both hands, stroking his neck and shoulders.

'It's not important,' she said. 'Not important at all.'

'To me it is.' His voice was strained, lumped with a thickness in his throat.

'You haven't told Hannah, have you?' she said, resigned.

'No,' he admitted.

'You said you would.'

'I couldn't, when it came to it.'

'You're not being fair.'

'I know.'

'So when are you going to do it?'

'Soon.'

'That's not an answer. You said that last time.'

'I mean it. Soon.'

'James.'

'What?'

'There's nothing wrong in being like other people. In crying, sometimes.'

Chapter Eleven

The basis of Collington's success had always been his attention to detail and his ability to select from company documentation and records intelligence he could use to his advantage. He had unwittingly been practising his craft when he co-ordinated freight rates with train schedules as a junior porter. Or even when he plotted the back alleys between the four sectors of Berlin or tramped the High Streets of Richmond and Hounslow and Kingston, deciding ahead of the demand what the public wanted to see in shop windows.

The consciousness developed during the expansion of SAGOMI and had been honed into a rare expertise by the time he attempted to discover why Russia was buying gold.

It took a week of double-checking and cross-referencing to complete the assessment, after his return from Italy. And there were, surprisingly, long periods when Geoffrey Wall was making an enquiry for him, when Collington had nothing to do except go over what had happened in Rome and conclude what a disaster it had been. They *had* made love, that night, and every night afterwards and in the afternoon before he left. They had done all the tourist things that she'd wanted, like drinking in Harry's Bar on the Via Veneto and throwing coins into the Trevi Fountain. They had taken a horse-drawn carriage ride at night to the Coliseum and the Victor Emmanuel monument and she had pretended to forget. But she hadn't, any more than he had. The memory had lain between them like a barrier, his embarrassment caused not so much by his momentary ineffectiveness in bed but by the thought of how close he had come to weeping.

He had actually been glad when it was time for him to leave, just as he was glad when Wall assembled the final piece of information and he was able to concentrate fully upon creating a picture and put the episode from his mind.

There was a small conference table in his office suite, and he displayed everything there, instructing his secretaries to hold all his calls and even locking the doors against any interruption.

Lloyd's of London had provided all the information necessary about the global movements of shipping. There was a lot of material, a file nearly an inch thick, but Wall had attached a summary and initially that was sufficient for Collington. He smiled, feeling the first stir of satisfaction at being proved right. He had insisted that the enquiry extend back a year and was glad, because the first three months provided the comparison. During that period there was hardly any movement of grain ships that could be logically traced between Soviet and American ports. The concentration had built up immediately afterwards, lists of ships and company charters, with routings to the Soviet Union's cold and warm water ports from America's East and Gulf coasts. Wall had been as efficient as Collington had anticipated, providing not merely the names of the vessels but their carrying capacity, so it was a matter of simple if somewhat lengthy arithmetic to compute, with an accuracy margin of a few thousand bushels, precisely how much grain Russia had imported from the United States over the previous nine months.

Collington turned away from Wall's report to a separate collection of documents he had ordered from SAGOMI's agricultural analyst. The information here was much more easily assimilated: a collection of figures and graphs showing the United States grain exports to Russia over the preceding years. During 1978 and 1979, 17,000,000 metric tonnes had been shipped. During 1980 it should have been 26,000,000, but Washington had embargoed sales at 9,000,000 because of the Soviet invasion of Afghanistan.

Collington frowned, going back to the figures he had computed from Wall's report. Believing he had miscalculated, he set them out again, sitting back and whistling through his teeth in astonishment at the results. In nine months, the Soviet Union had taken 37,000,000 metric tonnes.

He scribbled the figure on to the jotting pad from which he intended to prepare his report to the board, going back to the agricultural glossary, wanting confirmation of the conversion. A metric tonne was equivalent to 2205 lb, making a metric tonne of soya beans equivalent to 37 bushels, which was the same as wheat, but with corn coming out slightly higher at 39 bushels.

Collington pushed aside the second report, progressing to the one he had requested from America. It was divided again, to prevent those who had prepared it establishing any sort of link that might have led to gossip. The division — like the reports themselves — had been easy because the metal commodity markets of New York were quite separate from the grain commodity markets which were headquartered in Chicago. It was to the Chicago file to which Collington turned first, wanting a final confirmation of the grain shipments before moving on. It was detailed as Collington had insisted it should be, breaking down the sales into soya bean, corn and wheat, in bushels, against the identifiable purchasers.

Collington converted the figures back into tonnes, to make the sum easy. The United States government agencies had purchased a total of 45,000,000 metric tonnes and were committed, in future contracts on crops not yet harvested, to buy a further 35,000,000.

The metal file was the largest of them all, because Collington had extended the enquiry not just to America but to the markets throughout the world and then added a separate enquiry to their own mining divisions, to obtain three year figures of global gold production and sales. It was, however, upon America that he concentrated first. The figures increased as he went from country to country.

Because it was his business to be aware of such things, Collington had known of the United States government decision to make monthly, open-market gold sales, but he re-read the account from their mining analyst and then concentrated upon the additional material that had been provided. There was even a photostat of an article in *Fortune* magazine, quoting at length the United States Treasury Secretary, Henry Moreton, hinting at a bad miscalculation of America's gold reserves, and a graph alongside recording the increased strength of the dollar.

Collington returned to the list of figures he had made, setting out the gold purchases throughout the previous three years. He checked his figures, as he had done with the grain shipments, then sat back in his chair, shaking his head. There had to be a margin for error, but at five tonnes that would be over-generous. And even building that into the stocks necessary for the United States to maintain their sales at the levels currently operating without seriously weakening their gold holdings, there hadn't been a miscalculation.

A mystery, determined Collington. And as such it would have

remained, but for a conversation with a diamond merchant in Israel and the awareness of the cargo of a crashed Russian transporter in Amsterdam. Which made it perfectly understandable. Two countries had come to quite an ordinary commodities agreement, one to bolster its currency, the other to avert famine. Ordinary, that is, except for the fact that the Soviet Union had entered the contract with insufficient resources to meet its terms and was now involved in an incredible bluff, having to buy secretly upon the open market not just to avert starvation but to retain its international credibility.

Collington stood up from the table, stretching to relieve the cramp of concentration in his body. So what? he thought. SAGOMI owned maybe 2,000,000 acres of farmland, but there was little he could do to intrude into the arrangement for the company's benefit. And gold sales were government controlled, removing any opportunity for advantage from the Soviet difficulty. The only benefit would be political and that would be gained by the South African government, once he'd reported back to the board and Metzinger had in turn gone back to his cabinet informant.

The satisfaction had hardened as he had fitted the pieces together; it had been the return of an old feeling, like the pleasure he had known when he was working quite alone in Israel. Now it seeped away, leaving him dispirited and empty. He had proved to himself that he was as good as he had ever been. But there had been scant need for such proof, because it was not in his business life that he suffered self doubt.

He felt cheated.

Collington resealed the files with their pink binding tape, unlocked the door, released his calls and slouched back to his desk chair, waiting for his private secretary to take dictation for the report. A damp squib, he decided. Energising, while it lasted; but a damp squib, nevertheless. So what was he going to do about Hannah and Ann?

Igor Struve grew increasingly nostalgic about the era of Stalin. He conveniently forgot the paranoia and the purges. His recollection was of firmness, of a man strong enough to lead Russia through any crisis. Not that he regarded the crop failure as a crisis, because like most of the government élite he was quite unaffected by it. In Stalin's day, they wouldn't have gone running, cap in hand, to America; they'd have imposed rationing and demanded sacrifice and mourned the few who had died. But now the leadership was weak. That's why upstarts like Leonov got promoted beyond their station, allowed access to the offices of the minister himself. Struve was determined not to be victim of the difficulties that had arisen. The scheme would undoubtedly fail and there would be an enquiry and a search for scapegoats. And Struve had never been a scapegoat in his life. He had no responsibility for anything that had happened, he calculated, apart from providing the money. So the resolve was easy.

All he had to do was limit that, so he could later claim the foresight in anticipating the disaster and refusing to waste more where too much had already been ridiculously expended. And others would be blamed. It was a decision he had reached before the interview with Leonov.

Leonov had expected to meet Struve alone, but when he entered the office he saw that Vladimir Orlov was already there. Leonov greeted the official from the mining control as an equal and bent his head, in proper deference, towards Struve. The Finance Minister did not respond.

'What about the crash?' he demanded, at once.

'There's no indication of the gold having been discovered.'

'But you're not sure?'

'No.'

Struve turned to the other man. 'What about the mines?'

'Siberia is closed now, for five months,' said Orlov. 'It's going to take three months, at least, to repair the damage to Zod and pump out the water from the workings where the dam was breached. That brings our output there down to three tonnes, if we're lucky.'

'What about Muruntau?' persisted the minister. 'That produced eighty tonnes last year.'

'We've imported camp labour from the Potma prisons,' said Orlov. 'But it doesn't matter how many men you have: you can't replace a machine. And it's the machinery that's failing. We won't be able to replant for four months. We can't hope to resume even average output in under six.'

'So we continue as before,' said Struve, nodding dismissively to conclude the meeting. Except that he would gradually withdraw: this would be the last direct encounter.

'In my report, I made a request,' said Leonov, not rising as Orlov had done.

'For more money,' said Struve.

'Insufficient is being allowed,' protested Leonov. 'With the money available at the moment, we can't withstand a ten per cent price fluctuation. And there is a shortfall in the Ukraine to compensate for.'

'There hasn't been more than a three per cent swing over the last three months,' argued Struve.

'There must be a greater allowance for instability. And for the Ukraine.'

'I have allowed you two increases since this arrangement was made,' said Struve. 'The foreign currency available to us is not limitless: what you are allowed at the moment is greater than that being allocated to any other foreign investment.'

Slowly, anxious not to antagonise the man, Leonov said: 'The deal concluded with the United States of America has the full backing of the Politburo. It is at risk because of shortage of money.'

'Is that a threat?' said Struve, outraged.

'It is a simple explanation of the facts,' said Leonov.

'You will be allowed no more money.'

'May I ask if my request has gone forward to be considered by the Politburo?'

'No, young man. You may not!' said Struve.

Chapter Twelve

Because a balance had to be maintained in every aspect of the company's work, Metzinger's office suite in the SAGOMI building matched Collington's. The only difference was that it did not adjoin the main boardroom, but it still had to be approached through two separate rooms, each containing secretaries. The arrangement guaranteed complete privacy, when necessary, and Metzinger decided it was particularly useful after the meeting at which Collington had reported on his enquiry.

Metzinger was conscious that he was about to embark upon the most dangerous enterprise he had ever contemplated in forty years of business life and he was feeling a numbing lightheadedness: like drunkenness, he supposed. But drunkenness risked lack of control and Metzinger was confident he wasn't going to lose that. Which was why he had only invited Jan Wassenaar back to the office, excluding de Villiers from what he was going to propose. De Villiers was a clerk, nothing more; certainly he didn't possess the courage to take the risks that Metzinger was going to put to the Afrikaner sitting opposite. Wassenaar was clearly depressed: an understandable attitude for a businessman who had just left a board meeting at which it had become clear that there was no company benefit from what was happening with the gold purchases. How long, wondered Metzinger, would it take him to relieve that depression?

'Collington did well,' said Wassenaar in begrudging admiration.

'We have the organisation to provide the material,' said Metzinger.

'But he remembered Israel,' insisted Wassenaar. 'That was necessary. And he still had to interpret it.'

'He's a clever man,' conceded Metzinger, guiding the conversation. 'But maybe not clever enough.'

Wassenaar frowned at the remark, but instead of querying it said: 'When are you meeting Knoetze?'

'I'm not sure that I'm going to meet him, not yet,' said the deputy chairman quietly. Wassenaar's frown had deepened and he was concentrating fully on Metzinger. 'There's rarely been a discussion between us when you haven't spoken about our need for an advantage in this,' Metzinger reminded.

'But there isn't one,' said Wassenaar. 'We've just spent two hours deciding that.'

'Certainly not for the company,' agreed Metzinger.

'What then?' demanded the lawyer.

'There are two ways to alter the directorships upon the controlling board,' said Metzinger. 'The first is through the holding of 'A' shares in Witwatersrand. But precisely because that created an unacceptable control, there was built in the safeguard that whether they possessed 'A' shares or not, directors could be voted from the board if there were a sufficiently strong no-confidence vote from the shareholders.'

Wassenaar moved impatiently in his chair. 'I know the situation as well as you do,' he said. 'How can there be a no-confidence vote in this board? Every company we control is scheduled this year to distribute the highest dividend in its history . . . in some cases it's twenty-five per cent. We're one of the most successful multinationals in the world. And a no-confidence vote is against a board, not individuals.'

'Not necessarily,' said Metzinger quickly. 'If a director could be proved to have been working independently of the board, and against its interest and those of the company, then the vote could be personal.'

Wassenaar moved forward in his seat, intent upon what Metzinger was saying.

'We *have* an advantage,' said Metzinger. 'One that we haven't had the forethought to recognise. I came forward with some information that could only have come from one source. Collington checked it and found it to be accurate. So now he *believes*.'

'Believes what?' said Wassenaar.

'That there is a direct link between me and the government. He believes it but there's no way he can check it. He's entirely dependent upon my word.'

A smile appeared on Wassenaar's face. 'So if you went back and told him the matter wasn't closed, he'd think you were passing on the views of the Cabinet?'

'But more importantly,' completed Metzinger, 'being asked to do something with unofficial government support.'

Wassenaar shook his head, professionally doubtful. 'It's an appalling risk,' he said. 'To achieve a no-confidence vote, whatever we did would have to be shown, against Collington, to have affected the companies adversely. That sort of manipulation is blatantly criminal. And the conspiracy could be proved. We'd have to make the approach at a board meeting. We could go into closed session, certainly, but at any shareholders' meeting it would be our word against the directors supporting Collington.'

'I wasn't envisaging any boardroom discussion,' said Metzinger.

'I am as anxious as anyone for the control of SAGOMI to be vested in the proper hands,' said Wassenaar, sensing Metzinger's irritation. 'But I don't think that we should allow that ambition to override sensible caution.'

'Simpson's shares give us nothing, in any practical sense,' said Metzinger. 'It would be a great pity not to take advantage of an opportunity.'

'We'd have to be careful,' warned Wassenaar. 'Incredibly careful.'

'I intend to be.'

'What about Knoetze?'

'I'll say enquiries look hopeful, but there's nothing positive yet.'

'You're in a good pivotal position,' conceded Wassenaar.

'Are you with me?' said Metzinger, demanding a commitment.

Wassenaar hesitated. 'If we overthrew Collington, you'd be chairman,' he said.

'Yes.'

'Who'd be deputy?'

'You would.'

'I'm with you.'

Collington had hurriedly bought the Gucci handbag while Ann was in another part of the store, trying on shoes, and he felt the vaguest twinge of conscience, giving it to Hannah. Knowing his wife's simplicity of taste he had ruled against one with the familiar green and red motif, so that the only ostentation was the G of the clasp.

She was by the pool, wearing a patterned one-piece costume, her hair held back with a matching bandana. She took the gift, smiled and said, 'Your taste is improving.'

'I'm glad you like it,' said Collington.

'So you didn't get to London?'

Collington shook his head. 'That's why I stopped by, to see if you'd heard from Paul.'

'Not yet,' she said.

'I'll write tonight,' determined Collington. 'I don't want to be involved in anything that will clash with his visit.'

'You know the dates.'

'I thought you might have been planning something separately.'

'If I had been, I would have told you,' she said.

He dabbed a handkerchief against his face and slipped out of his jacket.

'Would you like to change?' she invited, indicating the cabin and the shower assembly. 'There are plenty of your costumes there.'

'No thanks,' said Collington.

'Oh,' she said, making no attempt to disguise her disappointment.

He eased himself on to the sun-bed opposite hers. He was suddenly aware of the difference in his attitudes to Hannah and Ann. With Ann he was constantly alert, trying to anticipate her enthusiasms — to show off, he supposed. With Hannah, there was no strain. If he wanted to, he could stretch out on the sun-bed and lie for thirty minutes without speaking and Hannah would be quite happy without conversation. There couldn't be that relaxation with Ann.

'Daddy has told me about himself and Janet Simpson,' Hannah announced.

'Told you what?'

'That he's seeing her and that they like each other and that they've even thought of getting married. It was all rather embarrassing — he made a special trip out here and from the way he behaved you would have thought he'd made her pregnant and was asking my forgiveness.'

Collington smiled at her description. It must have started before Walter Simpson's death. It was easy to understand how the shares had been secured.

'I'm giving a dinner party for them. I'd like you to come,' she said, looking at him intently.

Collington grimaced at the invitation. 'I'm not sure that would make for an altogether relaxed evening.'

'But it would be uneven, without a partner for me. And there's no one else I'd like to come.'

He wanted to be with her, Collington accepted. Just as he wanted to change and stay with her, by the pool. 'I'd love to,' he said.

'Friday then?' she said at once.

'So it was all fixed?'

'All except your coming.'

'What if I'd said no?'

'Like I said, it would have been an uneven evening.'

He stood and she shielded her eyes against the sun as she looked up at him. 'Going already?' she said, disappointed again.

'I've got a lot to do,' said Collington, conscious of the emptiness of the excuse as he spoke. Hannah was making it as easy for him as she possibly could, he thought, walking back through the house towards the front door. So why the hell couldn't he overcome the pride and ask her to take him back? The dinner party would be the occasion, he decided. But what about Ann?

Chapter Thirteen

Collington purposely arrived at Parkstown early so that he would be with Hannah to greet Metzinger and Janet Simpson. Both were aware of the separation, so he accepted that the gesture was meaningless, but he *wanted* to be a good host with her. He'd try to make her realise it, before the other two arrived. He parked in his accustomed place, but didn't immediately get out of the car. It was a pretence, he recognised. For what purpose? Social politeness? Or to impress Hannah? To impress Hannah, he decided, honestly. Since when had that been necessary?

She smiled up as he was shown into the small drawing-room and said, 'You're early. That was thoughtful.'

She was wearing a flame-coloured dress, backless and open to the thigh, showing the tan she had been cultivating during his visit two days earlier. 'I've made the drinks,' she said, nodding to the frosted pitcher that stood behind her on the trolley.

'So you expected me before the others?'

'Sort of,' she admitted.

'You look very lovely,' he said.

Hannah raised her eyebrows in exaggerated surprise. 'I can't remember the last time you paid me that sort of compliment.'

'And I can't remember the last time you played the coquette,' he said.

Hannah whirled around to show how the dress flared away, and Collington had a brief glimpse of her body and wondered if that had been her intention. 'Like it?' she said.

'Yes.'

She giggled, unable to stop herself. 'We're being a bit gauche, aren't we?'

'A little,' he admitted. He handed her the drink and as she accepted it, their hands touched awkwardly.

'I wrote to Paul,' he said.

'I haven't had a reply to any of my letters. Perhaps he doesn't want to come home for the holidays.'

'We'll sort it out,' he said confidently.

The outer door opened and they both turned towards it. Metzinger was framed there and Collington's first impression was of the man's embarrassment, which surprised him because he had never once thought of the Afrikaner being ill at ease. Metzinger stood back, ushering Janet Simpson politely ahead of him. Like Metzinger, Janet Simpson had an agelessness about her. She had been much younger than Walter Simpson at the time of their marriage, but Collington guessed she was nearing sixty now. She could have been ten or even fifteen years younger. Only the whiteness of her hair gave any clue. It would have been better if she had dyed it, but she was an unyielding, proper woman and considered hair colouring to be cheap. Her hair was arranged in formal, ridged waves around her oval face, and as she came nearer into the room at a sedate, almost grand pace, Collington saw that there was no make-up, apart from the palest of lipsticks. She wore a severe black dress, high-necked, long-skirted, and with full sleeves. She looked a formidable woman, which she was, and Collington qualified his initial impression. Metzinger *was* uncomfortable. But it was not because he was introducing a wife they never imagined he would take, rather that he was anxious for things to go right for her. Collington didn't think the other man should have worried.

Hannah went across the room to greet them. She kissed her father and then Janet Simpson. The woman moved further into the room, extending her hand and making it quite clear from the way she held herself that she didn't expect any more contact than that. Collington took her hand and said: 'Hello Janet.'

'Good evening, James,' she said. She had a clipped, precise way of speaking, as formal as everything else about her.

Collington looked sideways as Metzinger approached. The man *did* seem ageless, thought Collington. But more. The word to describe him was indestructible. It was impossible to imagine him suffering any infirmity.

The four stood in a loose circle, hesitating to initiate a conversation. A houseboy intruded with drinks, easing the tension and when he withdrew Hannah said to the other woman, 'I am delighted to see you both here.'

Janet relaxed slightly, allowing the briefest of smiles. 'I'm pleased too,' she said.

She looked at Collington, expecting him to say something, and he groped for the words. 'Congratulations,' he said.

'It's not quite got that far, yet,' qualified Metzinger.

'Were you surprised?' Janet said to Hannah.

'Very much,' said Hannah, matching the directness.

'I think a lot of people will be.'

'Is there going to be a formal announcement?' asked Collington.

'We haven't decided yet.' said Janet.

'I want Paul to come over to the farm when he gets back, so I can tell him,' announced Metzinger.

Metzinger had never been a hypocrite, thought Collington fairly. He had resisted his marriage to Hannah before it happened and maintained the opposition afterwards. He had allowed only one relaxation and that was his affection for his grandson. Paul matched it and Collington wondered if that was where the boy would prefer to spend his summer vacation, on Metzinger's farm.

'We'll see it happens,' promised Collington.

The meal was announced and they paired off formally, Janet taking Collington's arm and Metzinger escorting his daughter. Because there were only four of them, Hannah had ignored the large table which dominated the room, setting instead the smaller, round one which they had installed for overflow guests when they had given large dinners, or for children during equally large lunches.

There hadn't been either for a long time — not even in the months before their separation. In Collington's mind the split was fixed as a sudden, abrupt thing, a flurried Saturday afternoon departure with no suitcases and an air of unreality, because of the theatricality of it all. Hannah had expected him to come back and he supposed he had thought he would return. But when the moment had come he hadn't been able to lift the telephone to apologise, and so a week had passed and the trip to London arrived and the affair with Ann had suddenly seemed something more. Which it hadn't been, he accepted. He'd used Ann to live out some pulp fiction fantasy, even managing at one stage to convince himself that the separation had all been Hannah's fault. He had a lot of apologising to do, and apology seemed an insufficient description for it.

Hannah had ordered champagne and Collington realised that she meant him to propose a toast. Hannah then occupied the early conversation, recounting Paul's various successes at school but omitting the sudden absence of any letters. Janet Simpson talked of a recent visit to CapeTown, which started out casually enough, nothing more than an account of a week's holiday, but then she grew irritated, complaining of the difficulties not just in Cape Town but throughout the Union, because the proper separation between the people was being relaxed. Collington intercepted Hannah's warning look and smiled to reassure her that he wasn't going to involve himself in an argument about apartheid, but the response came from Metzinger on his right.

'Look what happened in Rhodesia!' demanded the other man. 'People create a civilisation where one didn't exist before, establish a country and a heritage and then get cast aside for their trouble. It's a warning! A terrible warning.'

Fleetingly Collington considered disputing Metzinger's interpretation of history and reminding the man of the ancient culture and ruins from which the country had got its new name but Hannah caught his eye again. Instead he said, intending nothing more than gentle mockery, 'But what happened in Zimbabwe won't happen here.'

Metzinger turned directly towards the other man, a flush colouring his face, and Collington realised the mistake and prepared for the outburst.

'No!' said Metzinger, brittle-voiced. 'It won't happen here. It won't ever happen here and life's going to be much easier when everyone realises it. The South African map will end up drawn as it was always intended, the Bantu nations separate to the east and South Africa occupying what remains as theirs by God-given right.'

It was fortunate that this came at the end of the meal. Hannah started to lead Janet from the room, leaving Collington and Metzinger with cigars and port.

Collington passed the humidor and the cutter and then the decanter, giving the older man time to recover his composure.

'I welcomed the chance to meet like this, when Hannah told me you'd be here,' said Metzinger. His voice was soft, all anger gone.

Collington stared curiously at the other man. 'Why?' he said.

'I wanted to tell you of my appreciation for what you did. I've been officially asked to thank you, very sincerely.'

'You could have told me that at the office,' said Collington. It sounded rude, which he hadn't intended.

Metzinger seemed not to notice. He shook his head. 'Better like this.'

Collington wondered what the government would do about the information. If there were a purpose to be served, Pretoria could cause a lot of problems, in the way they controlled the regular gold releases. 'Pity we couldn't have benefited more,' he said.

'I think there could be a way that we might,' declared Metzinger.

Collington concentrated on the man, aware that this was not a casual, after dinner conversation. 'What do you mean?' he said.

'The Sasol plant damage is very extensive: it will be at least a year before oil production is resumed.'

SAGOMI controlled five coal mines and Collington had already assessed the implications of the damage. 'It'll probably be the only division in which we don't declare a profit this year,' he accepted. 'But we could absorb the losses easily enough. I'm going to propose at the next board meeting that we make a planned reduction of output and stockpile. When Sasolberg and Secuna resume, we'll be ready with the supplies.'

'I wasn't thinking of the company difficulties,' said Metzinger. He was talking quietly, still staring intently at the glowing tip of his cigar. 'I was thinking of the country.'

'It's an inconvenience, probably a severe one. But nothing that can't be overcome,' disputed Collington. 'It's no secret that South Africa has got huge reserves in storage. I've heard periods of up to twelve months suggested. And they've bought successfully on the spot market for years.'

'But oil — at least, an unhindered, guaranteed supply — is the one natural resource this country hasn't got,' said Metzinger distantly.

'It's a problem that's always existed.'

'But one that's being discussed again, because of what happened at the Sasol plants. And because of your discovery of the gold-for-wheat arrangement. There's an attractive simplicity, pledging two commodities against each other.'

'It's common enough,' said Collington. 'And it must have occurred to the government a hundred times to make a gold-for-oil offer . . .' He hesitated, not wanting to arouse the other man's anger again. Knowing there was no way he could make the point without taking the risk, he said, 'The Middle East have got the oil and they don't want to sell it to us. Publicly, at least. I'm damned sure they know it comes here unofficially.'

Metzinger slapped his hand against the table and for a moment Collington imagined the anger of which he had been afraid. Then he saw that Metzinger was smiling and realised he was trying to emphasise his argument. 'Exactly!' Metzinger said. 'They won't do it publicly but don't care what comes in the back door. Why can't we regularise that?'

'I don't understand.'

'We're a multi-national,' said Metzinger, splaying his hand between them and ticking the points off against his fingers. 'Among the biggest, with separate, self-contained divisions, not just here in Africa but in Europe and America.'

Collington nodded, encouraging the man to go on. 'We've got the structure and the expertise to trade, country to country. The Middle East won't deal directly with South Africa. But what if a proposal could be put forward, removing that problem?'

'For them to supply a company registered and operating from England or America, you mean?'

'Just that,' said Metzinger, slapping the table again. 'England is an oil producer now, just like America. There wouldn't be anything suspicious in our forming independent, self-contained companies there.'

'It doesn't work, on two levels,' refused Collington. 'The shell companies would still be traceable to SAGOMI, and we're headquartered here, in South Africa. So the link is too obvious. But even more than that, to make the deal work we'd have to pledge gold in return for oil. And we can't sell gold. Only the government can do that.'

'You surprise me,' said Metzinger, shaking his head.

Collington realised the other man was patronising him.

'You're talking about rules,' said Metzinger. 'I've never known you to be particularly observant of them in the past.'

'In the past we've never considered anything of this magnitude,'

Collington argued back. 'And I'm not just talking about rules. I'm talking about the law. No deal, no matter how big, would justify our risking the whole structure of SAGOMI by doing something openly criminal.'

'It wouldn't be open. And there would only be a prosecution if the government saw fit to bring one.'

Collington smiled. 'And you're telling me they wouldn't.'

'I'm suggesting that the gratitude for ensuring a guaranteed supply of oil would match the effort involved.'

'How detailed have your talks been?' pressed Collington.

'Not at all,' said Metzinger unhelpfully. 'I'm reflecting attitudes and impressions. No one is committing themselves at this stage.'

'I would be, on behalf of the company,' pointed out Collington.

'You've done that before, with as much uncertainty.'

Collington shook his head. 'That was years ago,' he said. 'We're consolidated now, with a world-wide reputation. And even then I was negotiating for the company, not a government.'

'It's *still* the company,' insisted Metzinger. 'How would you assess a profit margin if we were allowed exclusive import and distribution rights throughout the country, with government tax aid for tanker and refinery construction.'

'Spectacular,' answered Collington at once. 'But I couldn't consider it without some sort of support. I couldn't risk SAGOMI without a government guarantee, no matter how unofficial.'

'We won't get it,' said Metzinger. 'It would have to come the other way. I'd need to go back with a firm proposal, supported by guarantees from an oil producer, before they would declare themselves.'

'That's not the way to do business. And you know it,' said Collington.

'It was once. It was the way the reputation of the company was established.'

'Times have changed,' said Collington, deciding the cliché was appropriate.

'Perhaps you have, too,' said Metzinger.

Collington smiled at Metzinger's attempt to goad him. 'Perhaps I have,' he said, refusing to respond. A company could not fail to make a staggering success with the operating concessions at which

Metzinger had hinted. But were those concessions too much to expect? Hardly, from a government which had always regarded oil as the worst economic weapon to be used against it. With whom could an agreement be attempted? Saudi Arabia, he supposed. That was the country with the biggest reserves. And although there was an occasional rumour, the ruling family appeared more stable than some of the other governments in the area. He had been right in stressing to Metzinger the dangers of an unsupported approach; it showed the proper business prudence from the head of a company with their responsibilities. He could justifiably and provably present himself to the Middle East as a businessman, nothing more. And as such return — hopefully with an indication of an agreement — to open talks with Pretoria.

It certainly justified another intelligence assessment from Geoffrey Wall. A further thought came to him. Only he could do it, in the early stages at least. So it would be personal involvement again.

'What we have been talking about is not for general discussion,' warned Metzinger.

'I understand,' said Collington. Metzinger was proud of his government connections, he thought. He wished he could identify them.

'I think it's time we joined the women,' said Metzinger, reminded of his new responsibilities.

When they entered the drawing-room, Collington saw Hannah had prepared the card table for bridge. They played for an hour, Collington partnering Janet. She played determinedly, openly correcting him when she considered he had made a mistake. By the end, they had won twenty rand.

It was Janet who suggested they should go and Metzinger immediately agreed. At the door Collington realised that Janet was still expecting nothing more than a handshake, to which she responded with dry-palmed firmness.

'Quite a woman,' judged Collington, as he and Hannah returned to the cardroom.

'I've never seen Daddy like it,' she agreed. 'If she said bark, I'm sure he'd do it.'

'I thought it was a successful evening.'

'Thank you for coming.'

'I enjoyed it.'

'This is all a bit unreal, isn't it?'

'Yes,' he admitted.

'If you need me to say it, then I will. I want you back. I want you back right now which means I don't want you to leave for that stupid apartment tonight.' The offer burst from her, in a gush of words. And then she came to him, expecting him to hold her, tensing slightly at his obvious hesitation. He felt her body against his, her breasts pressing into him and the hard pubic mound, and there was none of the difficulty he had known in Rome with Ann. He pushed her away, an act of refusal, leading her to a chair and sitting her down.

'I've got something to say first.'

'Oh,' she said.

He crouched at her feet, his hands cupped around her face. 'I love you, Hannah,' he said. 'I've come as near as I ever want to fucking everything up and now I'm going to put it right. But it's got to be the proper way.'

Her eyes had misted but now she blinked against the tears. 'I don't understand what you mean.'

'I have let things become confused,' said Collington, admitting it to himself as well as Hannah for the first time. 'I'm sitting on top of everything, like one of those carved figureheads they used to put on sailing boats. And with about as much practical use. I was bored and irritated and instead of recognising why, I imagined it was with our marriage, which it never was. And so I was stupid.'

He hesitated, at the moment of complete admission. She deserved the complete honesty after what he had done, but he was apprehensive about causing any more hurt.

'There was another woman, in London,' he hurried on, unable to look at her. 'She's worked for the company for a long time — Jenkins' personal assistant — and I'd known her socially and I was there, lonely and bored.'

'You don't have to make it sound like a rather bad film script,' she said, pulling away from him, rigid-faced.

'It *was* rather like a bad film,' he said. 'I behaved like a shit to her and like a shit to you. Which is why I'm not staying with you tonight, although I want to. I'm not coming back until I've been as honest with her as I have with you. And when I've done that I want to come back.'

'Bastard!' she said, in sudden vehemence.

He had expected tears, certainly, and then the forgiveness she'd promised. The different reaction startled him.

'It's been a game, hasn't it?' she said. 'Some stupid, male menopausal game. And you've caused Christ knows what damage to our son, buggered up some poor bitch in London and made me hate you . . . You're a bastard.'

It was becoming the disaster it had been in Rome, thought Collington. 'Is that what you do, hate me?' he said, wanting her to say she didn't and bring the mood around to forgiveness.

She gestured him away impatiently, turning her head into the corner of the chair. 'I don't know how I feel,' she said. 'Except that I don't want you near me.'

He scrambled to his feet, feeling self-conscious and stupid. 'I couldn't even explain it well, could I?'

'I don't think it was anything to explain *well*,' she said. 'And I don't like the self-pity, James. It doesn't become you.'

'I meant what I said. About wanting to come back.' He held out his hands in the first pleading gesture he could ever remember in his life. 'Please!'

'It's amazing,' she said, as if in some private conversation with herself. 'I never suspected it . . . I never thought you were screwing around . . .'

'I wasn't screwing around!'

'Then what the hell was it?'

It hadn't been like that, Collington thought. But there would never be a way he could convince Hannah. Nor Ann, either.

'You don't want to understand,' he said.

'Get out,' she said. She began to cry, her shoulders pumping with emotion. 'Christ! I even invited you to sleep with me, like some whore.'

'Stop it!' he shouted. 'You've taken everything I've said and turned it upside down.'

'Go away, James. Leave me alone.'

He strode away from the house, leaving doors swung wide open behind him. He took the driveway in the same anger, turning wide so that the car slid on the gravel, and he felt the shudder of the wing as it bounced off the gatepost. He'd tried a lie and it hadn't worked and he'd tried honesty and that hadn't worked either. He wanted Hannah, who didn't want him. And he didn't want Ann. Who did.

'Jesus!' said Collington, speaking aloud to himself in the car. 'What a fuck-up!'

It was after midnight when he got back to the penthouse, and had his thoughts been under their usual control he might not have called Geoffrey Wall so late. But despite the distraction of the episode with Hannah, he couldn't clear his mind completely of what Metzinger had said. Wall answered on the second ring, as alert and bright as always. There wasn't any irritation in his voice, either at the lateness or the request.

'It won't work,' warned Wall. 'There are regulations, rules . . .'

'I'm not particularly concerned about rules,' said Collington, parrotting what Metzinger had said. Perhaps he should have been: there was probably a rule against admitting unsuspected adultery to a wife at the moment she invited you back.

'What if it's impossible?'

'Your brief is to make it possible,' reminded Collington. He sounded like a parody of a multi-national executive — film dialogue again.

There was a momentary pause from the other end of the telephone. Then Wall said, 'How much time do I have?'

'Three days, maximum,' said Collington. 'Tomorrow, if possible.'

'We'd need an edge,' said Wall. 'A lever.'

'Find one.'

Chapter Fourteen

Geoffrey Wall had the Middle East assessments on Collington's desk by the middle of the following afternoon: a deliberately impressive performance.

'You said today, if possible,' he reminded Collington, just unable to keep the satisfaction from his voice.

Collington nodded across the desk, emphasising his gratitude.

Wall was almost a caricature of the rising American business executive, neatly barbered, Ivy-league suited; even the shirt was button down. Collington knew the performance was not quite as dramatic as the man was making it, because the intelligence unit maintained comprehensive records, but it would have been picky to show his awareness. He looked at the desk clock, establishing a time limit for himself.

'Two hours,' he said. 'Then we'll have a conference.'

Collington's middle-of-the-night instructions had been quite explicit, demanding an across-the-board examination, and so Wall had covered all the main oil producers. Only Iran had been excluded, because of its unpredictability. Collington started on the smaller suppliers, like Oman and Bahrain moving up to Kuwait and Iraq and the Arab Emirates of the gulf. A linking theme began to emerge early, which was why he left Saudi Arabia until last. It was the biggest producer and would therefore be affected more than most by the weakness which Collington detected.

He was tempted to hurry through the file, seeking confirmation of what he wanted, but he suppressed the eagerness. Attention to detail had always been the key to success and it would be here, if he were to translate Metzinger's suggestion to some practical benefit.

Collington was a man accustomed to dealing with cosmic sums of money, but even he was surprised at Wall's estimate that the Saudi Arabian Monetary Authority had £35,000,000,000 invested abroad. The figure was included in the facts-at-a-glance synopsis at the beginning of the file, so Collington flicked through until he found a more comprehensive budgetary analysis, because it was important for what he had in mind. Predictably, Wall hadn't made a mistake.

Collington went back to the beginning, noting the Saudi output at 9,500,000 barrels a day and agreeing the formula by which Wall had computed the income. Because of the price fluctuations, Wall had used a mean average, over three years, to assess the annual revenue. On a figure of twenty-six dollars a barrel for light crude, it put the yearly income at around £30,000,000,000. Yet even with these colossal earnings, the Saudis were running a budget deficit, largely because of the cost of the capital goods they imported and the massive development plans for the country. There had been a suspension of some of the work, but Collington saw that for the five-year period from 1980, the Saudi government had pledged themselves to spend £134,000,000,000.

The investment pattern came half-way through the file and Collington smiled as he came to it, tapping against the table edge the gold pencil he'd taken to make margin notes.

Until the Saudis had withdrawn control for themselves, their oil business had been run by the Arabian America Oil Company, which Collington supposed made understandable the decision to retain their monetary links with America. It was easy to be wise in hindsight as Collington was being, but in the beginning it would have been difficult for any financial counsellor to anticipate the danger of what had happened.

Of the £35,000,000,000 invested, more than half was in dollar holdings, in American banks and American investments: even direct bank holdings were denominated in dollars. Certainly in the last few months, since what he now knew to be the gold-for-wheat deal between the United States and the Soviet Union and the resulting gold sales, the dollar had strengthened. So it was proving a good investment for the Saudi Arabians.

But Wall had taken the figures sufficiently far back to provide a comparison. For more than a year before the resumption of the American gold sales, Saudi Arabia had been trapped in a ridiculous financial position. And trapped was the right word, Collington decided. They had been locked into a weak, falling currency, but to have attempted to shift such vast sums away from dollars and convert them to maybe marks or yen would have depressed the dollar even further and worsened a position from which he was convinced they would have wanted to escape.

It was a monstrous cleft-stick situation and Collington would have bet a year's income that the Saudi financiers were desperate for a way out. A gold offer, bypassing the uncertainty of paper currency, would seem very attractive to a nation which inherently trusted metal anyway.

Collington thrust back in his chair, sighing. It was a bargaining position, certainly. But it still didn't provide the lever that Geoffrey Wall had recognised as being necessary the previous night. Perhaps Metzinger's idea wasn't viable after all.

Wall's knock came precisely after two hours and Collington gestured him to a chair. The American perched on its edge, his body tensed forward, like a gun dog awaiting the order to go and fetch.

'What's the weakness?' demanded Collington, with a sweep of his hand encompassing everything that Wall had prepared.

'No secret about that,' said Wall at once. 'They're all locked into dollars. It's not so bad at the moment, but in the past it's cost them millions.'

Collington tilted back in his chair and looked at the ceiling. 'If you were a Middle East producer and someone came to you and offered gold instead of a paper exchange, what would you do?'

'Want to accept it,' said Wall.

'*Want* to?' queried Collington, isolating the reservation.

'It would be difficult from here,' said Wall. 'The oil embargo has been pretty flaky in the past. What you're suggesting, I think, is something new. Very new and very big. Since Iran, the Muslims have been feeling their power. I can't see any Middle East country risking the internal upheaval that would be caused if it became known that a deal had been made with South Africa. Better to lose millions than a throne, surely?'

Collington nodded at the political assessment; 'Unless there were a lever,' he said, using Wall's word.

'Which I might have.'

Collington sat up straight, staring across at the younger man. If Wall had found a way he should have announced it at once, instead of allowing the preliminary hypothesis. The man was trying to show how clever he was; worse, he had imposed some sort of test upon Collington, trying to gauge his ability. Collington looked for self-confidence in his senior executives but hoped that Wall wasn't going to over-reach himself.

'Then why haven't I got it?' Collington asked, showing his annoyance.

Wall blinked, taking the rebuke. 'I thought you wanted a general discussion first,' he said, in bad recovery.

'What is it?' said Collington, maintaining the edge to his voice.

'Prince Tewfik Hassan,' declared Wall. He'd prepared his presentation and refused to be deflected by Collington's irritation.

The composition of the Saudi government had been listed on the second sheet of the file Collington had read earlier. 'Minister for Oil and Development,' he identified.

'And the man confidently expected one day to get the throne.'

'What about him?'

'He was involved in the attempt to corner the silver market, with that Texan named Bains. Difficult to be absolutely accurate, but the guess is that he lost about £100,000,000.'

Collington smiled broadly, his anger at the other man evaporating. 'Now there's a thing!' he said. He leaned further forward across the desk. 'What's the full background?'

Wall took a photograph from the document case at his side, sliding it across to Collington. Hassan was pictured wearing the white robes which indicated he was a pilgrim who had worshipped at Mecca. He was staring, dark-eyed and unsmiling into the camera, a thin-faced, goatee-bearded man.

'Educated in Islamic and civil law at King Fuad University in Cairo,' recited Wall. 'Then quite a run around America. Law at New York University and Harvard Law School and then . . .' Wall looked up, smiling. 'And at this point he seems to have developed a negotiating technique, during a year studying psychiatry at Columbia University . . .'

'Strange switch,' said Collington.

Wall nodded. 'Not many friends, according to our divisions in New York and London. Parties a lot when he's in the West: Regine's, Annabel's, that sort of thing. Likes first nights, particularly Broadway. Described by those who've been up against him as a hard negotiator. Married for eight years to a wife named Leila.

Two children, both being educated locally but scheduled for English prep schools, when they're old enough . . .'

'How did the silver thing come about?'

'Unclear,' admitted Wall. 'Best guess is that he retained an association with Bains from Harvard. They were there together and there are reports of a friendship.'

'I wonder if it still exists.'

'Wouldn't think so.'

'And I wouldn't think he's equipping himself to be ruler. Sounds more like a playboy.'

Wall shook his head. 'I think that's misleading. He's as hard as hell, like I said. And the partying isn't too serious; certainly it's a secret well kept from Riyadh or Jeddah, so it doesn't matter. The money loss is more important. It's the first business mistake he's made. And it's a bad one. If he's going to foul up like that, so the criticism goes, what the hell's going to happen when he gets control over the whole pot?'

'What's the commission protocol?' demanded Collington, ahead of the other man.

'Couldn't be better,' said Wall. 'One of the biggest concerns in the government is the tendency towards corruption.'

'If Hassan could come in with a deal that lifted the Saudis from the uncertainty of currency fluctuation and at the same time recovered the £100,000,000, he'd have made a complete recovery, wouldn't he?' mused Collington. 'He'd have *proved* his ability to be king.'

'It would be a neat twist, if you could make it work.'

Collington thrust up from the table, the decision settling in his mind. 'It's worth a trip to Riyadh,' he said.

'That won't be necessary,' said Wall.

Collington had twisted towards the picture window, with its view of Pretoria. He turned back, waiting.

'Hassan is in London, for an indefinite stay. You won't even have to hang around for a visa; just an appointment.'

'And you've already applied for that?' anticipated Collington.

'I sent a cable to the embassy this morning. I guessed you'd want me to.'

The man was coming dangerously close to exceeding his

responsibility, thought Collington. But he'd done too well to be criticised. Collington hoped the mild confrontation would serve as sufficient warning.

'Thank you,' he said.

Since de Villiers' exclusion, Metzinger and Wassenaar had taken to having private meetings in addition to their monthly gatherings at the farm. Wassenaar listened intently to Metzinger's account of the after-dinner conversation at Parkstown, occasionally nodding his approval as Metzinger demonstrated the circumspect way he had made various points.

'How did Collington react?' Wassenaar asked immediately the account was over.

'At the dinner table, without much enthusiasm,' said Metzinger.

Wassenaar smiled, recognising from the tone of the other man's voice that there was more to come.

'But he's taken the bait,' completed Metzinger.

'How do you know?'

'I've got the switchboard monitored, so I know the calls he makes. He's had that whizz-kid American, Wall, working all hours. The company plane has been put on stand-by for a flight to London . . .' Metzinger smiled. 'And I couldn't be better placed there,' he completed. Metzinger had been worried when Hannah had told him that Collington was to be present at the dinner. Although it had presented the ideal opportunity for the gold entrapment, it had indicated some kind of a reconciliation, nullifying the hold he had over the Talbot woman. The concern hadn't lasted long, fortunately: when he'd spoken to Hannah the following day, she'd seemed more determined than ever upon a divorce.

'He goes to England every month,' said Wassenaar, cautiously.

'It's an unscheduled trip,' insisted Metzinger. 'He's got no appointments arranged through the London division. I know that for a fact.'

'What then?'

'I don't know,' admitted Metzinger. 'But I will.'

'You sound very sure of yourself.'

'I've got reason to be,' said Metzinger confidently.

Chapter Fifteen

Henry Moreton was a contented man, although he took great care to prevent the satisfaction at what was happening becoming obvious to anyone, even his wife. The cover profile in *Time* magazine had caught exactly the right note, from the very first sentence: 'The man fast becoming to money what Henry Kissinger was to foreign policy . . .' He'd worried, briefly, that the colour picture of him amid hills of gleaming ingots in the Federal Reserve Bank in New York might have indicated too much co-operation, as if he were enjoying the exposure, but there hadn't been any criticism. He made self-effacing jokes about it, inventing anecdotes to tell against himself, but it was nice to have his name recognised when he rang a theatre or a restaurant. Two nights ago, at the Kennedy Center, a woman had actually offered her programme and asked for his autograph. He'd been tempted to sign the thing, but it was a government function, with a lot of White House staffers around, and he didn't want it gossiped back to Pennsylvannia Avenue or appearing with some snide comment in the *Post*. So he had declined, with an explanation about the responsibility of his position. He would be quite happy for *that* to get back to the President; it was the sort of conservative response of which Pemberton would approve.

A small thing like refusing to scrawl his name for a pushy woman reflected the care that Moreton was maintaining: just as he recognised the satisfaction, he was aware of the danger of complacency. And it would have been complacent to imagine he had brewed some magic elixir simply by building up the gold reserves. There were still other things, too many things, that could undermine the confidence he was managing to achieve and Moreton was determined to cover every one of them.

Industry was a worry. The goddamned unions seemed to be growing increasingly contemptuous of the Taft-Hartley Act, threatening strikes and disruptions. A close-down in Detroit could create a nervous reaction in Wall Street and Moreton moved quickly to establish a monitor.

It was an indication of his growing power and reputation that the FBI responded within three days to his request, sending a division director to learn exactly what he wanted and undertaking, without referring back for higher approval, to provide a weekly file anticipating any difficulty that might arise.

Moreton knew, of course, that the chief danger was external, which was why he repeated the FBI request to the CIA. This time the response only took two days.

Moreton was cultivating the demeanour of an urbane, self-contained man. He sat silent behind his desk, studying the section head who had just been shown into his office, wondering if he should conduct the interview at all.

He had made his needs specifically clear when he had spoken to CIA Director Bradley Cowles at Langley and had expected a political analyst. Sidney Englehart had made it equally clear that he was attached to covert operations.

'This is not an operational requirement,' said Moreton, deciding upon an immediate challenge.

'We're aware of that, sir,' said Englehart. He had a pronounced vowel-bending drawl, maybe Tennessee or Georgia, and looked like a corn-fed country boy, thick-waisted and heavy. He used his hands a lot when he talked, as if he were juggling with the words.

'But you're from an operational division.'

'There was a full discussion about what we thought your needs might be. All the political intelligence is channelled through me, for dissemination elsewhere. For the speed you indicated was necessary, it was thought better not to wait until it got to analysis.'

He had said he wanted to know before, not after an event, remembered Moreton. So perhaps Englehart was the right man. But this way the intelligence would be raw and unrefined, imposing upon him the burden of correct interpretation.

'How long does analysis take?'

Englehart hesitated at the naivety of Moreton's question and then remembered he had not used the CIA before. 'Sometimes a week, sometimes a month.'

And sometimes got screwed up even then, like it had in Iran. He could always go back for confirmation, but it would be better if he relied upon his own judgment, decided Moreton.

'The only purpose is to be aware, in advance, of anything that might affect our currency,' said Moreton.

'So I understand,' said Englehart.

'Then understand something further,' said Moreton, leaning forward over the desk to emphasise what he was going to say. 'This isn't anything we can be half-assed and casual about. It's regarded of the highest importance, by the President himself.'

Englehart nodded and Moreton wished that the man would appear more impressed.

'You aware of finance, Mr Englehart?'

The CIA man smiled, apparently amused at the question. 'Not the sort of awareness that you're talking about.'

'When this adminstration came to office the decision was made to raise the value of the dollar. An arrangement about which you have no need to know was reached. And we've achieved the objective. We've restored confidence, but it's still a fragile thing . . .'

'I'm aware of the wheat crisis in the Soviet Union,' interrupted Englehart, impatient at the start of an obvious lecture.

Moreton wondered if the CIA man had intended impudence. It was obvious that Englehart would know, he realised, belatedly. It was from the Agency's satellite reconnaissance that they had received the first indication of the Russian crop failure. And impudent or not, it showed that the man was fully alert to the needs of the situation.

Moreton nodded, pulling a prepared list from a side drawer. 'That's the sort of intelligence I'm talking about. I want the cultivation areas of the Ukraine under constant surveillance . . .' He paused, expecting Englehart to make notes. Instead the man just nodded, encouraging him on. His gesture was patronising, but Moreton failed to recognise it as such.

'We're represented and involved, often through your agency, in a great many countries throughout the world, particularly in the Caribbean and South America and Africa. I want to know, long before it becomes a worrying factor, of any destabilising moves against any regime or government we support. I want that intelligence to be completely global. If there's a change in *any* major production affecting the world balance, I want to know . . .'

Englehart had initially had a faint air of condescension about him, Moreton thought. But not any more: it had taken longer than Moreton had expected but now the man was impressed with the sort of task with which he was being presented.

'. . . I want that gold monitor to extend to South Africa. I don't care how unimportant it may seem, but if there's a fluctuation, I want to know about it. And Russia again. I know the difficulty here. And I don't know how well you're placed to get the information. But if it's possible to discover anything about their production, then I want it on my desk within an hour of it reaching yours.'

'This is going to be very complete,' said Englehart.

'It's *got* to be very complete,' stressed Moreton. 'A variation in any of the things I've spoken about could cause a slide . . .' He smiled, about to offer a lesson in elementary finance. 'Bankers and money men are supposed to be hard-headed and intelligent and expert,' he said. 'Yet it would be difficult to find a group of men more susceptible to rumour and innuendo. Mere gossip can cost Wall Street millions.' He waved his hands, seeking an example. 'An attempted coup, in the Caribbean let's say, could create a panic . . .'

'I'll remember that,' promised Englehart.

'Something else,' said the Finance Secretary, discarding his earlier doubts and realising how the man could become a positive advantage. 'There are times, I know, when we ourselves consider destabilisation necessary . . .' He saw Englehart about to speak and raised his hand, stopping him. '. . . If your Director considers it necessary, then I'll get authorisation from the President. But I want to know, in advance, of any such decision affecting any of the countries with which we're involved. I'm not interested in the motives or the morals: only in the affect on the money.'

Englehart made a half-hearted gesture of assent.

'I want your assurance on that,' pressed Moreton.

'I'll need authority,' said Englehart.

'You'll get it, before the day's out.' An hour before, that sort of confident assertion would have caused the other man to smirk. Now Englehart sat subdued and straight-faced.

'Anything we've overlooked?' demanded Moreton, strengthening his control.

Englehart did not reply at once, aware that his opening attitude had been mistaken and not wanting to provide the wrong answer.

He brightened, abruptly. 'Yes,' he said, confidently. 'Perhaps the most uncertain situation of all.'

Moreton smiled with the other man, glad he had passed the test. He supposed it could have been dismissed as a juvenile trick, but it had been important for him to get a confirmation of Englehart's ability.

'Glad you realised it,' he said. 'Oil! And the Middle East. I want that whole area regarded as top priority: extra personnel assigned, if necessary. The West is paranoid about oil. At the slightest uncertainty, everyone goes for the panic button. I'll need practically a daily analysis, from the whole area.'

'You're going to be a busy guy,' said Englehart, admiringly.

And a successful one, thought Moreton.

The woman who was now named Brigitte re Jong had been born Svetlana Dallin in the town of Perm in the Urals, the industrialised area of the Soviet Union which is closed to all Western contact. It was from the Urals that Lenin had got the fiercest support for his revolution and the Dallin family had epitomised that fervour. Svetlana's father had fought in the siege of Leningrad and been wounded and returned home to become a party secretary for the local soviet. He had travelled to Moscow five times to be honoured with official placing in the May Day celebrations and had taken her with him on two of the visits.

They had been special outings, rewards not from her family but from her tutors. She had been selected for training as a 'sleeper' within a day of the unrecorded death, at the age of five and a half, of the real Brigitte re Jong in the Amstel Canal. At an age when most girls of her age were playing with dolls, Svetlana — now Brigitte — was learning Dutch. She was taught English, too. When her ability to learn was fully developed, she was crammed at the KGB school on the outskirts of Moscow, while in Holland preparations were made to provide a cover story sufficient to gain her admission into a university. This would confirm the grounding for the identity which was now fully established within her.

She displayed a particular interest in mathematics and economics and before she left Moscow it was decided that she should pursue that inclination, because financial interpretation of western economies was considered vital intelligence within the Soviet Union.

By the time she arrived in Utrecht to read economics, the assimilation was so complete that she *was* Brigitte re Jong. And even though she was only eighteen, she never once made a mistake. If she did attract attention, it was for her diligence. Her dedication to work impressed her lecturers and surprised her classmates, who tried but failed to interest her in socialising. She continually refused the invitations.

For over three years, there was no contact from Moscow. The approach came three months before her graduation with a first-class degree, directing her towards a brokerage firm.

The benefit of her education in economics wasn't fully appreciated until the grain crisis occurred in the Soviet Union and they needed to buy gold from the USA. By the time of the Ilyushin crash, she had been responsible for the undisclosed purchase of £250,000,000 worth of South African gold in a series of commodity trades remarkable for their expertise.

Brigitte was a completely dedicated woman, interested only in the business for which she had been infiltrated into Holland. She maintained acquaintanceships, not friendships, and it was fortunate that she had a low sexuality, because she withheld herself without difficulty from any serious involvement with men, permitting relationships, sometimes going as far as the bedroom but always ending them before anything serious might develop to endanger her role.

For most women it would have been a strained, unreal existence. But Brigitte had been trained in restraint since childhood. So she enjoyed what she did, every day of her life.

The first indication of Collington's arrival came as it always did, by the official telex to all department heads, and then there was the telephone call, inhibited because of the office surroundings but still personal. Ann snatched out expectantly when the telephone rang in her flat and waited, smiling in anticipation at the familiar blur of an international connection. Her expression faded the moment she recognised Metzinger's voice.

'We haven't spoken for a long time,' he said.

'No.'

'They were good situation reports.'

'Thank you.'

'Thank *you*, for sending them to me,' said Metzinger. There was a pause. Then he said, 'Collington is coming to London.'

'I know.'

'I want everything that happens while he's there.'

She didn't say anything.

'Did you hear me?'

'Yes.'

'It's important. Everything. Do you understand?'

'Yes, I understand.'

She replaced the receiver, but continued to stare at it. Not again, she determined. She wouldn't betray James again. Even if it meant losing him, she intended warning him what was happening. He'd understand, she decided; he was a complete and sophisticated man.

Chapter Sixteen

Collington knew that he had been running away from his problems. Because of the appointment at Paul's school in Hampshire and the late arrival at Heathrow there was a slim argument in favour of his having remained overnight at an airport hotel. But that's all it was: slim, too slim. There was no reason why he should not have continued on to Princes Gate and confronted Ann and admitted a mistake and told her it was all over. Except that he was avoiding it, even now.

But today was the day when the running was to stop. Ann was expecting him that evening. So that evening he'd tell her, and that would be the end of it. But what about Paul? To tell the child there was going to be a reconciliation might cause even more harm than had been done already, if it wasn't true. And Collington was unsure that it was true. He'd tried daily, since the night of the dinner, to arrange a meeting with Hannah and every time she had refused. He'd even resorted to the blackmail of Paul's visit, in an effort to get her to agree, and that had been the word she had used to describe it, in telling him to go to hell.

The chauffeur took the link road out of London airport, going through Hounslow to pick up the motorway to Hampshire and Collington gazed out of the car, remembering landmarks. Some of the shops from which he had got his washing-machine ideas still existed and he wondered if the same people were behind the same counters. In those days he had travelled on foot or bicycle and now he was in the back of a chauffeur-driven limousine or private jet. Which was quite a difference, he thought. But was he so different? He supposed his vision had expanded, so that now he thought in millions as easily as he had done in hundreds or even thousands, but that made him no different from any other self-made businessman who had developed with his success. Apart from that, Collington didn't think he'd changed.

What differences would he find in Paul, since the visit at which he had announced the separation? The absence of any letters indicated something, but he would have expected the headmaster to inform him of any real problems when he had telephoned for permission to take the boy out on a day not allocated for parent visiting. But Paul was a self-contained child; Collington was sure he could have kept his feelings hidden from the staff, if that's what he had wanted.

They arrived ahead of time, but Paul was already waiting. His fly-away hair had been wetted down in a forlorn attempt at neatness, and from the black traces which still lingered beneath his fingernails, Collington guessed the boy had been polishing his shoes. He obviously didn't do it very often and it hadn't really worked. The corduroy trousers were bagged and there was a darn in the elbow of his jumper.

The matron was waiting with Paul, which may have accounted for some of his forced reserve as he exchanged greetings with his father.

Collington nodded to her and said, 'When I bring him back I'll thank the headmaster for making the allowance.'

'We understand how difficult it must be for you,' she said. 'Supper is at six o'clock.'

'I'll have him back on time,' promised Collington.

The chauffeur held the door open and Collington gestured the boy in ahead of him. He was growing fast, decided Collington: he didn't imagine Paul would attain his height, but he'd probably top six feet.

'I won,' announced Paul, as the car moved off down the drive.

'What?'

'We had a bet in my form about the car you'd come in. Everyone said a Daimler, but I guessed a Rolls.'

'How much?'

'Ten pence.'

'Is it important?'

'Gambling?' frowned the boy.

'The sort of car I come in.'

'Not really,' dismissed Paul. 'It's just a game we play.'

Collington supposed that such competition was harmlessly natural but decided that next time he would use a less ostentatious vehicle: he didn't want Paul developing artificial attitudes.

'How are you?' said Collington.

'All right, thank you,' said his son. 'I had a cold sore on my lip, but the matron got it better with ointment.'

'How about lessons?'

'Next term I'm starting Latin. I got a B for biology, and low As for the rest. I'm sixth in the class.'

'How many in the class?' asked Collington.

Paul frowned again, at being caught out. 'Ten,' he said.

'Last term you were fourth.'

'I know.'

'So what happened?' Perhaps he should have expected Paul's schoolwork to suffer, thought Collington.

The boy made an uncomfortable movement. 'More difficult, I suppose.'

The car stopped outside the hotel where Collington had made the lunch reservation and Paul announced: 'Another ten pence. I said we'd come here.'

Collington stood slightly back as Paul entered the hotel, made his way to the dining-room and was shown to their table, aware of the boy's natural self-confidence. On the day he had hired the Rolls-Royce and persuaded the Birmingham marketing manager to sell washing-machines directly to him, he'd buttered his bread with a fish fork, remembered Collington.

Paul ordered an entrée between his first and main course and Collington said, 'You seem hungry.'

'Don't get the chance to eat much at school.'

'How is it?'

Paul made another of his doubtful movements. 'All right,' he said.

'Your mother isn't going to be very pleased about the dropped grades,' said Collington.

'How do you know?'

Collington began to respond automatically to the rudeness but then stopped himself. 'Because we're both proud of you and don't like it when standards start to drop.' He hesitated and then added pointedly, 'In everything.'

Paul was blushing, knowing he'd gone too far. 'You still talk then?'

The child's effort to appear adult was painfully obvious and

Collington almost laughed. He stopped himself, knowing it would be a mistake. 'Of course we do,' he said.

'Mummy wrote in her letter that you were still friends.'

'Why shouldn't we be?'

'Why aren't you still living together, if you're friends?' The boy was looking at him imploringly, his eyes filmed, the attempt at adult conversation faltering.

'I told you last time,' said Collington gently. 'There are occasions when a man and a woman need to be away from each other, to sort things out.'

'What things?' demanded the boy.

'Their relationship.'

'You said you were still friends.'

'People have got to be more than friends to be married.'

'What happens if you decide that it's been a mistake? Being apart, I mean.'

'Then you get back together again,' said Collington patiently. The opportunity was there, to say he hoped it would happen. Cautiously he studied the child's grave, open face, saw his need and said nothing. To have told Paul in the beginning might have been premature. To cause the pendulum to swing again would be positively cruel, unless he could guarantee it happening.

'Will you get back together again?' pressed the boy.

'It hasn't been decided yet,' said Collington. Paul had inherited his mother's directness, he thought.

'Do you want to?'

'That's a decision that two of us have got to make.'

Paul looked down at his plate and said, 'Are you in love with somebody else?'

The child would have tensed himself in preparation for it all, Collington guessed, rehearsing the questions in his unhappiness.

'No,' he said positively.

'Is Mummy?'

'No,' he said again.

For the first time the boy smiled, the hope obvious. 'So you just had a row?' he said. The naïvety was a sudden contrast to the earlier demands.

'A lot of rows,' said Collington.

For several moments they continued eating in silence and then

Collington said, 'You haven't answered our letters.'

'No.'

'Why not?'

'I wasn't sure what to say.'

'The examination results would have been something. And starting Latin next term.'

'I meant about the summer vacation.'

'There are a lot of choices about what to do.'

'Who would I be with, in Pretoria?'

'Both of us.'

'In the same house?'

More rehearsed preparation, thought Collington. 'It hasn't been decided yet.'

'Where do you live?'

'In the company apartment.'

'Do you want me to come home?'

This time Collington allowed the laugh, to show his surprise. 'Of course we want you to come home!'

'Won't it be unnatural, with *two* homes?'

Yes, decided Collington. He thought he would find it more difficult than Hannah. 'No,' he insisted. 'What happens to the other boys in your school, whose parents aren't together?'

'They spend most of the time packing and unpacking their cases. And getting two presents, instead of one.'

Collington frowned at the unexpected cynicism from a twelve-year-old. 'We'd be together for whatever trip you wanted,' he said. 'We could go down to the coast. Or on safari again. You enjoyed the safari last time.'

'You'll be together, just for me?'

Collington felt an impatience. 'Even if your mother and I were unfriendly, which we are not, we would do things together for you. Because we love you. And whatever is happening between us isn't going to affect that love. But as a matter of fact the holiday won't be just for you. It'll be for all of us.'

'There's a boy at school, John Reynolds. He says I could spend the summer with him, here in England.'

'Not without our permission, you couldn't.'

'I know. Would you let me?'

Collington pushed away his food, disturbed at the direction of the conversation. 'If you sincerely wanted to do that, rather than come back to South Africa, then I suppose so. It's not a decision I'll make now, without talking about it to your mother. She'll be very upset.'

'Don't you think it would be better, in the circumstances?'

'No, I don't,' said Collington positively. It would practically be making his son an orphan, like he'd been once. The analogy shocked him.

'You sound angry,' said the boy.

'I am.'

'I didn't mean you to be.'

'You've talked about what's happened, quite openly at school?' Collington wondered why he felt embarrassed.

'Only to Reynolds. He's my best friend.'

'And he's asked his parents if you could stay?'

'Not yet. I wanted to meet you first.'

'I'm glad you did.' Collington reached across the table for his son's hand and having done so regretted the gesture because it seemed awkwardly artificial.

'I want you to come home to South Africa for the summer,' he said. 'You seem to think that whatever is happening between your mother and I means that you have been abandoned. It doesn't mean that at all. We want you with us, with both of us.'

Paul freed his hand, looking around the restaurant to see if anyone were looking at them. 'Could we go to the Kalahari again? And camp?'

'If the game wardens said it was safe enough.'

'It was fun last time,' said the boy reflectively.

'There's no reason why it shouldn't be again.'

Paul looked up sharply, about to speak, and then appeared to change his mind. Several moments elapsed and then he said, 'I'll write this week. I promise.'

After their meal they walked through Lyndhurst and Collington asked his son if there were anything he needed. Paul said there wasn't, but as they were passing a sports shop Collington suggested a pair of cricketing gloves. 'But Mummy sent me some a month ago,' Paul said, and despite their feelings they laughed at the reminder of present duplication.

Collington returned the boy at the promised time, kissed him despite his obvious discomfort at the gesture in front of his schoolfriends and made him repeat the promise to write about the vacation within the week. The interview with the headmaster lasted longer than Collington had anticipated and he was glad that he had been prepared by the discussion with Paul about his examination results. Paul's work was showing a marked deterioration, complained the school head. The boy lacked initiative and concentration and there had been several punishments for insolence.

'He's even creating some infantile gambling syndicate and bullied some of the younger children into wagering their money.'

'He said something about gambling,' remembered Collington.

'Unless there is a marked and sustained improvement, we'll have to hold him back in his present form,' said the head. 'In a year he's due to sit his common entrance for a public school. A setback like this couldn't have come at a worse time.'

Collington was not a man accustomed to depression. He slumped morosely in the back of the car as he returned to London, too immersed in his thoughts when it left the motorway to bother with the once familiar sights around Richmond.

Paul's reaction, when he had told the boy of the separation, had been misleading: he hadn't expected his behaviour today. Hannah would blame him, when he told her: rightly so. It wouldn't help the relationship he was trying to restore between them.

He shifted in his seat, as last aware of his surroundings as the car turned off the Cromwell Road towards Hyde Park and his house. Ann would be waiting, he knew.

She was in the lounge overlooking the park. Her hair wasn't free, as it had been in Rome, but neatly arranged and her make-up had been applied carefully, too. She didn't hurry to him as she normally did, but remained on the edge of her seat, and Collington's impression was one of vulnerability. He was going to hurt her and he didn't want to — but it had to be tonight. He'd let things drift too long already.

He went further into the room and still she didn't get up to greet him. He saw she was wearing one of the dresses they had bought in Rome.

'Hello,' he said.

'Hello.'

The tension was immediately obvious to both of them.

'Good to see you again.' Fatuous conversation, he thought angrily. He wasn't glad to see her: he was uncomfortable and awkward.

'Yes,' she said. She'd been preparing for this, ever since her return from Italy, and now the moment had come and she was frightened to do it. But it had to be now. Whatever he did when she told him, it had to be now.

They began simultaneously. Ann started, 'I want to say . . .' just as Collington said, 'There's something I want . . .' and they both stopped, laughing uncertainly. 'You first,' said Collington.

He thought she was going to argue, but then she looked away and said, 'I want you to know about something. About me.'

Collington looked about him, as if unsure of the room, and then sat down, facing her curiously.

She continued to stare down at the carpet, her voice so quiet that he had to strain to hear her. 'There was someone else, when you weren't here,' she said. 'There wasn't anything to it — not love, I mean. It was just . . .' She stopped, jerking her shoulders. 'Oh, I don't know, one of those things that starts for no particular reason and then goes on, because it's easier than ending it.'

She imagined he'd arrived with a decision about them and wanted to empty the cupboards of skeletons, decided Collington. She was waiting for him to respond but he couldn't think of anything.

'It's over,' she said. 'Finished.'

She looked up and he realised she was close to tears. He'd never seen her cry, Collington realised; he'd never thought of her as the sort of woman who would. But then she'd probably thought the same thing about him, in Rome.

'I didn't have any right to impose conditions,' he said. She winced, and Collington knew it hadn't been what she had expected him to say.

'I thought you had,' she said, softly again.

'It wasn't what . . .' he tried again, but she talked across him.

'That wasn't all,' she said.

'What?'

'Metzinger found out. He had me investigated and he found out.'

'Metzinger!'

'Months ago. He said it would be grounds for a divorce from Hannah. And disgrace for me.'

There was no eruption of anger. Collington remained quite still in his chair, gazing across at her, expressionlessly. Months ago: yet Hannah hadn't known when he'd confessed on the night of the dinner. Why hadn't the man used the information if he'd gone to a lot of trouble to obtain it? And why the trouble in the first place?

'He didn't tell Hannah,' he said.

'That wasn't the arrangement.' She was avoiding his eyes, her voice even lower.

'Arrangement?'

'He said he wouldn't do anything, if I co-operated. If I told him what you were doing and what Richard was doing, here in London.'

'To spy?'

She nodded her head, in jerky confirmation.

'Did you?'

There was another head movement.

'Why?' Still there was no indication of anger and she wished there had been. She flinched at the control in his voice.

'I don't know,' she said. 'I read all the statements and there were pictures and then he came on to me immediately after the share thing which Richard wasn't in Pretoria for, and I told him what you'd said on the telephone to Richard . . .' The confession was bursting from her, in a confusion of words. She stopped, breathlessly and said, 'Oh Christ!'

'You should have told me.'

'Don't you think I don't realise that!'

'When?'

'When what?'

'When did he confront you?'

She made a vague motion with her hands. 'When Walter Simpson died . . . just before the funeral.'

'When was the last time?'

'Yesterday'

'Yesterday!'

'He knew you were coming to London . . . that we'd be together. He said I was to find out everything that was going on. And tell him . . .' She blinked up hopefully towards Collington. 'But I decided to tell you, instead,' she finished.

Metzinger would have found out anyway. So what was it, mistrust or something more? Something more about which he was going to have to be careful — even more careful than he had been over the share imbalance after Simpson's death.

'You haven't said anything.'

Collington looked at Ann again. There was none of the usual bounce and enthusiasm about her: she looked crushed, physically small in the chair. He felt sorry for her. He went to speak and then stopped, remembering what he had intended to say before her confession. He had an excuse now.

'No,' he agreed. 'I haven't said anything.'

'I'm sorry,' she said. 'I was stupid and I didn't think and I'm sorry.'

He was surprised, Collington conceded. He'd always thought Ann a professional, someone strong enough to resist the sort of pressure that Metzinger had exerted. She'd behaved stupidly.

'I don't like you looking at me like that,' she said.

'Like what?'

'Like you're disgusted.'

'It isn't disgust,' he said.

'Does it matter?' The hope was obvious.

'I had something to say too,' he reminded her. He wouldn't take the easy way out; he wouldn't run any more.

Her hands were tight against her knees, her body rigid.

'I told Hannah,' he said.

A smile sparked, briefly. 'That you wanted a divorce?'

'No,' he said. 'Not that at all.'

It was as if he had slapped her. She jerked back in the chair, her face momentarily flinching in what he realised was an effort to avoid more tears. 'Is that what you were going to say? That you wanted to end it, with us?'

'Yes,' he said.

Quickly she covered her eyes with her hands. 'So it would have ended anyway?' she said.

'Anyway?'

'Even if I hadn't told you about Metzinger?'

'Yes,' he said.

She snorted a laugh. 'I had it all worked out,' she said. 'I was going to confess and you were going to be angry and then you were going to forgive me and everything was going to be all right . . . just like a bloody fairy story.'

Once again he couldn't think of anything to say. She moved her head, as if examining the room. 'There's a lot of my stuff here,' she said.

'Yes.'

'I don't want to pack now . . . I don't think . . .' She gulped to a halt.

'You needn't leave . . . there are other rooms . . .' he started, thoughtlessly. And then stopped.

'That's ridiculous,' she said.

'I didn't think.'

'Will you be here tomorrow?'

'I don't expect to be.'

'I'll collect them then.'

'All right.'

Ann smiled, too brightly. 'We're being remarkably civilised, aren't we?'

'Yes.'

'I'll give Richard my resignation tomorrow.'

'You needn't,' he said. 'I'll shield you against Metzinger, now that I know.'

'That's stupid, too.'

'Not necessarily.'

'To me it is.'

'What will you do?'

She shrugged. 'I don't know.'

'Why not stay on, until you decide?'

'No.'

'I'm sorry I've hurt you.'

'I'm sorry about the spying. We both buggered it up.'

'Thank you for telling me. About Metzinger.'

'Is it important?'

'I don't know.'

'I hope it'll work out with Hannah,' she said. Almost at once her face quivered and the tears finally came. 'No, I don't,' she burst out defiantly. 'I didn't mean that at all. I hope it's a disaster.'

Collington wanted to comfort her but knew that if he reached out to touch her they would end up in bed. She snatched a handkerchief from her handbag and blew her nose and wiped her eyes. 'I didn't mean to say that.'

'It doesn't matter.'

'Nothing does any more, does it?' she said. 'Oh shit, that's self-pity, and I didn't intend that either!' She jerked upright, standing uncertainly before him. 'I think I should go.'

'Yes,' he said, rising with her.

'Goodbye, James.'

'Goodbye.'

'I'm sorry.'

'There's no need for you to be sorry. I'm sorry.'

'This is getting maudlin.'

He wanted to make some gesture, to kiss her, but knew that would be wrong, like trying to comfort her. She seemed held by the same uncertainty. Then, without saying anything else, she turned and left the room.

Collington remained standing for a long time, looking after her. When he finally moved, it was a decisive movement towards the telephone. He needed to be covered against Metzinger. Thank God Geoffrey Wall was so efficient. Having him in London helped, too.

Chapter Seventeen

The loss of £100,000,000 had done little to impair Prince Hassan's life style. Collington had expected a suite, perhaps two — certainly not the occupation of an entire floor. He allowed Wall to establish preliminary contact, to minimise the delay, but even so it took an hour for him to progress past squatting Arabs and be allowed by unidentified staff members to approach the Saudi prince. Collington remained patient throughout, recognising the psychology: Hassan wanted to appear the more important of the two of them. Collington wondered why he was making so much effort to assert something that was already obvious.

He was finally admitted to a large corner room, which would have looked out on to Grosvenor Square had the blinds not been drawn. There were three other Arabs there, all robed like Hassan. When the Prince rose to greet him, Collington saw that there was a jewelled dagger hilt protruding from a black cummerbund. An odour permeated the room, perfume rather than incense.

'Welcome to my temporary home,' said Hassan. There was a slight hiss in his voice, and just the vaguest trace of an American accent in some of the words. He didn't smile.

'I appreciate the honour of such a meeting,' said Collington, matching the elaborate courtesy. It was like eating chewy toffee, he thought.

Hassan indicated a couch upon which he had been sitting and Collington moved towards it. Having been kept waiting, Hassan was now attempting to treat him as an equal. As he seated himself, Collington became aware of another Arab entering from the direction in which he had come, carrying a tray with tiny cups of sweet red tea. They had obviously taken over a kitchen as well.

The tea was served and Hassan said, 'My humble apologies for your delay.'

Collington didn't imagine Hassan had ever been humble in his life. 'It was nothing,' he said.

'There are many demands upon me.'

'I can appreciate that. It was gracious of you to see me so quickly.'

'You are not unknown to us, by reputation at least. There is a saying that curiosity should be satisfied, before it begins to burn.'

Collington looked across at the other men in the room. They were following the conversation intently and he guessed they could speak English. It was the sort of protection he would have sought in similar circumstances.

'You will know then of my companies,' said Collington.

'So many companies!' said Hassan, in apparent admiration.

The Arab was manœoeuvring the conversation, Collington recognised, so that he was constantly having to follow the direction, the supplicant to the stronger man. Wall had warned him of the man's negotiating technique.

'Which I hope to expand even further,' he said.

'The prophets praise a man of adventure,' said Hassan.

Collington had no way of knowing, but he suspected that Hassan was making up the Arab folklore as he went along.

'Men of adventure need companions,' he said, entering into the charade and hoping Hassan wouldn't interpret it as a reference to the silver débâcle. 'And discretion,' he added quickly, looking around at the watchful Arabs. 'Great discretion.'

'Discretion is always of the greatest importance,' agreed Hassan.

'I came alone,' said Collington, pressing the point.

Hassan hesitated, taking it. Abruptly, he clapped his hands together, a single gesture, and the three men rose and filed from the room.

It had been easy, thought Collington: too easy. Just as it had been too easy for Wall to arrange the appointment in such a short time.

Hassan might be trying to conceal it, with the pretence before the meeting and the gluey verbosity, but he was an anxious man. Wouldn't he have been anxious, if he had dropped £100,000,000, Collington asked himself. He'd continue the ambiguity, forcing the concession of directness from the other man.

'Adventurous companions complement each other to mutual benefit,' he said.

'Is that why you come, for mutual benefit?' said Hassan.

It was the first time he had asked a direct question, giving Collington the advantage.

'Yes,' said Collington and stopped. He wasn't the supplicant any more.

Hassan shifted along the couch, seeming aware of the change of strategy.

'Do you approach me as my country's Minister for Oil and Development, or Prince Tewfik Hassan?' he asked.

'I approach Prince Tewfik Hassan, who is Saudi Arabia's Minister for Oil and Development,' said Collington, unhelpfully.

'I represent a country,' said the Arab. 'Whom do you represent?'

The shadow boxing was over, decided Collington, gratefully.

'Myself,' he said.

'Only yourself?' insisted Hassan.

'Only myself,' replied Collington.

'Could the position change?'

Anxious or not, Hassan was determined not to make any more mistakes.

'Not to the point of causing yourself or your country any embarrassment,' Collington said. He felt Hassan's eyes directly upon him. He met the stare, refusing to be intimidated.

'I think it's time you talked more fully,' invited Hassan.

He'd taken the bait, decided Collington. Now the man had to be played, like a nervous fish.

'Your country has a weakness,' he declared, conscious of Hassan's immediate frown at something which could be criticism. He hurried on: 'A weakness which could not be foreseen. And which is now difficult for you to confront.'

'What do you mean?' demanded Hassan sharply. The man was offended, Collington knew, but he was in the stronger position.

'The foreign investment reserves of your country are over committed to dollars,' he said. 'Even your bank holdings are denominated in American currency. And the dollar is over-burdened. All currency is volatile, but too much world trading is costed in American money. Your country is *losing* money with its investments.'

Hassan sat silent, digesting the assessment. 'The dollar is a rising currency,' he said.

'The strength has only been there for a few months,' disputed Collington. 'And even now, you can't have benefited. The rise began in June. For two years prior to that, allowing for every fluctuation, the overall loss represented eighteen per cent on all your investments. The current rise is twelve per cent. You're six per cent short.'

Hassan smiled, a different expression than before. 'You are a well-informed man,' he said, and this time the praise seemed genuine.

'It would have been an insult to make this approach without being so,' said Collington, falling back for a moment on verbosity and deciding it was time to make concessions himself.

Hassan continued smiling. 'What is your proposal, Mr Collington?'

'Gold,' declared Collington, purposely dramatic. 'A commodities agreement with Saudi Arabia, committing gold for oil.'

Hassan sighed. 'It seems so very simple,' he said wistfully.

'And could be,' said Collington.

Hassan shook his head. 'Saudi Arabia is the pivot in the Middle East,' he said. 'For years we've been the moderating influence, trying to dissuade the other oil producers from price increases which worsen the inflation in the West and so reduce their profits. Could we, as the leaders, consider breaking an embargo we were instrumental in establishing?'

For the first time Collington realised that neither of them had directly mentioned South Africa: he decided to take his lead from the other man's diplomacy.

'Earlier we used the word discretion,' Collington reminded. 'Just as I approached this meeting as well informed as possible, I considered the difficulties that might arise. I do not consider them insurmountable.'

'I need to be persuaded,' said Hassan.

'We are multi-national,' said Collington. 'We have divisions in Europe, here in London and in America. I propose the establishment of several, separate companies. Here in London there would be a division actively attempting to participate in the development of the North Sea, aiming to win a drilling contract from the British government. It would also, of course, be involved in purchasing.

There would be another purchasing company in America, headquartered possibly on the Gulf of Mexico. And in Rotterdam there would be a third.'

'Behind the cover of a legitimate company in Britain we would supply oil which would in turn be sold to a legitimate company in America, who would re-sell it to Holland and from Holland it would go on to a further destination?' queried Hassan.

'Everything would be legitimate,' qualified Collington. 'I'm suggesting nothing to contravene the rules or laws of any of the countries. The only unusual thing would be that once the oil was purchased, it would not be sold, re-sold and sold again, as happens at the moment.'

'Once more you make it sound so simple!' said the Arab. 'But there is still a flaw that makes it unworkable.'

Collington was surprised Hassan had lost £100,000,000. He was not a stupid man.

'Which is?' he said, anticipating the man's answer.

'You are a gold producer, not seller. You are forbidden, by law, to dispose of it. So there is no way — no legal way — that you could enter into this sort of commitment.'

'You, too, are well informed,' said Collington.

'I, too, wanted to avoid insult,' responded Hassan.

'What if a way could be established?'

Hassan looked at him blank-faced, but there was definitely a reaction, which Collington would have missed if he had not been regarding the man so intently. For a moment there had been an expression of greed in Hassan's eyes: that's what had cost £100,000,000, he thought. It was an expensive disadvantage.

'You spoke of representing yourself, no one else,' said Hassan.

'You are the minister of a country that has taken a public stance against another country,' said Collington. 'I regard this as an exploratory meeting: as I have already made clear, I wanted to introduce nothing that might have created embarrassment between us.'

'How confident are you of a way being established?' said Hassan.

'I would not have made this approach without such confidence,' said Collington. That was an over-commitment, he recognised, based upon his talks with Metzinger. But the Afrikaner was unquestionably talking on behalf of the Cabinet.

'Between whom would these contracts be drawn?' asked Hassan.

'An independently-owned company in England. And the oil company of Saudi Arabia,' said Collington, guessing the direction of the conversation.

'And who would be the negotiators?'

It was time for caution, recognised Collington. Hassan was almost landed, but the line would snap if he introduced talk of commission too openly: pride would dictate it, irrespective of the man's desperation.

'I have opened these talks,' he said. 'If they were to progress, then I would expect to remain involved. The representative for your country would be a matter for you to determine.'

'Were it not to be myself, then I would need to be in a position to brief my successor fully,' said Hassan.

'Of course,' nodded Collington, seeing the opening the other man had prepared. 'The companies would be established as I have already indicated. I would anticipate our purchases to be in the region of £500,000,000. All shipment, discharge and delivery costs would be borne by us . . .' Collington hesitated, appearing to remember something. 'There would be a commission, of course. In the circumstances, considering the importance of what we are discussing, I would fix that at twenty per cent . . .' He hurried on, as if the commission figure were a minor, unimportant part of the negotiations. 'There would be the complete discretion that I have indicated, the full knowledge of the transactions being confined to a limited number of the top executives.'

Geoffrey Wall might be an ideal man to run the operation, he thought suddenly. The man had been involved since the outset and Collington imagined it would be the sort of enterprise that would attract the American.

'You seem to have considered the details fairly fully,' said Hassan.

Where before Collington had interpreted greed in the man's look, now there was contentment. Collington had hesitated, fixing the commission figure exactly to match Hassan's losses, but now he knew it had not been a mistake.

'I have done,' he said. 'I would ask you to, also.'

'Will you be in London long?'

'My plans are fluid,' said Collington.

'Perhaps there would be an opportunity for us to meet again?'

'I would welcome that.'

'Our embassy knows the way to contact you?'

'At all times,' assured Collington.

Hassan rose to end the encounter, and Collington stood immediately.

'I have enjoyed the meeting,' said Hassan.

'So have I.'

'It would be pleasant if there were mutual benefit,' said Hassan.

'I sincerely hope there will be,' said Collington. The ending was going to be as formalised as the beginning, he thought.

There was another sharp handclap and at once the three men who had been excluded returned to the room. Collington wondered if they had been able to hear much from the ante-room. He followed them through the crowded corridors to the elevator and emerged into the rush hour. His car fidgeted through the central London traffic back to the City, where the SAGOMI building overlooked the Tower and the Thames beyond. Geoffrey Wall was waiting when Collington entered his offices.

'How did it go?' asked the American.

'Good, I think,' assessed Collington. 'He's certainly attracted.'

'Ran a check, just out of curiosity, while you were there,' said Wall. 'Difficult to trace his every movement, of course. But he's a pretty public figure, so there's usually some publicity somewhere. I reckon that since he fouled up on the silver deal, he hasn't spent more than a month in Saudi Arabia.'

Collington looked up from his desk, nodding appreciatively. 'Disgraced?' he said.

'Certainly that, although I think he's too high up in the pecking order for him to have been asked to get out. My guess it's a pretty frantic search for a way to recover.'

'I'd say we're in pretty good shape,' said Collington confidently.

'What do you think of these?' asked Wall. From velvet boxes on a document table the assistant took what appeared to be golden bells. It was only when Wall held them up that Collington became aware of the curvature in their design and the thongs, hanging down.

'What are they?' frowned Collington.

'There's a protocol shift at the second meeting,' advised Wall. 'It's present-giving time if you reach even tentative agreement. Hassan is a keen hawker. So I've had these rushed through: they're hawk caps, to fit over the bird's head when it's not hunting.'

Collington stretched forward, smiling, taking one of the tiny covers and weighing it in his hand, professionally. It was heavy carat gold and Hassan would recognise it as such. 'Bloody clever,' he said to Wall. If the deal went through, he would offer the man the chairmanship, Collington decided: he had earned it.

Collington expected Wall to smile at the praise, but instead the man remained solemn. 'There's been a personal internal memorandum, from Richard Jenkins,' he said.

'What?'

'Ann Talbot has quit. Jenkins said he would welcome some guidance from you.'

Collington hadn't expected her to move as fast as she had indicated at Princes Gate. 'She's to be allowed anything she wants . . . time to arrange her affairs, things like that. And the fullest severance pay . . .'

Wall was nodding, making notations with a gold pen on a small reminder pad.

'What about the enquiry agency?'

'I've found it,' said Wall. 'They're the best. I haven't made any approach, not yet.'

'Don't,' instructed Collington. 'I'm not interested in learning what they found out, just who they are in case there's a need for any pressure.'

'Anything else?' asked the other man.

There was. But Collington would pay her £100,000 from his personal account and send it to her privately.

Aloud he said, 'Yes. Make sure the resignation is not communicated to the office in Pretoria. I want the story spread that she's on an extended leave of absence.'

It was dark by the time Collington got back to Princes Gate. He went from room to room, conscious that it was a pointless tour because the staff would have cleaned anyway. But he didn't think it would have been necessary, even if there hadn't been other people in the house. There wasn't a trace of anything that belonged to Ann, nor any indication of where it had been before she removed it. It was as if she had never been into the house and lived there as his wife.

The distance between Hassan's hotel and the American embassy in Grosvenor Square was short, little more than four hundred yards, which meant that compared to other operatives throughout the world, the CIA men stationed there had one of the simplest jobs responding to the instructions Englehart had issued after his meeting with Henry Moreton. Englehart had attached a priority listing to the orders, because Moreton's clearance for information about any clandestine activity arrived from the President's office just two hours after his encounter with the Treasury Secretary and the CIA section head recognised power when it reached out, grabbed him by the balls and squeezed.

Collington's arrival, on Prince Hassan's floor, was noted, as every arrival was. He was photographed upon departure, and because he was a public figure whose picture had frequently appeared in newspapers, he was identified as James Collington within an hour.

A description of the visit, including its length and the fact that Collington had obviously been received in personal audience by the Prince, was included in the overnight diplomatic pouch that went from Heathrow to Andrews Air Force base. By the time Englehart reached his desk at 8.00 am American time, the file was carefully annotated and personal details about Collington had been added to the London report from the bank of information available about a businessman of such international stature.

Moreton's summons came before noon. Englehart had been expecting it, so he responded at once.

When he entered the financier's office, Englehart saw that everything else he had provided had been relegated to a document table on the side and that only Collington's dossier lay on the desk.

'What's this mean?' demanded Moreton.

'I don't know,' confessed Englehart.

'What's Collington into?'

'Everything,' said Englehart, nodding to the documents containing the information that lay before Moreton. 'One of the biggest multi-nationals in existence. He's a high flier.'

'But all the Saudis have got is oil,' mused Moreton.

'The politics are wrong,' argued Englehart.

'Politics is compromise,' lectured Moreton. 'If the pressure is strong enough, any principle will bend.'

'You think it's a problem?'

'I think it's something I want to know a lot more about,' said Moreton. 'I want a finger up the ass of everyone you've got in London. I want access to Hassan's suite and to wherever Collington is living. I want to know every meeting they have and everything that they say. I've got a feeling about this, a feeling I don't like.'

'Hassan was the yo-yo who got his fingers burned over the silver thing,' reminded Englehart.

'That's what I don't like about it most of all,' said Moreton. 'He's vulnerable.'

Back at Langley, Englehart looked up from the cables he was preparing to send to Grosvenor Square, thinking back to the meeting with Moreton. He'd encountered men like the Treasury Secretary before, trying to leave scorch marks wherever they went. They invariably burned themselves out. But they caused an awful lot of ripples first. And a presidential sanction, in two hours, was more than a ripple; it was practically a tidal wave. He hoped to Christ that Moreton fouled up soon. But until he did, Englehart knew that every time Moreton said jump, he was going to have to equal an Olympic record. And he'd never enjoyed sport, not even as a kid.

Chapter Eighteen

Dimitri Krotkov was an experienced intelligence officer and he had a clear, analytical mind. One of his first actions after learning of the grain crop failure in the Ukraine was to order a weekly summary of all applications necessary to travel within the country. It was a staggering instruction, considering the size of the Soviet Union: over two hundred men had to be assigned exclusively to the task and even then it would have been impossible without the aid of computers.

He also demanded reports from all the agricultural areas, anticipating the information. There had been a cumulative effect in the crop shortages. To maintain the wheat and cereal norms which had been imposed upon them, arable farmers had gradually been decreasing supplies to animal breeders. At first this shortfall had been made up by the American imports, although from the beginning this had been successful only in isolated areas because of the confused inefficiency of Russian bureaucracy. With the worsening of the grain production situation, the Agricultural Ministry had attempted the convenient way out, gambled that the difficulties would be quickly resolved and diverted the animal foodstuff to the consumer market. But the difficulties hadn't been resolved; they'd worsened, to crisis proportions. By the time of the Ukraine collapse, it had been decided to introduce rationing for wheat, grain, barley and soya. It was then discovered that there was insufficient meat, because the majority of the animals had starved to death for want of the food directed elsewhere by the agricultural authorities.

There was a purge within the ministry, and the director and two of his deputies were jailed for varying terms, on an umbrella charge of activities prejudicial to the interests of the Soviet Union. That did nothing, though, to cure the problem.

More rationing was introduced, this time for meat, in Gorky and Kuibyshev and Yaroslavl and throughout Kazakhstan and Siberia and the Urals, limiting the holders to two kilogrammes a week. Briefly the public believed the authorities were able to control the problem. And then it was realised that supplies weren't sufficient for even two kilogrammes.

No open restrictions were imposed in Moscow, where the Western embassies and journalists were concentrated. Periodic shortages were commonplace and hardly commented upon. But official restraint would have been. To conceal the truth of the situation, they actually put food on display in certain shops. It worked one way but not the other. No outside observer learned of the difficulty, but the rumours that there was food available in the capital spread into the countryside.

It was then that Krotkov's foresight proved itself. He learned of the upsurge of travel applications almost as soon as they started. In the short term, the danger was easily avoided: he issued orders throughout the country that fewer visas should be issued and only then when his officials were convinced that there was a genuine reason for the request, other than food buying. At the same time he flooded Moscow with informants and observers of his own. In two weeks there was an increase of fifteen per cent in the number of people arriving in the capital from the provinces, nearly all of them illegally. Extra guards were installed at airports, railway stations and bus depots to intercept those who had anticipated the checks and disembarked just outside the city, hoping to escape the net by finally arriving on local transport. There were too many offenders to impose penalties; they were simply refused entry on the grounds of insufficient travel documentation and returned, immediately, to the place from which they had begun their journey.

Krotkov waited until the facts were irrefutable before informing Nikolai Leonov. This time the Foreign Ministry official travelled to Dzerzhinsky Square and sat in the starkly bare office overlooking the Lubyanka jail, blinking rapidly at what Krotkov had to say. The KGB chief talked in an even, unemotional voice which heightened the seriousness.

'Oh God!' said Leonov. Increasingly, as his scheme foundered, Leonov was calling upon someone in whom he was not supposed to believe, just as the scientist had done at their first crisis meeting after the plane crash.

'What about the increased wheat purchases from America?' said Krotkov.

'I haven't been able to get any.'

'What!'

'To get wheat, I need gold. To get gold, I need foreign currency. I've virtually exhausted all I'm being allowed, even before trying to make up for the Ukraine shortages.'

Krotkov leaned earnestly across the desk. 'For the moment, I can contain what's happening,' he said. 'But only just. I'm stopping most of them, but some are getting through. At the moment, someone in the Ukraine thinks the problem is only local. He doesn't know it exists in Siberia and Lithuania and all along the Black Sea. And neither do the residents here. But now people are *meeting* in Moscow. From all those places; from everywhere. And they're going to talk and they're going to realise it isn't local but something affecting the whole country. And I can't contain that. The Politburo couldn't contain it and the Central Committee couldn't contain it and the damned Red Army couldn't contain it!'

'I'm not the one you have to convince,' said Leonov. 'It's Igor Struve.'

'Apply again.'

'I've made four applications already.'

'Make a fifth. And I'll support it with everything I've told you today,' promised Krotkov. 'And if he tries to block that, then I'll find a way around the damned man. He might be able to stop you but he won't stop me.'

For the CIA agents in London, the most difficult part of obeying Englehart's surveillance instructions was obtaining accommodation at Claridge's on the floor immediately below that occupied by Prince Hassan and his entourage. They finally resorted to direct embassy pressure, something they would have preferred to avoid, convincing the management that the would-be guest was an American with influential connections in Washington. Once installed, the eavesdropping was comparatively easy, because of the incredible efficiency of modern electronics. Microphones boosted by microchip circuits were attached to the ceiling throughout the suite, providing listening access to every room used by the prince. Listeners were equipped with antennaed earphones, which provided clear, undistorted reception. Yet in spite of their sophisticated gadgetry, it hadn't occurred to anyone that, among themselves, those above would speak in Arabic. Fortunately they had two tape recorders with them, initially intended just for back-up, so it was not a serious oversight. It just meant that there was a delay of a few hours while the material was translated.

It was far easier at Collington's Princes Gate home. They gained admission there by the very old but usually effective pretence of posing as Post Office engineers, checking a line fault. In the telephones on every floor they installed miniscule receivers that turned each instrument into an open microphone, relaying every conversation to a listening van parked a hundred and fifty yards away in Hyde Park.

Englehart was impressed that everything was done within twelve hours and said so in a congratulatory cable.

It was a pity that so much enterprise was wasted. The next meeting between Prince Hassan and Collington was to take place in the Saudi Arabian embassy.

Chapter Nineteen

The response came after three days and Collington calculated he was still in control. If the second meeting had to be in London at all — which it shouldn't have been — then Hassan should have strung it out for at least a fortnight, perhaps even waiting until Collington had tried to make contact again, either through the ambassador or personally, at the hotel. A proper negotiator, or one less desperate, would have considered a month the minimum of time. And then insisted that the conference be in Jeddah, which would have given him the psychological advantage of being on his own territory.

There was none of the artificiality of the first encounter. Collington's appointment at the embassy was immediately acknowledged and he was ushered without any of the previous hindrance to an office which he guessed, from the fittings and the drapes and the portrait of the king, was normally occupied by the ambassador.

Even Hassan had changed, literally. He was wearing a superbly cut, dove-grey suit of silk, a white shirt and a patterned, dark tie. Collington thought it made him appear more forceful than he had done in his traditional dress.

'I wondered if you would still be in London,' said Hassan after the greetings, and Collington guessed he was trying to account for the speed and make it appear a concession.

'I said my departure was fluid,' said Collington. He allowed a short pause and then said: 'I hadn't intended leaving for several weeks.'

Hassan's mouth was fixed in a tight line and there was a tightness about his face, too. 'I have communicated your approach,' he said directly.

'I appreciate the importance you attach to it,' said Collington.

'The response was that the dollar holdings are currently a good investment,' said Hassan.

If it had been, then he wouldn't have been sitting opposite the man in a flamboyantly decorated ambassador's office, Collington knew. 'Currently,' he picked up at once. 'But surely there was a more long-term interpretation of the advantages of my approach?'

'Yes, there was,' conceded Hassan.

'And an acceptance of the weakness in the past?' pressed Collington. The verbal minuet was over: now was the time for positions to be established. Hassan had assumed the role of negotiator. He'd been a royal prince the last time. Now it was different.

'That was also acknowledged,' said the Arab. He leaned back from the desk, wanting to recover. 'The official attitude within my government is that we should cut back, rather than increase, our oil output. As the demand and therefore the price increases, it is more valuable to us in the ground than in storage tanks or giant tankers.'

Collington had anticipated the argument. 'More valuable if it remains denominated in dollars,' he agreed. 'But that is not the point of this discussion, is it? Oil prices have fluctuated in the last year, from a scarcity high of thirty-five dollars a barrel, to an over-production low of sixteen. At thirty-five dollars, it makes good fiscal sense to leave it in the ground. At sixteen, you're only fifty cents ahead on your overall investment. You would have to reduce by at least $31,250,000 the development plan that is to run until 1985 because of a drop in anticipated earnings, and you would have to go deeply into your reserves, actually threatening the stability of the dollar from which you are at the moment benefiting, to maintain refinery and drilling equipment.'

The scope and yet the conciseness of Collington's knowledge momentarily silenced Hassan. He sat beyond the desk, clearly attempting to think of something to say and failing.

Collington saw the advantage and pressed it. 'There is only one commodity that remains consistent. No matter what the fluctuations, gold remains high. In the period during which the dollar has risen and fallen through a graph of twenty-two per cent and oil has climbed and dipped through twelve per cent, gold has shown an uninterrupted ascent. If, three years ago, you had invested in gold the £35,000,000,000 you have placed in currencies throughout the world, your valuation would have been £53,500,000,000. As it is, in real terms, £35,000,000,000 three years ago is today valued at

£29,000,000,000. As I said before, that is a bad return. As a businessman, I would regard it as unacceptable.'

'You advance a convincing argument,' said Hassan, in grudging praise.

'It is not difficult,' said Collington, 'It is based on indisputable fact.' He waited, leaving the other man at a disadvantage.

Hassan conceded his position. 'In principle, we are interested,' he declared. He watched for any reaction, but Collington remained impassive.

'I am very pleased,' said Collington.

'But only in principle,' stressed Hassan.

'I'd need your feelings explained fully,' said Collington.

'We both know of the potential danger to the stability of my country if this arrangement were to become public knowledge after an agreement were reached?'

Collington nodded.

'We are speaking directly, as businessmen. And as a businessman, I know you will not be offended by what I am about to say. We feel at the moment we are conceding too much, even by continuing the contact that has been opened, without the slightest proof that you can maintain your side of any proposal that is agreed.'

'I am not offended,' said Collington. 'In your position I would feel exactly the same way.'

Hassan smiled his quick, automatic smile and Collington was reminded of the up-and-down mouth of a ventriloquist's dummy.

'For this discussion to continue beyond today, there would need to be such a demonstration,' said Hassan.

'What?'

'Eventually there would have to be a contractual agreement, but we think it is too premature for that.'

'What then?'

'Practical proof.'

'Practical?'

Hassan hesitated, like a child about to risk swearing in front of a parent for the first time. Then he said, 'South Africa is shortly to make a gold release.'

Collington nodded. Hassan hadn't wasted the intervening days since their last meeting.

'Have it changed,' said Hassan, simply.

'Changed!' Collington's control slipped, momentarily, at the demand. It was the silver corner, all over again. But this time Hassan was sure of the odds. He was probably buying into bullion already, because whatever happened gold wasn't going to slump. And any sort of interruption in the South African release would cause a jump. Hassan intended to recover far more than this lost £100,000,000. He *was* a greedy bastard.

'A commitment to reserves, instead of a sale, has happened before, many times,' said the Arab.

There was a sudden confidence about the man, Collington decided. 'Not when a release date has been fixed,' he said. 'It'll cause a fluctuation.'

'Only temporary.'

Which was all that Hassan would want, Collington thought. 'I can't give any assurance,' he said.

Hassan's face registered an artificial look of sadness. 'It's the demonstration that my government seeks,' he said. 'Without it I doubt that they will be interested in continuing these negotiations.'

All Collington's previous satisfaction evaporated. Hassan had him trapped and knew it. 'It is unorthodox,' he protested.

'So is the conversation we are having,' said Hassan.

'There will need to be a channel through which we can maintain contact.'

'This embassy has proved satisfactory, up to now,' pointed out Hassan.

'I'll return to South Africa tomorrow,' said Collington.

'Yes,' said Hassan, assuming complete supremacy. 'The release is scheduled for a week from now. You'll have to hurry.'

Collington was on his feet before he remembered Wall's foresight in providing a gift. He took the boxes from his briefcase and said to the Arab: 'I would be honoured if you would accept these, as a token of our continued friendship and association.'

Hassan stood, reaching out with almost childlike eagerness for the gift. The greed was obvious in everything, Collington thought.

'I would like you to accept something from me,' reciprocated Hassan. From a side drawer in the desk he produced a single box and Collington took it, smiling his thanks.

He opened it in the car. It was a watch, over-ornate and heavy, the band as well as the body in solid gold. Collington knew he would have to wear it when he met Hassan again: he'd feel self-conscious, he decided.

'Are they amateurs!' raged Moreton. 'Idiotic, goddamn amateurs!'

'We never had any reason to believe it was official,' defended Englehart, concerned at the degree of the man's fury. 'It was a good bet that they'd meet again either at the hotel or his place.'

Moreton, who had been striding around the room in his anger, leaned forward over his desk at the CIA section head. 'We're not betting here,' he said softly. 'This isn't penny ante poker in the boys' locker room. This is business: big, serious business. And even now you haven't realised what the embassy meeting means, have you?'

Englehart frowned, trying to understand.

'You *said* it, for Christ's sake!' exploded Moreton. 'The embassy visit makes it official. So what, officially, is Saudi Arabia's Oil Minister doing with a multi-national business set-up like SAGOMI?'

'That's what we've got to find out,' said Englehart.

'That's what *you've* got to find out,' corrected the Treasury Secretary. 'And you've got to do it a damned sight better than you have done so far.'

It was whip-crack-and-jump time, recognised Englehart. Which was why, by the time the SAGOMI company plane returned Collington from England, a squad of twenty men had been drafted to Pretoria to put him under twenty-four-hour surveillance.

Chapter Twenty

The impending gold release imposed a time limit, and as it was the weekend it meant Collington having to see Metzinger at the farm, instead of the office. Collington drove preoccupied, still unable to decide what Metzinger was attempting by suborning Ann Talbot. Collington realised he would have to be careful not to over-respond. The Afrikaner opposition was an admitted, open fact. So there was a certain understandable logic in what Metzinger appeared to be trying to establish, creating a system from which he might discover advantages that could be used to continue their pressure for control. And now he was forewarned, Collington calculated that he had the advantage.

He certainly felt he needed one. And not just with Metzinger. He was unsure if Hannah would have agreed so readily to see him, if it hadn't been for his meeting with Paul. Certainly her attitude seemed to have changed from what it had been immediately before he went away. There had been no hostility in her voice when he'd telephoned; rather it had been a flat, blank neutrality.

The road looped and began running parallel to the perimeter fence of Metzinger's property. It was a huge farm, one of the biggest in the province. Metzinger's father had started it, just after the end of the First World War, but it had been much smaller then. It had been Metzinger who had expanded it to its present size and raised the quality of his cattle to championship level. In everything he did, Metzinger had to be the best, reflected Collington.

Collington parked in the shade of the barn in which Metzinger housed his Voortrekker wagons and walked across the intervening courtyard to the main house. Creeper had been encouraged to grow in such a way that it matted across the front of the house, and Collington thought it resembled an English country home. He didn't imagine Metzinger would have welcomed the comparison.

Collington had telephoned ahead and Metzinger was waiting for him, in the study off the main vestibule of the farmhouse. Even at weekends the man wore a business suit, a tie and a stiff, white-collared shirt. There were drinks on a tray beside the desk for visitors. Collington declined the invitation, wanting to conclude the meeting as soon as possible; he had only three hours before he was due at Parkstown.

'Was it successful?' demanded Metzinger.

'It could be,' said Collington. Until he learned completely of Metzinger's intention there was every point in apparent co-operation. Metzinger leaned intently across the desk as Collington recounted everything that had happened during his meeting with Hassan. Metzinger reacted first at the size of the commission that Collington had offered and then at the method Hassan had stipulated to prove that the approach had government approval.

'Couldn't we have offered less money?' said Metzinger.

'The figure was important,' said Collington. 'That was the amount he lost in the silver speculation with R.L.Bains.'

Metzinger nodded, accepting the argument, and said, 'So he'd want the commission up front, in advance of anything we might earn?'

'We didn't become as detailed as that,' said Collington. 'But I imagine that is what he would expect.'

'He would have our money and we'd have no guarantee of completion. They could renegue on the whole deal if they chose.'

'I think that's being overly suspicious,' said Collington. 'I said that's what he would expect, not what we would agree. His desperation is in our favour. I'd be prepared to give him half, no more. So they would have to go ahead for him to get the rest. And the necessity of a formal contract came from him before I had to introduce it. If we had their signatures on paper, they'd have to go through: they couldn't risk the embarrassment of any open litigation.'

'It wouldn't be *their* signatures,' said Metzinger. 'Surely they will set up front companies to provide us, just as we intend covering ourselves.'

'That would cover them against any casual business enquiry,' agreed Collington. 'But not the sort of investigation we could afford to mount if they attempted to pull out once the deal had been made. The risk of exposure would still be there.'

'I don't like the method they demand for proof of government involvement,' said Metzinger, moving on. 'It's gimmicky.'

'It's Hassan's idea,' said Collington. 'He's a crook.'

'Gambling on a rise?' queried Metzinger.

'Unquestionably,' said Collington. 'But it's that or nothing.'

'We'd benefit, too,' said Metzinger. 'Any upward movement in gold carries our share value up.'

He sat back expansively in his chair and Collington wondered if the man pictured on the wall behind him, a sepia-tinted print of a Boer, standing stiffly upright with a barrel-loading rifle beside him, were Metzinger's grandfather. According to Walter Simpson's account, the man had been one of de Wet's raiders, the mounted guerrilla group that had arguably caused the greatest British casualties during the Boer War.

'It's gone surprisingly well, hasn't it?' said Metzinger, coming as close as he ever would to praise.

'Now I think we should raise it at a full board meeting,' said Collington. 'I don't think it's ethical to continue any longer like this.'

Metzinger jerked up a warning hand. 'Let me consult first,' he said. 'We've done nothing yet but open up the most tentative negotiations. The potential is too great to risk any premature discussion. No one is going to criticise you for secrecy, if you present a signed and sealed agreement.'

'I think I should be involved in the government discussions,' pressed Collington.

'So do I,' agreed Metzinger, at once. 'I'll make the point.'

A clock sounded somewhere in the room and Collington realised they had been talking for an hour.

'To affect the change in date of the gold release, there will have to be talks this week,' said Collington.

'Of course.'

'You'll suggest expanding the discussions then?'

'Yes,' promised Metzinger.

'And get a decision about involving the board?'

'That too.'

Collington made a show of consulting his watch. 'I've another appointment, back in Pretoria,' he said.

Metzinger rose with him, walking him to the door. 'I appreciate your coming all the way out here at a weekend,' he said.

'I thought it was necessary, in view of the time.'

Metzinger nodded. 'I'll try to arrange a meeting for Monday,' he said. 'That should allow a sufficient period for any withholding announcement to be made.'

A perfectly ordinary business discussion, decided Collington, entering his car. He wondered what Metzinger's reaction would be if he learned that Ann Talbot had left the company.

Even though he knew there was little chance of his being late, Collington still drove fast and arrived early at Parkstown. Hannah wasn't on the porch to greet him this time.

The houseboy showed him to the drawing-room and Collington stood looking out over the undisturbed swimming-pool and the grounds beyond. It was still his, he supposed. He felt no sense of possession. Or pride, either. It had to be a character fault, not to feel anything. There was no purpose in working at anything, unless there was a reason for the activity. Without a focus for achievement, the labour became robot-like. So why did he do it? Why had he ever done it? Why hadn't he been content to remain on a railway station at Richmond? He would probably have been a stationmaster by now – maybe at one of the major London terminals, with a top hat to wear for visits by royalty. The stationmaster at Richmond had had one, wrapped in tissue and protected in its box, in the hope of further promotion.

He heard the door and turned to face Hannah as she entered. She hadn't made any concessions for the weekend any more than her father. She was wearing a severely cut, tight-fitting suit in muted grey. The stockings were grey, too, and she was wearing spectacles instead of her usual contact lenses. They were the heaviest she owned, horn-rimmed, and Collington decided there was a psychological reason for it. Whether consciously or not, she had worn them to create a barrier between them.

'Hello Hannah,' he said.

'Hello.'

It was the same voice as on the telephone, empty of expression. He wondered if she would offer her cheek to be kissed, as she had done before. He moved back further into the room, towards her.

She moved away from him to one of the side chairs.

'Have you been offered tea?'

'I didn't want anything.'

'Did you see Paul?'

She'd blame him, Collington knew. No matter how he attempted to explain it, the fault remained his and there was no way he could minimise it. It was selfish to want to try, he accepted. But it wasn't the blame he sought to avoid: it was any further deterioration in her feelings for him.

'Well?' she said impatiently.

He told her simply and chronologically, avoiding nothing, because he decided that if she later discovered that he had withheld something, it would make the situation worse. At the end, when he was telling her of his interview with the headmaster, colour began to flush her cheeks and he saw her hands tighten along the arms of the chair.

'Jesus!' she exploded, when he finished. 'What the hell have you done?'

She was being irrational, confusing her feelings about his admission of adultery with what had happened with the child, but there was no point in trying to make her understand that. Or in arguing, either.

'Perhaps I made a mistake in saying anything at all,' he said. 'I thought it best at the time. So did you.'

'What did you say? What have you told him?'

'About what?'

'Us!'

'Nothing more than I had already. I thought there had been enough harm, without wanting to raise his hopes by saying we might get back together.'

He thought she was about to challenge that but she didn't, just shook her head in some private thought. Then she said: 'He still thinks we're separated?'

'Yes.'

'So he's going to go on buggering about and risking his common entrance?'

'I don't know,' said Collington, feeling a sense of helplessness. 'I suppose that's the obvious conclusion.'

'I hope you're proud of all this!' she said.

'I told you the last time how sorry I was, and if you want me to, I'll say it again. I regret it, probably more than I've ever regretted anything in my life, and if I could go back and change it all, then I would. But I can't. So all I can do is try to repair it, as best I can.' As he spoke, Collington's head was bowed, and he became aware that his hands were shaking. 'I saw Ann in London,' he took up.

'Ann?'

He hadn't given her a name, remembered Collington. 'The woman I told you about . . .' He looked up at her. 'It's all over,' he said. 'Finished. She's even leaving the company.'

'Just like that,' said Hannah, snapping her fingers.

Collington was finding it very difficult to control his temper. There had to be a limit to her reproaches. 'How else can it be, for Christ's sake!' he said. 'I cheated, OK. And now I'm being honest, completely and utterly one hundred per cent honest. There isn't any different way that I can say sorry. I love you and I want to come back . . .' He held his hands out towards her. 'Now it's down to you. Now it's time for you to decide if pride and hurt or whatever are more important than anything else.'

'I don't know,' Hannah said. 'I just don't know any more. About anything.'

Soviet sleepers of Brigitte re Jong's calibre work under a system of clearly defined restrictions. One of the most stringent is that contact shall always come from Moscow, never to it. But it was becoming increasingly difficult for Brigitte to maintain this instruction. Twice in the past week she had purchased gold on a margin and twice had to surrender before settlement, because of insufficient funds to complete. She'd made a profit on each transaction, but she didn't want to develop a reputation within the trade as a speculator. If more money wasn't made available to her soon, she would have to disregard the basic rule and protest through the embassy to Moscow.

There would be annoyance, she knew: a rebuke, maybe. But it was ridiculous expecting her to continue as she was. The whole scheme was collapsing.

Chapter Twenty-One

Metzinger decided he had done well during the farmhouse meeting with Collington. He was confident that he had completely concealed his confusion at what the Saudis wanted to indicate that the approach had government support, advancing the arguments and objections that Collington would have expected.

But he had been confused because even as Collington was speaking he accepted there was no way he could arrange the sort of manœuvre required to maintain the conviction in Collington's mind that there was official backing. It was fortunate that it had been a weekend, with Saturday night and all of Sunday to consider it. By Monday, Metzinger wasn't confused any more. By Monday he had concluded that the theatricality of the situation couldn't be better suited to his purpose.

Knoetze came forward from his desk the moment Metzinger entered, leading him away from any indication of officialdom towards lounging chairs and a settee against the windows which had a view of the SAGOMI skyscraper.

'Your call was intriguing,' said the South African security chief.

'I hope you didn't mind me coming through at a weekend.'

'It's been several weeks since we found that South African gold was being bought by the Soviet Union,' reminded Knoetze. 'And apart from the information that came from you, about the reason for the Russian purchases, we've made no progress whatsoever. So I certainly didn't mind the call.'

It irritated him, having to show any sort of subservience to Metzinger, but Knoetze was sure he was concealing his real feelings.

Metzinger looked away from the other man as if there were an embarrassment. 'I want you to understand something,' he said. 'I want you to remember it and I want it made clear to anyone else in the government to whom you speak about this.'

He looked back to Knoetze, who nodded encouragingly. 'What is it?' he asked.

'You know what sort of a man Collington is,' said Metzinger. 'He's brilliant. He's innovative and resourceful and it's because of his drive that SAGOMI occupies the place it does today in world business.'

Knoetze was sitting with his head to one side, intent upon the praise.

'But it isn't easy,' continued Metzinger. 'He's an entrepreneur, a loner. And he always has been. That's how he came up with the information from Israel, making the gold shipment so understandable.'

'Why are you telling me this?' frowned Knoetze.

'Because I want you to appreciate fully what I'm going to say. I am going to tell you this morning exactly what Collington has told me. But I want you and anyone else to remember at all times that this is all I am doing, repeating what I have been told. I have no way whatsoever of being able to guarantee the accuracy of the information.'

'You doubt it?' demanded the security chief.

'No!' insisted Metzinger, immediately. 'Just making my position clear.'

'I understand,' assured Knoetze. 'And I will make sure that others do, too.'

Metzinger smiled appreciatively. 'Thank you,' he said.

'So what does Collington say?'

Still Metzinger did not answer directly; he'd rehearsed a sequence so that it would appear convincing.

'There is a similarity between us and the man whom Collington contacted in Israel. With intelligence links,' he said.

'The Israeli information came from the Mossad?'

Metzinger nodded. 'That's what I understand. As Collington understands what he's now been told. About the Sasol bombings.'

It had exactly the effect that Metzinger had expected. Knoetze started forward, until their knees were almost touching. 'Everything!' said Knoetze. 'I want to know everything!'

'I gather the Israelis have penetrated the Palestinian Liberation Organisation,' said Metzinger.

'They'd be fools not to have done,' said Knoetze.

'And it's been said publicly that the African National Congress guerrillas are being trained by them.'

Knoetze sat nodding and Metzinger could see the growing belief registering on the man's face.

'Certainly Russia is short of gold,' said Metzinger. 'But not as short as we first thought. It's not all being committed to grain purchase from America. According to what Collington has told me, some is being used to fund the attacks against us here, in South Africa. The Sasol bombing was directly financed by gold which went from this country to the Soviet Union. From Moscow, it went straight to Mozambique.'

Knoetze found it impossible to remain seated any longer. He stood up and began striding back and forth in front of the window. 'The cynical bastards,' he said.

'There's something else,' said Metzinger, stopping the man. Knoetze was in front of him, staring down.

'Collington says they've been promised more,' declared Metzinger. 'Presumably from this month's gold release. That's why I thought it urgent for us to meet.'

Knoetze sat down again. 'I'll repeat what I said before,' he said. 'I'm indebted to you. Deeply indebted.'

'And I'll repeat what I said. I'm merely a conduit in this.'

'It has a logic about it,' said Knoetze. 'A simple, damnable logic.'

'Will you recommend a postponement of the gold release?' said Metzinger. He had hesitated to suggest it openly, not wanting to go too far, but he decided that Knoetze was completely convinced and that there would be no risk.

'Of course,' said Knoetze. 'There will be outside protests, I suppose. But that's not important.'

'The Cabinet may not agree,' said Metzinger.

'They'll agree, if they think it will prevent something like the Sasol bombing,' said Knoetze. He reached across to put his hand on the other man's arm. 'You'll let me know if you hear anything more.'

'Of course.'

'And thank Collington for me.'

'I will.'

Knoetze smiled suddenly, as the idea came to him. 'Perhaps I should meet him myself,' he said. 'To thank him personally.'

Metzinger shook his head. 'We came together as Broeders,' he reminded. 'I don't think it would be right to involve the company any more directly than it already is.'

Knoetze nodded in agreement. 'You're probably right,' he said.

Metzinger stretched out in the back of the car taking him the short distance from Skinner Street to the SAGOMI offices, the satisfaction warming through him. It was working out more successfully than he'd imagined possible, when the idea of removing Collington from the board had first come to him. Even the timing was perfect: the annual meeting of the shareholders in three months was exactly right for what he intended.

Back in his suite, Metzinger gave instructions that he was not to be disturbed and then locked his office door to avoid any interruption he hadn't anticipated. He obtained an outside line and made his own connection to London, frowning when he was told that Ann Talbot was on a leave of absence. Unwilling to disclose himself by speaking directly to Richard Jenkins, Metzinger disconnected and booked the second call through to her apartment, tapping his finger impatiently at the unanswered ring. Finally he slammed the telephone down angrily. He'd make her suffer if this were some ridiculous way to avoid doing what he'd told her.

Moreton cast aside the report, dissatisfied with it. 'This doesn't tell me anything more than I already knew, apart from the fact that he's got some difficult relationship with his wife,' he said.

'There's nothing else to say,' said Englehart. 'Since he got back to South Africa he's done nothing but behave like a normal businessman.'

'What about Hassan?'

'Flew back to Jeddah, the day after their meeting at the embassy.'

'How are we placed in Saudi Arabia?'

'Good,' said Englehart. 'Got a deputy manager in the oil ministry directly on the payroll. He's already been contacted.'

'Something's going to break,' predicted Moreton. 'I'm sure of it.'

Two days later, South Africa announced the postponement of the gold release.

Chapter Twenty-Two

There were local variables, making a difference of one or two points, but on the metal markets throughout the world gold was averaged at $640 an ounze on the day South Africa made the announcement. The Pretoria government attempted to dampen speculation, insisting with supportive figures that there were no production difficulties, but the threat of scarcity bred the inevitable nervousness and the price jump was merely delayed, not prevented.

London exacerbated the problem. The market had anticipated the sale and was short on contracts. To cover itself, the metal was pegged there at $644, which was too high by at least two dollars. In Frankfurt and Zurich it was decided that London possessed information they did not. They settled at $648. The trend became infectious. Worried that its favourite investment was at risk, Paris valued it at $650 at the opening, was surprised by the scramble to buy and re-assessed at $655 two hours later.

After two days, Australia decided to take advantage of the situation and offered a ton of gold for sale, which the market hadn't expected. It was as though paraffin had been thrown on to an open fire.

In Washington, Henry Moreton received a telephone call from the President, congratulating him for his financial anticipation on stockpiling and confirming that with the addition of the Russian supplies to those which they already held, their gold holdings had in a week increased in value by two billion dollars. Moreton's campaign had been extremely effective. The American reserves were acknowledged in the financial centres of every capital throughout the world and the dollar rose, with its now accepted backing. Moreton recognised the effect and its cause the moment it happened. At $850 an ounze, he decided he could boost a market trend without the slightest risk.

He issued a statement, later praised for its authority by the *Wall*

Street Journal, criticising the nervousness of investors and asserting that the United States government had no intention of adding to the spiral, nor benefiting from it. So they were suspending their advertised gold sales.

That first day, Frankfurt and Zurich had reacted in the belief of secret information. The American decision, which came within two weeks of the news from Pretoria, removed any doubts: the governments in Bonn, Paris and London separately instructed their ambassadors to make official enquiries in Washington and the State Department's assurance that they were not working in concert with South Africa was received with scepticism by all three. The price reached $900, as Moreton had expected it to, and in newspapers there were pictures of people queueing outside the offices of metal merchants, wanting to sell jewellery and plate for melting down.

In Moscow, Igor Struve was dismissed. When the degree and the effect of the old man's obstructiveness was realised, the commodities operation was removed entirely from either Finance or Foreign Ministry interference. Leonov was placed nominally under Krotkov's control, but it was made clear that they were expected to work together more as equals. To reinforce that, Leonov was allowed access at all times to the Politburo secretariat and was allocated offices within the Kremlin complex. It was there that they met on the day their joint control became effective.

'What's your estimate of timing?' demanded Krotkov.

'Insufficient,' said Leonov at once. 'I've officially requested more grain to make up for the Ukraine loss. But it will be three weeks at the earliest, before the first ships arrive.'

'Food riots have started,' said Krotkov. 'There have been two in Kiev, and another in Odessa, which is worrying. It's a port used by foreign ships, the sort of place from which the news could leak out.'

'We're five tonnes short on the disposable gold available, to meet the contract with America,' disclosed Leonov. 'Through Amsterdam we're approaching bullion brokers direct, but even that won't be enough, unless South Africa makes a release.'

'Any indications that they might?'

Leonov shook his head. 'Nothing,' he said.

'Could we delay settlement?'

'Maybe for a month,' said Leonov. 'There would be suspicion if we tried to stretch it any further.'

'What ideas do you have?'

Leonov shrugged. 'None,' he conceded.

For several moments both men were silent. Then Krotkov said, 'I think we should do something in South Africa.'

'We're already doing everything we can.'

'There's little that Brigitte re Jong can do in Holland any more,' said Krotkov. 'She's a bone fide broker who would have a reason for going to South Africa. All we want is an indication of whether or not there'll be a release.'

Leonov stood up, walking aimlessly around the room as he considered the idea. 'If we did get the hint of a sale, it would enable us to establish firm order positions in advance of anyone else,' he said.

'And it would be something practical,' said Krotkov.

Leonov nodded. 'There's been too little of that, for too long,' he said.

Metzinger had been uncertain of Wassenaar's reaction, wondering if the man would consider he had gone too far. But Wassenaar had actually reached out to shake his hand in a gesture Metzinger found vaguely embarrassing and said, with soft-voiced sincerity, 'Masterly. Absolutely masterly.'

'There can be no criticism against me,' stressed Metzinger. 'I made it clear to Knoetze that I was relaying information and that I couldn't guarantee its veracity.'

'The mining division shares have gone up five Rand during the speculation,' said Wassenaar. 'It's spectacular.'

'It will appear to be an entire market manipulation for company profit by Collington.'

The remark appeared to register. 'When we mount the coup against Collington, there's going to be a loss of public confidence,' Wassenaar said. 'The shares will fall quite heavily.'

Metzinger smiled. 'I've anticipated that, too,' he said. It was an exaggeration, because the idea had only occurred to him fleetingly and he hadn't properly thought it through, but Wassenaar's enthusiasm encouraged him.

'What?' said the other man.

'We can time the announcement and therefore anticipate the drop, right?' he said.

'Right.'

'So there would be no risk in our going bearish, would there?' said Metzinger. 'If we placed automatic sell orders at, say, four points below market valuation and then reversed, with purchase orders at a low of ten, then we'd pick up ten points a share when the board was re-assembled and the value re-established at the former level. And it will rise: our holdings are too strong to suffer for any length of time. The fluctuation would be over in a matter of days. A couple of weeks, at the outside.'

Wassenaar was smiling, his head bent forward in concentration. 'If I sold at four and picked up at ten, I'd show a profit of almost a million and a half Rand.'

'And I would make over two million,' said Metzinger. 'Which I think is fitting reward for all the effort involved.'

'Do you know what I think is a pity, Marius?'

'What?' said Metzinger.

'That no one is ever going to know how clever you've been.'

Chapter Twenty-Three

Brigitte re Jong had determined to break the inviolable instructions and make contact with Moscow through the Dutch embassy on the Friday. And then, on Thursday, came the summons to Paris.

She guessed it would be with Nikolai Leonov, because it was he who had originally briefed her, all those months before. Then she had found him a strange contrast even to the limited number of men with whom she had allowed herself any relationship. He had been stiff and uncomfortable, appearing unaware of how to behave, and she had wondered at the time if all Soviet men were so awkward.

Brigitte went to Paris by an indirect route, checking automatically for any surveillance, and booked into the hotel which had been designated in her contact message, near the Opéra.

Leonov arrived the day after her and as soon as she admitted him to her room, she saw the change in his appearance. He was still fastidiously neat, as he had been at their first encounter, but his face was sagged and pouched with fatigue and he had a tendency to blink too often and too rapidly.

She sat on the bed, allowing him the only chair in the room.

'I'm sorry I had to bring you here,' he said. 'I came out through Czechoslovakia into Vienna. And then up by train. Paris seemed a good central spot.'

'It was no inconvenience,' she said. Even with his awkwardness, there had been a forcefulness last time. Now that seemed to have disappeared.

'I'm sorry, too, about the restriction of funds,' he said.

'Have there been difficulties?' she anticipated.

'Incredible difficulties,' he said. Slowly, anxious for her to know everything, he told her of the opposition he had been experiencing immediately before the Ilyushin crash and how it had intensified afterwards.

'Were they mad!' she exclaimed, when he finished.

'Jealous men guarding empires,' judged Leonov, all anger at what had happened gone now. 'Everything has been centralised to myself and Krotkov.'

'When it's too late,' she said.

'How much of the five tonnes can we get direct from bullion dealers?' demanded Leonov. 'There are no financial restrictions now.'

Brigitte frowned at the note of desperate hope in the man's voice. 'Some,' she said. 'It would be at a massive premium: probably more than $1,000 an ounze. We definitely couldn't get it all. That's an enormous amount in the present circumstances. I don't honestly think that much is available on the open market. Gold is worth more in a vault at the moment.'

'We need an indication of whether the South Africans are going to maintain the suspension,' insisted Leonov.

'Yes,' she agreed.

'That's why I want you to go to Pretoria.'

'Me!'

'You're a broker: that's perfect cover.'

'It's the government who decide the sales,' she reminded. 'The producers might not know.'

'It's worth a try,' he said. 'Anything is worth a try.'

She frowned again. 'There are a lot of producers to cover. And it won't be easy, getting to the level of people who might know. There's Anglo-American, Consolidated Gold Fields, SAGOMI, Rio-Tinto Zinc, Union Corporation, Charter Consolidated . . .' She tailed off. 'And they're only the major ones,' she added.

'How soon could you leave Amsterdam?' he said.

'Monday.'

'Try for the first plane.'

Englehart had left instructions in the cipher room in case a message arrived and he knew from the look on his wife's face, as he stood with the telephone in his hand, that she suspected him of arranging it purposely.

'I've got to go out,' he said.

'Mother's coming, for pot roast,' Ruth said evenly.

'I'm sorry. It's important.'

'You weren't here last time.'

'It was important then.'

'What shall I tell her?'

'That I'll try to get back.'

'You promised that last time.'

'This time I really will,' he said, shrugging into his jacket as he left the house. Even before he got out of Georgetown, the telephone in the car purred with the location of Henry Moreton and Englehart nodded, deciding he might be able to keep his promise to Ruth after all. He used the Agency insignia and identification to bluster his way past the parking restrictions outside the Kennedy Center, striding impatiently up and down in the vestibule while an attendant went into the auditorium to find the Treasury Secretary.

Moreton hurried out, programme still in his hand. He was wearing a dinner jacket and black tie and Englehart guessed it was some official party.

'I thought it was something you'd want to know right away,' said Englehart, in apology.

'What is it?' said the man.

'Important,' assured Englehart.

Moreton looked uncertainly around the crowded building and Englehart said, 'My car's right outside.'

The two men hurried towards it. Englehart negotiated his way out of the forecourt and set out aimlessly around the capital. 'We got a message from our man in the Saudi oil ministry,' he announced bluntly.

Moreton twisted around to look across the vehicle. 'What?' he demanded.

'Collington is offering the Saudis a commodity deal, gold for oil.'

'Son of a bitch!' exclaimed the Treasury Secretary.

'Is that bad?' asked Englehart.

Moreton had his head bowed against his chest. 'The majority of our oil supply comes from there,' he said simply. 'If there's a cutback, there'll be an industrial panic. And if there's an industrial panic, the dollar goes down the tube. Just like knocking down dominoes.'

The analogy had been used before, remembered Englehart;

Vietnam had been a disaster, too. 'I thought the South African government controlled the gold.'

'They couldn't risk a direct approach, could they?' said Moreton. 'Collington is obviously an emissary.'

'He's certainly big enough,' reflected Englehart.

'It would be a complicated set-up,' said Moreton. 'Lots of sideways movement before it got to one place from another . . .' He looked across the car again. 'You're right,' he agreed. 'Collington's got the organisation for a set-up like that.'

'What are we going to do?' asked Englehart.

'We're going to screw it up, that's what we're going to do,' declared Moreton.

Chapter Twenty-Four

Marius Metzinger and Jan Wassenaar calculated their share disposal with the care that R.L. Bains had shown, six months earlier, when he set out to corner the silver market, although their operation was miniscule by comparison and stood no risk of exposure.

There were three farmhouse meetings, to consider the effect upon every portfolio they held of the coup they intended against Collington. The multi-national spread of SAGOMI was vast, from a fast-food chain in the Middle West of America to a ball-bearing factory in Marseilles to a pasta-manufacturing plant in Naples, and the first conference was solely concerned with the elimination of those companies likely to be unaffected.

And it was at that first meeting that they decided it was going to be easier than they had expected. Both agreed the drop and rise was going to be brief, reflecting nothing more than automatic nervousness from outside investors at the uncertainty of a boardroom battle, and that if there was any movement in the peripheral holdings it would be too small to provide a profit and could therefore be ignored.

That narrowed the operation considerably and made it completely manageable. The chief shifts would obviously be in SAGOMI, the parent company. Metzinger had 40,000 shares and Wassenaar 37,500 and on the day of their initial discussion, the value of each share stood at R4-50. There would be matching selling throughout their mining division and here their ownership was more widely spread, through diamonds to copper to uranium and gold. The share value was equally varied, at the lowest R3-75, up to a gold high of R50. Once more Metzinger was slightly ahead in ownership, with a total of 57,000 shares to Wassenaar's 46,500.

The second meeting was the most important because it was there that they calculated the risk involved against the profit expectation. Metzinger started out proposing the figures that had been mentioned when the idea first came to them, selling at four points below valuation and buying back in when the drop reached ten, giving them a six point profit per share when the prices stabilised. Wassenaar invoked his lawyer's caution, arguing that the six points between four and ten was too wide a gap, leaving them too vulnerable if the panic was not as great as they anticipated and the fall didn't reach ten points.

Greed had begun to infect Metzinger and he was reluctant to abandon the position, and it took several hours of concentrated argument for the lawyer to convince him. They finally agreed upon a compromise, raising the selling figure to two points below valuation and buying back in at seven. On a profit margin of five points, they each stood to make a profit of well over a million Rand.

The practical operation of the coup was entrusted to Wassenaar because of his expertise in company law, and when they debated the method at their third gathering, they discovered again that it was going to be easier than they had expected. SAGOMI was quoted on the London and New York exchanges, as well as in South Africa, enabling them to spread the sell orders thinly enough to avoid the slightest suspicion. The mining shares were more centralised and therefore more difficult, but at Wassenaar's suggestion Metzinger agreed that the instructions should be placed through a Zurich broker, taking any focus away from themselves as local shareholders.

It was late when they finished and Wassenaar sat back in the chair in Metzinger's study, physically aching from the effort of concentration.

'There's nothing we haven't anticipated,' he said confidently.

'Just one thing,' corrected Metzinger. 'Janet Simpson.'

Wassenaar frowned. He had half expected Metzinger to raise it.

'She gave us her absolute support the last time,' reminded Metzinger. 'I think she should be allowed to benefit, like we are.'

'It spreads the knowledge beyond us two,' protested Wassenaar. 'What we are doing is technically a conspiracy . . . an illegal act.'

'She needn't know,' argued Metzinger. 'You're a lawyer. Couldn't she entrust certain portfolios to you, with power of attorney?'

Wassenaar stared down into his lap, considering the suggestion. 'It's possible,' he said doubtfully.

'Then she could be included?'

'Would she do it, without asking any questions?'

'If I suggested it,' said Metzinger, confidently. 'She trusts me implicitly.'

'What are her holdings?' asked Wassenaar, guessing that the other man would have briefed himself.

'Twenty thousand in SAGOMI,' said Metzinger, at once. 'Thirty thousand spread elsewhere, throughout the mining companies. They could be absorbed without any curiosity.'

Metzinger was right, conceded Wassenaar. And Janet Simpson had allied herself to them when it mattered. 'I suppose we should,' he said.

Metzinger, who had been expecting a more protracted argument, smiled quickly at his success. 'You'll arrange all the documentation then, authorising you to act on her behalf?'

'I'd hardly entrust it to anyone else, would I?' demanded the lawyer.

'How long will it take to set up?'

'It's a completely straightforward situation,' said Wassenaar. 'I would expect to have all the orders placed within a week. A fortnight at the outside . . .' He hesitated. 'For the scheme to work, they will have to be automatic sell and buy orders,' he said. 'It's going to be a worrying time.'

'Big prizes aren't won by small men,' said Metzinger.

'Collington isn't called "Tiny" for nothing,' reminded the lawyer.

'It began as a joke,' said Metzinger. 'And that's how it's going to end.'

The need for power and prestige affects people in different ways. Some men have the intellectual capacity to grow and expand with it, but in others the desire to succeed becomes distorted, so that they are unbalanced by the craving. The doubt about Henry Moreton's reasoning came abruptly to Englehart while he was in the Treasury Secretary's office and stayed with him, a worrying, nagging doubt. And a pointless one, he conceded. Because there was not a damned thing he could do to challenge the instructions. The CIA had a presidential order to accord Henry Moreton *carte blanche* in everything he wanted. And until that was rescinded from the White House, the man could call any shot he liked. Englehart had seen it before and knew bloody well that his ass would be in the nearest sling if he attempted to raise doubts through the Executive or even with the Director himself. And with five years to go before retirement to the clapboard bungalow at Cape Cod, Englehart had no intention of bucking the system.

'It's time to teach people lessons,' said Moreton. 'Don't you think?'

He had taken to walking magisterially around the office as he spoke and there was frequently a patronising tone in his voice, Englehart recognised. 'I'm not sure I know what you mean,' he said cautiously.

'I mean that Hassan has got to be shown where his loyalties lie and that industrialist has got to learn that even as big as he is, he can still get his fingers burned.' Moreton finally sat behind his desk. 'That's what I mean,' he said again.

'How?' said Englehart, nervously.

'I was scheduled anyway to go to Paris, for a meeting of the International Monetary Fund,' disclosed Moreton. 'OPEC are meeting at the same time in Vienna.'

'Hassan will be there, representing Saudi Arabia,' said Englehart.

'He's agreed to meet me,' said Moreton. 'I had confirmation this morning from the embassy here. Crafty bastard seems set on playing all the ends against the middle.'

'There's no way you can let him know what we've learned,' said Englehart, immediately regretting the remark when he saw Moreton's expression.

'I've no intention of letting him know what we've learned,' said the Treasury Secretary. 'I'm going to convince Hassan where his best markets remain. And that he shouldn't risk a transfer to any other customer offering any other sort of commodity.'

'A risk, in gold?' queried Englehart, trying to score back off the other man.

'In the *supply*,' qualified Moreton.

'How can that be uncertain?'

'Because we're going to show it to be,' said Moreton simply.

Englehart sat silent, unable to ask the question, and Moreton smiled at him across the desk. 'How much increase has there been in guerrilla activity in South Africa, since the blacks took over Mozambique and Zimbabwe?'

'Quite a lot,' conceded the CIA man.

'Quite a lot,' echoed Moreton. 'They've bombed the oil-from-coal plants and they've sabotaged rail links and they've fomented protest uprisings not just by the blacks, but by the coloureds as well.'

'You're going to speculate that the gold mines are an obvious target?' asked Englehart.

'I'm going to suggest the possibility,' said Moreton. 'And you're going to see that it happens.'

'*Me*!'

'How long have you had people there, watching Collington?'

'About a month.'

'So they're well established?'

Englehart nodded.

'How much infiltration . . . manœuvrable infiltration, do we have in the protest groups?'

'Some,' allowed Englehart.

'Enough, if they were properly guided by your people, to hit the mines?'

'I'd guess they're well guarded.'

'The Sasol plants at Secuna and Sasolberg were well guarded, too. They got those,' snapped Moreton, irritated with the man's objections.

'There had probably been months of planning.'

'Are you telling me we couldn't do better than a bunch of guys living in huts, in the bush!'

Englehart pinched the bridge of his nose, using his hand to conceal any reaction to Moreton's dismissal of guerrillas who probably had degrees from Moscow University equivalent to the man's own.

'What I am saying is that the scope of covert activities has been greatly curtailed since Chile and the mistakes that were made backing some of the regimes in the Caribbean.'

'Are *you* telling *me* what Administration policy is?' demanded Moreton.

'I'm advising caution,' said Englehart.

'And I'm saying that I want an attack on the gold mines controlled by Collington. I want it done so that Hassan will get the point. You understand that?'

'Yes, sir,' said Englehart.

'And I don't want any foul-ups. This isn't going to become an embarrassment, like Chile and the Bay of Pigs. It's to look Communist planned, like everything else. That's why I want you there personally, on top of everything.'

Englehart's stomach churned in turmoil. 'It's not usual for a section head to go out into the field.'

'What we're doing isn't usual,' rejected Moreton. 'We're trying to protect a major source of energy supply to the United States of America. Do you want the authority of the Director on this?'

It wouldn't be much protection, but it would be something, thought Englehart. 'Yes,' he said. 'I do.'

'Don't you go cold on me over this,' said Moreton threateningly.

'I will do my job,' said Englehart, refusing to be frightened.

'Then make sure you do it well,' said Moreton. 'This is an annoying interference and I'm going to get it removed.'

This time it took longer for the confirmation of Moreton's influence to register. It was three hours after he got back to Langley before the co-operation instruction came from Bradley Cowles' office. The demand to go operational again and be involved in field work frightened Englehart more than the thought of losing a pension and the cottage on the Cape, and so he placed a formal request for an interview with the Director. It was refused.

Janet Simpson was pleased at the way her relationship with Hannah was progressing. The girl had tried hard the night of the dinner, even arranging the cosmetic attendance of her separated husband, and at the meetings that followed had shown no resentment at the possibility of Janet becoming her stepmother. Janet was glad Marius had agreed to her being the one to tell Hannah about the wedding. That was the way it should be, woman to woman. Explained properly, Hannah would understand the need for two lonely people to get together, just as Janet understood how impossible it was for someone with Hannah's background to remain with someone like Collington. Janet hadn't pried about the marriage break-up, but Marius hadn't any doubts that it was all over. Play-acting, he called the trial separation. And Janet decided he was right. Certainly at their last meeting, just before Collington went to London, Hannah's feelings against him seemed to have hardened: there had even been an occasion when Janet had thought she was on the point of weeping openly, which had surprised her.

The car pulled into the forecourt of the building where Jan Wassenaar had his lawyer's practice and Janet checked the time from the dashboard clock, over the chauffeur's shoulder. There was still an hour to go before her luncheon appointment with Hannah.

It was thoughtful of Marius to have Wassenaar examine the mine and parent company portfolios, to see what improvements could be made in the holdings. But then it was typical; he loved her, after all.

Chapter Twenty-Five

Collington had allowed two weeks to elapse after the suspension of the gold sale, wanting the approach to come to him from the Saudi embassy in London. When it didn't, he had Wall make contact. Another two weeks passed and still there was no response. Collington tried to curb his frustration, recognising that Hassan was at last behaving as he had expected him to after their initial meeting, delaying to improve his bargaining position, and that it was therefore illogical to become affected by it. There was speculation of an oil price adjustment at the forthcoming OPEC meeting in Vienna and it would have been impossible anyway for them to have discussed an arrangement in detail. Having made himself face that reality Collington extended his objectivity to accept that it wasn't Hassan's delay that was of immediate concern to him.

Collington had wanted to call Hannah a number of times. Once he'd even lifted the telephone and stood uncertainly for several moments with it growling in his hand before replacing it, conscious that he would have nothing to say when Hannah answered. This wasn't a business deal, with each of them attempting some miniscule psychological superiority. He knew he didn't have a position: the approach had to come from her because she was the one who had to make the decision.

It was six weeks precisely from the day of his return from London when Hannah's call came.

'I thought it was time we met,' she declared bluntly.

'When?'

'What are you doing now?'

'Nothing,' he said. He supposed she had the right to make him run, if she wanted.

'Why not tonight then?'

Was her voice as expressionless as before? Collington couldn't be sure. 'If you'd like me to come,' he agreed.

'Yes,' she said. 'I'd like you to.'

There had definitely been a softening that time, Collington decided in retrospect. The daytime traffic had lessened and most of the lights were in his favour, so he made good time to Parkstown. She was waiting for him in the room in which they had played bridge, the night of the dinner with Metzinger. Had she chosen it because it was the place where he'd blurted his affair with Ann?

She was dressed less severely than when they had last met, in a long-skirted cocktail dress, but she didn't come forward to greet him when he entered the room.

'I've been waiting for your call,' he said.

'It wasn't easy to make.'

'I still want to come back,' he said. 'Nothing's changed.'

'There can't have been many times when you've said sorry,' Hannah reflected.

'Do you want me to say it again?'

She didn't answer him directly. 'You hurt me, James,' she said. 'Do you know what I felt like, aware that there's been another woman? Inadequate. Like there was something missing.'

Collington considered the words, wanting to say nothing that would annoy her. 'It wasn't that,' he said. 'Never that.'

She shrugged her shoulders. 'Maybe not,' she said. 'But that's how it made me feel.'

'And now?'

'Don't be naïve, James. You've never really believed I wouldn't take you back.'

'It took you long enough to decide.'

'I said *you* wouldn't doubt it; I didn't say I was so sure.'

'Terms?' he said.

She made an impatient, flicking-away motion with her hand. 'You're not in a boardroom now: you're with your estranged wife trying to patch up a marriage and you don't patch up marriages by imposing conditions and regulations.'

'What is it you want, then?'

'Honesty,' she said, simply. 'Not like the last attempt, when it was too late. If you meet anyone else again, I want to know. I'm not going to be put on trial, compared one to the other. You'll have to make up your mind. And stick with it. I'm not going to go through anything like this again. It's bloody near crucified me and it's going to take me a long time to forget, even though I'm going to try.'

'Are you doing this because you want to? Or because you think it's the way to put Paul back on track?'

'How long do you think he would be fooled by a bullshit arrangement like that?'

'Long enough, if he were only here for the holidays.'

She looked steadily at him and for a long time she didn't speak. Then she said, 'I made all sorts of resolutions. I wasn't going to make any concessions or let you know what it's been like, what it's really been like, and now I'm with you I can't go through with it! I *tried* not to want you. I tried to think myself out of love and to do what Daddy wants and get a divorce and start all over again, but I can't. I'm not doing this for Paul. I'm not doing it for anyone, except myself. For Christ's sake, come back home.'

She stood looking at him, near to tears, and Collington gazed back, momentarily unable to react to what she had said. He had come not knowing what to expect, but certainly it hadn't been this. Not so abruptly, anyway. He moved at last, reaching out for her, and she came to him, buried her head into his chest, the emotion vibrating through her.

'I gave in,' she said, her voice muffled. 'I wanted to make you beg, but in the end I couldn't do it.'

He eased her head back from him so that he could kiss her. 'Thank you,' he said. 'For having me back.'

They made love there, on the floor, entangled in pushed-apart clothing and furniture legs. He rolled on to his back, keeping her on top of him and they collided with a wine table, skidding it into a bureau against the wall. She tensed, tightening around him, and said, 'The servants will come in.'

'I don't care.'

'Let's go upstairs.'

'Not yet.'

'Please.'

'I'm not ready yet.'

'I am!' she said, trying to hold the rise in her voice, and then she fell over him, nibbling at his neck and saying, 'James, oh James' over and over again. They stayed enmeshed, uncaring about discovery. She moved slightly off him to make herself more comfortable and said, 'Don't ever do anything like it again, will you? I thought I'd lost you and I didn't know what the hell I was going to do.'

'I promise,' he said, meaning it.

'I've done nothing for the past four months, except think of us. And do you know what I realised?'

'What?'

'How limited you are.'

He twisted his head to look at her. 'What the hell does that mean?'

'I'm not criticising,' she said hurriedly, feeling out and putting her finger to his lips. 'But think about it. You don't do anything except business. And earn money. Even Daddy's got that stupid museum, but you've got nothing. You don't play golf or sail . . .' She jerked her head towards the pool. 'Or even swim, particularly well.'

'So the affair was a surrogate hobby.'

'I'm not attaching labels to it. But why go on, so hard? Why be there, every morning at eight, if there's nothing for you to do? And if there are so many people to look after things, why don't you get home until eight at night?'

'Habit, I suppose,' he said.

'But you don't *have* to any more. Would Europe be any less efficient or America not work so well, if you didn't keep flying off every five minutes?'

'Probably not,' he admitted.

'You're a marvel, James. A legend. People write about you in magazines and newspapers and millions of people must read it and envy you. But you haven't enjoyed a bit of it, have you?'

She was exaggerating, Collington thought — but not much. He wondered if there had been a similar conversation to this all those years ago, when Walter Simpson had taken to staying longer and longer in England with his first wife and almost lost the company.

'I'll take a long break when Paul gets here.'

'I wasn't talking about a three- or four-week vacation. I was talking about all the time.'

'I'll think about it,' he said.

They finally moved apart and Hannah said, 'Now let's go to bed and do it properly.'

'Wasn't that proper?' he asked. He felt very relaxed and contented to be back with her.

'It was highly improper,' she giggled, as they climbed the circular staircase that went around the edge of the vestibule. 'What do you think Daddy would say if he heard his daughter had got laid beneath the card table?'

Collington laughed with her. 'Probably that you were being raped and what else could you expect, from someone with my background.'

He undressed her and they came together again, unhurriedly this time, enjoying the feel and touch of each other's bodies.

'Daddy will be disappointed when I tell him,' she said, pulling her mouth away from his neck. 'He actually asked me if we were getting back together, after the dinner party.'

Collington had been letting his mind drift. He began to concentrate on what she was saying. How close had the man been to using the information about Ann, Collington wondered.

'They're getting married, he and Janet,' Hannah continued. 'We had lunch a couple of days ago, especially for her to tell me.'

'Have you been seeing a lot of her?'

'Maybe once a week,' said Hannah. 'I quite like her. I think her politics are cock-eyed, like Daddy's, but she's a straightforward lady. I think they'll be very happy.'

Collington didn't reply, his mind still preoccupied with Metzinger's enquiry. It would have been a natural enough question for a father to ask of a daughter going through a separation, but Collington looked for hidden reasons in everything Metzinger did.

'Should I do anything about *my* shares?' she said.

'What shares?'

'I'm not sure, precisely,' said Hannah. 'Janet was very proud about how Daddy is looking after her. She said that upon his advice she was having her mining portfolio adjusted by Jan Wassenaar — giving him the power of attorney, apparently.'

She sensed his physical reaction and pulled away, to look up at him. 'What is it?' she said.

'Nothing,' he said, irritated. 'I don't think there is any reason to worry about your holdings.'

'If you say so,' she accepted immediately.

'And Hannah.'

'What?'

'Don't tell your father yet, about our getting back together.'

'Why ever not?' She propped herself up on her elbow and looked straight at him.

'I just don't want him to know. Not yet.'

She waited for him to say more but when he didn't she said, 'Sometimes I think you and he behave towards each other like a couple of kids.'

'Just don't tell him, for the moment. Please,' said Collington.

'Kids!' she said again, exasperated.

Before he began the enquiry, Collington accepted the possibility of his being over-cautious. He hadn't been cautious enough about Simpson, and for that he considered the investigation justified. But there was further cause, beyond that. His examination of Simpson's holdings — and therefore his widow's inheritance — might have been too late to prevent Metzinger's boardroom coup, but it had been recent enough for Collington to remember the general state of the portfolios. And his recollection was that there was no need for any adjustment, in the mining shares least of all. Since the postponement of the gold sales, they had gone up four points.

He had summoned the files from records by mid-morning, concentrating first upon the mines and then scrutinising every holding that Janet Simpson possessed. And by mid-afternoon had confirmed his original impression. Her portfolios had been meticulously created by her late husband and there wasn't the slightest need for her to do anything but accept the dividends. Certainly there was no need for the sort of movement indicated by going beyond a broker, nor to vest power of attorney in Jan Wassenaar who wasn't, Collington noted from the files in front of him, her normal lawyer anyway.

It was the link between the woman and Wassenaar that intrigued him most of all. They had combined, with Metzinger and de Villiers, to defeat him once before. And they appeared to be combining again. But for what? He went through the Simpson file again and then that of the corporation lawyer, adding and subtracting and re-allocating, trying to hypothesise a share grouping that could be used in some board manœuvre. Finally he abandoned the effort, pushing the folders away. There was nothing, Collington decided; absolutely nothing.

He had been doodling all the while on a jotting pad, isolating words that didn't link. There was Janet Simpson's name and Wassenaar's and lawyer and broker. Around broker he assembled a pattern, festooning it with whorls and curlicues and then he began to concentrate solely upon that word. It didn't fit: it jarred the picture. Why had Janet Simpson bypassed a broker and gone to a lawyer?

It was an impulsive reflection, coming from nothing but instinct, but the more he considered it the more it seemed worthwhile pursuing. He thought of using Geoffrey Wall, but changed his mind, wanting no traceable association with the company.

Instead he used the lawyer whom he had briefed for his separation from Hannah, using the reconciliation as the initial reason for the interview and then supplementing the fee the man would have earned for the abandoned divorce action with a different brief. In three days, with the lawyer acting as nominee for the enquiry, Collington got confirmation of his hunch. Precise figures were difficult, because brokers in Pretoria and Cape Town and Johannesburg were showing the same discretion as the lawyer. But there had been firm indications — two brokers even offering contracts — that approximately 66,000 shares in the SAGOMI parent company and in the mining division were shortly being offered for sale, through a base vendor in Zurich.

Collington went back to his statistics and at first considered there had been a mistake. The combined holdings on the South African exchange of major and subsidiary shares held by Janet Simpson and Wassenaar only came to 46,200. Then he remembered the original power struggle and added Metzinger's South African holdings. The total came to 66,200.

Collington rose from his desk, standing against the office window with its view of the capital. It was unquestionably another manœuvre. But to what purpose? From the figures Collington knew all three were retaining their 'A' and Preferential shares, disposing only of the ordinary ones. And the ordinary holdings were ineffective either at parent board level or in any of the subsidiary mining companies. Their only worth was their monetary value. And at the moment, because they were mining shares, that monetary value was greater than any other that they held. Which made it nonsense to sell. The illogicalities echoed in Collington's head: compared to this, the solving of the mystery of the gold shipment from Amsterdam had been easy. Turning his thoughts outside South Africa, Collington remembered the Zurich vendor and this time his action wasn't dictated by instinct, but by practical business deduction.

No South African broker had been able to provide a date for the disposal, but Collington recognised a time limit of sorts and decided he could not risk going personally either to London or New York. He used the telephone from the Parkstown house, not confident of the security of the SAGOMI switchboard, holding the connection to England and America for over an hour while he painstakingly briefed lawyers to carry out exactly the same investigation there as he had instigated in Pretoria. By the week's end, he had replies from both countries. It was a pointless calculation, but he did the sum anyway, intent upon every last detail. Metzinger's holdings in their publicly quoted parent company and their mining divisions throughout the world amounted to 97,000. Wassenaar had 84,000 shares, and Janet Simpson 72,000. And the total number of shares being offered, on value drop orders in Pretoria, London and New York, was 253,000. Collington didn't need a calculator to make the addition. For two further days he tried to reach anything but the obvious conclusion, but couldn't. It had to be a conspiracy. There was no way he could work out how they intended to achieve it, but clearly the three of them were gambling on a share drop and were mounting a bear operation to sell high and buy back low on a falling market, to make a killing when the value rose again.

The decision to oppose them was automatic. And probably, he thought in passing, illegal. The difficulty was in assessing the gap through which they intended letting the shares drop, so that he could accurately place his automatic purchase orders to intercept them on the way down. A prudent businessman is satisfied with a profit of one per cent. But there was nothing prudent about what the Afrikaners were attempting, so he estimated they were reckoning on a higher return than that. For a long time he played with figures, going as high as ten and coming back as low as one and then accepted there was no way any sort of intelligent assessment could be made: it was as great a gamble as sticking a pin in a race card and picking a 100-to-1 winner. Having thought of ten as his maximum, Collington compromised and determined upon five.

Although he was domiciled predominantly in South Africa, Collington's mind still worked in sterling. On the quoted price of the shares on the three main exchanges, the total value being offered was £9,500,000. In London, Pretoria and New York he placed automatic purchase orders for all SAGOMI and mining division shares that dropped five points below their quotation, all on a ten per cent margin. That meant that if £9,500,000 were offered, he immediately spent £950,000 and then had twenty-eight days to raise the remainder of the purchase price. Through London merchant banks he arranged stand-by credit of £15,000,000 to support his personal fortune, offered against his shareholding in SAGOMI and its other divisions and the property he personally owned in South Africa and London.

On paper, it seemed perfectly simple. But Collington recognised the danger. Other ordinary shareholders might be influenced by what the Afrikaners intended and sell at the same time. And his instructions to the brokers meant he would pick up those shares as well. Collington accepted that he was ridiculously exposed, in a position he would normally have dismissed as insane, even with his tendency to take risks.

Collington used the benefit of the time differences between South Africa and the other countries, and the evening he got authority for his credit arrangements and certificated confirmation of the purchase orders was the first time he had returned to Parkstown before nine.

'I thought we'd talked about your working less,' protested Hannah mildly.

'This is unusual but necessary,' said Collington.

'And I suppose next week there will be something else that's unusual but necessary,' she said.

'I hope not,' said Collington, sincerely.

Brigitte re Jong worked with dogged persistence to get past the middle management barrier to the directors and officials of the gold mining companies who might have some knowledge of government thinking and be able to give an indication of when the gold release would start again. And while she waited for appointments to be confirmed, she toured bullion brokers, ostensibly to buy any few ounzes that might be available but also in the hope of picking up some rumour.

Leonov had established a liaison system with Moscow through Angola, and she learned from that source that they had succeeded in amassing two and a half tonnes in short-term futures from brokers, but at a swingeing premium.

The communication was at a fixed time, so Leonov scheduled meetings with Krotkov immediately afterwards.

'Any news?' demanded the KGB chief, before the other man had closed the door behind him.

'General expectation that there will be a release soon. No one knows the date.'

'Two and a half tonnes to go then?' said Krotkov.

'I can probably bluff, for that amount,' said Leonov. 'I calculate I've got four to five weeks before it becomes critical.'

'Something has to happen in that time,' insisted Krotkov, angrily. 'It's just got to.'

'Yes,' said Leonov, cynically. 'But what?'

In final desperation, Metzinger cabled Ann Talbot in London, demanding that she contact him. He waited four days for the call and when it didn't come decided positively that she was running away. Stupid little bitch. He'd warned her what would happen and he'd meant it. Disclosing the divorce material to Hannah would be the *coup de grâce*, after manipulating Collington's disgrace at the shareholders' meeting. Metzinger was annoyed he couldn't do it at once. But it would be foolish to hurry. He had all the time in the world. Stupid little bitch, he thought again.

Chapter Twenty-Six

Sidney Englehart was a worried man. It would have been an exaggeration to label him a buck-passer, someone who attempted to avoid responsibility; if that had been the case he wouldn't have made section head and run covert operations so successfully for the past three years. Rather he was careful, a Washington professional who knew how important it was to watch his back. The foul-ups before his appointment had helped. Nervous of the inefficiency that was being exposed publicly, there had been an official policy to reduce the number of clandestine activities. Less operations meant less chances of screwing up. Which suited Englehart just fine. So did the edict on things that were sanctioned. They had to be planned meticulously and executed with the same care, the criterion being to abort up to the last moment if success began to look doubtful.

And that was why Englehart was worried. Moreton had short-circuited the system. And if the shit hit the fan Englehart knew he wouldn't just be sprayed: he'd be the fall guy trying to scrub it off the walls with a toothbrush.

The sort of operation upon which Moreton was insisting should have been planned over two months, not weeks. They were fully briefed on the guerrilla organisations, certainly; they had even infiltrated sufficiently to be able to influence the attacks, if the situation arose, as it had now. But that still wasn't enough. A successful sabotage wasn't achieved by planting a stick of dynamite or a wad of plastic in a guy's hand, pointing out the target and catching the early plane home. You had to be sure it was the hand of the right guy — not some loud-mouth high on threats from the safety of his home territory, but weak on follow-through when he was given the chance to prove his macho. You had to plan separate back-up strikes, in case the first one came unglued. You had to carry out independent reconnaissance, keeping your groups and your attacks separate, so that if one were intercepted, the capture of those that followed wasn't automatic. Most of all you had to have protection, to insulate yourself by a chain-link of groups and cells from the men who did the job, so that the finger pointed a different way if it went wrong. And having set everything up and guaranteed it was perfect, you had to do it all over again, just to make one hundred and one per cent sure.

Moreton's superman routine meant that Englehart had been unable to do almost any of that. He took extra operatives with him to Pretoria and withdrew some of the men who were already there watching Collington, because they knew what the industrialist was doing and there wasn't much point in continuing such close surveillance. He drafted black CIA operatives into Angola, Namibia, Zimbabwe and Mozambique to make links with the African National Congress and SWAPO guerrillas, and he also brought blacks to South Africa to liaise between the guerrillas across the borders and those who had, over the years, established themselves in the mines. Then he waited until they were activated.

Considering the limited time available, the mobilisation was comparatively trouble-free, the only real difficulties being the communications between himself in Pretoria and his people in the countries to the north, and the uncertainty that came from not being able to test the people who were going to carry out the sabotage.

The ease with which they established themselves did little to reassure him. Because there was a deeper concern, greater than the uncertainty created by Moreton's ridiculous insistence upon speed. The extent of the sabotage being demanded by the Treasury Secretary meant that people would die. And that alarmed Englehart, more than anything else. Because never before, in anything he had initiated or participated in, had Englehart been responsible for taking a human life. And he didn't want to start here, on some half-assed idea.

The chance of reducing the casualties occurred to him two days after he arrived in Pretoria and was attempting to brief himself, as fully as possible in the time available, about gold mining. He learned that some of the workings in Witwatersrand were as deep as 3500 metres, and that the rock temperature, at that depth, could be as high as 54 degrees centigrade, so that to make it humanly bearable there had to be extensive refrigeration.

It was standard procedure for the covert section head to be fully informed of the technical and scientific developments made at Langley and on the fourth day of the operation there arrived at Johannesburg airport from Washington a container supposed, according to the manifest, to contain light engineering equipment. Englehart retrieved it without difficulty and by that evening the contents were being distributed throughout the guerrilla groups. It was basically dynamite, but within the tube that housed it there was also a detonator. It was operated electrically by a minute battery containing just sufficient energy to explode it. The contact wires were held one millimetre apart by gelatine wax. The bomb went off when the wax melted and the wires touched.

The OPEC conference in Vienna was scheduled to last three days and Moreton's meeting with Prince Hassan was arranged for the day after it ended. Knowing how important it was to the Treasury Secretary that the sabotage coincided with his encounter with Hassan, Englehart timed his emplacements from the opening of the oil producers' gathering. By the time of the final communiqué, when oil was pegged at the price that had held for the previous three months but was threatening to rise at their next meeting, Englehart reckoned that throughout the five SAGOMI mines in the Witwatersrand he had twenty bombs planted. They had issued sixty, but Englehart was a realist and calculated that two-thirds would have been thrown away or hidden long before their carriers reached the minehead, either through last minute fear of detection or because they had agreed to be saboteurs only as long as it took them to be handed the bribery money.

Englehart telephoned Moreton before he left Paris for the meeting with the Saudi prince, frowning at the artificiality of the enthusiasm which Moreton managed to project.

'Everything OK?' demanded Moreton.

'As good as it will ever be.'

'What's the matter?' demanded Moreton, detecting the reserve in the CIA man's voice.

'It's been too rushed. Panicked almost.'

'I asked for a demonstration,' said Moreton. 'Not a replay of Hiroshima.'

'There've been too many corners cut,' insisted Englehart. 'I don't like cutting corners.'

'There's nothing wrong with that, once in a while,' said Moreton glibly.

'The last time I tried it, I got a ticket for traffic violation,' said Englehart.

Uninvited, Wassenaar helped himself to more brandy for the third time and Metzinger frowned across at his friend, concerned at his obvious nervousness.

'I didn't expect we would have to wait this long,' said the corporation lawyer. 'I thought it would be over, short and sharp, just like that.' He brought the heel of his right hand into the palm of his left, in a chopping motion.

'It's taking longer than I expected,' admitted Metzinger. 'We'll just have to be patient. The length of time doesn't alter anything.'

'The shares have been exposed for a long time,' protested Wassenaar. 'Maybe too long.'

'We've taken a position and we'll have to stand with it,' said Metzinger. 'It would be ridiculous to change course now. As soon as Collington gets something in writing from the Arab, we can leak the disclosure and the rest is inevitable.'

'It's got to happen soon,' insisted Wassenaar. 'If there isn't anything within the next week or two, then I'm going to cancel my sell orders. You can go on with the risk if you want to, but I'm getting out.'

'It could cost you a lot of money,' said Metzinger.

'It would be worth it, for peace of mind,' said Wassenaar.

Chapter Twenty-Seven

The oil-producing countries which form OPEC had taken their predictable positions at the Vienna meeting, the extremists led by Nigeria and Libya insisting upon higher barrel prices and the moderates, fronted by Prince Hassan, arguing that any increase would be self defeating, heightening in the West the inflation which devalued the money they were paid for their oil in the first place. Hassan won, the victory only slightly marred by the face-saving compromise in the communiqué stating that charges were likely to rise after their next gathering. The debate and its outcome were closely monitored by the IMF meeting in Paris, and Henry Moreton left the conference for Austria with the unofficial authority to thank the Saudi prince for what he had done.

As he had been among fellow Muslims, Hassan had worn robes, and he maintained the dress for his appointment with the American Treasury Secretary. Initially it was a formal grouping, Hassan sitting with his deputy and the director of their oil development corporation and Moreton accompanied by the American ambassador to Austria and the US trade attaché. The speeches were as governed as the arrangement. Moreton expressed the gratitude of the Western nations for Hassan's control, to which the Arab sat nodding in ready acceptance. Then Hassan delivered the stereotyped speech about the need for the oil-consuming nations to control inflation, the need for which Moreton readily acknowledged. There was red tea and assurances of continued friendship.

The private unrecorded meeting was planned for the afternoon and both men relaxed visibly as their officials and secretaries withdrew, leaving them alone.

'I appreciated your earlier remarks,' said Hassan.

'They were sincerely meant,' said Moreton.

'But I cannot guarantee the control forever. It might even be impossible at the next conference, in three months' time. Our revenues are being constantly eroded,' Hassan replied.

Moreton controlled any expression of satisfaction at the direction the conversation was taking. 'That surely isn't the case in recent months,' he said gently. 'The dollar has hardened constantly.'

'Only in recent months,' qualified Hassan. 'Before that time the pricing of oil in United States currency was detrimental to every OPEC producer. And could be again, if its value were to drop.'

'I come to you as a friend and give an assurance as a friend,' said Moreton. 'There is no likelihood of that happening, according to every estimate and expectation we have. There will probably be fluctuations, but not through more than one or two points. At the Treasury we have created a base of solid stability.'

'Upon gold,' said Hassan abruptly.

Moreton was momentarily silenced by the directness. Was Hassan just showing off his fiscal awareness or trying to make some other point? Fiscal awareness, decided Moreton; he supposed the Arab's mind would be preoccupied with gold, after Collington's approach.

'There was a surprising miscalculation of our reserve,' said Moreton, advancing the official explanation.

'Many countries must envy such a mistake. And your good fortune,' said Hassan.

Moreton decided it was going to be easier for him to make the point than he had expected. 'It is one from which we expect to continue to benefit,' he said.

'I don't understand,' said Hassan, taking the bait.

'It is not unknown to you that our State Department is staffed by political analysts whose function it is constantly to forecast ahead, so that my country may attempt to anticipate events and reduce the possibility of being affected by any sudden change.'

Hassan's forehead creased slightly at Moreton's pedantic, almost patronising delivery.

'There are only two sources of gold. South Africa. And the Soviet Union. Certainly Australia is a producer, but not on a level sufficient to meet world demand if any difficulty arose with the other two suppliers.'

'Do your analysts predict difficulties?' demanded Hassan.

Moreton shrugged, a man speaking generalities rather than

specifics. He was sure that the deal with Russia put him in strong control of the situation. 'The Soviet Union will always remain an uncertainty,' he said. 'But statistics show that during the last year, far less was offered on the open market than at any other time.'

'Which is why, surely, the world looks to South Africa for a guarantee of its supply?'

'But what does it see, when it looks?' said Moreton. 'South Africa is a country surrounded by hostile neighbours, ostracised by many countries and riven by internal dissent because of its policies.'

'I am *aware* of the international situation,' said Hassan, discomforted by Moreton's tendency to lecture. 'And it is by no means a new situation.'

'Not new,' accepted Moreton. 'But worsening dramatically.'

'Are you predicting a serious interruption of South African gold production?'

Moreton avoided the question. 'South Africa is more advanced than any other country in the world in the process of extracting oil from coal,' he said. 'Their Sasol plants are accorded the highest security classification because they are so vital to the economy of the country . . . .'

'Yet despite that protection, they were successfully attacked by terrorists,' said Hassan, anticipating the point.

'There has long been a belief in South Africa that no cohesive opposition could ever be mounted against apartheid because of the tribalism of the people, splitting them into too many rival, squabbling groups. But the opinion in my country is that such a belief is no longer valid. We think the African nationalist parties are becoming better organised and that South Africa's difficulties are going to become more severe.'

Hassan stretched back in his seat. 'We seem to have digressed into quite a detailed discussion about the political future of South Africa,' he said.

'Because it is relevant to what we were discussing earlier,' insisted Moreton. 'I talked about it being a situation from which the United States will automatically benefit. We *have* a gold reserve. And are known to have it. The dollar went up through eight points when South Africa suspended its gold sales. Were there to be a serious cutback, I would expect it to treble that jump. And not drop appreciably, either.'

'Are you expecting a cutback?' pressed Hassan.

Moreton made a helpless, open-handed gesture. 'I'm talking in the most general terms,' he insisted. 'But I think it could be the logical, sensible conclusion to be drawn from what is happening in South Africa at the moment . . . .' He paused, as if a thought had just occurred to him. 'And our logical benefit from the dollar strength would be that of the oil producers too, wouldn't it? United States currency would remain the best pricing and payment, for your crude.'

'Is this an informal discussion?' said Hassan, determined to clarify the terms in which they were speaking.

'Absolutely,' assured Moreton. 'A conversation between friends, on subjects that might be of mutual interest.'

'I appreciate the trouble to which you have gone, travelling from Paris to make it possible,' said Hassan.

'The journey from Paris was to express gratitude, from myself and others,' said Moreton. It had been a convenient development, providing an understandable reason for the meeting.

'It is good to know that there is such friendship between our two countries,' said Hassan.

'It's our hope that it will continue for a long time.'

The principle of refrigeration is to compress Freon gas until it liquefies and then direct that liquid through an evaporator. The act of evaporation creates the coldness, reducing the liquid to gas again, to be recycled through the system. For the compression to work, the circuit has to remain sealed.

Observing another law of covert operations, Englehart segregated those who planted the explosives from those whom he intended to activate them.

Calculating the time difference between Austria and South Africa, Englehart realised he would have to act during the evening shifts at all the mines. In some he was better placed than others. In Witwatersrand One he had seven clandestine members of the African National Congress and in Witwatersrand Five there was a fanatical group of six. In both Witwatersrand Two and Four he was sure of four guerrillas, but in mine Three there was only one man.

Their instructions were identical and simple. Four hours after the commencement of the shift, they had to puncture in as many places and at as many levels as possible the refrigeration lines, taking care that they holed the return section, carrying the gas that had to escape, and not the supply line, where the gas would have converted to liquid. The back-up, emergency installations had to be attacked in the same way, making it impossible for the managers to control the temperature for at least an hour.

Witwatersrand Three was the first to go and ironically, with only one man to activate the explosives, the effect was the most dramatic. The man succeeded in damaging the first and secondary systems on the second level, where the earlier saboteurs had managed to secrete three sticks of explosive. The temperature began to rise after fifteen minutes and before the hour was up the night manager realised there was a crisis and sounded the evacuation order. As a precaution he took all the workers from the third, lower level which was fortunate, because when the bombs went off they shattered a reinforced section of number two shaft where the SAGOMI geologists had earlier predicted a river course. The entire second level and part of the third were flooded and but for the manager's caution, the death toll would unquestionably have been high. As it was, not one man died. As soon as the flood alarm sounded, the upper section was cleared and the pumps activated automatically.

Predictably, the refrigeration was damaged most badly at Witwatersrand One. It malfunctioned on all three levels and once again, as Englehart had calculated, the mines were cleared of workers in advance of the explosions.

Witwatersrand Five suffered from the fanaticism of the group there. They concentrated too long upon the first system and when they moved on to the emergency back-up in three places they holed the liquid rather than the gas supply. Damage on the second and third levels was minimal, but on the top section the roof was brought down over a distance of fifty yards.

Overall, the most extensive damage was at Witwatersrand Two. There was dynamite at all levels and the refrigeration was destroyed throughout the mine. There were roof-falls and wall cave-in on levels two and three and on the upper section the sticks had been wedged beneath the cart lines, so that the whole supply equipment was wrecked.

Witwatersrand Four was damaged least of all. The guerrillas there were only able to affect the refrigeration on the lower level. And there was only one stick of explosive. It ripped up a section of tracking and caused a minor roof-fall, but the most serious damage was to the cooling equipment itself.

The explosions, which began in mine Three, progressed like a linked firecracker through the SAGOMI mines, all happening within the space of an hour. An incredible statistic, from which only Englehart was to derive any satisfaction, was that because of the way he chose to make the detonations, a total workforce of over 5500 men was cleared from the mines before the explosions, and in the final count only two men died and eighteen were injured.

It was midnight when Collington's telephone rang.

Chapter Twenty-Eight

Collington was alerted immediately and automatically about any emergency. He was already on his way to the airstrip, responding to the alert about Witwatersrand Three, when the second call came about mine One. By the time he got to the company helicopter there was news of Five and Two and before they received control tower clearance, the pattern was complete, with the explosion at Four.

'What the hell is this, a war?' demanded the pilot.

Collington was in the co-pilot's seat so that he could fly connected to the earphones and receive the latest bulletins. He didn't respond to the pilot, instead gazing down at the necklace of lights around the capital and the velvet blackness of the veld beyond. It couldn't be this! He was prepared to believe almost anything about Metzinger. But he could not conceive that the Afrikaner had in some way arranged with Wassenaar and Janet Simpson the simultaneous bombing of the company's five mines, in order to affect the share balance. The Afrikaners might be determined to upset control of the company, but it was preposterous to consider them capable of something like this: this was elaborate, co-ordinated sabotage, something beyond their ability and resources. So what in God's name had happened? It didn't make sense, any of it. There was only one thing of which he was certain and the knowledge frightened him. The share fluctuation was going to be far more dramatic than he had ever calculated. The mine holdings were vast, extending beyond gold: there was coal and copper and uranium and diamonds and all of them would be affected by an attack like this. There were four thousand issued shares in gold alone, spread in pockets of varying sizes amongst small investors who would hear the news of the bombing on their morning radios and, by the time the market opened, would be sitting by their telephones, waiting to see what would happen.

And Collington knew what would happen. Across the board, in all their mining divisions, there would be a shiver of nervousness. The first effects would be felt upon the shares of the parent company. The moment the SAGOMI shares dropped, the mood would spread to the separate companies. The quickest and severest dip, inevitably, would be in the gold. It would go below five. Collington had prepared himself to pick up the 253,000 combined holdings of Metzinger, Janet Simpson and Wassenaar. But not the thousands of others that would be offloaded in those first hours of panic.

By complete and utter accident, by placing automatic purchase orders at five points below market par, Collington had assembled the most effective barrier against the sort of panic that would arise from the disaster towards which he was flying. The value *couldn't* drop below five. Because he was buying at that valuation. In a day or two, a week at most, the market confidence from his buying would bring the strength back to the shares. It was an impossible assessment to make so soon, but Collington calculated that by then he would have exhausted his personal commitment of £4,000,000 and probably drawn upon the majority of his £15,000,000 stand-by credit. And if he spent a total of £19,000,000 on ten per cent margin purchases, that meant that within twenty-eight days he would be required to pay out a further£171,000,000 to settle his brokerage orders in full.

Which he didn't have. Nor did he have any way of raising that amount without the support of the company. And he couldn't seek company backing until he had clarified the involvement of Metzinger, Wassenaar and Janet Simpson. There was an escape, Collington recognised. He could be ready, when the brokerage offices opened. And withdraw the buy orders. He would not be able to cover them all before the trading began, but he could minimise his losses.

But if he did that, the block would be removed from the selling. Millions would be wiped off the value of the companies. And the Afrikaners would succeed in their coup.

So what was he going to do? Gamble? Or run? It wasn't a question, Collington thought at once — not one that he had to consider, anyway. He'd gamble on being able to beat them, in a twenty-eight-day time limit. And if he failed, he'd go bankrupt.

He'd aimed high, all his life. To go broke for £171,000,000 was high enough.

The radio crackled, blurred by static, and Collington tensed forward. He had demanded the information before they had taken off and smiled in fleeting relief when it was relayed. No one had been killed at either Witwatersrand Three or One and only eight of the injuries were regarded as serious. As the machine was putting down at Three, Collington heard of the first death at mine Two, but that hadn't resulted directly from any blast: an elderly timekeeper had suffered a heart attack and died.

There was pandemonium at Witwatersrand Three. Six hundred men had been brought up safely from the mine and were milling aimlessly around the shaft-head. The alarm siren had echoed through the black settlements where the workers lived. Wives and relatives of those on the shift were flooding in, imagining their men trapped below, and the off-duty miners came as well, some out of curiosity and others to help with any rescue attempts. There were rumours that there were some people still trapped below and the women who couldn't immediately locate their men began to panic and scream, setting up the ululating African wail of grief. Only immediately around the shaft entrance was there a cleared area, a radius of little more than twenty yards created by a linked-arm cordon of South African security police.

Collington clawed his way forward, pushing and thrusting people aside. At the police barrier, an officer threw his arm across Collington's chest and just as roughly Collington swept it aside, shouting his identity into the man's face and demanding to see the officer in charge. The man went for his baton and Collington shouted his name again, then that of the company. He would probably have been clubbed down in the confusion, but for the nearness of the superintendent. The man nodded and led him through and Collington hurried across the floodlit area, squinting at the brightness towards the knot of mine officials.

There he was recognised at once. The local manager identified himself as a man called Jorgensen and introduced the mine engineer as Becker. It was obvious both men had just come up. They were still wearing their lamp helmets. Their protective clothing was mud-slimed and soaked, clinging to their bodies.

'How bad?' shouted Collington.

'Bad enough,' said Becker. 'The river's breached on the middle level. Water's maybe four feet deep and would be deeper if it weren't going down into the third section.'

'What about the pumps?'

'They'll be able to reduce it, but not appreciably. And it'll only need one or two pump failures for us to fall behind. We'll have to seal off the river.'

'How long?'

Collington thought the man was going to swear at him for the stupidity of the question. There was a visible tightening of Becker's mouth as he controlled himself. He said: 'I've got four teams working down there now. It's impossible to give an estimate. There's God knows how many thousands of gallons to be pumped out, even if we dam the river.'

'Is it true the other mines have been attacked?' Jorgensen demanded of Collington.

'Every one,' confirmed Collington. 'All within an hour of the first explosion here.'

The superintendent who had allowed Collington to enter the closed-off area had joined the group. 'Goddamned Communists,' he said, as Collington confirmed the extent of the damage.

'What proof have we here?' demanded Collington, turning to the man.

The security officer looked back at him in apparent bewilderment. 'Who else could organise something as widespread as this, apart from one of the black organisations?'

'It was definitely planned explosions, down here anyway,' said Becker.

'I'm going to the other sites,' Collington said to the man. 'I know it won't be easy and I know I'm asking a lot, but I want as complete a report as possible by midday tomorrow on the extent of the damage, the length of time it is going to take to make the necessary repairs and how long it will be before we can begin even partial production.'

Because he knew that every one of their mines had been sabotaged and that there was no point in maintaining a sequence, Collington ordered that they fly to the nearest, in a direct line. That was Witwatersrand Five and it proved a fortunate choice, because it was one of the least damaged. Control was better there, the crowd cordoned back not just from the mine-head but to the sides as well, so that a roadway had been formed. The engineer was a man called Robertson and the manager someone named Walton or Wilton, which Collington didn't even attempt to clarify in his impatience.

'We seem to be luckier than most,' said Robertson. He lifted his hand and Collington saw he was carrying a short-wave radio; he guessed contact had been established between all the mines by now.

'What is it?' he said.

'A few rock-falls, on the second or third. Maybe two or three days to clear and check the cart-tracking,' reported Robertson. 'Worst damage at number one. The tunnel is completely blocked here and we don't know yet how far it goes back.'

'I want to go down,' said Collington.

The manager shouted towards the time-keeper's hut and a lamp helmet and cover-alls were hurried out and handed to Collington with a grin of embarrassment. They were much too small for him, ending a good foot and a half above his ankles and cutting into his groin.

'Let's go,' said Collington, careless of his appearance.

The main electricity supply had been cut, as a precautionary measure against fire, and the cage was lowered by an emergency generator. Collington was almost immediately conscious of the heat and turned to Robertson. 'What's happened to the refrigeration?' he asked.

'That was sabotaged, too.'

'By the explosion?'

'No,' said the engineer. 'Something else.'

The cage came to a lurching halt and they emerged on the first level. Temporary, battery-powered illumination had been strung along the shaft, giving an incongruous appearance of party lighting. Although it was three hours since the explosion, dust was still swirling in the air, catching the back of Collington's throat and forcing him to swallow. As he approached the men already working at the main blockage, he saw several were wearing breathing apparatus.

'Here,' said Robertson.

Collington went towards the equipment against which the man

was standing, straining up to see what he was pointing at. Then he saw the punctures in the gas return pipes.

'Looks like a pick edge. Or a spike of some sort,' said Robertson. 'And look here.'

Collington followed the man to the emergency system and saw the stains where the suddenly released liquid had spurted out at the sudden moment of release.

'What's it mean?' he demanded.

'It would have made us inoperative,' said Robertson. 'We'd have been unworkable until we repaired it. But it wouldn't have been as prolonged as the sort of shutdown the explosions will have caused.'

'Could they be independent acts?' asked Collington.

'Unlikely, don't you think?' said Robertson. 'This looks very organised to me. Not haphazard. And they've found the same thing at Two and at One. There's a connection, but I can't think what it is.'

Robertson moved away for a muttered conversation with the men attempting to clear the main blockage and then returned, shaking his head. 'Still no idea how far it goes back,' he said.

'What are the other two levels like?'

'Much better, like I said,' reminded Robertson. 'I've got men working on both of them. I reckon we could clear both sections to get some sort of production moving within twenty-four hours. It'll probably be more difficult to repair the refrigeration.'

'They did it on every level?' said Collington.

'Always the same,' confirmed Robertson. 'Something sharp, driven into the pipe so that we lost compression and the gas leaked out.'

They were winched slowly and in darkness, apart from the narrow beam from their helmet lamps, back up to the surface. The heat and the extra layer of clothing had soaked Collington with sweat, so that his clothes hung about him as wetly as they had upon the officials at the first mine. The manager had obtained a car from somewhere, so Collington did not have to walk back to where the helicopter was waiting, its rotor arms hanging like the limp wings of some insect. As soon as he got into the cabin, the pilot gave him an updated report of the damage. Collington decided to visit Witwatersrand Two next.

By the time he arrived, a plan had already been thumb-tacked to a blackboard set up at the shaft-head, to brief the damage experts before they descended. The manager stood, pointer in hand, tracing it through the cross-section illustration of the mine, indicating the destruction they had so far discovered on each working.

'How long to get the first level back into production?' demanded Collington, at the end. 'It only seems to be tracking.'

'It's *all* the tracking,' said the man. 'And all the drive motors. The refrigeration is shattered. I'd say a fortnight, working non-stop.'

Collington frowned at the pessimism. 'What about the rest?'

'Longer,' said the man. 'Much longer. Three months, I'd say.'

Collington's depression increased when he got a similar estimate from the engineer at mine One. He asked if he could make a personal inspection again and the man shook his head, doubtfully. 'No problem on the first, because nothing happened there, except to the refrigeration. On the second level we've counted at least eight roof-falls and it's still dropping, at the slightest disturbance. Third level is incredible: there's hardly a recognisable shaft visible.'

Because the damage was slightest at Four, they remained there for the briefest period of time, just long enough for Collington to gauge a production resumption date and confirm that the greatest difficulty would be cooling the mine.

Dawn broke as the helicopter lifted off and set course for Pretoria, a great orange and peach blush spreading over the skyline and warming through the veld below, changing the blacks and browns into ochres and yellows. A family of sedate giraffe skittered nervously as the sound of the helicopter reached them; and a herd of elephant prepared themselves for the heat of the day in a dust bowl, scattering the red earth over their backs with their trunks.

Collington returned to the cabin, taking a clipboard from a side pocket and strapping it to his thigh, so he could make his assessment while they flew. Witwatersrand One and Two were probably the worst, with Three submerged in an unknown quantity of floodwater and therefore not much better. Five was quite good and Four could be back in production within a week, if they could rush the refrigeration equipment through.

Collington arrived back in Pretoria gritty-eyed through lack of sleep, his face stubbled by beard. His suit was mud-caked and concertinaed by dried perspiration at every fold and crease, but he decided against wasting time at Parkstown. Instead he went straight from the airstrip to the SAGOMI building. There was a still, expectant mood throughout the building; people were gathered together in gossiping groups, seeking either sensation or reassurance.

Collington thrust into his set of offices, shouting for Geoffrey Wall to follow him. The American was in step almost immediately, and they entered Collington's private suite one behind the other.

'OK,' said Collington. 'How bad is it?'

'Something like an avalanche, when trading started,' said his personal assistant. 'It's amazingly difficult, trying to read a pattern. It steadied at six, immediately lifted to five, and there it's stayed for the past hour. Currently we're four below last night's market par, on both SAGOMI and the mines.'

Collington sank gratefully into his chair, leaning forward to cup his head in his hands. He was too weary to make the conversion himself, so he said: 'Tell me, in sterling, the total value of the shares that were offered for trading.'

There was a moment's quiet while the man made a calculation and then he said, still cautious, 'It'll be an estimate, you understand.'

'That's all I want,' said Collington.

'I guess about £120,000,000.'

Not as bad as he had calculated, but it was going to be a lot of money to raise in a short time.

'All the directors, apart from Mr Jenkins, have come in,' said Wall. 'They want an immediate meeting.'

'I bet they do,' said Collington.

'Sensational,' said Moreton, his enthusiasm echoing down the telephone line. 'Absolutely sensational. I'm going to recommend a commendation to the Director personally. Absolutely sensational.'

'Thank you, sir,' said Englehart. Objectively he supposed only two dead was something approaching the miraculous, but he still felt it was too many.

'It'll make the point to Hassan,' said the Treasury Secretary, and

Englehart winced at his carelessness on an open telephone line.

'I'm wrapping the whole operation up,' he said. 'I want to get the people out as soon as possible, even though things have gone so well.'

'No!' said Moreton, at once.

Englehart felt a wash of helplessness sweep over him. 'Why not?' he said.

'Be wrong to get out too soon,' said Moreton. 'This is going too well to leave it. Just stay where you are. Enjoy yourselves. We'll talk about it again in a few days.'

In a few days, thought Englehart, Moreton would be safe in the comfort of Washington. And he'd be here with his neck on the fucking block, five thousand miles from home. And five thousand miles from the clapboard house at Cape Cod and the retirement pension.

Brigitte re Jong had been finding sleep increasingly difficult and so she had taken to listening to the earliest newscasts. It was there that she heard the first flash about the mine explosions, driving away any chance of rest for the remainder of the early morning. She got out of bed and lit a cigarette and sat with it smouldering in her hand, considering the implications. Speculators and investors and bullion dealers and everyone else who wanted to get in on the act would link the South African suspension to their expectation of an attack that had materialised. There would be an automatic assumption of a gold starvation and the price was going to be uncontainable.

By midday, she was proved right. At noon the quoted price for an ounze of gold was $1300.

It was ironical that it was the very day she had arranged to visit SAGOMI.

Chapter Twenty-Nine

While Wall assembled the staff he wanted, Collington went up to the penthouse to clean himself up. He shaved and then showered, remaining under the water for a long time to try to drive the fatigue from his body, face against the jets as he went through the instructions he had just issued and attempted to think of anything he might have overlooked. He had transferred most of his clothes back to Parkstown, so he descended to the working level wearing jeans and a bush-shirt. Everyone was waiting and Collington saw gratefully that Wall had remembered coffee. He poured it black and sat with a cup between his hands, staring out at them over the desk. The first priority was public confidence and share stability, and the quickest way to achieve that was through the media.

He had rehearsed the statement in the returning helicopter and again under the shower. He went through it generally with the public relations director and then dictated it to one of the waiting secretaries. He purposely chose not to begin with the mines. Instead he set out the scope of SAGOMI holdings, emphasising the mining shares only as a fraction of its overall wealth. Having established that they were big enough to suffer the setback, he described the damage and then added to the release the time that he would personally give a press conference, to go into greater detail.

He ordered Wall to liaise with the engineers on the five sites and then have the helicopter collect the reports he had demanded, to be back with them in Pretoria before he met the press. He told their communications division he wanted open telephone lines as well as telex maintained between London and New York so they could constantly monitor the share movement, and he entrusted Wall with the task within the country. As he finished, the message came from London that Richard Jenkins was already on his way but would not arrive until the next day.

Collington had agreed to hold the board meeting at noon. They were all there when he entered the room. No one was sitting and

Metzinger started forward, towards him. He was pebble-eyed, his face flushed, and Collington decided he had never seen the man so out of control before, not even when Simpson had defeated him for boardroom control.

'Why weren't we alerted, when it happened?' demanded Metzinger. 'I learned about it first from the radio. And then when someone from the Rand *Daily Mail* telephoned me for a comment!'

Wassenaar had moved with the deputy chairman. He had a better hold on himself, but his nervousness was obvious too. 'When I tried to get into your office this morning I was told you were in conference. It's monstrous to treat fellow directors like that!'

Collington stood gazing between the two men, trying to make a judgment. There would have to be an act, if they were in any way involved. But it would have been of concern, not outrage. On his way to Witwatersrand Three, when his mind had been fresher, he had decided Metzinger wouldn't go as far as this, Collington remembered. Could they have been caught out, intending some other sort of market play? It was the obvious conclusion from their behaviour. Whatever the answer, it would be premature for him to make any challenge.

'I was not being discourteous,' said Collington, purposely keeping his voice even to contrast with the excitability of the other two men. 'There were things I considered more important, to regain stability . . . .' He looked beyond Metzinger and Wassenaar. 'Shall we sit down?' he invited.

For a moment Collington thought Metzinger and Wassenaar were going to remain where they were, blocking his further progress into the boardroom, but they moved backwards, towards their usual seats.

'The market movement has been enormous,' said Metzinger, at once.

'Which is why stability was the first importance,' repeated Collington. He had got an update from Wall, moments before entering the room, keeping the value in sterling. 'Up to half an hour ago, £122,000,000 had been offered for trading.'

'Good God!' said de Villiers, always impressed by figures.

'But it hasn't been a protracted slide,' said Platt, who had waited in the tape-room. 'There was only one concerted fall below six. That was the greatest volume, I'll concede. But then it steadied at five with a spread of buying. My view is that the heat has gone out of the trading. In London, for the past hour, we've only been two below market par, which is astonishing.

'How bad is it?' demanded Jamieson.

'Bad enough,' said Collington. He had brought into the boardroom the clipboard notes he had made in the helicopter. Referring to them, he set out the damage and repair estimates to each mine, going into far greater detail than he had done in the press release. Everyone in the room was grave-faced by the time he finished.

'Terrible,' said Metzinger, shaking his head. 'An absolute disaster.'

'No it's not,' said Collington, allowing his irritation at the other man's exaggeration to show. 'I've said it's all repairable, in three months at the outside. It could have been far worse.'

'Only the South African mines,' mused Jamieson. 'The one in Zimbabwe left untouched.'

'In a black-controlled country,' said Wassenaar, impatient at the other man's inability to understand. 'They've no reason to prove their strength there, have they?'

'No doubt about it being Communist guerrillas,' said Metzinger, and Collington looked at the man closely, looking for the unease he would have expected had Metzinger had positive knowledge of the cause. The attitude wasn't there.

'That was the provisional assessment,' he said. 'I'm having more detailed reports brought in this afternoon, before the press conference starts.'

'What press conference?' asked de Villiers.

'I'm giving a press conference, at four.'

'Shouldn't that have been a board decision?' persisted the accountant.

'It should,' conceded Collington. 'I'll repeat what I've already said. The primary consideration now is confidence and stability. That's why, without over-elaborating, I've set out the damage in the first release. And why I'm not going to try to avoid the press. We're going to suffer far more from rumour and innuendo than we are from honesty. We've gained a lot, from the buying that has matched the selling. We've got to build on that confidence.'

'I agree,' said Platt and Brooking entered the discussion for the first time and said, 'So do I. It's the obvious thing to do.'

Collington looked at the Englishman, fleetingly surprised by his definite opinion.

'It would seem that the action of the chairman has done much to avoid this being the disaster it could have been,' said Jamieson, reinforcing the other two.

If only they knew how much, thought Collington. From Wall's latest figures, he had already spent £12,200,000. The brokers would be getting nervous soon, demanding he increase his maintenance margins. Collington didn't think he would be able to raise merchant bank loans to give him extra liquidity at under eighteen per cent.

'If we need a formal vote of approval for the conference, then I propose it,' said Brooking, continuing his unaccustomed outspokeness.

'Seconded,' said Platt.

It had been a meaningless objection, with even de Villiers giving his approval when it was put to a formal acceptance.

'I have another proposal,' said Collington, once the vote had been recorded. 'The statement I have already issued is purposely slanted to show the overall strength of the group. At the annual shareholders' meeting, a month from now, we were due to announce our dividend payments in SAGOMI shares. I propose we go into reserves and declare a dividend of twenty-five per cent, at once.'

Platt let the air out noisily from between his teeth. 'That's a gambler's throw,' he said.

'No it's not,' Collington immediately challenged. 'Although if you want to make the analogy, it's the throw of a gambler who holds all the cards. We've got the money, in reserve. And overall we *are* strong. We could sustain a complete closedown of the gold mine for *six* months, and it wouldn't affect the group by more than about a half per cent. The only point of the dividend would be to provide practical proof of what we are saying.'

'How much would a twenty-five per cent dividend cost?' said de Villiers.

'Twenty-five million Rand,' said Collington, his argument prepared.

De Villiers looked up at him, frowning. 'That's a lot of money,' he said. 'Too much.'

'It could backfire,' said Metzinger, coming out in predictable opposition. 'What if the markets interpret it differently, as *being* a bluff?'

'I don't think that's likely,' said Collington.

'It's a possibility,' disputed Wassenaar. 'I don't think the risk is justified.'

'I think it's an intriguing idea,' said Platt. 'But I still think there's an element of gamble about it. It could be misinterpreted.'

Platt was against him, assessed Collington. And Jenkins' departure from London had been too hurried for there to be any proxy allocation. So he couldn't go to a vote.

'I simply offered it for consideration,' he said, in unusual acquiescence. Tiredness was pulling at him, so that he kept stretching his face to prevent his eyes from closing. He would have to go upstairs to sleep soon, if he were to perform properly at the press conference.

Seizing the retreat, Metzinger said, 'Do you wish a vote?'

Collington shook his head wearily. 'It was a proposal offered for discussion, nothing more,' he repeated. 'I do formally propose, however, that we meet again tomorrow. Jenkins is arriving from London and in another twenty-four hours there might be a better picture from the engineers' reports.'

'Seconded,' said Brooking, knowing the agreement would be a formality.

After the drama throughout the night, Collington thought there was a strange anti-climax about this meeting with the directors. He hadn't known what to expect when he entered the room, but definitely something different from this. But how could it have been different? he asked himself objectively. It was the most preliminary of meetings, to pass on the most preliminary information. If there were to have been something out of the ordinary, then it should have come from Metzinger and Wassenaar. There *was* an attitude but it wasn't one of guilty awareness; it was of concern, going far beyond that being shown by the rest of the people in the room. Collington was sure they'd been caught out. The difficulty was going to be in proving it.

Collington walked stoop-shouldered from the room, back to his offices. Geoffrey Wall was waiting with the latest share figures. South Africa seemed to have settled at four below par, with London fluctuating between two and three and Wall Street steady at two.

'Somebody must know something that we don't,' said the personal assistant. 'If there hadn't been such immediate and heavy buying, we'd be in bad shape.'

'What about the mine reports?'

'Helicopter is scheduled back at three-thirty.'

'I'll need some clothes from Parkstown.'

'I've already sent the driver,' said Wall. 'Your wife said hello and told me to say she'll expect you when she sees you.'

'I'm going upstairs to sleep,' said Collington. 'I'll want a call at three.'

'There is one more thing,' said Wall.

Collington turned at the door.

'There was something else in that message from London, apart from Jenkins' arrival. Ann Talbot says we have over-calculated her severance settlement by £100,000. She's returned the money.'

Too late Collington realised it had been a mistake anyway. Ann Talbot wasn't the sort of woman one should attempt to buy off.

Metzinger and Wassenaar faced each other across the deputy chairman's office like two purposely enraged dogs about to be released for a fight.

'Why didn't you stop it!' demanded Metzinger.

'Don't try and throw the blame on to me,' rejected the lawyer. '*I* was the one who argued the stupidity of remaining in such an exposed position. You know damned well that to cover ourselves, we had to work through a Zurich broker. The time difference meant there were two hours of open trading on the exchanges here. By the time I got to him the nervousness had spread, even though London and Wall Street weren't properly operating. There were off-market disposals, before he could get to the London and New York brokers with whom he had arranged the automatic sell. He was lucky to withdraw what he did.'

'How much?' asked Metzinger, his voice hollow.

'A total of eighty thousand of yours and seventy-two of mine.'

'Dear God!' said Metzinger, despairingly. 'What about Janet?'

'Forty thousand,' said Wassenaar.

'Do you know the prices?'

'All at five below par. That's when the big buy started.'

'I've lost a million and a half Rand,' said Metzinger, dully. 'And Janet is down over half a million.'

'Mine is a million, too,' said the lawyer.

Metzinger thrust up from his desk, walking jerkingly around the room. 'Why did it happen?' he said. 'Why the hell did it have to happen, just when we were so close?'

'We were never close,' said Wassenaar, refusing to allow the man any escape. 'There hasn't been any approach from the Arabs for weeks. We *knew* the danger. We should have scrapped the whole thing.'

Metzinger came back to his desk but he didn't sit down behind it. Instead he went round to the front, so that he was staring down at where Wassenaar was sitting. 'I'm not going to lose,' he said. 'I'm going to go on, to remove Collington. And I'm going to get my money back, every last Rand of it.'

'You're mad,' said Wassenaar. 'Absolutely bloody mad.'

'No,' said Metzinger. 'I'm just determined.'

Although he had only managed two hours sleep, Collington awoke without the cotton wool feeling in his mind. There had been no appreciable share movement while he was asleep and the provisional engineers' reports went little beyond what he already knew, merely adding measurements and slightly reducing the repair estimate in mines One and Two. They had managed to plug the breach in the river wall in Witwatersrand Three and auxiliary pumps were being installed to speed up the extraction of the water. In all five it was being suggested that a great deal of refrigeration trunking could be repaired, rather than wait for entire replacement, and if that proved possible then working could resume sooner than the estimates already given.

The press were assembled in the ground-floor conference room and initially Collington was surprised at the number until Wall identified the European and American journalists, as well as local reporters and television crews. Collington had prepared blackboard displays of each mine. He made an opening statement, repeating what he had made clear in his earlier release about the group strength, and then went from display to display, pointer in hand, illustrating the damage. He refused to be drawn about re-opening dates, not wanting to give a commitment which circumstances might prove over-optimistic, and he said, in response to a flurry of questions, that every indication so far was that it had been a concerted terrorist attack. He concluded by quoting the share value of the mining division on the world exchanges as evidence of the confidence of investors. The conference lasted for over an hour and Collington had insisted it be video-recorded, to enable him to watch an instant playback. He and Wall sat before the television screen in the penthouse office and at the end Collington said, 'Well?'

It was an objective question, insistent upon an honest answer and Wall said, 'I can't help thinking we were a bit too open.'

'Rather that than rumour and supposition,' said Collington, repeating his earlier argument.

'You've been absolutely honest,' said Wall. 'What if the interpretation is that you're covering up and that it's worse than what you say?'

'Today's Friday and apart from Wall Street, the markets are already closed,' said Collington. 'I'm drafting extra people to clear Witwatersrand Four over the weekend. We can repair the refrigeration trunking rather than replace. On Sunday I want a press release distributed to every journalist and television crew who were present today, inviting them to an on-site inspection for Wednesday. That story will be carried in Monday's papers and stem any uncertainty at the beginning of the week. The markets should hold until Wednesday and then there will be the reports and television pictures, showing a virtually undamaged mine. And that should bring us to Thursday and even Friday. After a week, the interest will be diminishing. We should end on a high.'

Wall listened admiringly. 'That's clever,' he said, honest still. 'That's very clever.'

'And necessary,' said Collington.

'It's going to be a busy weekend,' said Wall.

'I expected that.'

'By the way, there's been a personal call for you from Louis Knoetze.'

'Knoetze?'

'The Security Chief. He wants a meeting.'

'Of course,' agreed Collington at once. 'Would he agree to Saturday?'

'It was his idea.'

'Fix it,' ordered Collington. 'His convenience.'

Wall started sifting through the other messages that had been held for him during the conference by his secretary. 'Even getting brokers from as far away as Amsterdam,' he said, as an aside.

'What?'

'Nothing,' said Wall, uncomfortable now that he'd attempted any lightness. 'Just a request for a meeting from a determined woman from Amsterdam. Doesn't seem content with middle management.'

If it hadn't been for the mention of Amsterdam, where the bullion plane had crashed, and Collington's recollection of Metzinger identifying the Soviet purchase broker as a woman, Collington would have ignored what his assistant was saying. Instead he leaned forward, intently, and said: 'What's the name?'

Wall had progressed on through his messages. He frowned, his regret at raising it at all increasing. 'Brigitte re Jong,' he read.

'I'll see her,' said Collington.

Chapter Thirty

When the Saturday appointment had been confirmed, Knoetze had spoken of evidence, and so Collington went to Skinner Street with evidence of his own. It was too much of a coincidence for the Soviet purchase broker to be in South Africa, Collington decided. To his satisfaction, it was confirmation that she knew the identity of her customers when she made the purchases and he expected Knoetze to think so too. The security chief would probably be annoyed that she had managed to enter the country undetected, although the uncertainty up to now would have made any sea or airport alert to immigration officials too premature.

Collington had expected to find the security chief in uniform, but Knoetze was casual-suited. He was a chubby-faced, soft-fleshed man, given to smiling at the end of everything he said, as if nervous of getting the other person's agreement to an opinion. It seemed oddly to fit a man in his position.

'At last!' Knoetze greeted Collington. 'This meeting should have been much earlier. And in pleasanter circumstances.'

Collington accepted the offered hand, slightly confused at being treated like an old friend at their first meeting.

'I suppose there's a danger of Marius taking offence,' continued the security chief, leading Collington to the window-seats with their view of the SAGOMI building. 'But this is an escalation. I wanted to hear your views personally, not passed on by a third party.'

'I understand,' said Collington. And did, more than the man had intended. Collington had assumed, because of the circumstances of the gold discovery and Metzinger's confirmation at the board meeting that it was a security file, that Knoetze would in some way be involved with Metzinger's discussions with the government. He had never imagined the man to be the *direct* link.

'Could they have found out about your helping us with the information about the gold?' demanded Knoetze. 'That's the obvious conclusion, as they only hit your mines.'

'It's a possibility, I suppose,' answered Collington, cautiously. Was that why the woman was pressing for a meeting beyond middle-management level, to issue threats?

'We've confirmation that the explosives were Communist in origin,' disclosed Knoetze. He went to his desk, returning at once holding some charred, indistinguishable shapes. Clean cardboard tags were attached to all of them. 'These were recovered from Witwatersrand Four, One and Two,' said the man, turning the cards over to remind himself. 'They're containers . . . .' He stretched forward, pointing to a particularly blackened part of the piece recovered from Four. 'Our forensic people think that's some sort of wax.'

'What's the significance of that?' said Collington.

'It might link with the interference with the refrigeration, if the devices were activated by heat in some way,' said Knoetze. He picked up another piece. It was badly burned, so the lettering was difficult to read. 'It's Spanish,' he identified. 'Obviously Cuban. Russia directs a lot of her activities throughout Africa that way.'

It would be the most bizarre irony, decided Collington, if his discovery of the gold use had brought about this retaliation and ruined whatever scheme Metzinger, Wassenaar and Janet Simpson were devising. The reflection passed at once. Despite the indications to the contrary, there was no way Russia could have discovered a three-hour dinner in Jerusalem with a business contact: even Levy didn't know the importance of the information he had provided. So why Communist bombs in their mines? And the immediate approach from Brigitte re Jong? Mystery was compounding mystery, swamping his normally clear mind with too many conflicting questions.

'Your Mossad contact didn't give any hint that the gold mines might be the next target, after the Sasol plants?' demanded Knoetze.

The story was continuing to unfold too confusingly for someone even of Collington's quickness. 'Mossad?' he queried.

Knoetze held up his hands — an apologetic gesture — and the quick smile came and went. 'I wish to cause you no embarrassment,' he said. 'You must know that anything you say in this office will be in the strictest confidence. But Marius did tell me that your man in Israel had intelligence sources.'

Collington supposed it might have been an exaggeration by Metzinger, to impress the other man. But the need to impress seemed pointless. 'Certainly he has access to information,' said Collington guardedly. 'But our conversation about gold was entirely concentrated upon the Soviet Union and its difficulties.'

Knoetze frowned, head to one side, as if there were a misunderstanding between them. 'But wasn't there a discussion about the gold coming from here being used for some fresh outrage, after the Sasol bombings?'

That wasn't an exaggeration by Metzinger, Collington thought: that was a downright lie. Little glimmers of awareness kept coming to him, like a curtain twitching sideways in a darkened room on a bright day. Perhaps Knoetze had more information to impart than he imagined.

'There was an assumption,' said Collington, striving for an ambiguity the man would accept without suspicion.

'I don't think I would have recommended the suspension of the gold release merely on an assumption,' said Knoetze, allowing the irritation to become obvious. 'Perhaps it was not a good idea for Marius to oppose our meeting for so long.'

Collington agreed. If Knoetze had urged the suspension of the gold release for that reason, he didn't know anything about the negotiations with Prince Hassan, guessed Collington, with stomach-churning suddenness. And if he didn't know, then neither did anyone in the government, upon whose behalf he was supposed to be talking. The curtain swung apart, letting in more light. So what was the conclusion? There was an obvious one and Collington felt a physical chill, as if he had been exposed to an unexpected blast of coldness.

The initial information about the gold shipment had come from Knoetze and Metzinger had used it to intrude himself like a filter, removing or distilling things he wanted neither side to know. Collington's mind blocked with a contradiction. But why? Why lie to the government about terrorist finance and to him about secret oil supplies? The contradiction washed away as Collington thought back to everything that had been said since he entered Knoetze's office. Always the onus had been upon him, never Metzinger. The man could have represented himself as the innocent go-between, never the guarantor of the information. So whatever the outcome he, not Metzinger, would be shown to be a liar. And a liar, too, in his dealings with the Saudi prince. There was no authority, even unofficial, to offer gold in exchange for oil.

If he were right, then the manœuvre which had seemed so inpenetrably confusing was really worryingly simple. Metzinger was attempting to set up a situation to expose him as a charlatan and a liar, to disgrace him publicly and bring about a shareholders' removal at the annual meeting. SAGOMI would have been disgraced, too, by association. Which would have created a share stir. And Metzinger had been greedy, mounting a bear operation on the side, which had gone wrong because of some inexplicable attack upon their mines. The scenario swamped Collington, numbing him. There was a lot of supposition, perhaps too much. He became aware of Knoetze's concentration and forced a response. So far the indications had come from the security chief by accident. From now on it had to be by design.

'It's proved an accurate assumption,' Collington set out, carefully. 'But I think the nearness of confusion proves the importance of our dealing directly with each other in future.'

'I agree the need for personal contact, but not the assumption,' said Knoetze. 'Why only your mines? That's an incongruity. It makes it a personal attack, rather than one against the country.'

It was important to keep Knoetze curious and open to an approach, Collington decided. 'It *is* an incongruity,' he agreed. 'And one I can't explain. Although we must concede the possibility, as I did at the beginning, I can't honestly believe that anything I did in Israel could have been discovered. By itself, the information meant nothing. It only provided the answer for the gold purchases when I assessed it in connection with other things.'

'Then the attacks are even more bewildering,' said the security man.

It was time to set a more direct test, to establish absolutely whether or not Knoetze knew about Hassan.

'Bewildering,' said Collington. 'But not overly serious. I can get back into operation within three months, which is better than the Sasol plants.'

Knoetze jerked his head in a gesture of agreement. 'Nine months, if we're lucky,' he conceded. 'It's fortunate there's an oil glut on the world markets. Oil is available, at a price.'

'I'm imposing greater security at the mines,' disclosed Collington. 'Ahead of the point where the men collect their tools, I intend installing the sort of metal detectors that operate at airports, to show if anything is being carried in.'

'It'll be a deterrent, if nothing else,' said Knoetze.

'But Sasolberg and Secuna were already worked under the strictest security. What else can you do to prevent such attacks happening again?' said Collington.

'Additional guards, extra spot checks. Apart from that, nothing more than we were doing already,' admitted Knoetze.

He was almost there, decided Collington. 'So there will always be a reliance on the world market?'

'A need to keep the contacts open, certainly,' said Knoetze.

Knoetze's response would have been inconceivable if he had known about the Saudi negotiations. So that *had* been how Metzinger had intended to expose him. And still could, Collington supposed. His mind ran on, considering the implications. Hassan was a government minister and a potential future ruler. And Collington had met him, as a representative of SAGOMI. So his reputation and integrity were at stake if he attempted a hurried withdrawal. The alternative presented itself and Collington immediately recognised another gamble. But was it? What if he *pursued* the opening he had made with Hassan? And brought it to a successful conclusion, without Metzinger being aware? The rewards to the company would be astronomical, and there would be a supreme victory, defeating Metzinger with the very method the Afrikaner had evolved to bring about Collington's destruction.

He'd go on, decided Collington, the gambler. But he would also attempt some insurance, at once.

'What do you imagine the government's reaction would be to the offer of a stable, guaranteed market?' he said.

Knoetze wasn't displaying his camera shutter smiles any more. In a country like South Africa a security chief is as much a politician as a policeman and Knoetze was able to recognise an oblique approach when it was made.

'I would imagine there would be extreme interest,' he said.

'Such an arrangement would not be easy, of course.'

'I accept that.'

'There would need to be an intermediary situation . . . a large multi-national, for instance.'

'That would probably be essential.' Knoetze permitted himself another smile, but it wasn't the grimace of before. It was the reaction of a man getting more than he had expected.

'And there would also be the need for discretion,' said Collington. 'Absolute discretion.'

'Essential,' said Knoetze, eagerly. 'That would be understood, I'm sure.'

It wasn't much, thought Collington — hardly anything at all, in fact. And because this was an unrecorded meeting, Knoetze could deny the entire conversation, if it became necessary for him to do so. But Collington decided he was in a slightly safer position than he had been unknowingly when he entered the room. He hadn't disclosed the presence of Brigitte re Jong. And didn't intend to, not now. The need for a bargaining position might arise: protection even. He'd given Knoetze enough for one meeting. There was a glaring weakness in Knoetze's association with Metzinger. And to try to lessen it almost nullified the insurance he had just attempted by hinting at an oil arrangement with the security man. But he had to do it.

'About discretion,' he urged. 'There must be complete understanding between us both. For the moment, this conversation must reach no one beyond us two.'

Knoetze nodded, quickly.

'*No one,*' emphasised Collington. He hesitated, as if making a decision, then he said, 'There are times when negotiations are well advanced before they are even brought to the attention of my board.'

Comprehension registered in Knoetze's face. 'My vocation is security,' he said, lessening the tension of the exchanges between them. 'What's arisen in this conversation will remain between us. And *only* us.'

Unaware of Knoetze's antipathy towards Metzinger, Collington wondered which would prove stronger: that promise or Knoetze's feelings for Metzinger, Broeder to Broeder? He'd taken it as far as he could, he decided.

'I appreciate the guidance about the source of the explosives,' said Collington. 'I'll naturally pass on anything that my engineers come up with during the examination and the repairs.'

Knoetze took a piece of card from his pocket and handed it to Collington, and Collington saw it had the man's private, unlisted telephone number both here in the office and at home. 'I'd welcome that,' he said. 'I think it's obvious that there should be further meetings between us.'

'I think so, too,' agreed Knoetze.

Collington drove unhurriedly back to the SAGOMI building. He felt like a man half-way across a bridge, suddenly becoming aware that the ropes were being cut at either side of the chasm. At least the encounter with Knoetze had provided him with some sort of safety line, but he was unsure if it were strong enough to support his weight if he fell. The supposition he'd reached about Metzinger fitted everything that he knew, so far. The problem was that he didn't know enough. He wondered if the meeting with Brigitte re Jong would provide any more.

She came politely but confidently into the room, a petite, compact woman: Collington's impression was one of business-like efficiency. Closer, he saw what he thought were signs of tiredness around her eyes, only partially concealed by her spectacles. The glasses suited her, he thought. She smoothed the skirt of her silk print dress sedately over her knees and carefully placed the large, almost briefcase size handbag alongside her chair. It was crocodile, Collington saw, and matched her shoes: the Russians hadn't stinted. How much benefit did that knowledge give him? Until he discovered the purpose of her visit, that was an impossible question to answer. At least he wasn't at a disadvantage. He wasn't apprehensive, either. Which he should have been, he supposed. It was difficult to think of her as anything but a reasonably attractive woman.

'I'm very grateful for your agreeing to see me, particularly at a time like this,' she said. The accent that overlaid the English was impossible to identify.

Was she attempting to make some point immediately? He would have to be cautious against forming instant judgments on every remark. Collington smiled and said, 'Having scheduled the weekend for work, I actually found there was not a lot to do, once the repairs had been agreed and started. And I was intrigued why someone should fly all the way from Amsterdam to speak to us.'

'I hardly imagined I would be fortunate enough to speak to *you*,' she said flatteringly. 'And the visit is hardly surprising, surely, after the upheaval on the bullion markets. For anyone committed to contracts, the effect of the mine attacks, so close after the bullion suspension, was catastrophic.'

Again the directness, thought Collington. Yet there was almost an innocence about it. And he knew damned well she wasn't innocent. As she spoke she answered his smile and Collington saw she had perfect teeth.

'The bullion suspension was a government decision, as it would have to be,' said Collington, wanting to separate the two things.

She put her hand up to the side of her head, making some unnecessary adjustment to her glasses and said, 'I've seen quite a lot of producers — Anglo-American, Consolidated Gold Fields, Rio-Tinto Zinc. All say the same.'

'What else could they say?' demanded Collington. 'We supply to the government, according to the law . . . .' He paused, alert for her reaction to what he was about to add. 'The decision on what or what not to release on world markets is entirely a political decision.'

She met his look, giving no facial response. 'Surely there is consultation, from time to time?'

'Of course,' said Collington. 'But there wasn't on this occasion. Not with my company, certainly.' There was a lack of formality about the conversation, quite different from what he would have expected. If she wasn't going to attempt it, then he would have to take some lead. 'Why have you sought this meeting, Miss re Jong?' he asked bluntly.

She blushed at once, and Collington got the impression of genuine embarrassment. 'In Holland I have created a very successful business,' she said. 'I have a number of customers committed to a future position on bullion contracts: some could be seriously embarrassed by the shortage and the continuing uncertainty, driving prices up as high as they are.'

'That's the major peril of commodity dealing,' encouraged Collington.

'A peril,' she agreed. 'But not a necessity. I've built up a reputation by being able to provide my customers with the absolute maximum information, taking as much of the gamble out of it as possible.'

It was a convincing performance, thought Collington. Normally he would have been impressed. 'And you value that reputation sufficiently highly to come all the way to South Africa?'

'To be able to advise my people whether there was going to be a further withholding or a release, within a few days or a few weeks, would probably be the single most important piece of information I could pass on,' she said.

'Haven't you approached the government sources?'

'Of course,' she said. 'The official reply is that no decision has been made.'

'So you are attempting the unofficial?'

'I would have thought it a possibility that producers might get clearer advice. And that I might be able to get some impression of that advice.'

'Have you?'

She shook her head. 'The best I've been able to get is some nebulous impression that there'll be something soon.'

'I've known commodity contracts agreed on less,' said Collington.

'Not commodity contracts that I recommend. I don't just want the maximum information. I want the maximum *accurate* information,' she retorted.

There should have been something by now, Collington decided. Hardly an open threat, but a nuance at least. He set out to force the pace. 'I'm afraid you've come to an unproductive source, literally!' he said. 'Since the Communist attacks, I can't even produce gold.'

She faltered, just slightly, and if it hadn't been for Collington's presumption about her true identity it would have meant nothing. 'Communist?' she queried.

'There's been an official statement,' he reminded her.

'I didn't see anything about proof,' she said, recovering.

'There's been sufficient material recovered to confirm it forensically,' he said.

There was the slightest pause while she digested the information, and again it would have been meaningless but for his knowledge. Collington sat, waiting. He had created an ideal approach for her. All she had to do now was choose the innuendo and let him know the mistake he had made to cause the mines to be sabotaged in such a planned, detailed manner.

'In one day, those attacks caused a price fluctuation of $30 an ounze,' she said.

She'd ignored it! She had had an opportunity which it was impossible for her not to have seen or to have used, and she had responded with some empty remark about fluctuations. The inconsistencies began piling up, like snow in a drift. The Soviet Union was short of gold and being forced to buy on the open market. So it would have been insanity for them to mount such an outrage so soon after a bullion suspension which had already affected prices so much that their commodity deal with America must be bleeding them of resources. Only hours before he'd *seen* an explosive canister with Cuban markings. And Cuba behaved in Africa as it was instructed by Moscow. Yet not eight feet away from him sat a woman whom he was convinced was an agent of the Soviet Union, behaving as if she had been totally unaware of the staging of the attacks. Collington felt a surge of depression. He had left his meeting with the South African security chief believing that things were becoming clearer. With this woman he was becoming increasingly confused, by the minute. Then through the mist came a sudden moment of clarity, an advantage he hadn't realised before. Knoetze had confirmed his influence, making it clear that the suspension had occurred following his recommendation. Collington was convinced he had impressed the security chief sufficiently to orchestrate another decision, if he chose to do so. That gave him a position of incredible power over the woman and those whom she represented. *If* the mine attacks had been Communist in origin, it gave him an insurance he hadn't appreciated before. It was time for Brigitte re Jong to be offered some innuendo.

'A $30 fluctuation will be miniscule, compared to what will happen if there's a continuation of the gold suspension,' he said.

She frowned, unable to stop her reaction to such a possibility and said, 'I accept it's a government decision, removed from you and every other producer, but what's your *opinion*?'

'I think things have changed since the sabotage of my mines,' said Collington.

'I don't understand,' said the woman. She was staring at him, intently.

'I've already told you I had no foreknowledge, on this occasion, of the suspension,' said Collington. 'But quite obviously there was contact between the suppliers afterwards. My impression was that the full commitment to reserve was a limited decision and that next month there would have been a normal release.'

'And now?' she asked urgently.

Collington decided to make it appear a boastful indiscretion, that of a man wanting to impress an attractive woman. He smiled, indicating a confidence. 'Since the attacks, my contact has been more direct,' he said. 'South Africa sees gold as one of its strongest weapons in world affairs. I wouldn't be surprised if the suspension isn't continued until the inference is taken and international pressure is applied against the countries supplying the guerrillas with ammunition and expertise to attack us.'

Collington accepted it was a flawed argument and one that he could have improved, had he had more time for consideration. But perhaps it benefited from the rough edges: if there had been no inconsistencies, it might have appeared too contrived.

'Another suspension would create a positive starvation,' protested the woman.

'And achieve precisely the effect I've spoken about,' said Collington. Would it be going too far to indicate that he was in a position to affect the decision?

'It could mean something like $1500 an ounze,' she said, in awe, more to herself than to him. 'That's preposterous.'

She had provided him with an opening and Collington decided to take it. 'Even with the production loss SAGOMI is going to suffer until we get our mines back into operation, such a decision would affect us enormously.' He hesitated, to create the impression of continued boastfulness. 'I actually said I didn't know if it were justified for us to make such a profit. We'd be the only ones to benefit in a practical way.'

Her eyes had been averted while she considered the implications of a continued suspension, but at the indication of personal consultation she came back to him, intent again.

'Perhaps I'm saying too much,' he laughed, guessing that would be the behaviour of a conceited man. 'I never imagined any advantage from the attacks, but it seems I'm being allowed access to a limited degree of official thinking. It's rather flattering.'

'What was the reaction to your view about it being justified?' she said.

She would not have asked a direct question like that an hour ago, Collington knew. So she had accepted the impression he was attempting to convey, an over-promoted man anxious to impress.

'Flattering again,' he said. 'I know it's difficult to be sure, but there was a definite inference that my views carried some weight. I think they expected my opinion to be utterly different, as I was the victim of the outrages.' He'd gone far enough, Collington decided. Apart from his difficulty in maintaining the charade much longer, he wanted to stop far short of allowing her any suspicion. He still found it difficult, believing her true identity and her true function. He made much of consulting his watch.

'I've a mine tour very shortly,' he said.

She took the hint, leaning to gather the briefcase handbag. 'Again I want to say how grateful I am for the time you've allowed me,' she said. 'It's been useful: very useful.'

There was just one final thing, thought Collington. 'How much longer are you staying in South Africa?'

'I haven't really decided, not yet.'

'Are you enjoying it?'

'There's been little apart from work.'

'That's a pity,' said Collington, trying to maintain the image he had created for her. 'There should be some time for socialising.'

She stared at him across the desk, remembering to smile just in time. 'That would be very nice,' she said.

'Where are you staying?'

'The Burgerspark.'

Collington made a show of noting it on his jotting pad. 'Maybe we'll meet again,' he said.

'I would like that.'

And so would he, thought Collington. But not for the reasons she believed.

'How the hell did she get in to see the chairman himself?' demanded Krotkov.

'I don't know. And it's not important,' said Leonov, impatiently. 'What's important is that according to the man, we initiated the explosions.'

'What!'

'Positive, forensic proof.'

There were hundreds of operatives in the field, thought Krotkov, and a lot of nationalist guerrillas in Africa whom they supplied but whose actions they couldn't monitor from day to day.

'There've been no instructions,' protested Krotkov. 'On my honour. It would be an inconceivable thing for me to do.'

'It was inconceivable to have been denied money for so long. But it happened,' said Leonov. Anticipating the man's burst of rage, he said, 'I'm not suggesting you ordered it. What about someone else?'

'I'll find out,' guaranteed Krotkov. 'And if I discover someone operating on his own initiative, he'll spend the rest of his life in Lubyanka.'

In Pretoria, Brigitte re Jong sat submerged in the bath, confused by what seemed to be happening. It would be outrageous if one section of Soviet intelligence were working against the other. It made any chance of rectifying the shortfall virtually impossible, without bothering to calculate the next amount for which they were contracted in a few months' time. Her thoughts moved on to her meeting with Collington. He had surprised her. She had expected a mature man — sophisticated even. Instead of which he had behaved like a fool, interested only in impressing her. She wondered what he would be like in bed. That would be the inevitable result of any further contact from him. And she'd have to do it, in case there was some benefit. She wouldn't enjoy it, she knew.

Collington would have preferred to find some better way of continuing to off-balance Metzinger, but there was nothing else, he decided, approaching the deputy chairman's office. Metzinger was alone, sitting alert behind his desk, when Collington entered.

'Thought there was something you should know,' said Collington. 'Hannah and I have decided to get back together.'

Metzinger said nothing.

'I imagined you'd be pleased, for Paul at least,' said Collington, heavily.

'Of course,' said Metzinger. At least, he thought, there was something positive he could do about that.

Chapter Thirty-One

The helicopter was waiting on the airstrip. Collington belted himself into the co-pilot's seat and stared out of the window as the machine lifted off. There had been a lot of improvisation during his encounter with Brigitte re Jong. And with Knoetze, too. Collington couldn't recall an occasion when he had acted with less preparation and the awareness worried him. He thought he had ended ahead on both encounters, but he couldn't be sure. He wasn't even sure what he had hoped to achieve with the woman. She could be an advantage, certainly. But also a danger. On balance, perhaps more danger than advantage, if Knoetze ever discovered that he had been aware of a Soviet agent on South African territory and withheld the information.

Collington felt as if he were staring down at the disjointed board of a jigsaw puzzle, with all the pieces split apart, but without the picture to guide him. He needed the key and he needed it quickly. Behind every meeting he had and every action he took lay the awareness in Collington's mind that he had £103,000,000 to raise in less than a month.

His arrival at the mine was radioed ahead. The manager of Witwatersrand Four, Walter Shaw, was waiting on the airstrip. Beside him was the mine engineer, whom he introduced as William Kruber.

The instructions to hurry the repairs had been given the previous day, and in the Landrover taking them to the mine-head Collington explained the reasoning.

'A press party, for Wednesday?' asked Kruber. From the way he spoke it was obvious he thought the idea ridiculous.

'Television, too,' said Collington. 'They're to be given a complete tour of the mine. I'm printing maps to be issued before they descend, so they will be able to compare and know they're being shown everything . . . I want every section operational during the tour . . . .' He turned to the manager. 'I shall be coming, too,' he said. 'At the end of the tour I want some sort of facilities for a press conference. The keynote is going to be absolute openness.'

They got to the mine and Collington once more struggled into protective clothing that was too small for him. There was illumination as they went past the two first levels, but only the emergency lighting was in operation on the lowest level, where the electricity had been isolated because of the damage. Because it was the deepest part of the mine, the heat was greatest at that point. Generator-driven fan coolers had been installed, but even so the area was only just workable.

'We're using brief shifts,' explained Kruber, as they progressed along the shaft. 'Thirty minutes on, one hour off. Thanks, incidentally, for the extra men. It wouldn't have worked without them.'

They stopped where the roof had collapsed. The debris had already been removed and the shaft ceiling shored up, timber bulkheads supporting metal plating. The twisted tracking had already been lifted and welders were crouched over torches which were adding to the heat, fixing new sections into place.

'Should be completed by tomorrow, at the latest,' promised Shaw.

'Which leaves the refrigeration,' said Kruber. 'Because of the need for speed, I'm not going to attempt to replace. It was punctured in eight places. I'm going to patch the lot, internally as well as on the outside, for extra strength.'

Collington nodded agreement. 'Once the press visit is over, you can close down the lower section and replace what's necessary,' he said.

The heat was taking his breath, making him pant. As they moved back towards the cage, Collington saw that Shaw had thermos cases packed with water, for the men to replace their sweat loss.

'That's a good idea,' he said.

'It's necessary,' said the manager.

Collington emerged gratefully at ground level, gulping for air. 'We can get the repairs done without too much difficulty,' he judged.

The two men nodded.

'But what about the men who did it in the first place?'

Shaw shook his head. 'The investigations have got nowhere,' he said. 'Three men failed to turn up for work, which might indicate that they've run, thinking we'd discover they were involved. But we can't be sure there weren't more.'

'It's going to be quite pointless working like this for three days and then having the whole thing wrecked by another explosion,' said Collington. 'If we're attacked again it would cause exactly the opposite effect to that which I'm trying to achieve. By tomorrow I'll have the detection devices here. I'm also going to send in medical staff. After the men have gone through, I want a physical check. The obvious way to get dynamite sticks into the mine and still beat the detector is for them to be carried internally.'

'Anal examination?' queried Shaw distastefully.

'You won't have to do it,' said Collington.

'But it would take hours,' protested Shaw.

'No it won't,' rejected Collington. 'The first day it will be for everybody and there'll be heavy delays. The following day everyone will know how stringent the checks are and won't consider carrying anything anyway, so we can reduce the intensity. By Wednesday, we can come down to spot checks, sufficient to show we're not relaxing but insufficient to cause any serious hold-up.'

'What about hospitality?' asked Shaw, suddenly. 'For all the people who will be here on Wednesday.'

Collington hesitated, nodding at the forethought. 'Keep it simple,' he instructed. 'I don't want anyone imagining they're being given the treatment to be conned. No booze, just soft drinks. And keep the food simple, too. Nothing more than sandwiches.'

'Any thoughts in Pretoria on why our mines were singled out for attack?' asked Kruber.

'Not yet,' said Collington.

'What about the explosives?' demanded the engineer and Collington remembered that one of the shattered canisters Knoetze had shown him that morning had come from this mine.

'Cuban markings,' he said.

'No doubt it was Communist then?' said Shaw.

'Doesn't appear to be.'

'Bastards!' said Kruber viciously.

'Yes,' agreed Collington, less forcefully. 'They're bastards.'

Collington flew back to Pretoria, encouraged that his idea with Witwatersrand Four was practicable. If he could maintain the confidence until Friday, then the danger of any concentrated pressure upon the shares would be over. And seven days would have passed, bringing nearer the time he had to pay in full for the shares he had bought on the ten per cent margin. After two weeks, Collington reckoned that he could dispose of perhaps fifteen thousand shares, in small pockets spread all over the world markets, without causing any noticeable fluctuation. If they maintained their present price, that would mean each share going at four points above what he had paid for them, so he would have a cash profit of maybe £10,000,000. With that liquidity he might be able to borrow another £15,000,000. Which still left him hopelessly short of the settlement figure.

He shrugged aside the calculations. He still had almost four full weeks and a lot could happen in that time: there were other and more immediate things to occupy him.

The board meeting had been scheduled for the evening to allow for Jenkins' arrival. Everyone was assembled by the time Collington got to the SAGOMI building and unlike the previous day, he didn't bother to shower and change before going into the boardroom.

He entered looking intently at Metzinger and Wassenaar, believing he now knew the reason for their previous day's behaviour. Both appeared to have recovered their composure: indeed, there was something approaching a stiffness about them, as if they were making a conscious effort to show no emotion whatsoever. He would have to alter that, he decided. Uncertain, they might make a mistake and provide another part of the picture he was trying so desperately hard to complete.

Collington shook Jenkins' hand and formally called the meeting to order. For Jenkins' benefit he repeated the engineers' reports from all five mines and then widened the discussion to include those directors who had heard them before by setting out his intention regarding Witwatersrand Four.

'Will it work?' demanded Jenkins, at once.

'I've just come back from there,' said Collington. 'I don't think there's any problem.'

'It would underpin the confidence beautifully,' said Jamieson, admiringly. 'It's an excellent idea.'

'What about the investigations?' said Metzinger.

Collington turned to the deputy chairman. Because of his association with Knoetze, it was more than likely that Metzinger had contacted the security chief. Would Knoetze have maintained his undertaking? he wondered.

'Parts of explosives have been recovered from Witwatersrand One, Two and Four,' he said. 'They're Communist in origin.'

'Why us?' demanded Brooking.

'If I knew the answer to that, then a great many things might become clearer,' said Collington, pointedly avoiding looking at either Metzinger or Wassenaar as he spoke. 'There seems to be no apparent logical reason.'

'How much are the repairs going to cost?' demanded de Villiers, wanting information about which he could feel comfortable.

'It hasn't been costed in detail yet,' said Collington. 'The estimate is about R7,000,000.'

'Seven million!' echoed Platt. 'What about insurance?'

'We've got two-thirds cover, on a political sabotage policy taken out through Lloyds of London. The canisters will provide a proof of claim. I'll brief the lawyers tomorrow.'

'Still a lot to make up,' complained de Villiers, as if he were personally being asked to make up the shortfall.

'What do you think the shares will do when the markets open on Monday?' asked Brooking and Collington was conscious of a stir of movement from his left, where Metzinger and Wassenaar were sitting.

'Normally there would be a drop,' he said, glad of the question because of the discomfort it caused. 'Investors would have had the weekend to sit and worry. That's why I'm timing the press announcements. Today, for use in the Sunday papers here and in England and America, we're issuing a statement saying that the damage doesn't appear as serious as was first thought. Tomorrow, for the morning newspapers that will be read a couple of hours before the markets start, there's going to be the announcement about the re-opening of Four and the press visit. On Monday we'll release in detail the damage to Four and how it was repaired and that should carry us nicely through to Wednesday.'

'Beautiful,' said Jamieson.

'And no one will be able to accuse us of lying,' said Collington. Knowing that for Metzinger, Wassenaar and Janet Simpson to recover their money, they had to hope the shares would go below the five points at which they had lost on Friday, he added, 'By Wednesday I would expect us to be at par or maybe a point or two above. At worst, I can't see us dropping more than two in the other direction.'

He looked to his left as he finished speaking, so that he caught the look of annoyance that went between Wassenaar and Metzinger. Had they quarrelled? It was a possibility that hadn't occurred to him until that moment but he supposed it was likely, now that the scheme had gone wrong. From his knowledge of the number of shares on offer, Collington knew that de Villiers hadn't been included. What was the reason, he wondered, for the accountant's exclusion?

'I think it's been a great salvage operation,' said Jenkins. 'I'd like to propose a motion of gratitude to the chairman.'

'Seconded,' said Brooking, speaking fractionally ahead of Jamieson. All the hands went up, Metzinger and Wassenaar slightly behind the others.

Collington nodded his thanks and said, 'I don't see anything happening to justify us meeting tomorrow. Why don't we remain flexible during the coming week, so that we're all available if the need arises.'

There were gestures of agreement around the table and Collington looked at his watch, realising he would be able to get back to Hannah earlier than he had anticipated. He was tired, he realised — not the physical fatigue that had followed the sleepless night when he had visited the bombed mines, but a mental weariness, trying to produce the right conclusion from the confusion of the past two or three days.

He rose, formally breaking up the meeting, and as he moved away from the table he became aware of Metzinger at his elbow. 'Can we talk?' said his father-in-law, and Collington was conscious of a change in the man's customary attitude. Had he not known Metzinger so well and therefore been aware that such a thing were impossible, Collington would have thought of it as meekness. Whatever the definition, it showed that the man was worried.

'Of course,' he accepted.

He led the way into his adjoining offices, with Metzinger following. There was still a stiffness about the man, thought Collington, as Metzinger seated himself.

'There's a lot of official concern over this,' announced Metzinger.

'I should imagine there would be,' said Collington. A worried man about to make mistakes, he thought.

'I've been approached, to make that clear,' said Metzinger.

'Shouldn't you have mentioned it in there?' asked Collington, nodding towards the boardroom they had just left.

'I thought it best to keep it between ourselves, in view of the other circumstances.'

'Other circumstances?' said Collington, determined to back Metzinger into as tight a position as possible.

'The oil negotiations,' said Metzinger.

Which I now know to be bullshit, thought Collington. His guess that morning in Knoetze's office, that Metzinger intended to use the oil negotiations for some sort of public humiliation, *had* to be right for the man to force the matter at a time when five of their mines had been bombed and they should have been considering nothing else. Collington thought back to his reflection an hour before in the boardroom. They had obviously intended to buy back somewhere lower than the five points at which he had snapped up the shares they had on offer. To recover the money, Metzinger had to continue with his oil idea, unaware of Collington's purchase barrier which would always defeat him, hoping that he could buy substantially at a sudden dip below five and then make his profit when they rose again in value. Having been burned once, badly, it was an act of desperation. And also unnecessary. Collington was fairly certain that Metzinger would have been able to withdraw some of the shares, but even if he had lost all of them, the money would have been unimportant to someone of his wealth. And then Collington thought of the sort of man he recognised Metzinger to be, after all the years he had known him. Desperate and unnecessary it might be, but it was completely in character. Metzinger had always found it impossible to lose anything, whether it was money or an argument or a boardroom dispute. Or even a daughter.

'Has there been some discussion about the oil negotiations?' he said, pushing Metzinger further back into a corner.

Metzinger nodded. 'The mine attack, so soon after the Sasol bombings, seems to indicate an escalation in the terrorism. They're anxious to secure an agreement as soon as possible. A guaranteed supply would remove a lot of uncertainty.'

'I understand,' said Collington. 'But there's nothing I can do. I've taken the approach as far as I can. The next contact must come from Hassan.'

'It's been *weeks*,' said Metzinger.

'I'm aware of the time,' said Collington.

'Couldn't you make the approach?' urged Metzinger.

Anxiety was practically leaking out of the man, thought Collington. He shook his head. 'I don't think that would be good tactics, do you?'

'Normally, no,' agreed Metzinger. 'But the government feeling is that we should try to force the pace a little. Get a commitment.'

But for his encounter that morning with Louis Knoetze, he would have regarded this as a logical argument, thought Collington. He made another doubtful gesture. 'I wouldn't want to drive Hassan away. Or make him think he can increase the pressure upon us because we are desperate.'

'If he did want a higher commission, I think they might be prepared to pay,' said Metzinger.

This from a man who had queried the figure when he had announced it a few weeks earlier, remembered Collington.

'I'll remember that,' said Collington. 'I think we should try to get past the immediate crisis first.'

'Let's keep in touch about it,' said Metzinger. 'I don't think it's a situation we should let slip out of our hands.'

'I won't let it slip out of my hands,' assured Collington.

He telephoned ahead, so Hannah was expecting him when he got back to Parkstown.

'You look exhausted,' she said.

'I am.'

'And you smell!'

'It's bloody hot at the bottom of a gold mine.'

She stretched up to kiss him. 'I don't mind your smell,' she said.

Collington held her tightly, staring over her shoulder. Thank

Christ they had got back together before it had all happened, he thought. He wondered if he would ever be able to tell her what was happening between himself and her father. He'd promised complete honesty, he remembered.

'How is it?' she said, pulling back.

'Containable, with luck,' he said. 'I've worked out something to try to stop a share slide.'

'In for the evening?'

'I hope so.' As Collington spoke, the telephone beside them in the hallway rang and she said, 'Oh no!'

Collington felt a flicker of apprehension and then reached out to pick up the instrument. Immediately he recognised Geoffrey Wall's voice. There had been a message from the Saudi Arabian embassy in London, said the personal assistant. Prince Hassan would welcome another meeting.

Henry Moreton had always prided himself on being a realist, but even at his most objective he would not have forecast the success he had achieved. In less than a year he had turned the weakness of the dollar into something approaching an unchallengeable strength, earned the respect and friendship of the President of the United States and become practically as well known as Henry Kissinger had been. Life was an unblemished success. He frowned, questioning the assessment. Not quite unblemished. There were some private things that could be improved. Increasingly Barbara was boring him. But she was accompanying him less and less to official functions. He wouldn't risk an open split, of course, because of the political embarrassment it would cause. Those sort of arrangements were accepted and understood in Washington.

Chapter Thirty-Two

The carefully orchestrated publicity achieved precisely the effect that Collington intended. There was no drop at all at market opening in South Africa and the day ended with a two point, across-the-board average rise. They lost two points in initial trading in London, then the market stabilised and closed three above par. In Wall Street the final figure was one point up.

Nothing was found during the Monday security check at Witwatersrand, but the workers who had failed to report for work the day after the explosion remained absent. Police swooped on their homesteads and found they had disappeared. It took a further day to establish their membership of the African National Congress. A government announcement was made in Pretoria, stating the fact as positive proof that the mine sabotage had been Communist inspired.

Collington went to Skinner Street guessing that the security chief would imagine that the confirmation of the ANC involvement was the point of the meeting and, for the first fifteen minutes, Collington let the discussion with Louis Knoetze concentrate upon the investigation of the security forces. Several times he mentioned the company's gratitude at the speed of the enquiry, rightly assessing Knoetze's pride in identifying it as a political act.

'It still doesn't resolve the inconsistency of why it was only your mines, though,' said Knoetze. 'SAGOMI is not even Afrikaner-controlled, which is another intangible. Why not Anglo-American, which is? Or Union Corporation?'

They had been through it all at the weekend meeting and nothing that had happened since was going to clarify it any further, Collington thought. So it would be a conversation into a cul-de-sac.

'Has there been an opportunity since our last meeting for you to discuss with anyone else the other matter we discussed?' he asked.

Knoetze regarded him warily. 'Other matter?'

'That of energy supply.'

'I said at the time that I imagined there would be some interest,' said Knoetze, avoiding the direct answer. The smile clicked on and off, an almost apologetic expression.

'If an approach had been made, then, to some company sufficiently large to undertake the amount of organisation involved, you don't foresee any objections to it being pursued?' said Collington. Why was there the necessity to open diplomatic discussions with such ambiguity? wondered Collington. It was practically a replay of his London hotel meeting with Hassan.

'The government is always interested in beneficial trade links between this country and others,' said Knoetze.

It was like playing tennis with a superior player, constantly having the ball returned into his own court, thought Collington. He didn't think he would be able to get any firmer insurance if anything went wrong.

'I'm going abroad in a day or two,' he said.

'How long do you expect to be away?'

'Only briefly,' said Collington. 'Just a few days.' He allowed a pause in the conversation, uncertain whether or not to go on. Then he said, 'There was an understanding between us. About discretion.'

Knoetze frowned, an unusual expression for the man, and Collington thought momentarily that he might have offended the Afrikaner. Instead Knoetze said, 'This conversation won't go beyond the two of us.'

It would probably seem gibberish if it did, thought Collington, on his way down to street level in the lift. That was juvenile bitterness, he reflected. He had been over-confident in expecting any reaction other than that which he had got from Knoetze. So it had been a pointless encounter. Yet not quite, he decided.

Although they'd mouthed the words like students learning a foreign language, Knoetze wasn't in any doubt now about what he was talking about. How far the man would be prepared to come out and support him if things went wrong was a different matter: probably not at all. But there was no uncertainty in Collington's mind that he had been given the nod to continue with whatever he was doing.

There had been several conversations between the embassy in London and Pretoria since the weekend contact. Hassan had apparently remained in Austria to ski after the OPEC meeting, and so the meeting was scheduled for Vienna. The Arab had stipulated the Sacher hotel. After his meeting with Knoetze, Collington had Wall confirm the Thursday appointment and then concentrated upon the press visit to Witwatersrand Four. There had been over a hundred applications to attend, which had surprised him. He increased the number of maps produced for distribution at the mine-head, and he double-checked the transportation arrangements to ensure that they returned in sufficient time to transmit pictures and stories to whatever newspapers they represented. Helicopters were provided for the television reporters and, as an afterthought, Collington ordered that more should be chartered, in case there were any disruption or delay in the other transport.

He went down the mine ahead of everyone else, touring the three levels with Shaw and Kruber. The bright replacement patches on the refrigeration trunking and the newness of the track which had been ripped up in the explosion were the only obvious signs of what had happened.

'Photographers expecting a sensation are going to be disappointed,' predicted Shaw.

'Which is exactly what I want them to be,' said Collington. 'The message I want to get across is that everything is one hundred per cent normal.'

He was at the shaft-head to meet them. He displayed the body-checking equipment that had been installed and said that the physical body searches were to be continued just as intensively, allowing himself an exaggeration. For ease of movement the journalists were split into three groups. Collington accompanied each group on the underground tour, posing for photographs whenever they were requested, and he finally confronted them all in the mess hut which had been set aside for the conference. He showed no trace of his anxiety to be away and aboard an aircraft to fly him to Europe. The conference lasted an hour, with three separate interviews in side rooms with television reporters.

'I think it went well,' said Wall, in the helicopter taking them back to Pretoria.

Collington agreed, but he said, 'We'll see from the coverage.'

'Sure you don't want me to come to Austria?' asked Wall.

He would have welcomed the younger man's support, thought Collington, realising how much he had come to rely upon him in recent weeks. He shook his head and said, 'You'll be more use here, as a liaison!'

'Anything specific?'

Collington looked directly at his assistant. 'Watch everything,' he said.

Collington had packed before leaving Parkstown that morning and taken his luggage to the SAGOMI building. He had arranged the meeting with Metzinger for five and arrived fifteen minutes early, giving him the opportunity to check the world-wide prices in the SAGOMI and mining division shares in the tape-room. There had been a rise of two points in London, but elsewhere there was little movement. Nowhere had there been a drop.

'How did the conference go?' demanded Metzinger, as he entered Collington's office.

'Very well,' said Collington positively, determined against giving the man any hope of recovering his money. 'I've just checked the prices. We're holding up well everywhere.'

'I know,' said Metzinger. There was no satisfaction in his voice.

'I'm going to Austria tonight,' announced Collington, purposely dramatic.

Metzinger started, momentarily confused.

'Hassan has made another approach,' said Collington.

Metzinger's face brightened in palpable relief. 'He wants to go ahead?' he demanded, too eagerly.

'I won't know until I meet him.'

'When?'

'In Vienna, tomorrow afternoon.'

'I'll let my people know,' promised Metzinger.

'Why not wait until we see what his proposals are? With all the board here, we could make the announcement to them as well.'

'We'll have to let the government determine the announcement,' said Metzinger, hurriedly.

'Of course,' agreed Collington.

'You'll contact me, the moment you get back?'

'Of course.'

'I thought it might have been all over,' admitted Metzinger.

For one of us, thought Collington, it could still be all over.

Metzinger caught Wassenaar at his office and hurried immediately to see the corporation lawyer. Wassenaar listened blankly, failing to respond to the deputy chairman's enthusiasm.

'I told you I wasn't interested,' he reminded.

'A million Rand,' said Metzinger slowly. 'That's what you lost. A million.'

'I don't need the reminder,' said the lawyer.

'You need a chance to recover,' insisted Metzinger. 'I'm giving it to you.'

'To regain a million? Or lose another one?' said Wassenaar.

Metzinger started up from his chair, moving aimlessly around the room.

'How the hell can that happen?' he demanded. 'All we've got to do is place purchase orders. If we buy on a ten per cent margin, we'll have recovered our money before the month's out, for full settlement.'

Wassenaar hesitated, his resolve weakening. 'It's less involved than before,' he admitted.

'Look what's happened since the mines were bombed!' said Metzinger, continuing the pressure. 'We're level or a point or two above par on every exchange you can name. If we're that buoyant, how long do you imagine it will take for the shares to lift after we've embarrassed Collington?'

'I've the contract with the Zurich broker,' said Wassenaar. 'What orders do you want me to place for you?'

'What I lost,' instructed Metzinger, at once. 'Eighty thousand. And forty thousand for Janet.'

'When do you want them placed?'

'As soon as you can.'

'What position?'

Metzinger frowned, trying to decide. 'Two below par,' he said.

'They would have to go three above, for you just to be even.'

'I'm not going to end up even,' said Metzinger confidently. 'I'm going to end up as I intended. Ahead. And in control.'

Chapter Thirty-Three

Hassan had taken a whole floor of the Sacher and, as in London, the corridors and outer rooms were crowded with berobed Arabs, few of whom appeared to be doing very much. Unlike his initial meeting with the Saudi prince at Claridge's, Collington did not go through the ceremonial delays. His admission was as swift as it had been at the embassy and as he was announced Hassan hurried forward to greet him.

'It's good to see you again, my friend,' said Hassan. He retained his grip on Collington's hand, leading him further into the apartment. It was a large suite, adapted as an office: there was even a muted tape machine discharging its thread of information in one corner. Collington remembered that this was one of Metzinger's affectations.

'And you,' responded Collington. Their relationship seemed to have progressed since the last meeting, he thought.

There was a handclap and the tea came, and Collington sipped dutifully.

'I was sorry to learn of your misfortune,' said Hassan. 'Although it doesn't appear to have had the effect I would have imagined.' As he spoke Hassan indicated the tape machine and Collington wondered which price index it was linked to.

'We were lucky, in the circumstances,' he said. 'We've been able to re-open one mine already.'

'So I understand,' said Hassan. 'Your production won't be badly affected, then?'

'There will be full resumption within three months,' assured Collington.

'I'm pleased to hear it.'

'And a resumption of the normal gold release next month.' It was an over-commitment, but he wanted to get the discussion on course. If there was to be no reserve between them, then there shouldn't be the usual word play either.

'I regret the delay,' said Hassan, spreading his hands to indicate that the reasons were beyond his control. 'The OPEC meeting was not an easy one. There were many discussions necessary in its aftermath. And the need to consult my own country.'

'I hope those consultations went beyond the OPEC debate and included the proposals we have considered,' said Collington, maintaining the pressure.

Hassan smiled, moving to resist it. 'My first impression upon arriving in America for my education was of the directness of the people there. I'm reminded of it in you.'

Collington refused to be deflected. 'I think it is necessary for us to speak directly,' he said. 'If we are to go forward, I don't think we should allow any possibility of a misunderstanding.'

'Are we to go forward?' said Hassan.

'I hope so,' said Collington.

'I am assured you have the backing of the government?'

'Yes,' said Collington. Another over-commitment, he recognised. 'Do you have the approval of yours?'

'There has been a detailed consideration,' admitted Hassan. 'I have been asked to explore it further.'

And pick up £100,000,000 when passing 'Go', thought Collington. 'What further guarantees can I give, beyond those we have already discussed?'

'It would be important for us to be absolutely assured of adequate protection,' said Hassan. 'The companies you spoke about in England would have to be formed and staffed and trading would have to be commenced for us to be sure of your sincerity. And those in America, too.'

It was understandable caution, Collington reluctantly conceded. The oil industry was an insular, jealous collection of companies and organisations, each alert and suspicious towards any new entrant. It would be necessary for any front corporation to operate successfully for several months before actively entering the full arrangement with Saudi Arabia. It would mean leasing refinery space. And tanker charter, until it was clear that the Arabs intended going through with the scheme and it became economical to build their own. The expenditure was going to be enormous and based on the word of a man he suspected of manipulating the bullion suspension and whom he had already described as a crook.

'That would involve substantial capital outlay,' said Collington.

'For eventual substantial capital reward,' parried the Arab.

'I am responsible to my shareholders,' said Collington. 'I would need a document before I could consider such an investment.'

Hassan shook his head, recognising that the bargaining had begun. 'But if such a thing fell into the wrong hands, it could cause an upheaval within my country that can hardly be contemplated,' said Hassan.

'I would not insist upon it having the authority of the government behind it,' said Collington, in apparent concession. 'I would accept a letter from you to me.'

'I am still my country's Oil Minister,' said Hassan.

'And I am a businessman with as many interests outside South Africa as I have within. There would be no provable direct link,' said Collington. It was almost time to give another gentle twist of the screw.

'Upon the lips of provocateurs, there would be no need for a direct link,' insisted Hassan.

'There was talk between us at a previous meeting of a commission,' said Collington, aware of the flare of interest in Hassan's eyes.

'I don't remember the details,' said Hassan dismissively, as if it were unimportant.

'My estimate was that the figure would amount to something around £100,000,000.'

'A considerable sum of money.'

'And one which we could not consider paying, in addition to all the other expenditure, until after a full contract had been agreed between the companies I intend establishing and actual shipment had begun.'

Hassan's face closed in anger at the realisation that it could be a year or maybe longer before he received any payment. 'I do not think that would be acceptable,' he said stiffly.

'With such sums involved as those that we are considering, it would be unfortunate for any agreement to founder upon such an amount,' said Collington, appearing surprised at Hassan's outright rejection.

'It was not the sum, it was the principle,' said the Arab, too eager in his annoyance. 'There has been a considerable amount of work involved in bringing the discussions this far.'

'Believe me, I understand!' said Collington, raising his hands in a gesture of assurance. 'But it is exactly the principle, the business principle, that I *am* considering. Payment of commission is normal upon completion of a contract. But I haven't got a contract: I haven't even got a letter of intent.' Collington waited for the other man's greed to come to his assistance.

'Would you consider a letter of intent a contractual document?'

'I would regard it as an exploratory document,' qualified Collington. He paused, then threw the man's own conditions back at him. 'Quite clearly, to guard against the embarrassment you are so anxious to avoid, any such letter would be in far too general terms to be regarded as a contract.'

'What would the commission qualification be?'

Collington seemed to consider the question, then he said, 'I think half payment would be equitable.'

'I think that would be acceptable,' said Hassan, once more too quickly.

It was time to reel the line in too fast for Hassan to realise he was hooked, decided Collington. 'I would be prepared to make it clear in a responding letter that it was part payment. If you would appreciate the guarantee, I would even go so far as to make my letter specific enough to be legally binding as a contract.'

Hassan looked hopeful again, at his belief of an over-generous concession, but before he could speak Collington went on, 'And of course, the payment would be in gold.'

'Gold!'

Collington remained expressionless at Hassan's momentary lapse of control. The man was lying on the bank, gasping and waiting to be gaffed, he decided. 'It would show my measure of good faith,' said Collington. 'And at the same time act as proof to you and to your government, should you wish to make the arrangement known, of the South African government's tacit acceptance of the agreement.'

Collington purposely set out what he intended to do, offering the man his escape so there could be no subsequent accusations of trickery. He waited for Hassan to realise it. But instead Hassan said, 'I think we have reached an agreement, my friend.'

'I'm very pleased,' said Collington.

'Would you like to take the letter of intent back with you?'

'It would enable me to make arrangements for payment, which would have to be government authorised. And enable me to compile my reply, once that has been done.'

'I have secretaries in an adjoining room,' offered Hassan, anxious not to lose his imagined advantage. He rose, hurrying past the quietly churning tape machine and Collington relaxed back in his seat. Hassan had probably calculated a ten per cent rise, in a full year, on his half payment. And had let himself be blinded by a £5,000,000 commission increase to the insurance Collington was manipulating to protect himself both from the Saudi Arabians and the South Africans.

Collington intended to stipulate gold in his contractual reply to whatever Hassan was composing in the nearby room. As a legally binding document, it would be referenced. And that same reference would head the formal approach he made to Pretoria. He would register his copies in London, and if ever the arrangement became embarrassingly public he would have documentary proof that he was acting as an intermediary between two governments.

Hassan returned very quickly. He carried a top copy and a duplicate and Collington signed the duplicate for Hassan's retention. Hassan offered his hand and Collington shook it. 'To a successful business partnership.' he said.

'I sincerely hope so,' replied Collington.

Hassan relaxed, arms spread along either arm of his chair, a magnanimous victor. 'You spoke about payment arrangements,' he said.

'Of your choice,' agreed Collington.

'I think Switzerland,' said Hassan. 'They have such admirable banking laws.'

'That will be very simple for us to arrange,' said Collington.

'And all I have to do is trust in gold,' said Hassan, flippant in his satisfaction.

'There can't be anything safer in which we can place our trust,' said Collington, responding to the man's lightness. If the audience were terminated within the next hour, Collington calculated he could be airborne and on his way back to South Africa by mid-evening.

'Doesn't appear to be the view of every expert,' said Hassan.

'Then I'd hardly regard the man as an expert,' said Collington.

'A great many people do,' said Hassan. 'Henry Moreton has created quite a reputation for himself.'

'The United States Secretary to the Treasury!' said Collington. How could a man who had underpinned his country's currency with the gold deal with Russia decry its value? Surely not another mystery?

'He wasn't under-estimating its worth,' recalled Hassan. 'Rather its availability.'

Collington forced an attitude of calmness, not wanting the other man to detect his interest. Why was Moreton intruding in contradictory arguments about gold? There was an obvious answer, but Collington found it difficult to accept.

'Why should he doubt availability?' he encouraged the Arab.

Hassan shrugged, an artificially doubtful gesture. 'I thought you might be able to tell me.'

'I don't understand.'

'There was some talk of Communist infiltration into South Africa. And then the Communist bombing of your mines.'

Hassan was looking directly at him and Collington realised that they were once again involved in a verbal minuet.

'When did you meet Moreton?' he asked.

'Friday,' replied Hassan.

'The same day as the bombings,' remembered Collington, pointedly.

'The coincidence occurred to me, as well,' said Hassan equally heavily.

The picture of the jigsaw puzzle was slowly forming, thought Collington. Moreton had somehow discovered the Saudi negotiations and recognised them as a risk to the US oil supplies. How? The Saudi court was the most obvious — as obvious as the attempted warning to the Arab prince about the attacks on five specific mines. It removed the baffling inconsistency about the selection, which no one had been able to resolve. Until now. It might even have worked, Collington conceded, if Hassan hadn't been so desperate for £100,000,000. The word stayed with him, an irritation. Wasn't there also a desperation about America, albeit disguised, mounting attacks on South African territory? He'd replaced one inconsistency with another. But this time, he thought he knew a way to resolve it.

'An amazing coincidence,' agreed Collington. He wouldn't talk his suspicions through with Hassan. It might frighten the Arab off completely and Collington wanted the agreement settled before his other confrontation with Metzinger.

'We'll continue to use the London embassy for consultation,' decreed Hassan.

'Fine.'

'*Is* there a serious problem with the guerrilla incursion into South Africa?' demanded Hassan.

'South Africa has one of the most efficient security forces in the world,' replied Collington. 'There'll be times when they're defeated. Like Sasol. And like the SAGOMI mines. But don't misread it as a country on retreat.'

'You sound as if you approve of the policy,' said Hassan.

Collington looked up, startled at the assessment. 'I'm philosophical about it,' he corrected.

Collington was aware that he was about to involve himself in an activity in which he was an amateur and uncharacteristically his confidence wavered. Yet he thought he knew enough to defeat Metzinger, and that he was even in a position to bring off the oil deal, as well. The most sensible course of action would have been to alert the security chief to Brigitte re Jong's presence, tell the man about Moreton's conversation with the Saudi prince and let professionals take over. But he wanted to win in everything, just like Metzinger. Which he recognised as dangerous, his usual confidence overflowing into conceit, but he couldn't curb the desire. He remained uncertain throughout the morning, wishing there was someone with whom it was safe to discuss what he hoped to achieve, and then, at noon, he picked up the telephone and called the Burgerspark Hotel. She answered immediately, her voice neutral when he identified himself. The only sound of surprise came when he invited her back to the SAGOMI building and then he remembered the flirtatious impression he had attempted at their first meeting and which he now recognised to have been pointless, guessing that she had expected some continuation. His earlier behaviour worked in his favour. The woman entered his office more confident than on the first occasion, anticipating a repetition and sure of her ability to manipulate the encounter.

'I'm surprised,' she announced at once. There was a feigned petulance about the protest.

'What about?'

'It took so long for you to call.'

She was very good, decided Collington. Had he been the sort of man he had parodied a few days earlier, he would have imagined a conquest.

'Sit down,' he said, curtly.

Her composure faltered slightly, but the coquettish smile remained in place. Slowly, the slowness indicating her curiosity, she lowered herself into the seat to which he had gestured with an almost irritable flick of his hand. Collington had rehearsed the meeting, determined to gain immediate control. He let the silence build up to increase her uncertainty, waiting until she actually began to shift uncomfortably in the chair.

'In Amsterdam you run a business the main function of which has, over recent months, been to purchase gold on the Western market with which the Soviet Union is maintaining a commodities agreement with the United States of America, necessary because of Russia's own disastrous ore production in recent years . . . .'

He stopped, needing breath. He expected his assault to have an immediate effect, for her to wilt under the weight of the accusations. There *was* a discernible change. But not what he expected. The coquettishness went, abandoned like the pretence it was. But there was no collapse. She continued to look at him steadily, refusing any response until he had exhausted the accusations. He was confronting a complete professional, he accepted: she was going to let him fire every shot and mount every charge before she attempted to defend herself.

'Several months ago,' he resumed. 'An Ilyushin airfreighter, carrying £150,000,000 worth of gold to Moscow, crashed in Amsterdam. That shipment was discovered.'

For the first time she gave a reaction, the slightest wincing frown.

'I know why you're here,' said Collington. 'I know your desperation for gold. And I know you'll be exposed if there isn't another release within the next few weeks . . . .'

He let his voice trail, wanting the maximum effect. 'On my word alone, the gold sales will be resumed. Or stay suspended. Whether or not the Soviet arrangement with the United States of America continues or collapses, as the sham it is, depends entirely upon me. And what I decide to recommend to the government depends, in turn, upon you.'

Collington stopped, purposely composed, waiting to see what she would do. It was a measure of her complete professionalism that the woman made no attempt to argue, feigning outrage or astonishment or scrabbling for some retreat. She actually smiled, a faint, defeated expression, and then was immediately realistic.

'You haven't had me arrested,' she said. 'Why not?'

'It wouldn't have served my purpose,' announced Collington. 'I want your help.'

The reversal caused exactly the astonishment he had planned. Her mouth opened fractionally and, guessing her bewilderment, Collington resumed his demands. 'I know it wasn't the Soviet Union who initiated the attacks upon my mines. You've got the facilities to prove it. And I want that proof. I want documents and photographs. And I want it quickly . . . within days . . . .'

She was showing no reaction, trying to calculate an advantage.

'You could run, of course,' said Collington. 'I suppose, if we really want to be melodramatic, you could even cause me some harm, imagining I am some threat to you. Run. Or try any sort of attack against me or any member of my family and I will ensure that South African gold not only remains withheld, but that all the details of your commodity arrangement with the United States are made public. Consider, just for a moment, the effect of that.'

'I don't have to,' capitulated Brigitte, at once.

'I didn't think you would have to,' said Collington. His tension dissipated, leaving him feeling physically sick. He had taken a near preposterous gamble, bludgeoning her into submission. And got away with it. By her failure to deny anything, she had confirmed the Soviet association. Perhaps he was the slightly better professional after all.

'You haven't left me with very many alternatives,' she said.

'I didn't intend to leave you with any,' he replied.

'Who was it?' she demanded.

'The United States of America,' he announced.

Collington knew he was in complete command. She appeared almost visibly smaller in the chair, head turned away from him as she digested the information.

'I don't think it was to affect the arrangement with you: I don't think they suspect your inability to provide the gold to which you're committed.'

'You want proof?' she repeated, fixing the demand in her mind.

'If you provide it for me, then I'll do nothing about making the arrangement publicly known. I'll get a gold release. And I'll show you a way to get over your payment difficulties.'

'That's a sweeping promise,' she said.

'Which I can meet.'

'What if I can't get the proof?'

'You know the answer to that, without my having to tell you,' said Collington.

It was almost as though he were receiving some sort of divine inspiration, thought Henry Moreton. He'd sensed Englehart's irritation at being kept in South Africa, but it was proving the proper decision, just as everything else he had determined in the last months had been one hundred per cent right. Like retaining the surveillance on Prince Hassan after their meeting in Vienna. If he hadn't done that, then he wouldn't have learned of Collington's visit. And if he hadn't discovered the visit while Englehart and his team were still in South Africa and the neighbouring countries, then he wouldn't have been able to hit the son-of-a-bitch again. Some people never learned, thought Moreton. But Hassan was going to. And so was Collington.

Chapter Thirty-Four

Hassan's letter was short, not more than four lines of type, but Louis Knoetze remained hunched over it, apparently reading, while Collington waited patiently before the security chief. The apprehension Collington had known before his meeting with Brigitte re Jong hadn't diminished, despite his belief that he had been successful. Instead it had worsened, as the extremes to which he had gone kept presenting themselves in his mind, like nagging children demanding attention. In little over three weeks he was required to pay £103,000,000 he didn't have for shares he couldn't offer for re-sale, because of the certainty of market depression. His provisional purchases anyway contravened the company laws in at least two of the countries in which they had been made. And not two hours earlier he had actively entered into a conspiracy with someone he knew to be the agent of a regime publicly labelled responsible for sabotaging five of his company's gold mines. Collington was grateful that Knoetze had agreed so readily to meet him: it was time to start covering his positions.

Knoetze's head came up at last, one of his smiles coming on like a signal. 'This is an interesting document,' he said guardedly.

'And one I would like you to convey to the appropriate people,' said Collington.

Knoetze nodded. 'There will be a lot of questions.'

'The arrangements will have no connection whatsoever with South Africa,' said Collington, the assurances already established in his mind. 'SAGOMI will extend the existing shipping division in England to include oil and to be initial handlers. The Saudi oil will be processed through America, re-sold through different holding companies and finally returned to Europe. There will be a purchasing company established in Amsterdam which will buy, apparently on the spot market, through Swiss nominees. The tankers will be re-routed in transit to Durban and any other port that is specified.'

'A labyrinthine process,' said Knoetze.

'But a practical one,' said Collington. 'One that will be virtually undetectable.'

'What would you want?' demanded Knoetze, continuing with practicalities.

'Exclusive distribution rights throughout the country,' stipulated Collington. 'Government aid in creating refinery, storage and distribution arrangements.'

'Our dependence might become less when the Sasol plants are rebuilt.'

'I would expect, in recognition of the efforts to which my company is going during these times of difficulty, for us to be awarded greatly increased contracts for our coal mines,' said Collington.

A smile wisped across Knoetze's face. 'So you'll be covered both ways.'

'Few businessmen enjoy gambling to this extent,' said Collington. Except me, he thought.

'It wouldn't quite be true to say the arrangements would remain unconnected with the government, would it?' challenged Knoetze, isolating the point that Prince Hassan had missed during the Vienna discussions. 'Unless you intend purchasing £50,000,000 worth of gold on the open market to meet the agreed commission, then the authorisation and indeed the bullion would have to come from us.'

'I would look to the government for some positive indication of support,' said Collington.

'Confined to the gold provision?'

Collington shook his head. 'There would have to be some contractual understanding,' he said. From the inside pocket of his jacket he took the letter he had prepared before he left the SAGOMI headquarters. 'Here is the formal offer, on behalf of my company, to provide oil within the country of South Africa.'

Knoetze opened the unsealed envelope. There was one more line of type than in Hassan's letter.

'Admirably discreet,' said Knoetze.

'Acknowledgement of which I am sure my board would consider sufficient to commit the necessary expenditure and resources.'

'I'll forward your approach,' undertook Knoetze.

Almost there, thought Collington. 'I've undertaken to respond to Prince Hassan within a few days,' he exaggerated.

'I don't imagine it would take long for a reaction,' said Knoetze. He took a folder from a side drawer and carefully filed both letters.

There was still the gold release, Collington remembered, but this wasn't the moment to raise it.

'You'll be in Pretoria for the next week?' asked the security chief.

'I am available at any time,' said Collington.

Knoetze stood, to end the meeting. He extended his hand and said, 'We'll be in touch again, very soon.'

Collington arrived back at the SAGOMI building an hour early for his meeting with Metzinger, but almost as soon as he entered his office the intercom sounded and his appointments secretary said the deputy chairman was waiting. Collington had prepared for the encounter, perhaps more than for any of the previous meetings that day. The card house was almost built – but it would only take the slightest shake of the hand to bring it all tumbling down.

Metzinger flustered into the room, his uneasiness immediately registering with Collington. 'I've wanted to see you since this morning,' he complained at once.

'There isn't much for you to know,' said Collington.

'What happened?' said Metzinger, the concern obvious.

'The explosions worried him.'

'What do you mean?'

'He wanted an assurance that we could guarantee supply.'

'Damn!' said Metzinger.

'I told him it wasn't serious: that if we came to an agreement with the government, they could guarantee supply anyway, not just from our mines.'

'Did he accept that?'

'He seemed to,' said Collington, letting the doubt show.

'He wasn't prepared to enter into any sort of written undertaking?'

'Good God, no!' said Collington, as if the idea were ridiculous.

'Then what the hell did he want to see you in Vienna for?'

'An assurance, like I told you.'

'Which you gave him,' reminded Metzinger.

'And which he's taking back to Jeddah,' said Collington. It was time to extend the lure, to make Metzinger think it would still all work and hopefully to neutralise him against any action while Knoetze responded. Once he had a government document, Collington knew he would be safe.

Judging by the man's anxiety, it was obvious that Metzinger intended to complete his coup at the annual meeting, just three weeks away. The exposure would cause the share dip from which the man would ensure his financial recovery. The outrage to the shareholders would have to be staged just before that. So a fortnight would be the right timing, decided Collington.

'How long is that going to take?' demanded Metzinger.

'We left it loose,' said Collington. 'There was vague talk about a couple of weeks.'

He was intent upon the other man: the relief was visible. Collington hurried the meeting on. 'I see from the engineer's report that they expect to get Witwatersrand Four into production by the weekend,' he said.

'I read it,' said Metzinger, disinterestedly.

'The shares have settled,' said Collington. The idea of apparently anticipating the stockholders' meeting came abruptly. 'There should be a vote of appreciation for what we've done,' he said.

'There should be a vote,' said Metzinger heavily, and Collington decided he'd succeeded here, as well. It had been quite a day.

They lay side by side in the darkness. Collington knew she wanted him to make love to her and knew equally well that he couldn't.

'There was a letter from Paul today,' she said.

Collington wondered why she had waited until now to tell him. Not more than a fortnight ago it had been the predominant subject between them. She had delayed purposely, he recognised, to emphasise his lack of interest. In everything.

'What did he say?'

'He's looking forward to coming home. And that he's glad we're together.'

'Good.'

She stirred beside him, as if she were irritated by his response. 'We still haven't decided what we're going to do.'

He hadn't given any thought to that, either, Collington realised.

'He didn't say what he wanted?'

'He said he'd be happy, whatever we decided,' said Hannah. 'Either a safari or the coast.'

There was a possibility that in three weeks he wouldn't be able to afford either. He'd never before imagined himself without money. As a railway porter, £1 a week had been a fortune. The £7,500 from Berlin *had* been a fortune. Ever since then he'd had money. In increasing amounts, until he had ceased to be aware of it. Who would find it easier to adjust to being poor, he or Hannah? It was fortunate she had a personal fortune independent of his. For herself, of course. Collington knew he couldn't ever contemplate living off Hannah.

'Things haven't been easy lately,' he said, in clumsy apology.

'Don't you think I know that?'

'It's *because* you know that I said it. This hasn't been much of a reconciliation, has it?'

'There have been some things missing,' she said lightly.

He felt out for her hand, to show his gratitude for her gesture. He was suddenly overwhelmed by the need to confide in somebody. The words burst out, without coherence. 'I've extended myself, incredibly,' he said. 'There's a possibility that it will all work out. But an even greater possibility that it will go wrong and I'll lose everything . . . the money . . . the companies . . . everything.'

She moved suddenly and the light snapped on. She was supported on an elbow, looking down at him. 'The mine bombings?' she said.

He shook his head, almost irritably. 'That's only part of it.' He was sorry she had put the light on because his eyes flooded and he remembered that night with Ann in the hotel room in Rome.

There's nothing wrong in being like other people, in crying sometimes, she'd said.

'Everything?' she repeated, as if she wanted to be sure. 'Money, the companies, everything?'

'It could happen,' he said.

He saw a smile form on her face. 'I don't think that would be at all bad,' she said.

'You don't know what I mean,' he said.

'I think I do,' she said. 'I think it's you who doesn't know what it could mean!'

Chapter Thirty-Five

Krotkov had a fat man's nimbleness in everything he did. After the South African accusations over the mine bombings, he had moved people into Namibia, Mozambique, Zimbabwe and Angola to supplement those he had there permanently. Brigitte re Jong's message, following her encounter with Collington, gave him the focus for enquiries which were already underway. He flooded in more operatives, not from Moscow or any satellite country, which would have taken too much time, but south from the Ogaden, where Russia was helping the Ethiopian government in their secession war against Eritrea and where he had men to spare.

The Russian teams had been working for a week before Englehart, in Pretoria, was instructed by Moreton to mount another sabotage operation against the SAGOMI mines.

'It's not possible, not like before,' protested the section head, careless in his desperation that it was an open line.

'I want it done,' insisted Moreton.

'They've improved their security — it would never work.'

'Collington saw Hassan again,' said Moreton. 'Neither got the message, so it's got to be repeated.'

'Has this been cleared with the Director?'

'It doesn't have to be: don't challenge me, Englehart!'

Moreton had flipped, decided the section head. He was being manipulated by a megalomaniac and he had to attempt something to get out from underneath when the collapse happened. To argue with Moreton was pointless.

'It'll take several days,' he said cautiously.

'As quickly as possible,' insisted Moreton. 'I don't want those two bastards coming to any agreement that's going to endanger our oil supplies.'

'I'll do my best,' promised Englehart. To abort the whole damned thing, he thought.

What he intended was insubordination. The Langley orders had been quite explicit that he act under Moreton's instructions, so to challenge them was the equivalent of going against an edict of Bradley Cowles himself. But Englehart was convinced he was justified in doing it.

Communications for Englehart were more difficult than they were for Krotkov. In the Communist-sympathetic bordering countries, the Russians could move freely and were assured closed telephone and telex lines. The American had to use couriers to reach the supervisors controlling his people in Mozambique and Zimbabwe and instruct them to continue the chain, sideways into Namibia and northwards into Angola.

It took two days for Englehart to get acknowledgement from everyone, and he flew from Pretoria to the Seychelles, unaware that his alert to his team in the Mozambique capital of Maputo had been intercepted and that his controllers in Angola and Zimbabwe had been identified.

On the Wednesday following Moreton's telephone call, four CIA agents of supervisor rank flew from their separate postings into Victoria on the main Seychellois island of Mahe, and on each of the aircraft that carried them there were shadowing Russians.

Englehart had chosen the Mahe Beach Hotel, on the far side of the island from the main township, correctly guessing it would be quieter there and better suited to his purpose.

Freed from the need to maintain the false identities under which they had been acting in Africa, details of which the Russians already had, the Americans registered under their correct names and nationalities. It took two Russians to occupy the desk clerk's attention and another to feign difficulty reloading a complicated camera, for the fourth to get photographs of the registration particulars including the passport number of each man.

The Americans were photographed in groups on the open-sided terrace, and separately around the cliff-side pool overlooking L'Islette. It was on L'Islette that Englehart had gathered his people for the conference because it was a miniscule island where security could best be maintained. He decided to brief them one night when his group were the only people eating in the sole restaurant on the island; the other couple, who had come across in the following boat, seemed content to remain in the thatched bar, far enough away from the eating area not to overhear any of the conversation. Even so, Englehart kept his voice low as he disclosed Moreton's instructions and how he intended to oppose them.

'Another attack wouldn't work,' insisted Hank Barrett, who controlled the group in Mozambique. 'Four of the mines are without refrigeration anyway, so we couldn't use the devices we employed last time.'

'You'd still be taking a hell of a chance,' warned Walter Blake, who had come from Angola. 'Moreton carries a lot of weight.'

'That's why I called you here,' said Englehart. 'I want your support for the objection I'm going to make.'

Around the table there were varying shifts of unease from men who had reached a certain echelon in the agency, knew the politics of Washington and realised the danger to further promotion of bucking a system so openly.

'I'm not asking for a positive endorsement,' said Englehart, sensing the reluctance. 'I want to say in my objection that none of you consider the operation feasible and would confirm that if Langley required you to do so.'

'I'd do that,' said Nelson Siebert, who was based in Salisbury.

'You're wrongly placed to make the proper sort of argument,' warned the fourth man, Peter Grant. 'Langley are bound to check with Moreton, knowing the power he has with the President. And Moreton will screw you for going behind his back. And you're thousands of miles away, not able to fight back.'

'Maybe so,' agreed Englehart objectively. 'But the protest will be registered. It'll give us some protection if we're ordered to go ahead and the whole thing fouls up.'

There was fresh movement around the table as the assembled men belatedly recognised the advantages as well as the disadvantages of supporting Englehart.

'It's a bastard,' said Barrett. 'Whatever happens, we're caught in the middle.'

'Why's Moreton in a position to do this anyway?' demanded Siebert. 'What's he trying to achieve?'

Another standard instruction, thought Englehart; the need to know factor. It was an extension of the cell protection idea, not allowing people — even senior operatives — to know more than they need, for fear of future embarrassment. If he were seeking their help, Englehart supposed he should tell them. But enough rules had already been broken.

'Classified, above your ratings,' he said.

They all knew the regulations as well as he did. There were nods of acceptance from the men around the table at his refusal to tell them.

'But we need insurance,' stressed Englehart, assessing the shift in his favour.

'If you like,' said Siebert extravagantly, 'You can name me in the first objection.'

It acted as a challenge to the other three supervisors. For several moments none of them appeared to want to meet the eyes of the others. 'It'll go wrong, a second time,' said Barrett, as if he were arguing with himself. 'So we'll need protection.'

Englehart remained silent, knowing there was no further pressure he could impose. It was a relief to deal again with sane men.

'Include me in,' blurted Barrett. 'The way I see it, we're fucked either way.'

'We'll seem divided, if all the names aren't included,' said Grant.

'And we're not,' came in Blake.

'Name me,' said Grant.

'And me,' said Blake.

Englehart looked around to each of the men before speaking. Then he said quietly, 'Thank you. Thank you very much.'

'I'd like to think this would have some effect,' said Siebert. 'Like getting it aborted.'

'It's amazing how often it happens, some guy going maverick and people at the top not being able to see it,' said Barrett.

'They're going to see it soon,' said Englehart. 'I'm going to make them!'

'We hope so,' said Grant.

Only yards from the restaurant the sea lapped into a tiny bay and they carried their brandy there, staring out over the darkened water. 'This would be a great place for a vacation,' said Siebert.

'After this, we're all going to need vacations,' said Englehart.

Until his arrival in the Seychelles, Englehart had been the only American agent unidentified. On the aircraft carrying him back to South Africa there were three Russians, maintaining the surveillance which had now been established. All the photographic evidence went immediately back to Moscow.

Englehart timed his return so that the plane would arrive early in the day, not wanting to waste any time in attempting to block Moreton. Until now he had worked independently of the embassy, obeying the standing instruction that covert operations should be kept separate from any diplomatic mission, because of the risk of embarrassment. Breaking cover and identifying himself to the CIA Resident in the Pretorius Street consulate was therefore in direct contravention of normal behaviour, as well as being the first provable open challenge to the Treasury Secretary. The second came very quickly. From the secure communications room, Englehart opened up a telex link with Langley, attaching a priority coding to his message and setting out in complete detail the instructions he had been given by Moreton. Against them he listed his objections and added the named support to those objections of the four field supervisors. It took him an hour and when he sat back he was drenched in sweat, despite the air-conditioning. He'd risked it all, thought Englehart. The pension. And the cottage, with the sea fishing available just across the boardwalk. Everything. It seemed difficult to remember that only a few weeks before everything had seemed so assured.

The embassy-attached CIA man offered Englehart lunch but he refused, pleading the after-effect of airline meals, although knowing it wasn't anything he'd eaten which was causing the sick feeling. Twice he started forward when the machine twitched into operation, but on both occasions it was just normal State Department traffic. When the reply did come it was brief and, although he had anticipated it, there was still a sweep of nausea, far worse than anything he had experienced up until now. He was to proceed with the instructions that he had been given. And upon his return to Washington present himself for a directorate enquiry into his conduct. Englehart swallowed against the sickness and the defeat, thanked the embassy staff for their assistance, and emerged blinking into the sudden brightness of the mid-afternoon sun.

The photographs of Englehart entering and leaving the embassy completed the file and provided the most damning evidence. Until then, the pictures had been of American nationals. With the American consulate in Thibault House clearly defined on at least six prints, there was now a provable link with the government of the United States.

It was nearly midnight in Moscow when the final photographs arrived there. Krotkov was still in his office, though. And so was Leonov.

'It's been a very complete operation,' praised Leonov.

'So now what do we do with it?' asked Krotkov.

'What do you mean?'

'The woman is too exposed. And Collington has got too much control.'

'If he'd wanted to cause a problem, he could have done it just by disclosing her to the South African authorities. Why have us do all this?'

'I don't know why. Which creates an uncertainty. And I don't like uncertainties,' said Krotkov.

'We've got to meet his demands,' said Leonov, answering the original question.

Krotkov nodded, accepting the inevitability. 'But I think I'll keep the men who followed Englehart back to Pretoria in South Africa, to back her if she needs any help.'

'What are you going to do about the American groups?'

'Arrange their arrest,' said Krotkov. 'We're well placed in every country.'

'What about Collington?' pressed Leonov.

'Go along with what he asks,' said Krotkov. 'What else can I do?'

One thing, he remembered from Brigitte re Jong's initial message, was to provide a satisfactory explanation of the way in which such material could come into the industrialist's possession. The aircraft upon which it would have been carried, had it been in the diplomatic bag, arrived at Cairo at 6 am. By seven, the Soviet authorities had lodged a protest with the Egyptians, alleging that articles under consular privilege had been tampered with. Krotkov was unaware that the close proximity to Israel would help Collington even more.

Chapter Thirty-Six

Collington sat forcing the composure into himself, knowing that he was within fingertip reach of achieving at least partially what he wanted, but knowing equally well that if Knoetze reacted wrongly, it could all be snatched away from him. He was curious at the feeling of hollowness in his stomach: he had never known that degree of uncertainty — not even sitting at a prohibited cross-roads in Berlin in a darkened lorry, waiting for a torch to flash and knowing that a misinterpreted signal would mean the blare of klaxons and a cross-fire of section guards. Perhaps he had never taken this degree of risk before.

It hadn't seemed a risk, three hours earlier, when Brigitte re Jong had walked into his office with a file that confirmed more than he had ever hoped, let him read the accounts and look at the photographs and then demanded that he keep his side of the bargain they had reached. But now it did. Collington realised he would have to be careful of every word and every nuance of every word.

'Am I to assume this comes from the same source as your original information about the Soviet gold difficulty?' demanded the South African security chief.

There was no flickering smile and Collington realised the mannerism had always been an act, an attempt to lull whoever he was confronting into the belief of some superiority. 'Yes,' he said.

Knoetze looked pointedly at his watch. 'The Soviet protest about diplomatic interference at Cairo was made less than twenty-four hours ago,' he said. 'Your influence astonishes me, Mr Collington.'

'To learn what I did about the gold shipment, I had to let the Israeli authorities understand I was acting in a semi-official capacity,' said Collington. 'They regard me as a conduit.'

'To me?'

'To someone with influence within the government.'

'What do they want?'

'Information in return.'

'About what?'

'The next gold release.'

'Why?' Knoetze was snapping the questions out, trying to force the pace of the conversation.

'To emigrate from the Soviet Union to Israel, Jews have to purchase exit visas. Money, for that purpose, is supplied through the Dutch embassy in Moscow.'

'I am aware of the procedure,' said Knoetze.

Collington hadn't been, until Brigitte re Jong had told him when they had rehearsed the story earlier that morning; then it had seemed more acceptable than it did now.

'In the past weeks, Israel has used the Russian gold shortage. They've paid for visas in gold, using the Soviet desperation to force up the numbers being allowed to leave.'

Knoetze nodded, but it was impossible to gauge from the gesture whether or not he was accepting the explanation. 'And they want to know how much longer they can exert the pressure?'

'That's the inference,' said Collington. It was difficult, while he stood confronting this suspicious man, to imagine he had thought of the previous seven days as inactive. Even compared to his normal activities, they had been hectic. He had toured the mines twice. And held on-the-spot meetings with the respective engineers. He had chaired two board meetings at which they had considered the continued steadiness of the shares and tentatively agreed an agenda for the annual meeting, now little more than a fortnight away. And he had provided personal guarantored assurance to brokers in London and New York that he was in a position to complete in fourteen days the purchase of £103,000,000 worth of shares, which he wasn't.

'There seems to be the need for a lot of inference,' said Knoetze heavily. 'And unquestioned acceptance.'

'It was obviously my duty to pass the information on,' said Collington, indicating the file now neatly reassembled in front of Knoetze.

'Obviously,' agreed Knoetze. He looked down at the folder, without reading it. He sat like that for several moments. At last he came back to Collington.

'You have provided me with invaluable information,' he said simply. 'Information for which I am grateful and for which others in the government will be grateful . . . .' He paused, opening a drawer and taking out a letter. He held it in both hands, not offering it to Collington. 'This is the government's response to your offer to supply oil. It's an acceptance. And an agreement, too, to release sufficient gold for you to conclude the commission agreement with Prince Hassan.'

Knoetze shifted his grasp so that he was holding the letter even tighter. 'Your help over recent weeks to my government has been quite remarkable,' he said. 'If the oil negotiations are successfully concluded, then it will continue to be so . . . .' He stopped again, looking down at the file once more.

'You're a man with a reputation, Mr Collington,' he resumed, without looking up. 'A reputation for the unorthodox . . . .' He indicated the letter in his hand. 'Which would seem to be justified from this.'

He looked up suddenly, abruptly coming to the point. 'I would not like that unorthodoxy to become an embarrassment. To the government. To myself. Or to you.'

Collington's instinctive reaction was to confront the innuendo, but he controlled it. In every business negotiation there was the time for argument and the time for compromise. Just six feet away, being kept firmly from him, was the document with which he could defeat Metzinger's move. It was the time for compromise.

'I've always been particularly careful to avoid any sort of embarrassment,' he said.

'I hope it continues that way.'

'I intend it to.'

Knoetze lifted the letter in front of him, as if still debating what to do with it, and then slid it across the desk towards Collington. As Collington reached out for it, Knoetze said, 'Gold sales are going to be resumed in three weeks. There is to be a formal announcement in a week.'

Collington pocketed the letter securely, then offered his hand across the desk. Knoetze rose to take it. 'Thank you, Mr Collington.'

'Thank you,' replied Collington. It had been close, he decided. But he had got away with it. There was still a long way to go for complete victory, but the feeling of hollowness wasn't with him any more. But there wasn't a sensation of success, either.

Although they had discussed it generally during the meeting in the Seychelles, it wasn't until the positive directive came back from Langley that Englehart fully considered the practical difficulty of staging another attack against the SAGOMI mines, because until that moment he had hoped the instructions would be countermanded. And by then it was too late, because his judgment was impaired by the threat of the directorate enquiry. The almost inevitable outcome would be his dismissal from the service and his only consideration was to get back to Washington as soon as possible, to mount a defence to prevent that happening. Everything in his training dictated that he should have employed a different method of sabotage from that used on the first occasion. But he had wasted a week in fruitless objection, and it would have taken at least another week to move different material in from America.

The African National Congress had the greatest concentration in Mozambique and so it was to Hank Barrett in Maputo that the instruction went. Barrett, who was more rational than Englehart and who had been the one to warn against using the heat-activated devices again, wanted to dispute the order. But Englehart had stipulated a time limit, because he was sending messages to the other groups, pulling them out, and Barrett knew there was insufficient time to argue, since they were still using couriers and that meant a minimum delay of three days.

The ANC controllers in Mozambique still believed that Barrett's infiltrators were passing on instructions from Moscow and they responded immediately. The unquestioned order passed southwards through their command structure to the undetected guerrillas they still had working at Witwatersrand Four. There were three.

Here the mistakes which had begun with Englehart's misjudgment were compounded by further but more understandable human error. Two of the terrorists wrapped their explosives in bread carried in their meal tins, naïvely believing that the dough would be a sufficient barrier against the metal detection devices. The third attempted to smuggle it into the mine concealed internally. It was this man who was chosen by the medical staff for an anal examination in a spot check. When they saw him being led away, after he had passed safely through the detector, the following two panicked and tried to flee the check line. When the security men started to chase them, one actually threw his meal tin away in an effort to get rid of the evidence. It burst open and the bread split revealing the dynamite.

In Pretoria, Englehart received reluctant confirmation from Barrett that the sabotage would be carried out. The message made him decide it was time to reduce the strength of his team in South Africa. During the day he ordered the twelve operatives who had worked under him to rebase to Washington. The last left on the lunchtime flight. Alone, Englehart spent the time pacing his smoke-filled room, never more than a few yards from the constantly tuned radio, tensely waiting for the news flash which never came. He didn't even hear about the arrests, because Knoetze imposed complete censorship.

By the evening Englehart realised something had gone wrong and his nerve finally snapped. As overall controller, he should have been the last to quit and his intention had been to remain a further two days until those in the neighbouring countries had followed his instructions and he had received confirmation from Langley that they had all safely rebased. Instead, he tried to run. He thrust his belongings into a suitcase, telephoning Johannesburg airport for a seat on the first outgoing flight, which happened to be to England, with stops at Salisbury and Zurich. He booked as far as Switzerland, intending to change there for America.

As a result of the folder which Collington had produced, Englehart's name had been alerted to every air- and seaport, and even while the American was standing with the telephone to his ear, waiting for flight confirmation, the immigration computer hitched by link-line into the larger machine, in which all reservations were processed, was throwing it up with a priority listing.

Englehart sat hunched in the taxi taking him from Pretoria to the international airport, his suitcase clutched protectively against his knees. He was sweating so badly that he stank and chain-smoking, thrusting one half-burned cigarette against another and stubbing out the stump in a shower of sparks and split tobacco. He tried to force rational thought, to convince himself that the absence of news didn't mean there was a failure or detection and that even if there had been arrests, there was nothing whatsoever to link him with them. But there was no cohesion. Between every logical sequence he attempted there intruded images of Moreton, posturing in the Treasury office, and of Ruth, going with him all those weekends to the Cape, until they found the cottage they wanted at a price they could afford.

The seizure was perfectly co-ordinated. Englehart was immediately identified the moment he entered the embarkation hall, but they allowed him to approach the ticket desk, to identify himself and become preoccupied with signing the credit card docket before they moved. Before anyone spoke Englehart became aware of the encirclement. He whirled around, crouching, the despair whimpering from him when he saw how many there were.

Knoetze had helicoptered from Pretoria, assessing the political importance of the arrest and determined to organise it personally. 'If you try to run,' he said, 'we'll shoot you. Not to kill, of course. To cripple you. I want you alive.' The customary smile wasn't there because there was no need to trick this man. He was beyond tricking: beyond everything.

Because of the Russian influence in the other countries, the earlier arrests had been as complete, if slightly less efficient. Hank Barrett had been seized with five men at Maputo airport: he'd booked for the Seychelles again, intending to sneak an unofficial weekend vacation before returning to Washington. As international air routings were easier from Salisbury, Peter Grant had taken his group of six across the border from Namibia into Zimbabwe by road. There he linked with Nelson Siebert and twelve of them had a farewell lunch at the Meikles Hotel to celebrate the end of a successful operation. During the arrests afterwards at Salisbury airport, two of them tried to run: one had his leg broken by a bullet, and the other actually got outside the building, where he was quite accidentally knocked down by a taxi.

Walter Blake and his group almost made it. They got through passport and immigration control at Luanda airport and were waiting for take-off when the security men stormed aboard. Literally belted into their seats, the Americans accepted that any sort of resistance was pointless: at the same time a Swiss businessman had a heart attack, and when he was undressed in hospital, it was discovered he was attempting to smuggle £10,000 worth of diamonds out of the country.

Back in Pretoria, Englehart was subjected to a physical examination for self-destructing drugs that was far more painful and extensive than anything contemplated at Witwatersrand Four. At the moment he entered the cell, stripped of tie, shoelaces and belt, to find he was going to share it with two guards remaining *inside* the ten-foot-square rectangle, Brigitte re Jong was entering the residential penthouse of the SAGOMI building. Since his reconciliation with Hannah, the servants had been re-assigned to Parkstown, and Collington considered it the safest place for the encounter after Knoetze's warning.

Brigitte wondered if, after all, he was going to attempt some sort of seduction. She hoped not. Despite all the obvious reservations, she had begun to admire him.

She refused wine and then spirits and even coffee, anxious to maintain a distance between them, and so Collington stopped bothering, finally sitting down opposite her and telling her simply of the gold release.

'Three weeks?' she queried.

'A normal sale,' he confirmed.

For the first time there was an indication of relief: she appeared to sag physically, as if the tension had been released.

'How much are you short?'

She hesitated, reluctant to concede anything more. Then she realised it was a pointless reserve and said, 'Two and a half tonnes.'

'It's a lot,' admitted Collington. 'But if you buy into short-term contracts, you should cover it, at a cost.'

She nodded. 'I'm grateful for your help.'

Remembering Knoetze's suspicions, Collington said, 'Will you be going back to Amsterdam immediately?'

'Yes,' said Brigitte.

'What's happened has only relieved your short-term problem,' said Collington.

She had started to rise, to leave, but she relaxed back into her chair, realising the meeting wasn't over. 'What do you mean?' she asked.

'Another fluctuation, for whatever reason, and you're extended again.'

'I know,' she accepted.

'Ever thought of another commodity, to replace gold?'

'Like what?'

'Oil,' said Collington.

'America has its guaranteed supplies,' said the woman.

'For the moment,' said Collington.

Chapter Thirty-Seven

The Cabinet meeting had been underway for an hour when Knoetze arrived and they were already planning to use the arrest to its maximum advantage, to impress world opinion with South Africa's readiness to co-operate with the black governments to the north. When the completeness of Knoetze's information was realised, the decision became unanimous. Messages were sent to Luanda, Salisbury and Mozambique, and because of the speed with which South Africa responded, their ambassador in Washington was able to lodge the formal protest note with the American State Department by mid-morning.

Having complied with diplomatic protocol, a limited statement was issued to alert the news media, and then a full press conference called, headed by the Prime Minister and supported by the Minister for Internal Affairs. Here the photographs of the Seychelles meeting were released, and the accusation made by both ministers that the United States had attempted a conspiracy in four countries within the continent.

Because it had happened at Salisbury airport, the shooting had already been reported, with no explanation. Zimbabwe issued a full statement within an hour of the South African release, and because it had the heaviest concentration of foreign press, the coverage there was more extensive than from Angola or Mozambique. Anticipating this, the official South African news agency was supplied with additional information through Knoetze's department.

The American State Department had originally rejected the South African Note, correctly insisting that they were completely ignorant of the affair. That ill-considered action compounded the diplomatic embarrassment which was overwhelming the administration of John William Pemberton like an avalanche.

Pretoria publicly complained of the treatment of its accredited representative and instructed that the protest, unchanged, be delivered again, ensuring that there was television and newspaper coverage of the diplomat's arrival. It was coincidence that the media were still at the State Department when Zimbabwe made its official objection. By then the statements had been made in Africa and the other two countries confirmed that they were demanding official explanations.

Russia had waited, to gauge the international repercussions of the incident. By mid-afternoon it was assessed to be a major difficulty for America and one from which the Soviet Union could substantially benefit politically. In Moscow, a statement was issued through Tass, insisting that the Soviet Union were interested only in peace and the non-involvement in the affairs of other nations. What had happened in Africa finally identified the true instigators of violence and interference which had for too long been wrongly blamed upon Communist influence; the United States seemed to be a country determined upon colonialisation and undermining, by deceit, the established governments of the world.

The besieged offices of the Secretary of State and the Foreign Affairs adviser sought advice from the President. Pemberton realised he was in trouble. Like the true professional he was, he moved immediately to find someone else to blame publicly.

The Central Intelligence Agency had been monitoring the outcry from the moment of South Africa's first announcement. An analysis was prepared for Bradley Cowles, but he knew already — as he travelled from Langley to the White House — that the Agency was facing the biggest potential disaster since he had assumed its Directorship. He would have to be careful.

Cowles had expected it to be a full meeting, perhaps even of Cabinet number, and so he was surprised when he was shown into the Oval Office and found Pemberton alone. His normally immaculate waistcoat was unbuttoned, there weren't any smiles and the man's hair was disarrayed, as if he had been running his hands constantly through it.

'What in the name of Christ is going on?' he demanded, before Cowles had an opportunity to sit down.

It was self-protection time, recognised Cowles. 'I was hoping you would be able to help me, Mr President,' he said.

'Me!' exploded Pemberton. 'What the hell do I know about a guy called Englehart and whoever else is involved?'

'But these men were assigned upon your specific instructions, sir,' said Cowles. From his briefcase he took the presidential order allocating Henry Moreton covert staff and the presidential endorsement entrusting Moreton with full authority over them. The documents were photocopies. The originals were carefully secure in a safe at Langley, the combination of which was known only to Cowles and his immediate directorship.

'Moreton!' said Pemberton incredulously. He snapped down his call button, managing to control his voice for the outside staff, and demanded that the Treasury Secretary be summoned immediately. Then looked up at the Director. 'He's the Secretary to the *Treasury*,' he said, as if to reassure himself.

From the same briefcase Cowles took records of all Englehart's protests, passing them to the President. 'You will see that there were numerous attempts by my officer to question the instructions he was being given,' said the Director. 'On every occasion he was over-ruled by Mr Moreton, upon your authority.'

'That was for a particular thing,' insisted Pemberton desperately.

'It was a standing instruction,' Cowles pointed out. He didn't give a damn who carried the can – it wasn't going to leak out all over him.

'All the charges are right,' said Pemberton faintly. 'We've mounted a covert operation, not just in one but in four African countries!' He sat heavily in the high-backed chair, as if his legs were suddenly insufficient to support him. 'Can you imagine what that means? How it's going to screw any chance we might have had of maintaining any influence anywhere in the whole goddamn continent!'

'Yes, Mr President, I can,' said Cowles. 'I think it's an absolute, unmitigated disaster.'

Pemberton's head came up and Cowles met the look, steadily. It was the President who looked away first and Cowles knew that without a word being spoken the point had been established; he was personally fireproof.

'We've got about twenty-five men in the slammer,' said Pemberton, as if it were necessary to keep repeating the facts to inscribe them in his mind. 'One of them is the head of the covert division, for God's sake! What out have we got?'

'None that I can immediately foresee,' said Cowles.

A buzzer sounded on the President's desk with the secretary's announcement of Moreton's arrival and Pemberton rose up to confront the man, supporting himself forward over the desk in a stance of immediate challenge.

In recent months Moreton had cultivated a languid ambiance, an attentive diffidence to the constant praise for his monetarist policies which had consistently worked on the country's economy. The change in the Treasury Secretary was as marked as it was in Pemberton. Moreton was sweating openly, and he kept opening and closing his hands, as if he were practising strengthening exercises.

'From you,' said the President, 'I want an explanation. And it had better be good.'

Moreton attempted a desperate defence, avoiding Pemberton's demand and turning instead to the CIA Director. 'Your men fouled up!' he said, his voice just below a shout.

Cowles stared back, neither frightened nor impressed by the attack. He pointed towards the President's desk, where Englehart's objection lay uppermost. 'The man appointed to work under your direct control sent a positive memorandum pointing out the dangers of what he was being asked to do. It was not an isolated, personal view. It was supported, by name, by the supervisor of every group that was despatched to Africa upon your insistence. They warned that what they were being asked to do was impossible and that there was a grave risk of failure and detection . . . .' From the briefcase Cowles took his last document. 'This is a copy of your response to that objection,' he said, offering it not to Moreton but to the President. 'It is an insistence that the operation be continued.'

If there were a congressional enquiry, Cowles was confident he could make the cable about a directorate enquiry appear to be not into Englehart's behaviour but into the wiseness of the action. He would then come out of it even more secure.

'There is a law in this country,' said Pemberton, speaking slowly and to Moreton. 'It states that the President has personally to approve of any covert action. Under the Hughes-Ryan amendment, it must go through eight separate congressional committees for confirmation, which hasn't happened. Do you realise I could be impeached for this?'

'During the past year I have stabilised the currency of this country more effectively than at any time during the past fifteen years,' said Moreton. 'I discovered a situation which I considered might seriously interfere with our oil supplies and jeopardise that stability. I acted accordingly.'

There was complete silence in the Oval Office. Both Cowles and Pemberton gazed at the Treasury Secretary, simultaneously aware that the man did not appreciate the enormity of what he had done. And never would, in his conceit.

'You started a private, fucking war!' shouted Pemberton.

'I thought it important that warnings should be given,' said Moreton stubbornly.

Cowles looked away from the man, appearing embarrassed. 'What about my men in the field?' he said to the President. 'Can I have the State Department seek consular access?'

'No!' refused Pemberton at once. 'That would imply some responsibility for what's happened. This thing has been out of control for too long. Now it's containment time.'

'We're going to have to make some kind of announcement,' insisted Cowles.

'And I've decided what it's going to be,' said Pemberton, as the escape route widened before him. 'It will say that enquiries are continuing into an episode of which the American government was absolutely unaware . . . .' He turned to Moreton. 'Which is the truth,' he finished.

'Were you surprised that he kept his word?' asked Leonov.

'Yes,' admitted Krotkov. 'I thought there would be some trickery.'

There was vodka between them for a celebration, but neither man had drunk very much, each aware that the knowledge of a gold release date didn't completely solve their difficulties.

'I wonder what this solution is that he's talking about?'

Krotkov humped his shoulders. 'From the way he's behaved so far, it might be worth considering,' he said.

Leonov added to their glasses and then corked the bottle. 'What would you have done if he hadn't been straight with us?'

'I kept the men who followed Englehart in Pretoria,' reminded Krotkov. 'If he'd done anything . . . exposing Brigitte, for instance, I'd have had him killed. After all, we'd have had nothing to lose, would we?'

'No, I suppose not,' agreed Leonov. How long had it been since that sort of obscene brutality had ceased to horrify him?

Metzinger was clearly growing increasingly desperate. Collington realised first with amusement and then with apprehension that Metzinger was monitoring his movements, not just with unscheduled telephone calls and visits to the office in the SAGOMI building, but with apparently innocent calls to Hannah at Parkstown. If Metzinger learned of a trip outside South Africa, the only interpretation would be that it was to finalise details with Prince Hassan. And if he publicly leaked the negotiations, he could still cause the upheaval and manipulate the no-confidence vote at the shareholders' meeting.

Collington calculated that he needed two uncharted days and planned to get them with the precision of an army assault. He reckoned the analogy was appropriate: he *was* fighting a battle. What was it that Jamieson had said, after Metzinger had succeeded in getting Janet Simpson's voting strength on to the Afrikaner side of the board? Something about a battle not being a war. This time it would be, Collington determined: this battle was going to be decisive for one of them.

He recognised that Hannah was unwittingly a danger. He knew he could ask her to lie over his whereabouts, but she would obviously have demanded an explanation for the deceit and he wanted as much as possible to keep from her the impending confrontation between himself and her father. It was far kinder to remove her as a threat in another way: she'd actually enjoy it, he knew.

'Why don't you make a quick trip to England, to bring Paul back?' he suggested on the Saturday night, at dinner.

Her enthusiasm was immediate. 'What a marvellous idea!' she said.

Chapter Thirty-Eight

Collington started on Sunday in the study of the Parkstown house and then rehearsed throughout Monday for the encounter with Metzinger, needing a situation the older man would regard as ideal but not wanting to make it too perfect and arouse his suspicion. Finally satisfied, he didn't wait for one of Metzinger's unscheduled visits. He summoned the deputy chairman and when Metzinger entered the office, Collington rose to meet him, the excitement obvious. 'Hassan has agreed!' announced Collington.

For a moment there was no reaction from Metzinger. The look on his face was one of faint disbelief, a man not able to accept that everything he had hoped for was about to be realised. 'When?' he asked, curbing any over-enthusiasm.

'A message this morning, from London.'

'He's actually signed a contract?'

Collington shook his head. 'But he's indicated he's ready to.'

'When?' said Metzinger again.

'Saturday, in Zurich,' lied Collington. The timing would have suited everything that Metzinger wanted. The negotiations would have been disclosed at the beginning of the week, creating embarrassment and producing government denials, and by mid-week the shares would have dipped, then risen, allowing him to recover his money before Friday's annual meeting, at which he could have made his public disclosure and invited the shareholders' reaction to Collington's unapproved discussions.

Metzinger was holding himself rigidly under control. He showed no response.

'I'll need to be able to promise something from the government here, once I've got Hassan's written word,' said Collington.

'I'll arrange it, the moment we're sure he's committed,' promised Metzinger.

It wouldn't have been the sort of arrangement he would have expected, Collington knew. Hoping he wasn't going too far, making the denouncement appear almost laughably easy for the man, Collington said: 'Why don't I telephone from Switzerland?'

'That would be a good idea,' agreed Metzinger.

Collington stared across the desk, feeling a flicker of reluctant admiration for the man's negotiating ability. Inwardly he must be euphoric, imagining everything unfolding exactly as he wanted it, but outwardly he remained impassive. It was time to move on, Collington thought, giving Metzinger the impression that he would have an unhindered week in which to finalise the coup.

'Hannah is going to England to fetch Paul home for the long vacation,' said Collington. 'I'm going to take her to Johannesburg. I thought I'd stay over, because it's so central, and inspect the mines from there on Wednesday and Thursday to bring us up to date on the repairs. I'll go to Switzerland Thursday night.'

'Seems sensible,' said Metzinger.

'I'm very hopeful of this,' said Collington, enjoying the ambiguity.

'It seems to have worked well,' said Metzinger, and Collington wondered if he were enjoying the same personal amusement.

'It should mean that we're able to disclose the creation of an oil division at the annual meeting.'

'That and the dividend declaration should make for a lot of contented shareholders,' said Metzinger.

Metzinger lied well, thought Collington. But then, so did he. And he had reluctantly to continue withholding the complete truth at the lunch with Richard Jenkins in the business club near the Union Buildings.

'You want me to demand a board meeting for Friday?' queried the man whom Collington considered the strongest director on the board.

'Without giving a reason,' emphasised Collington. 'Just like Metzinger, when he announced the gold discovery.'

'Is there a connection?'

'Yes.'

Jenkins sat waiting, his knife and fork poised in front of him. When Collington didn't continue, Jenkins said, with characteristic bluntness, 'Well, what the hell is it then?'

'I don't want to tell you, not yet.'

Jenkins frowned, pushing the plate aside. 'What's going on?' he demanded.

'I have personally taken a very great risk,' said Collington, regretting that he sounded conceited. 'I don't want to involve anyone else, not prematurely.'

'You are involving me,' said Jenkins.

Collington shook his head. 'There can't be any embarrassment to you, simply summoning a meeting.'

'There will be when I'm asked to give the reason for the meeting and I don't know it.'

'You won't provide the reason,' said Collington. 'I will.'

'Why don't you summon the meeting?'

'Because I won't be here. Officially, anyway.'

'So Metzinger will be in the chair?'

'He'll believe himself to be, until just before the meeting starts.'

'This is nonsense,' protested Jenkins.

'I know it seems to be,' apologised Collington. 'But believe me, it's not. It'll become clear on Friday. Then you'll see there's a reason.'

'There'd better be,' said Jenkins, unimpressed with the assurance. 'I like my affairs straight, not wrapped up in mumbo jumbo.'

'After this they will be,' said Collington, wondering even now if he were able to give that sort of assurance.

'We've been associated for a long time,' said Jenkins. 'I know your integrity and I know you've never let me down yet. Not me. Nor the company. I'll do what you ask, on this occasion, because of what's happened between us in the past. But this isn't the way I do business. I won't expect this sort of request to be made of me in future.'

'I don't anticipate there'll be the need, in the future,' said Collington. He had expected Jenkins might object, but hardly with this vehemence. Bruce Jamieson would have been more easily persuaded. But Collington had purposely held back from involving his partner in the Zimbabwe mine. He wanted the board meeting demand to be a distraction, something by which Metzinger would be puzzled. If Jamieson had made the request, Metzinger might have guessed his involvement and been alerted to a counter manœuvre.

'When Metzinger called his meeting, you held back from asking him the purpose because you considered it bad tactics,' remembered Jenkins. 'What do I say if the Afrikaners make a positive approach?'

'Refuse it: you've every right.'

'They'd have cause to seek a delay, if they genuinely thought you to be out of the country.'

'Insist it goes to a boardroom vote,' said Collington. 'I just want them all in the same room on Friday morning.'

'Never again,' repeated Jenkins.

'Never again,' promised Collington. From the luncheon club he went back to the SAGOMI building. He gave instructions that he was not to be disturbed and then locked his doors against any chance intrusion. Collington was not a good typist and it took him a long time to complete an unspoiled foolscap page, referenced against the one he had received from Knoetze, agreeing the terms of the Arab's letter of intent and confirming payment in gold. Once that was in Hassan's possession, Collington knew he was safe from any boardroom or shareholders' accusations that he had been involved in unauthorised negotiations and therefore behaved in such a way as to earn a censure vote.

Two days, he thought: it was going to seem a long time.

He left the office early, warning his personal staff that he would not be available for the next three days, and drove home to Parkstown. Hannah was already packed, excited at the thought of a reunion with Paul sooner than she had expected. Because of the journey she was undertaking the following day, they went to bed early. They made love, comfortably relaxed, each wanting to please the other. When she felt him quicken, she pushed her hands gently against his chest, slowing him down; she raised her head to kiss him, taking over the pace. They burst together, driving against each other to prolong it, and finally he rolled wetly on to his side.

'Even when you told me about the other woman, I couldn't stop loving you,' she said, still breathless, in the darkness. 'I don't think there's anything that would ever make me do that.'

Would that remain true, when she discovered what he had done to overthrow her father? he wondered.

Collington had made Hannah's reservation on an early flight, for his convenience more than hers. Ironically, it was to touch down in Zurich on its way to London, but he stood patiently behind the barrier, waving her off, before going to the ticket desk and collecting his own documents for the flight two hours later. He bought newspapers and a paperback book from the kiosk, but found it impossible to concentrate, either in the departure lounge or even once he was aboard the aircraft.

From his window seat he attempted to see the private section and the SAGOMI plane upon which he normally made overseas flights, but his view was obstructed. Metzinger would undoubtedly check upon any flight plans for the aircraft and be reassured when he learned it was being readied for a Thursday flight; there was no way he could learn that it would be taking gold to Zurich, for a deal by then concluded.

Collington tried to sleep, but found that as impossible as his attempts to read. To occupy the time he started to watch the in-flight movie, but the earphones hurt his ears, so he abandoned that too, and sat in the semi-darkened plane watching the silent, unintelligible behaviour of the actors on the miniscule screen. They staged at Lusaka and Cairo and Collington, who was unused to so many stops, found the journey interminable.

It was late when he got to Zurich and as soon as he had checked into the Baur au Lac, he telephoned the Prince's floor to confirm his arrival and their meeting for the following day. He had whisky delivered, but discovered that he didn't want alcohol any more than he did food. Collington was an accomplished traveller, untroubled by climate or time changes, but tonight was an exception. He was tired from the flight, which was unusual, but he couldn't get to sleep. He dozed fitfully, always on a level of half-awake consciousness, his mind drifting from dreams to reality as he tried even at this late stage to isolate any flaws in what he was trying to do. He decided against breakfast, even coffee, using a toothbrush glass to drink water from the tap and hurrying to the lift that was to take him up to the Prince's quarters.

By now Collington was accustomed to the pomp of entire floor reservations and the appearance of a bedouin tribe, occupying the rooms. For this occasion Hassan had reverted to tradition and robes. His greeting was firm-handed and once again accompanied by several declarations of friendship.

Collington showed Hassan the South African government's letter upon which his was based, not letting the man consider them at the same time in case he became aware of the duplicate reference numbers providing the protecting link.

Hassan identified the Swiss Banking Corporation in the Paradeplatz as the place to which he wanted his initial commission sent, producing the authority of the numbered account unmarked and obviously opened within the previous few days.

The Arab offered his hand again and Collington took it. Hassan said, 'We have an agreement. Let's hope we both profit.'

It was time to complete the jigsaw puzzle, Collington decided. 'Despite the effort of those who sought to make it fail,' he said.

'Sought to make it fail?'

'The South African government has confirmed the association between the United States Treasury Secretary's warning to you and the attacks upon my mines,' exaggerated Collington. 'The American arrested at Johannesburg made a full statement saying they intended to keep you in line.'

'Keep me in line!' Hassan's outrage was immediate, his eyes flaring with anger.

'I meant no disrespect,' said Collington, appearing confused. 'I was using the wording the American employed to describe the operation.'

'Is this going to be made public?' said Hassan, the apprehension immediate at the possibility of fresh humiliation after the silver débâcle.

Collington shook his head reassuringly. 'The men in the bordering countries weren't apparently told *why* they were devising the attacks. Only the man in Pretoria knew that. Quite clearly South Africa will do nothing to impair the agreement we've reached. The man will be tried *in camera*, with no details of the evidence.'

The Arab's tension seemed to diminish. 'Keep me in line,' he repeated. 'The impudence of it; the incredible impudence!'

'They appeared to regard your country practically as a satellite state,' said Collington, stoking the fury. 'The man's statement talks of the ease of manipulating members of your government.'

Hassan's nostrils were opening and closing as if he were having difficulty in breathing. 'This was all written down?'

'That. And a lot more,' said Collington. 'But I am assured it will never be disclosed publicly.'

'Will it be read out in court?'

'Presumably,' said Collington.

'Then some people will know: there could be rumours.'

'I've been asked to assure you of the complete discretion of everyone involved: having established these contacts, we're anxious to remain friends.'

'America described itself as our friend.'

'I think it is for you to judge, from recent behaviour, who are true and who are false friends.'

'And for others to discover also,' said Hassan vehemently. 'When can you arrange the transfer of the commission payment?'

'Immediately,' said Collington. 'I have the government's guarantee: you've seen it yourself. It will be lodged in Switzerland by Thursday.'

'You're returning immediately?'

'Tonight,' said Collington.

Hassan straightened in his seat, a man who had made a decision. 'We will continue contact through the embassy in London,' he decided. 'I will expect to be kept fully informed of the company developments: my government won't move until we are completely satisfied with the progress.'

'I fully understand that,' said Collington.

Hassan stood, Collington rising with him. 'I have enjoyed our negotiations,' said the Arab. 'I think they have been honourable.'

'And they will continue to be so,' said Collington. Unless Metzinger discovers what's happening, he thought.

'He's given us the rope to hang him!' insisted Metzinger.

'It would seem so,' agreed Wassenaar, still showing faint reluctance.

'Because he thinks I'm in negotiation with the government, he's going to call me from Switzerland,' said Metzinger. 'We'll be able to plant the stories while he's on his way back and within a couple of days have a full-scale share wobble on our hands. It's all a foregone conclusion.'

'It almost seems too good,' said Wassenaar.

'Have you placed the purchase orders for Janet and myself?'

'I promised I'd do so,' reminded the company lawyer.

'What are you going to do, personally?'

Wassenaar didn't reply at once, his indecision obvious. 'It was a lot of money to lose, the first time,' he said.

'How many more times do I have to show you the way to get it all back?'

'No more,' said Wassenaar positively.

Chapter Thirty-Nine

Three days after the crisis broke, a snap poll questioning the leadership qualities of John Pemberton showed a drop of five per cent. South Africa increased the pressure on Washington, withdrawing its ambassador and refusing to deny newspaper speculation that serious consideration was being given in Pretoria to the question of breaking off diplomatic relations completely.

The government of Zimbabwe hesitated, calculating the extent of American aid following independence, then decided their position was strong enough — because of their chrome upon which the United States was so dependent — and issued a statement that they, too, were reviewing their continued relationship. Moscow fully utilised the situation. The Soviet government took up a long-neglected invitation for their President to make an official visit to Mozambique, to re-affirm friendship not just with the Maputo government but throughout the African continent. The Soviet ambassador in Luanda worked frantically in response to instructions from the Kremlin and succeeded in getting the Angolan government to issue a similar invitation to a Russian delegation. The Soviet response was immediate. The announcement that the Russian President would go direct from Mozambique to Angola politically elevated the visit to a triumphal procession.

The dollar tottered. Its first slump was against the stronger currencies, like the German mark and the Japanese yen. Because of the political nature of the crisis, the central banks were reluctant to come in with immediate support. The sag continued against the English pound and then the peripheral currencies, creating an unacceptable comparison with the collapsing confidence in the American administration.

The international developments were sufficiently worrying by themselves. Then the crisis began to grow internally. A hostile congress, which had waited a year for the opportunity to criticise the President, opened a censure debate and the pressure grew for a committee of enquiry to determine whether there were grounds for an impeachment against Pemberton.

Pemberton chaired an almost continuing session of meetings, the panic obviously rising as they progressed. He saw the Secretary of State and the Foreign Affairs adviser and the party leaders in both Houses, first separately for a personal position assessment and then in joint session, to achieve a consensus opinion.

When nothing better was suggested, he put forward the idea which had begun to form in his mind during that initial meeting with the CIA Director and Henry Moreton. Pemberton argued another piece of American political lore: the benefit of appearing honest with the people, a leader big enough to admit a mistake and then show he had redeemed himself by solving it. The most obvious drawback was that it conceded a weakness in Pemberton's control, but he insisted that this would be overwhelmed by the openness and then the magnanimity he intended to express.

Pemberton prepared the way with care. Through his family's Boston banking connections he succeeded in getting a directorship for Henry Moreton, on the positive agreement that after six months, when the affair had become history, they could dispose of him and that all directorship fees and severance pay upon dismissal would be indirectly met by the Pemberton trust. And then he set about bulldozing Moreton into agreement. For the meeting this time he assembled a group of Cabinet size, including the Secretary of State and the Foreign Affairs adviser, to impress upon the Treasury Secretary the full extent of the damage he had caused and force him, by sheer weight of argument, to agree what was being demanded. Moreton sat outnumbered and confused at the completeness of the personal opposition. He tried, as he had with the President before, to argue a justification for what he had done, and was defeated on every point. When he realised the degree of public humiliation in what was being proposed, he refused the resignation being insisted upon with the reasons that had been so explicitly outlined. It was here that Pemberton cleared the Oval Office, leaving just the two of them. Without witnesses, Pemberton presented the complete ultimatum. Either Moreton resigned, with an apology and allowing the reasons to be published, to take up the $100,000 a year directorship with the Boston Bank. Or he would be fired, still with the reasons being stated, but without a chance in hell of getting a junior clerk's job.

Moreton asked for time to consider and Pemberton refused, insisting upon a written acceptance and the letter of resignation before he left the White House that day. When, finally, Moreton mutely nodded agreement, Pemberton produced the resignation letter already typed upon Treasury Department notepaper, with the signed reply he intended to release to the press. Even before Moreton had passed through the White House gates on his way to clear his desk, Pemberton had summoned his press secretary, insisting on peak-time television for an address to the nation, to be followed by a full, televised press conference.

Pemberton dressed carefully for the appearance, a dark suit and matching tie and at the top of every page of his prepared script, he added a note reminding himself not to smile throughout the address. It was later estimated that not since Nixon's resignation speech after Watergate had there been greater viewing figures.

Three speech-writers had attempted the text and the final version included a great many alterations in Pemberton's own hand. Certainly the beginning was entirely his.

'I stand before you, this Nation, tonight a sad and unhappy man. And a contrite one, too. Contrite because I have failed, on a personal, human level. I misplaced my trust and you, the Nation, have had to suffer . . . .'

Pemberton looked down to his notes, not so much for a reminder but apparently to control a moment of emotion. When he looked back at the camera again, he disclosed abruptly that he had that morning accepted the resignation of the Secretary to the Treasury, Henry Moreton. He recalled the length of their association, the loyalty that the man had shown through the build-up to his candidacy, his election and then in the year of office. And then he spoke of the strain of office, the demands that are constantly made upon public figures and the sometimes physical, sometimes mental breakdown that can happen. There had been such a breakdown, he said. He accepted, fully, that what Moreton had done had grossly exceeded any function of his position, but after a full and searching enquiry he had concluded that throughout the man had believed he was doing the right thing. At a time when no one had suspected the severity of this mental problem, an arrangement had been permitted, giving him access to certain facilities of the CIA. There had been a misunderstanding by the chief of covert operations, a horrifying, terrible misunderstanding that would never be possible again because of fail-safe checks that Pemberton had already introduced. But because of that misunderstanding, Moreton had been allowed to initiate activities in other countries which were wrong and for which, as President of the United States of America, he was publicly apologising. So convinced was he of Moreton's innocence of any intended criminal intention that he had decided to grant him a presidential pardon for what had happened. Moreton was voluntarily entering a sanatorium to rest and to recover his health. Pemberton managed to achieve the perfect note of regret when he declared that Moreton's illness made it impossible for the man to consider any future in public political life. After his release from hospital, he intended to move to Boston where his abilities had already been recognised with an offer of a directorship from one of the city's most prestigious banks.

The television address overran by five minutes and the press conference that followed occupied a full hour. Pemberton had expected the request for a meeting from Cowles: having decided to abandon the men in Africa, he had purposely excluded the CIA Director from any discussions, apart from that initial conference with Moreton. Pemberton agreed to the meeting, wanting to conclude the whole episode.

'My men have been dumped,' complained the Director, at once.

'They committed illegal acts, for Christ's sake! What *could* I have done? There had to be sacrifices, to de-escalate this thing.'

'Will we attempt consular access now?'

'As soon as we resolve the diplomatic representation, of course.'

'And arrange defence lawyers?'

'They're American nationals; they're entitled to that.'

'It won't be much.'

'It's the best we can do.'

'They'll all be jailed.'

'Obviously.'

'What about some diplomatic release, when the heat's gone out of it?'

'When the heat's gone out of it,' half-promised Pemberton. 'But that will take a while. I think tonight went well, but I'm not sure we've contained it as much as I would like to have done.'

Pemberton's speech restored his prestige politically, causing an immediate jump in the popularity polls. But financiers and bankers think with calculators and computers, not with their hearts, and their reaction was apprehension at a presidential admission that for a year the United States economy had been under the direction of a man who was mentally unstable. That uncertainty might have waned with the gradual realisation that there were no more embarrassing disclosures to be made. But it wasn't given an opportunity.

The presidential address had been carried world-wide, so Prince Hassan saw it in Zurich, an hour after his meeting with Collington. Hassan put through a telephone call to Jeddah, where he spoke personally to the king, and Saudi Arabia subsequently announced publicly that it was reducing by twenty-five per cent the oil it supplied to the United States.

This withdrew the final prop for the dollar. In forty-eight hours the run was going to be so extreme that it ended two points below what it had been when Pemberton had assumed office.

Collington caught the night flight back to South Africa and missed both the Saudi announcement and its abrupt affect upon the dollar. By the time he landed at Johannesburg, the dollar slide had already begun and was worsening.

Collington decided against returning to Parkstown. It was mid-evening when the SAGOMI building would be deserted apart from the watchman, so he went to the penthouse apartment. Jenkins responded immediately to the telephone call, relieved to hear of his return. Metzinger and Wassenaar had both separately demanded to know the reason for the unexpected board meeting and Jenkins complained again at the stupidity he had felt, parrotting the answers Collington had suggested.

'It'll all become clear tomorrow,' promised Collington.

'It had bloody well better do,' said Jenkins.

Collington smiled, unoffended by Jenkins' brusqueness. He cleared the line for his second call to Louis Knoetze.

Chapter Forty

Collington slept well, which surprised him, but he woke early. There was a vague light groping its way from the windows and he guessed it was about four. Six hours, then, until the confrontation. He lay, hands cupped behind his head, waiting for the satisfaction. For days, weeks even, his mind had been filled with thoughts of defeat or victory, battles instead of wars and winning rather than losing.

He'd outsmarted Metzinger. So victory applied. Winning, too. Maybe even war, because if it went exactly as he anticipated, he could probably oust the deputy chairman from the board. Yet there was no sensation of triumph — just a blankness, which was even more of a surprise. He'd always felt *something*, no matter how mundane the eventual negotiation. Perhaps it would come later, when the moment actually arrived.

He tried to rehearse everything that would happen in the coming day and then abandoned the attempt, because his mind was becoming blocked with conflicting ideas. At last he rose from his bed and went to the bureau to make notes of advice on the day's events.

The apartment was not scheduled for occupation so there was no food, but Collington decided it didn't matter. He was not hungry. Breakfast would have simply been an activity, a way of occupying the intervening time. He bathed, leisurely, and then shaved, equally unhurriedly, pausing to stare at his reflection, looking for the strain signs from what he had been doing. His eyes appeared pinched but then maybe they'd always been like that. Certainly there was no apprehensive paleness or twitching nerve end, blinking a signal of the tension under which he had been working. In fact, Collington thought he looked quite fit.

The most obvious exit from the apartment, leading directly into the publicly used part of the building, was via the elevator. But there was also a fire escape, descending the length of the building through enclosed, little-used corridors, and that was how Collington went to the executive level. Re-entry back into the building was by a door conveniently close to his personal offices and Collington was satisfied that he negotiated the short distance without being identified. There were five secretaries, apart from Geoffrey Wall. He warned Wall about his appointment with Knoetze and told everyone else that his presence was not to be acknowledged anywhere in the building, irrespective of who made the enquiry.

Wall was waiting in the foyer for Knoetze's arrival and hurried the security chief immediately to Collington's suite. The man entered lounge-suited and with the habitual half-smile hovering ready at the corner of his mouth.

'We've caused chaos in Washington,' he said.

'So have the Arabs,' said Collington.

'How was it with Hassan?'

'Little more than a formality, really,' said Collington. 'But now everyone is contractually bound.'

'How long do you imagine it will take you to set everything up?'

'Not as long as you might think,' said Collington. 'We can lease tankers. Storage space, too. We own accommodation both in London and New York. We'll have to acquire something in Amsterdam, but that can be rented easily enough. The delays will really only be with company formations and assembly of the necessary administrative staff.'

'So we'll be ready to start according to Hassan's timing of six months?'

'I hope to have an operation of some sort underway in three,' said Collington. 'By the time we start shipping here in bulk, I want all the initial difficulties ironed out. Hassan insists we trade elsewhere to provide them with the necessary protection and I think it's a sound idea.'

'Our involvement has been quite different from my usual function,' admitted Knoetze. 'I've enjoyed it. At some stage in the future there are other members of the government who would enjoy meeting you personally.'

Now that all the danger had passed, thought Collington uncritically. 'I would enjoy that,' he said. 'I'm sorry that I had to ask you to come here today, as I did.'

'I understand the reason perfectly,' said Knoetze at once.

Not completely you don't, thought Collington. And he never would.

The clock on Collington's desk was a digital affair and during the conversation with Knoetze he had constantly been aware of the seconds flickering by. At five minutes to ten he said, 'It will be necessary for me to go in alone initially. I want the secretarial staff, apart from my own personal assistant who can take limited Minutes, to leave before you are admitted.'

'That's something I would insist on,' said Knoetze.

Collington waited until the hour had registered, wanting all the other directors to be seated before he made his entry. He went into the boardroom quietly and because the doors were recessed, providing miniscule corridors on either side, the other directors were momentarily unaware of his presence. Metzinger concluded his formal reading of the motion calling the meeting, turning to Jenkins as he did so.

'Perhaps now you'll provide the reason,' said the deputy chairman.

'Because I asked him to,' said Collington, from his concealment.

It was overly dramatic, dictated by the circumstances with which he was presented, and Collington continued into the room with a faint feeling of embarrassment. Only Metzinger and Wassenaar showed astonishment at his presence. Jenkins had known about it anyway and the attitude of the rest of the board was simply mild curiosity, imagining a perfectly understandable explanation.

'But . . . you are not supposed to be here . . . .' flustered Metzinger.

'Things changed,' said Collington. He stopped almost too close to the chair he normally occupied, so that he was bearing down upon the man. 'Shall we revert to normal board procedure,' he said.

Metzinger half stood, crabbing sideways around the table. Everyone else moved up, so Collington sat in his accustomed position, allowing the silence to further unsettle the two Afrikaners who had conspired against him. Then he said, 'I wish to propose the exclusion of all the secretarial staff, with the exception of Geoffrey Wall who can comply with the Minute requirements.'

Metzinger and Wassenaar exchanged looks and the mild curiosity of everyone else deepened into something stronger.

'I'll accept the arrangement enforced the last time this request was made: that an amendment can be put to revert to normal secretarial attendance if, in the opinion of the rest of the board, the reasons are unacceptable,' added Collington, moving to block Metzinger's escape routes.

'Seconded,' said Jenkins, more curious than the other non-Afrikaners because of his involvement so far.

'I object,' tried Metzinger, thrusting at shadows. 'The board should be given a reason, both for the request and for the bizarre manner in which this meeting was convened.'

The Afrikaner had recovered, Collington assessed. And was frantic. He would do everything he could to wreck the meeting, to give him time to discover what was happening and the danger that existed in it, for him.

'No reason was given for the closed session convened at your request,' reminded Collington. 'It is *precisely* that I wish to offer an explanation that I want again to go into private committee . . . .' He permitted just the right amount of pause and then made what appeared to be his concession. 'And on this occasion I have agreed to the presence of a Minute clerk, which didn't happen the last time . . . .'

'Seems fair to me,' said Jamieson.

'And me,' said Platt.

Seeing the way the meeting was going, Metzinger said hurriedly, 'I propose an amendment to the motion. That this board meeting does not go into closed session. And that it is postponed until the chairman provides a written explanation for his behaviour.'

'Seconded,' said Wassenaar at once.

'Is there any wish to talk upon the amendment?' invited Collington. Metzinger had shown his panic, he decided; he was sure he'd get the vote. There were negative movements from around the table.

'In favour of remaining in open session and postponement, for a formal explanation,' summarised Collington.

The hands of Metzinger and Wassenaar jerked up at once and Metzinger said, 'I carry the proxy vote of Mrs Simpson.'

De Villiers was frowning between the two sides. Metzinger turned to him pointedly, and with apparent reluctance the third Afrikaner raised his hand in support.

'Against?' said Collington.

Five hands went up simultaneously.

'For closed session?' said Collington.

Five hands went up again and he said, 'The original motion is carried.'

He sat back while the room cleared, forcing the smile and the attitude of relaxation further, to disconcert Metzinger. The Afrikaner was hunched sideways, his ear only inches from Wassenaar's whispered conversation. Wall had overseen the departure of the secretaries. He came back into the room, nodding, and Collington said, 'Shall we proceed?'

There was a movement of expectation around the table. From his document case Collington took the photostats of the letters of agreement from the South African government and the Saudi prince, together with his response to both of them, and he handed them to Wall for distribution. Momentarily all the heads were bent away from him. Metzinger was the first to look up, his face purple with fury at the first awareness of how he had been outwitted. 'This is improper . . . .' he started, but Collington cut him off.

'Not any more,' he said. 'There might have been some impropriety when the negotiations commenced, and if you would like to talk further to the members of this board about that, then you are at liberty to do so. But for the last weeks I have acted as the agreed emissary between the government of South Africa and that of Saudi Arabia. The need for an intermediary will remain. Both governments are agreed that SAGOMI should provide that intermediary.'

The anger was shuddering through Metzinger, initially at his awareness of how his coup had been turned against him now that Collington had South African government support, and then with the realisation that there was nothing he could do to argue against the man, because he would be damning himself out of his own mouth.

'Some time ago,' took up Collington, 'I was given to understand that the government in Pretoria was anxious to obtain a guaranteed energy supply.' He stopped, looking pointedly at Metzinger. The gaze of the deputy chairman wavered and fell to the photostats on the table before him. Collington started speaking again, encapsulating the negotiations throughout Europe with the Prince and the arrangements he had agreed, both for payment and for the shipment of the oil, through English, American and Dutch cover companies.

'We will have grant aid for refinery and tanker construction and full and exclusive distribution rights throughout this country,' Collington concluded.

'But that's fantastic!' said Jenkins. 'The profit will be enormous.'

'Providing the arrangements continue as they have begun, in absolute secrecy,' qualified Collington.

'You seem to have anticipated that,' said Brooking.

'I have an unusual proposal to make to the meeting,' said Collington. 'But first I want to establish if it is the wish of this board to remain in closed session.'

As he spoke he looked towards the Afrikaners. Metzinger continued to gaze at the table. Both Wassenaar and de Villiers shook their heads. Collington turned to Wall and nodded. The assistant went to the door connecting the boardroom to Collington's office, everyone straining around from the table to see what was happening.

A sound came from Metzinger when he saw Knoetze, a gasp which seemed to stretch into a groan. Collington rose to introduce the security chief to the assembled directors. Wall offered the man a chair, but instead of sitting down Knoetze remained upright. He smiled familiarly at Metzinger, nodding and greeting the man by name; as Metzinger struggled for a response, a faint expression of curiosity passed over Knoetze's face.

'I welcome the invitation to come to talk to you today,' said Knoetze. 'Firstly to express my personal admiration and also that of my government for the conduct throughout the negotiations of your chairman, James Collington. But more so to impress upon you the delicacy of their nature. It is vital that they remain as discreet as they have been so far. We are already witnessing in America the effect of an international embarrassment. South Africa does not want a repetition of that happening here. We have decided to progress because we are convinced that the integrity of your chairman extends to the managing board. It goes without saying, of course, for any public knowledge of this arrangement would cost your various companies untold millions. You have the assurance of my government that you will remain absolutely protected. We seek the same assurances from you.'

And there was the door, closed, locked and firmly bolted behind Metzinger, thought Collington. He had not expected the security chief to be as eloquent. There was an almost uncomfortable silence around the table and Collington said, 'I have already given my personal assurance. I now invite the board to respond.'

From around the table there were movements and gestures of assent. One of the last was Metzinger. Collington was staring at the man, waiting, and as he made the pledge Collington decided that he had secured the windows, as well as the door. Strangely he had expected it to take longer. But then the meeting wasn't over yet.

Knoetze looked to where Wall was sitting at the side table. 'I would appreciate there being no record of my attendance here,' he said.

'There won't be,' promised Collington.

Knoetze hesitated, wondering if there were any more for him to say and then nodded generally towards the table. Wall stood to escort him from the room.

Jenkins was the first to respond. 'I think the chairman deserves a vote of thanks from this board, for what appears to be a highly original but successful negotiation,' he said.

Jamieson was about to react, too, but Collington raised his hand, stopping the man. 'I have something further to say.'

There had been a relaxation from the English side of the board, but now they turned to concentrate upon him again.

'Some weeks ago,' said Collington, moving the early morning reminder notes from his pocket, 'I came to suspect that there was an improper share proposal being mounted against a certain division within the SAGOMI holdings . . . .' He stopped, looking around the table. There had been expectant smiles when he had begun talking, but now they were fading.

'. . . I concluded that it was a bear operation,' resumed Collington. 'I estimated the number of shares involved, initially, at 253,000, all from our mining divison . . . .'

He was looking directly at Metzinger and Wassenaar. They were completely still, gazing up the table at him rigid-faced, knowing they had been caught.

'Why weren't we informed?' demanded Platt.

'For me to have discussed it openly without a vestige of proof would have laid me open to an accusation of libel. Instead, I decided personally to oppose any fluctuation within the company by creating a protection. I placed automatic purchase orders at five points below par.'

'Which came into operation after the bombings?' remembered Jenkins.

'But America caused the sabotage: they've admitted it,' frowned Jamieson.

'The bombings were quite coincidental to the share coup,' said Collington.

'Are you suggesting,' said Platt slowly, 'that you suspect some directors, either of the parent company or of a subsidiary holding, attempted to engage in some illegal manipulation?'

'I believe that my action, in view of the paper profit so far accruing on the purchased shares, could be construed as such. It is for that reason that I am making this declaration now and intend a full statement at the shareholders' meeting next week. I propose today that an independent firm of auditors is called in immediately. I will make available to them all details of my share holdings and dealings in recent weeks. I want all purchases and exchanges to become public for discussion at the annual meeting.'

'Such an investigation should disclose the vendors of the 253,000 shares,' said Platt quickly.

'Yes,' said Collington, regarding Metzinger again. 'My dealings form the reason for the audit and the audit will provide the proof I wasn't able to assemble.'

Wassenaar looked abruptly to Metzinger, expecting the man to react in some way. The deputy chairman made an ineffectual movement with his hands. 'There could be an explanation,' he volunteered weakly.

'Then it can be offered to the shareholders,' said Collington. 'I intend throwing the meeting open for a full vote of confidence.'

'I second the motion to call in auditors,' said Platt.

'Any other views?' demanded Collington, looking to the Afrikaners' side of the table. No one moved.

'I would like a recorded vote,' said Collington mercilessly. Neither Metzinger nor Wassenaar could abstain and they would be voting for their own destruction. Reluctantly the hands went up to form a unanimous decision. Still Collington hadn't finished with them. 'There is a final matter,' he said. 'The share block was created on margin purchases. I provided the money for that, but there is an outstanding settlement debt to brokers of £103,000,000.'

'Can we legally provide liquidity?' asked Jamieson.

'As a company, to prevent improper share speculation, we can,' assured Collington. 'At current stock parity I would like to offer, for company absorption, the shares for which I have made myself responsible.'

'That's five points above what you paid for them,' protested de Villiers.

'On a £15,000,000 loan,' reminded Collington. 'The share sale profit will pay the interest for which I am liable on that loan. I will personally make no financial profit whatsoever. Nor do I seek to.'

'I'll make the purchase a formal proposal,' said Jenkins.

'Seconded,' said Platt.

'Earlier in this meeting, I also suggested that the chairman be thanked,' reminded Jenkins. 'That motion was not proceeded with. I would like to propose it again: I think what the chairman has done in protection of this company has been magnificent.'

'I hope everyone feels that way,' said Collington.

Wassenaar and Metzinger went immediately from the board meeting to Metzinger's offices where Wassenaar burst out in anger; he quickly subsided when Metzinger refused to argue back. The older man sat bent forward over his desk, eyes fixed upon some point in the carpet.

'What are we going to do?' demanded Wassenaar. 'We're trapped. Completely and utterly trapped.'

'I know,' said Metzinger dully.

'Any audit will disclose our sale orders. And he can guide them to it. He *knows*. How else could he have quoted the number that we placed?'

'I'm sorry, Jan,' said Metzinger slowly. 'I led you into it and I'm sorry.'

The contrition momentarily silenced Wassenaar: he was conscious for the first time of the completeness of Metzinger's defeat.

'Marius,' he said, his voice quietly coaxing. 'We've got to do something. I know company law and I know criminal law, where it's applicable. We've committed a crime we could be tried for. And we will be, if the audit goes ahead.'

Metzinger stirred himself, the effort obvious. 'There *is* nothing,' he said.

'A deal,' said Wassenaar, his legal training emerging. 'We've got to offer a deal.'

Metzinger tried to concentrate. 'To make a deal, we'd have to have something to offer,' he said emptily. 'We haven't got anything.'

'Yes we have, Marius.'

'What?'

'Our places on the board. And the 'A' shares.'

'Oh no!' The despair groaned from Metzinger at his acceptance of the sacrifice.

'It's a possibility,' insisted Wassenaar eagerly. 'They don't want any more upheavals after everything that's happened. Collington said so himself. That's our bargain. Our resignations in return for cancellation of the audit. And with no public disclosures, there would be no public damage. Either to us. Or the company.'

'He'd win,' said Metzinger.

'He's *won*,' corrected Wassenaar.

'I can't do it.'

'Would you rather have the disgrace of a trial? Maybe even a jail sentence? With Janet involved as well?'

Metzinger leaned forward against the desk, his head in his hands.

'No,' he said again.

'If you don't make the approach, then I will,' said Wassenaar.

Metzinger looked up at him and Wassenaar saw the man's eyes were wet. 'So you're abandoning me?'

'No, Marius. I'm saving myself.'

Metzinger looked away, staring towards the internal intercom machine which linked his office with that of Collington. He pushed his hand across the table towards it, stopping just short of the button that would connect him to Geoffrey Wall.

'The only way,' urged Wassenaar, by his side.

Jerkily, Metzinger depressed the button. Wall's voice came on the line at once.

'I'd like to see the chairman immediately,' said Metzinger, his voice dry.

'He's expecting you,' said Wall.

'So the panic is over?' said Krotkov.

Leonov nodded, realising that for the first time in months that he wasn't knotted with tension. 'They couldn't give a damn about gold any more. All they want is oil. And we're in surplus.'

'What's involved in changing the contracts?'

'Hardly anything, having both agreed. Cultural attachés could exchange signatures at embassy level.'

'And they're not attempting to alter grain levels against us?'

'The reverse,' said Leonov. 'They've allowed an escalator clause for us to increase the importation if our needs go up.'

'Can we trust Collington that his only advantage is the obvious one — the profit he'll make from shipment?'

Leonov hesitated. 'We've had no cause whatsoever to doubt him so far.'

'What's the decision going to be, do you think?'

'The Politburo directorate have already made it,' disclosed Leonov. 'The oil companies which the man is forming are to be offered, through the Amsterdam brokerage, exclusive transportation rights.'

'He'll make a lot,' said Krotkov.

'He risked a lot,' reminded Leonov.

Chapter Forty-One

It was a subdued meeting: Collington had anticipated an atmosphere, but not one of embarrassment. Yet that was the predominant attitude from the directors whom he had reconvened for the second board meeting in one day.

'I'm astonished,' said Jenkins, breaking the silence after Collington had disclosed his encounter with Metzinger.

'If we agree to the terms, we'll be concealing a crime,' said Platt. 'We can't do it.'

'We've no proof of a crime at the moment,' said Collington. 'And we haven't yet briefed auditors. If we rescind that decision, and if the board is satisfied that I have provided a full explanation of my involvement, then technically we're not in breach of the law.'

'That's debatable,' argued Platt.

'It's also practical,' said Jenkins. 'Amazingly, in recent weeks we've withstood a number of events which might seriously have disturbed the confidence of our shareholders. If this were made public, it would cause the slide we've so far avoided.'

'There's also the undertaking we gave at the earlier meeting to Knoetze,' reminded Jamieson. 'There would be no way we could announce what Metzinger and Wassenaar have been attempting without the negotiations with the Saudis becoming known.'

'And the deal would be wrecked,' said Collington, coming out in support.

'The only effect would be one of upheaval,' said Brooking, assessing the majority feeling and moving with it.

'They've shown a certain honour by offering their resignations,' said de Villiers, attempting a vain defence.

'They've taken the only way out for them to avoid criminal prosecution,' said Platt. 'There's no honour in that.'

'What's the effect of their resignations?' demanded Jenkins.

'They offer the 'A' voting shares for the agreed disposal of the rest of the board, by vote.'

'What about Mrs Simpson?' asked Platt.

'Metzinger exonerates her completely: she acted entirely without knowledge of what was going on. She put her affairs, at Metzinger's suggestion, into Wassenaar's hands. His was the decision to place her shares for sale.'

'So her 'A' shares are not included?' persisted Platt.

'No,' said Collington. Of them all, he supposed Platt was being the least hypocritical, openly acknowledging the opportunity to achieve absolute British supremacy.

'I do not consider that anything would be gained by bringing this affair into the open,' said Jenkins. 'Rather, I think it would be detrimental to the interests of SAGOMI. I move we accept the resignations. And close the matter there.'

'I second,' said de Villiers.

'Before a vote,' said Platt, 'I'd like to discover if anyone has any views on the disposal of the 'A' shares.'

'There are two hundred,' said Collington. 'I propose they are equally divided between the remaining directors.' He could afford to be generous with the disbursement: there was no possibility, ever again, of the Afrikaners gaining control. Where, wondered Collington once more, was any feeling of triumph?

The response, surprisingly, came from de Villiers, a concession of absolute defeat. 'That's very fair,' said the accountant.

With an almost bullying tenacity, Platt persisted relentlessly. 'I think another approach should be made to Mrs Simpson, offering a board absorption, for equal disbursement, of her two hundred 'A' shares,' he said.

There was no reason for his feeling of reluctance, Collington knew. Everything he had done had been for this moment: after the battle that decided the war, it was always necessary to pursue the enemy in defeat, mopping up the stragglers and ensuring, absolutely, that there could be no unexpected counter-attack. Metzinger and Wassenaar were disposing of two hundred shares. If Janet Simpson — shortly to become Metzinger's wife — retained her two hundred, then through her Metzinger's influence would not have diminished at all.

'I have an amendment,' he said, stirring himself at last. His control was absolute and everyone in the room looked towards him, waiting. 'I consider that we should refuse the resignation offers of the deputy chairman and Wassenaar unless they include the disposal offer of the 'A' shares held by Mrs Simpson.'

'But you said she was uninvolved,' said de Villiers, in weak protest.

Everyone in the room recognised that Collington was determined to remove for ever any possibility of Afrikaner control by taking the shares from Simpson's widow. He waited for anyone to take up de Villiers' point. No one spoke and Collington said, ignoring the remaining Afrikaner, 'That is my amendment.'

'Seconded,' said Platt. He smiled towards Collington, as if grateful for the man's decision to remove any danger in the future.

'Amendment for discussion?' invited Collington. He spoke to de Villiers, knowing there could be no other opposition. The Afrikaner accountant collapsed further, shaking his head and refusing to meet Collington's stare.

'The amendment to be voted upon,' decided Collington. He had expected de Villiers to be the last to vote, but his hand went up first.

'Until there is a response from the two absent directors, I suggest that the auditors' examination be deferred,' continued Collington. Again the vote was unanimous.

'You went soft,' complained Platt, as they left the boardroom.

'Disinterested,' corrected Collington.

Two days later, there was solicitors' confirmation that Janet Simpson's shares were offered for disposal. They were equally divided at a board gathering convened the day before the annual general meeting.

At the meeting, the expansion of the London division passed unremarked. Collington declared an overall dividend of twenty-two per cent, which was an increase of seven per cent over the preceding year. The resignations of Metzinger and Wassenaar were recorded as being for personal reasons; Collington proposed a vote of appreciation for their work for the company during their directorships and the vote was unanimous. There was an unopposed acceptance of the chairman's report and of the statement of accounts. The meeting ended with a vote of confidence in the SAGOMI board in general and James Collington in particular.

'You should feel very satisfied,' said Jenkins, as the meeting ended.

'Yes,' said Collington. 'I should, shouldn't I?'

Why then, he wondered, didn't he?

In the first days of his vacation, Paul had been suspicious, looking to see if their togetherness was an act for his benefit. And so there had been a pretension, everyone performing with rehearsed attitudes. Collington had held Hannah back from over-reacting, knowing the child had to make his own decision. If they attempted to intervene, it might delay rather than hasten the process.

By the time of the safari, the child's acceptance was practically complete. Collington had bought him a movie camera and they shot gazelle, giraffe and once, surprisingly, an ostrich. The white hunter later concluded that it had lost its mate and, instead of running away in its grief, as it should have done, it had charged straight-necked at them, splitting its beak against the observation lorry. After that it could not have eaten properly, so they had to kill it. Paul wept and Hannah cried with him.

Collington deferred to the hunter, agreeing that they should run the perimeter of the desert edge, to give them time to acclimatise. By the fourth day they had adjusted to the need to rise by four and rest beneath the awnings during the breath-sucking heat of midday. And that night they camped, laager style, around a camp fire. They had insect lamps to trap the mosquitoes, and after the campfire supper they put Paul to bed in the air-conditioned, shower-provided, flush-toiletted camper.

So much alcohol was unwise, even though the heat had gone from the day and the problem of dehydration didn't exist, but Collington needed the help. And then he told Hannah of the confrontation with her father and what he had done to win, uncertain of her response. The acceptance surprised him, as so much had surprised him in the final, decisive days. There was no anger. No accusation of falsehood or trickery or deceit. She just seemed sad. For a long time she sat head bowed while the cicadae chirruped about them and the thorn trees scraped in the bullying wind and then she said, 'It never ended, did it?'

'What?' he said.

'The war. He still thought it was 1900, with his stupid wagons and his stupid mementoes. Nothing has happened for him since then.' She looked up. 'He tried to stop it happening, you know — our getting back together. During all the trouble with the mines.'

'How?'

'Enquiry agent reports.'

'What did you do with them?'

'Threw them away, without reading them.'

'Thank you,' he said.

'I did it for me, not you.'

Paul learned to stamp a camp area, to clear it, by the vibrations, of snakes and then rake it for scorpions, and on the Monday of the third week the hunter awarded him the prize that went to every child on the Monday of the third week, attesting that he was fully qualified in safari survival technique.

And on that Monday, amid secrecy so complete that no knowledge of the hearing emerged until the government made it public in a terse, four-line statement a fortnight later, Sidney Englehart appeared before a Pretoria court, charged with espionage. He was sentenced, after a four-hour hearing at which his complete confession was read out, to seven years' imprisonment. He was to serve four, two under hard labour, before a diplomatic exchange was surreptitiously arranged. During his imprisonment his wife divorced him, and because the President had declared the operation unofficial and therefore unauthorised, his pension rights were lost. Englehart became the security officer for the Flagler dog track in Florida and his luck held during his ten years of employment: until he died from a heart attack which caused a two-mile traffic jam on Biscayne Boulevarde, there was never a security problem. That employment finally produced a pension of $5000, but there was no one to whom it could be given. It went back into the fund.

Of the operational staff he was the luckiest. There were four operatives under Hank Barrett. They were all imprisoned in a jail in Massangena. Barrett and two others contracted malaria, but it was really the malnutrition which broke their health and when it became obvious that they were terminally ill the Mozambique government returned them to America where all three died within four months. Siebert, always the most volatile, collapsed under the unremitting pressure of his hard labour sentence and became insane. Peter Grant led an escape, after eighteen months of his imprisonment, succeeding in getting eight of the Americans out of their jail and into the bush thirty miles from Bulawayo. Without a compass, they fled the wrong way into the jungle. They were already emaciated and suffering from malaria and it only took a week for them to die, predominantly from exposure. Only Grant survived and when he was discovered, he was so deeply infested with parasites that his left foot had to be amputated. There were five men sentenced in Angola with Walter Blake. All contracted dysentery and before proper treatment could be provided, three of them died. Blake was the first.

It took three years for Nikolai Leonov to get the ambassadorship he sought and there were times when he despaired of ever receiving his reward. It proved a worthwhile, if ironical wait. He was posted to Washington just in time to attend the swearing-in ceremony of John William Pemberton for his second term of office as President of the United States of America.

Henry Moreton began watching the ceremony on the small portable television in the Boston department store where he had managed to get a job as senior costing clerk after his dismissal from the bank. After thirty minutes the memories became too much for him, so he backed away through the crush of people around the screen and went back to work. No one in the store was surprised; he had the reputation of being a dedicated worker.

Because of the executive echelon she had occupied at SAGOMI, Ann Talbot had a reputation among multi-nationals with offices in London and had no difficulty in obtaining a job, although not initially as a personal assistant. It took her three years to achieve that rank. She resisted any romantic attachments, which gave rise to rumours about frigidity and even, briefly, lesbianism.

Even if it hadn't been part of her function, she would have monitored SAGOMI. She read the announcements of Metzinger's and Wassenaar's resignations and guessed that Collington had outmanœuvred them. She even considered writing to Collington out of professional curiousity, but discarded the idea, recognising its stupidity.

She got a board appointment at forty and took a positive career decision, subjugating her sex drive to her ambition. The commitment was absolute. The chairmanship came at forty-six, with disconcerting publicity. She endured it for the benefit of the company, but she didn't enjoy it. There were numerous congratulations and she hoped there would be one from Collington. There wasn't.

At the press conference to which she agreed on the day her appointment was announced, a television reporter asked, 'Do you consider yourself a complete, satisfied woman?'

'Yes,' Ann replied at once. Frequently afterwards, she wondered if Collington had seen the interview. She hoped he had: she'd watched the video recording and knew the response sounded completely honest.

Epilogue

There had been times in those early months after his resignation from SAGOMI when Janet had been concerned at Metzinger's mental health. She knew it came from his complete humiliation in her eyes: he'd even suggested cancelling the wedding, unable to accept that she would still want to marry him after the way he had failed her. She had hoped her insistence upon the ceremony would have helped, but it hadn't. He became increasingly withdrawn and taciturn, hardly speaking to her and spending hours among his Boer memorabilia: once she had even surprised him on the driving box of one of the wagons, the reins in his hands.

The Broederbond appointment saved him. His election as society chairman came unexpectedly and he seized it with an excited eagerness that had surprised and then pleased her. It gave them a social life again, frequently with some government involvement, and Janet enjoyed that. She made herself their social secretary, always making discreet enquiries to ensure that neither Collington nor Hannah would be present at any occasion to create an embarrassment. Sometimes she regretted the lack of contact. Not with Collington, of course: she hated him as much as Marius. But she genuinely liked Hannah and had wanted to make a friend of her.

The couple were never mentioned in the household. Nor would they have been, Janet supposed, but for the announcement of Collington's knighthood. Even then, she waited for her husband to remark upon it.

'Not bad, for a bastard,' said Metzinger, throwing the newspaper down.

'Was he?' asked Janet, remembering Collington's orphanage upbringing and momentarily misunderstanding the remark.

'Yes,' said Metzinger bitterly. 'An absolute bastard.'

She waited for him to continue, but he didn't. She knew everything else, but she wouldn't know about this — not the final defeat. The Broederbond chairmanship had been his chance to beat Collington. It would have taken a long time to create sufficient opposition to the companies, but he knew the organisation was powerful enough to destroy them, finally. And to have destroyed Collington he would have done anything. That had been the first thought when he knew the appointment was to be his, and he carried it with him through the initial meetings and then the induction ceremony. It would have been through Knoetze, he supposed, that Collington had learned of the chairmanship: the security chief was the obvious source, from what he now knew.

The package had arrived a week after his election. Photostats of all the share transactions, dated so the attempted share manœuvre and his part in it was clearly, criminally, identified. It had been anonymous, but Metzinger hadn't needed any explanation for the warning. Because not everything was unidentified. The file had been assembled by the same enquiry agents who had discovered so much about Ann Talbot, which he supposed Collington considered clever.

'Bastard,' he said again.